The Beekeeper Diaries

Kevin Carey grew up in London. He moved to Norfolk as a young man, when he married, and spent his time designing and building beautiful homes, classic and contemporary furniture, and travelling Europe with his family. He has been writing short stories for most of his life, and after completing an advanced Creative Writing course with the Open University, moved to Buckinghamshire. This is his first novel.

To Dr Elleman

Best wishes

Kevin Carey

The Beekeeper Diaries

Kevin Carey

Cover designed by KDP Cover Creator

This book is a work of fiction. Names, characters, places, and incidents either are products of the author's imagination or are used fictitiously. Any resemblance to actual persons, living or dead, events, or locales is entirely coincidental.

Author: Kevin Carey

Printed in the United Kingdom

First Printing: December 2017
Amazon KDP Direct Publishing

ISBN-9781973486916

To my friend, my muse, my wife.
I know no other like you, and I love you.

Kevin Carey

ACCORDING TO WESTERN TRADITION HONEY STANDS FOR ELOQUENCE, IMMORTALITY, AND SHEER PLEASURE. THE BEE, THE HONEYMAKER, WORKS FOR THE COMMON GOOD, AND CAN BE NO MORE BRIBED OR CORRUPTED THAN A FLOWER. THEY ARE NEITHER SENTIMENTAL NOR ROMANTIC. NEITHER ARE THEY PHILOSOPHICAL; ALTHOUGH THEY INSPIRE PHILOSOPHERS; NOR DO THEY RETIRE IN CONTEMPLATIVE SOLITUDE. ONE BEE IS NO BEE

Bee by Claire Preston

Prologue

Meadowsweet, Wraysbury, Berkshire June 2008

MUMMY IS DYING. I tried to put that thought out of my mind as I quietly closed the door leading from the kitchen to the garden, and I stepped out onto the old stone patio. As the early evening air prickled my skin, long forgotten aromas wandered about me, and I closed my eyes as I breathed in the familiar smells of early summer blossoms of English rosebuds and freshly mown grass; I was sure that I could also smell the beehives, but maybe it was my imagination.

I breathed in again, and the tiredness faded a little. In spite of everything, I was pleased to see the house, and I placed my hand on one of the old oak timbers by the door; the feel of it's rough, dry texture strangely agreeable. My mother was certainly pleased to see me, but it had become clear since I had returned home, that my sister had mixed feelings. Well, I was here now, so we would just have to make the best of it, for Mummy's sake.

I stepped onto the lawn and walked across the garden, past the old wooden table and chairs. They had long ago lost their colour from years of dry sun and wet rain, and they were beginning to lean like an old man struggling to straighten his back. The flower borders were slowly filling once sparse voids with green leaf and softly blushing colour, and I stopped to take in the image, and then I looked back at the house. The French doors facing onto the garden had been left open for most of the day; I remembered how hot the living room used to get from just a little sun, and now the tall conifers along the boundary were beginning to cast their shadows onto the south wall of the house, their tops swaying softly in the high, gentle wind. The oak frames in between the lime rendered panels of the house grumbled as they cooled after a long day in the hot sun, and I changed the purpose of my journey and wandered over to close the doors, eager to preserve the heat of the day. It took several, as quiet as I could be, attempts before they shut properly.

The old house was looking tired, but it was strong; I knew Meadowsweet was strong. My great Grandfather had been a master builder; Mummy passed the story down about how he had built the house single-handedly. I had never known him, but my grandmother Constance, my namesake, had often recounted the stories to my mother of how he had refused to let any other craftsman work on the house. She had said his philosophy was, if you get it right the first time then it will last a lifetime, and as part of his life's work he had built Meadowsweet out of green oak taken from the trees felled in the meadow.

I continued my journey toward the end of the gardens, where there was a wide gap through the conifers that led to a large white painted gate which opened into the meadow, and when I reached it, I slid my hand through and grabbed at the worn rusty bar holding it closed, and I pulled it back with once remembered ease. I paused, looking for childhood memories, and I saw my mother with her warm, familiar smile, and for an instant there was my father; then he was gone.

The low groan of the gate as it opened interrupted the stillness, and although the light was fading more quickly now, it still played with the trees as it danced across the meadow's tall grass and cast eerie shadows onto the painted hives of Meadowsweet, where the bees, heavy with pollen, flew unsteadily with legs swollen, past birds no longer singing; silent wings taking them home.

My Great grandmother had named the house after the herbs growing in the meadow; it was during the summer months that their strong, sweet smell would fill the house with their fragrance. Vases and bowls of every description were employed to place the graceful, creamy white flowers around the rooms, and later they would be dried by hanging them from the beams in the kitchen and made into potpourri. My Mother had been named Philippa Mary, after the herbs Latin name, Filipendula Ulmaria. The herb was also known as Lady of the Meadow; all three generations of the Swan women had adopted that title in their time. As I stood in the still, damp air of the meadow, wearing my Mother's white hat which glowed softly in the remaining delicate light, I wondered who that title might belong to when Mummy was no longer here. What would happen to the meadow now she was so ill, was hard to say, but for today this Lady of the Meadow would take her royal gift, and I wandered, albeit nervously, toward the beehives, but with a sense of purpose, gently swinging Mummy's old metal bucket as I went. She would use it to collect odd pieces of honeycomb that had broken off in the hives.

My sister Jemima had told me earlier that the man who came to cut the grass was worried by the bees, and now it was getting too high in the meadow. He would only take his lawnmower in there when it was cold, as the bees were more reluctant to venture out. The hives were also in need of painting. My great Grandfather had built them before they had even built Meadowsweet; many generations of bees had long since come and gone, but Mummy used to tell me that they passed the stories of our ancestors down to their offspring, and that it would bond them to each Lady of the Meadow. She had hoped that they would speak to her of her own past, and bring back the memories that now eluded her, and standing here in the meadow, I wondered if perhaps they would speak of my past.

It had been many years since I had paid a visit to the meadow, and I thought about why I had come here today, to the hives; and the reason for my reluctant journey to the meadow, and the home of the bees. I had come home to be with my Mother, and it had become clear, after returning from Milan three days ago, just how ill she was. Only yesterday, we had had quite a lucid conversation; for all that she couldn't remember, she knew that she might not have long; not just to live, but to remember; to be herself, and she had asked me to go to the bees for her whilst there was still time.

I had come to the meadow with Mummy on many occasions, but that was so long ago; when she would tuck her long, gorgeous hair into the soft woven hat that she had discovered in a charity shop many years before. The hat had probably been the subject of many a conversation at weddings; when worn by its previous owner, but as far as Mummy was concerned it was perfect for visiting the bees. Whenever she wore it she would often forget to pull down the muslin mesh she had once carefully sewn around the wide brim, but now, as they danced a welcome around me, and the hive buzzed with excitement, I dropped the mesh down from the same hat; not feeling quite as confident. New bees would be in the hive every day, but Mummy would say that that the older ones would also dance to the others so that they would always recognize us. I repeated the greeting that I had heard my mother say for so many years. 'Hello my babies.' I said softly, 'and how are you today?'

There were six hives altogether. I took the smoker out of the bucket and gently blew some around the blue hive Mummy had described, to calm the bees. I placed my gloved hand onto the lid, and I could feel the bees vibrating their wings with excitement. I lifted the lid from the hive and placed it to one side, and my stomach clenched with anticipation. as I caught the fullness of the sweet aroma, and I remembered the first time I had come here. Mummy had been busy in the kitchen; she may have been pouring the honey into glass jars, or possibly cooking; I can't remember which, but I had wandered through the open kitchen door into the garden, where I had seen her walk across to the large white gate many times before; I had wanted to know what was on the other side.

I blew some more smoke around the hive, and turned my attention to the super; the box in which the frames are hung. I found that it was glued to the super below, so I took the old thick-bladed knife from the bucket and softly prised the box away so as not to disturb the bees too much.

Back then I had not been tall enough to see over the tops of the new trees on the boundary that day. They had been planted to screen the meadow from the gardens, but I had been able to clamber underneath the gate and was soon into the meadow exploring its wonders, and like any curious young lady of three, when I had seen the large painted boxes I had wanted to know what might be inside them.

When the super became loose enough to move I put my hands on each side and attempted to lift it. Just as on my first journey into the meadow, the bees were everywhere around me now, and the sound was all at once magical and forbidding. I wasn't sure that I wanted to stay, but at the same time I was drawn in by their song. Mummy had given me very clear instructions, and had described where to look in the hive. She had also told me that what I found would also help me to understand the past; now I was here, I wasn't sure that I wanted to know. It had taken me a long time to find a good place, a comfortable place to be; to survive.

The super came off with a little easing, and I placed it carefully to one side. I then tried to remove the next super containing another layer of frames. They were full of honey, just like the top box; it was possible that the honey hadn't been taken last season, and I wasn't here to do that either. It was too soon to take the bees harvest. By the look of the gardens, there was going to be a good nectar source this year, and I wondered if Mummy would add another super on the top to cope with the honey flow. That seemed unlikely.

That box was also glued firmly to the deep super at the bottom, and so I followed the same procedure of using the knife to work my way around the edges of the box. It eventually loosened, and I lifted that super off and placed it next the top one.

My mother had long ago filled in the memories of that first visit to the meadow; telling me how she had been in the kitchen and had heard the most dreadful screams coming from outside; she had known instinctively where she would find me. When she did discover me, she found that I had been stung so many times on my face and my body that it had been difficult for her to recognize her young baby.

It is said that pain has no memory, but I flinched at the recollection as I lifted the queen excluder off the deep super. The light was fading rapidly now, so I would need to be quick.

Then there was the fast drive to the hospital and the long boring days on the ward, and the look of disbelief on my mother's face when I came home, because the first thing I did was to run across to the meadow and stand at the white gate. When Mummy had followed me, I had made it clear that I wanted to go into the meadow again, and so she took me to the bees. I don't remember what she said, but she spoke to them in a soft, smiling voice, and even then, as now, I knew that her world was one of magic and dreams. Would knowing about her life answer the questions I had?

I waited for the strain of lifting the boxes to dissolve and then I looked into the bottom of the hive in anticipation of what it contained. There were two frames missing from the super as Mummy had described, and I squeezed my eyes into narrow slits and peered into the darkness of the lower box as if it were the lair of some demon or dragon. But instead I found a writhing mass of bees, and lying deep within them, between the frames, and carefully wrapped many times over in oiled brown paper; tied with several pieces of string, were my Mother's diaries.

Chapter 1

The sun broke through the small high windows along one side of the tiny Italian church, sending several shafts of light through to the other wall. I looked up from my seat on the cool wooden bench at the back in an effort to find a brief respite from the droll emotion of the eulogy being read out, and I couldn't help but notice the thousands of tiny dust particles dancing across the space. The thick white walls of the building left the room cool, maybe even cold, but I could imagine that if I were able to rise the twenty feet or so to the windows, I would be bathed in the heat of the Italian sun.

The shafts of light also accentuated the starkness of the occasion. In what seemed to me to be a cruel twist of nature, the harshness of the light caused the scene to be devoid of all the colour that life had to offer. And I knew that the subject of the eulogy, an artist of some distinction, would not approve. In contrast, any renaissance artist would have wished to capture the scene on canvas, such was their preoccupation with death as an art form.

I glanced to my left and saw that Lucinda, my boss, was trying to discreetly read an email on her phone. I knew that she would be completely distracted until the email had been answered. My boss lived for the moment; work came before everything, including the death of a client. Even if he was an artist of some distinction.

At that instant, my phone gave a very audible trill indicating the receipt of a message, and the audience, including Lucinda, turned as one to express their annoyance. I wondered if I should ignore it, or at least find out who the message was from.

I chose the latter. A few minutes later I found myself pacing outside the small Italian church, patiently waiting for Jemima to answer the phone. My sister's message had simply said, *Mummy not good; urgent.*

Chapter 2

The flight from Milan to Luton had not been a pleasant one. There was a two-hour delay because of bad weather, and then the cold train journey to Windsor, and now I was being driven through the dark and wet roads of Wraysbury by a taxi driver who didn't seem to know where the hell he was going. I watched drops of rain each choose their individual paths down the glass which just made my eyes feel even heavier. The conversation with Jemima had not gone so well. We hadn't spoken in several years, and it was obvious that she was still full of resentment. Our relationship had always been strained at best. I gave a deep sigh. Weren't twins supposed to be the best of friends?

'Ah, I think this is the right way Madam.'

The driver roused me from my thoughts, and I peered through the rain beyond the glass as I tried to make out the road signs. Ten years of living in Milan had dimmed even my memories of the area. Then I saw the Colne Brook as we quickly drove over it. 'There; just there!' I shouted. 'Turn right; right for goodness sake!' The taxi braked sharply and veered around the next turning causing a protest of horns from the surrounding vehicles.

And I knew that I was home; I could almost smell the Meadowsweet honey.

The taxi drove along Coppermill Road, and I pointed to the right. As we travelled through the gates of Meadowsweet and along the drive I glanced to my left and could just make out the white gate to the meadow through the darkness and the rain. I wondered who was looking after the bees, and I surprised myself at the pang of concern I felt for them. We had not parted in good company either.

I could still remember the day I had left, and I felt the pain of that parting now. I knew, in truth, that there had been many reasons to go; not the least of them being to have a life of my own. As the taxi pulled up outside the large open porch of the house, I knew it would be Jem who would open the door, and I shivered. We had been close once. It had always seemed that even though we were twins, everything was against our ever having a relationship. We looked nothing alike; we had completely different interests, and I felt so much older than her. The bees, in contrast, were so similar; thousands upon thousands of twins; all working together for the common good. And somehow, like the bees, we were going to have to work together for the common good of our mother.

As I climbed out of the taxi into the dark rain, I had forgotten how cold this country could be, and I ran into the porch for shelter. It was supposed to be late spring for goodness sake.

The porch light came on and the door opened abruptly, startling me. 'Connie.' My sister's beaming face sent another shiver through me, and I smiled back in practiced efficiency.

'Jemmie. It's good to see you.' I turned back to the taxi as if I had forgotten something. 'Let me just get my bags.' The taxi driver had already unloaded them and was bringing them into the porch area. 'Oh, thank you,' I said as I handed him a bunch of notes, knowing that there was a generous tip in the amount.

He smiled appreciatively. 'Thank you, Madam.' He stepped away; stopped momentarily, and turned back to face me. 'Would you like me to take the cases into the hallway?'

'Yes please, that would be very helpful.' The temporary distraction allowed me to breathe normally again, and I turned to my sister, who seemed to be frozen in the moment. Our eyes met, looking for a connection; but I couldn't find one.

'You look stunning Connie.' Jemima eyed me up and down, as if she were appraising one of the artworks from my boss's gallery. 'So slim and glamourous; not the Constance I remember.' I ignored the comment, and we stood in silence for several seconds. 'And look at your thick dark hair; it used to be so thin and mousey.' So, she could still insult me whilst throwing in a supposed compliment. She still had her long red locks which had never changed; and her arms looked thin through the fine wool cardigan she was wearing.

'How is Mummy?' I broke the silence, and as the taxi driver slid past and silently climbed into his vehicle, Jemima moved forward.

'Connie,' she said abruptly, and without warning, she broke into soft tearful sobs and threw her arms around me. 'I've missed you Connie.' After a short while she pulled back, holding onto my shoulders. 'You're shivering.'

'It's so bloody cold in this country, I replied.

'Come inside,' she said as she pulled a tissue from the sleeve of her cardigan. 'I'll make us both a hot drink.'

Walking through the long, wide hallway, with its tall ceiling, and ornate plasterwork, I caught the familiar fragrance of Meadowsweet, and I noticed a bowl of faded white flowers on the large oval table in the centre of the hall. Beyond that, were the oak stairs with their highly-polished handrail. I felt a sudden urge to run up the stairs and slide down the rail, as I had done many times as a young girl. Instead, we turned to the left, and went into the kitchen. It was always the warmest room of the house, and the smell of the heat from the Aga made me think of toast. I was hungry. We stood in awkward silence while Jemima made some hot chocolate, but no toast, and then went back through the hall and across to the drawing room, where we sat in the high back armchairs either side of the fireplace. I tucked my legs up onto the armchair and cupped my hands around the hot mug. Jemima opened the door of the woodburner, placed two small logs into the flames, and I began feel the heat penetrating my skin as the orange glow danced across the dimly lit room. Familiar memories came flooding back; some not so good. I broached the subject of Mummy again. 'How is she doing then?'

'I'm not sure where to start really.' She shifted uneasily in her chair. 'She's not doing so well.'

'What's the problem Jem?'

'The truth is Connie, she's dying.'

I sat up forcefully, nearly spilling my chocolate. 'What do you mean?' I asked. 'Why didn't you tell me this earlier Jemmie?'

'Because it's not the kind of thing that you share in a text message or a phone call; at least not if you can help it.'

'Yes, you're right. I'm sorry.'

'Are you? I mean, are you really Connie?' she replied.

'What is that supposed to mean?'

Jemima stood up and walked toward the woodburner. 'I've been looking after mother for the past eighteen years and....'

'Don't you mean that she's been looking after you?'

'Well that's a moot point really. I mean, maybe in the beginning, when the children were younger, but she's become increasingly dependent on me.' When she turned toward me she had tears in her eyes again. 'She keeps asking for you.'

I looked up at my sister in stunned silence and thought about the impact of that. I had left home under a cloud some time ago; and, in truth, Jemima had been left behind too. I remembered the tears from both of them when I walked out of the front door with my suitcase. Mummy had begged me not to go. Jemima had stood silently, and it was that that I could never forgive her for.

'What is she....?' I didn't know how to ask the question.

'Her heart is failing,' Jemima said. 'The muscles in her heart are dying.'

'What does that mean? I asked. 'Is she awake?'

She explained in more detail that Mummy had a heart condition that had most likely been there from birth, but it was only showing now because of her age. She also revealed that there were other problems, but that she would prefer that I speak to the Doctor after his visit in the morning.

I had not slept well. I woke up to soft sunlight filtering through the open curtains. Since living in Milan, I had grown accustomed to having a constant connection to the outside world, even during my sleep hours, as the city was never quiet. To misquote Dickens; it could be the best of places and the worst of places all rolled into one. The contrast of the weather from the previous night could not have been greater; although the hot sultry summer I had left behind would eventually lead to a cold, maybe foggy winter. I glanced at the bedside clock. 7:20 am. The last time I had stayed in this bedroom, my bedroom, I remembered yearning for a quiet life as Jemima's two children, also twins, charged up and down the corridors. And it was the twins that had eventually driven me away. Not because of the noise. It was more the constant reminders of my sister's betrayal.

Now I would welcome the sound. Everywhere felt so deathly quiet. In the current circumstances, an unfortunate choice of words. I got out of bed and walked over to the long open window, where reassuring sounds of spring filtered through to the bedroom, and I felt at peace with the house. I could see the meadow, and I tried to pick out any solitary bees who may have been searching for nectar. A pair of buzzing wings flew past the window, causing me to jump back. The busy streets of Milan would have disguised any such sound. I bent my knees slightly and pushed the sash window further up. The honeysuckle and clematis climbing up to and past the room were beginning to bud, and leaning slightly over, I could see several of the bees foraging around and then making their way off in obvious disappointment. It would be a little while before there were any rich pickings to be had. Just then, two familiar characters landed on the ledge, as if curious to know if there was anything of value within. 'Hello my babies,' I said to them softly. 'And how are you today?' Mummy had so many times said the same words to the bees. Soft tears blurred my vision.

'Talk to them,' she would say. 'Tell them the stories of your life. They want to know all about you.' Mummy said that she had told them all about the birth of Jemima's twins. 'A boy and a girl you know,' she had said to them, 'and they are so much alike; not like Constance and Jemima at all.' She would say how important it was that they knew when somebody lived, and somebody died.

'Did you tell them when we were born?' I had asked her.

'I did,' she replied. 'They know many things about our family; if you ever want to know anything about your past then ask them; ask the bees.' I had found it difficult to relate such folklore to my demanding job at the De Luca Art Gallery in Milan, entertaining clients and helping to catalogue artwork. I left the bees on the window ledge and sat down on the edge of the bed. A knock on the bedroom door brought me back to reality.

'Breakfast is ready Connie,' Jemima called through the door.

We sat at the large oak kitchen table and tucked into the egg and bacon Jemima had cooked. I removed the cloth from the jar of honey and used a small spoon to drizzle the golden liquid over my bacon.

'You know, Mummy still does that,' Jemima said.

'Has the Doctor been yet?' I asked, ignoring her comment. 'As I really would like to see Mummy.'

'He's with her now. If he thinks that she's well enough then she will come down for breakfast.'

'I'd forgotten how quiet it is here,' I said.

'Very quiet,' she replied. 'Especially with the twins away at Uni.' Jem looked at me as if she wished she hadn't mentioned them.

'How old are they now?'

'Nineteen this year.'

'Are they enjoying university?'

'To be honest I hear so little from them. They have their friends I suppose, so they don't need me so much.'

'Does their father....'

'No,' she replied, and she turned her back to me and wandered over to the sink.

There was a slight tap on the kitchen door and it slowly opened, revealing first a hand clenching the panel, and then a rather nervous looking man peering around the side. 'Er hello, I mean, good morning. I'm the Doctor; that is Doctor....'

'Yes, we know who you are,' interrupted Jemima in obvious irritation.

I rose from my chair and walked over with an outstretched hand. 'Hello Doctor. I'm sorry, but we haven't met.' I gave a sideways glance at Jemima as the doctor took my hand. His hand shake was limp and slightly clammy. I could see instantly why this man would irritate her. He was old enough to be our father but lacked any air of authority whatsoever. His build was slight and his gaze ineffectual and wandering. 'I'm Constance Hunter.'

On hearing my name his nervousness seemed to dissipate somewhat, and his face issued a beaming smile. 'Oh, hello Miss Hunter; Mary, that is your mother; of course, you know that; anyway, she has told me all about you.'

'Wonderful,' I replied. 'Anyway, Doctor?'

'Oh, er, yes. I'm Doctor Sidle; as in idle; although I don't get much time to be idle these days.' He laughed with a small repetitive snigger.

I cast my sister another sideways glance; but this time one of understanding. 'Doctor Sidle.'

'Er yes; yes, Miss Hunter.'

'Perhaps you could tell me how my Mother is this morning.'

He straightened and took on an accomplished, serious demeanour. 'Of course, of course. Well I have suggested that she rise for a while, but she tires easily so I would recommend that it is only for a short while.' He took a step forward and leaned slightly toward me, as if wishing to share a confidence. 'She has asked to see the bees. Perhaps just a few minutes won't hurt if she is agreeable.'

Jemima rose and went over to the Aga. 'I'll make her some tea.' She turned to me and smiled graciously. 'Perhaps you would like to take mummy some breakfast.'

'Of course,' I replied.

He clasped his hands and began rubbing them together. 'Right. yes, well I'll be off. Same time tomorrow then?'

'Just one thing Doctor.' I took his arm and led him into the spacious entrance hall, where I caught a glance of Mummy's portrait on the stairs. 'How bad...?'

'That's very hard to say Miss Hunter, but she has deteriorated since I saw her, and her heart is very weak, and her body is finding it harder to fight off infections. She is quite confused now. There are moments of recognition and then they go. The only thing I have seen that calms her are the bees. That's the only reason I can recommend that kind of effort. Otherwise just be patient; and please don't be shocked by some of the things she may say.'

'Thank you again. Your concern and attention are very much appreciated.'

'You are very welcome Miss Hunter. Your mother is a very kind person, and she cares very much for those around her. That is not always very evident with dementia.'

Dementia? And how long has that been....?' I asked.

'We have known for some months now, but it's really only in the past few weeks that there has been a marked deterioration. We have only had a few conversations, and I can say that some of the time the dementia would be difficult to notice. She remembers many things from the past and, I must say, she has led a very interesting and almost magical life.'

Despite his self-consciousness demeanour, he had a great deal of respect for my Mother and obviously cared very deeply about her. 'Have you been her doctor for long?' I asked.

'I would say around ten years.' He replied.

So, you know her well then. Once again, thank you,' I said. 'Perhaps tomorrow, if you have the time, we can discuss some of the things that she has spoken about.'

'You're very welcome Miss Swan. Goodbye.'

I closed the front door and stood holding on to the handle for a few minutes. The whistle of the kettle on the Aga brought me back.

∞ ∞ ∞

Mummy was asleep and had not woken since I had entered the room. This bedroom had previously been my Grandmother's, and Mummy had said that it brought her great comfort to be in here. She looked too peaceful and serene to disturb. Living and working in Milan had taken away any opportunities for quiet reflection, and I envied that one thing about her. I had so much to tell her, about my life, and my work, and about Gabriel. Had we really been dating for three years? Such an old-fashioned word. But he was an old-fashioned kind of man. And his family were the same. He was always reciting old sayings from his Mama, and I knew better than to question them. I hadn't contacted him since I got here; I hadn't even sent him a text to let him know that I'd arrived safely.

He would be worrying; I knew that, but I hated being fussed over. Perhaps not calling him was my way of staying in control, but he hadn't contacted me either, and that bothered me; even though he had said that he wouldn't disturb me; telling me I had to focus on my family; and when I had protested, he had held onto my shoulders and said, 'My Mama, she always say, *'se vuoi piacere a tutti, devi alzarsi presto.'* Which roughly translated as, 'Those who want to please everyone have to get up early.' In this situation, it would be impossible to keep everyone happy. Since moving to Milan ten years ago, I had grown used to working hard to do just that. I had spent the first seven years when I left home wandering from job to job in London, and I had chanced upon an art exhibition whilst on holiday in Milan, which is where I met my current boss, Lucinda. Warding off amorous Italian admirers had become something of a pastime. And that was what had attracted me to Gabriel. Apart from an occasional warm smile, he had shown little interest in me from the moment we met, that is, in the way Italian men show an interest, and I had felt somewhat insulted.

I placed my hand on the teapot and it was barely warm, so I leaned forward and gently touched Mummy's hand to wake her. After a few minutes, she stirred and opened her eyes; blinking rapidly for some time as she focused her gaze on me. She smiled and spoke softly. 'Hello.' I expected more, but nothing came; just a warm smile. I breathed in to speak; breathed out again and waited. I glanced at the clock several times before she slowly roused herself. Old habits.

'Hello dear, and how are you?' Mummy said.

'I'm fine,' I replied, and coughed lightly as my throat went dry. 'More importantly, how are you?'

'Oh me; well I'm not doing so well. But I am pleased to see you.'

'You are?'

'Oh yes dear. I've been waiting for you.'

'You have?'

'You answer everything with a question.'

'Do I?'

She smiled and clasped my hand. 'It's alright dear. Would you like to help me out of bed and then pour me a cup of tea Connie?'

I breathed out a large sigh, and a single tear fell along the curve of my cheek.

∞ ∞ ∞

I carried the tray down the stairs. Mummy and I had chatted briefly, but I had stopped when I saw her eyes closing several times. I told her that I would come and see her again in a couple of hours. It was good to see the portraits again; I had barely glanced at them on my journey up the stairs earlier. Familiar faces of family gone by smiled back at me. I could hear Jemima in the kitchen, so I sat on the bottom step for a few minutes. She had told me that when she had received the diagnosis from the hospital her first instinct had been to contact me, but that it had taken her a few weeks to find the courage to do so. It was too soon for me to know what kind of life she had had since I had left. Getting pregnant and marrying that loser had not been a good start. But that hadn't been my fault. So why did I feel so guilty? And why did Jemima resent me? Was it because I had left her to make the best of things?

The sound of china shattering woke me from my thoughts, so I left the stairs and the portraits and moved quickly through to the kitchen with the tray of uneaten breakfast. Spread across the floor was the aftermath of a thrown cup. 'Whatever is the matter?'

I placed the tray on the oak worktop and bent down to pick up some of the pieces of the cup. One of them had my lipstick on it. Jemima looked at me and picked up a tea towel to wipe her face. 'You wouldn't understand.'

'Probably not; but it might help to talk.'

She stood in silence for a while.

'We're going to have to sell Meadowsweet,' she suddenly blurted out.

I stood up. She had a look of shock on her face, as if she had just been told this revelation herself. 'Why?' I asked.

'The money's running out. We can't afford to stay here.'

'But Mummy owns the house. I don't understand.'

'Look around you Connie; the house is falling apart.'

'It's not that bad, surely.'

'it's worse than that; you don't see the bills.'

We stood for several moments, both taking in what she had said.

'How long....?'

'A year; two at the most.'

'What about the bees?' I asked without thinking.

She joined me in collecting the remainder of the broken shards. 'That's a big part of the problem; Mummy cares more about them than she does me.'

'It's just that she's not herself Jem. You can hardly blame her for....'

'That's just the point Connie; she always has done.' She stood and threw the broken pieces into the bin. 'Even the twins used to say that their Nan was more interested in the bees than them.... Did it never bother you? Really.'

'Well, to be truthful; no, it didn't. I always thought it was a natural part of our lives. If I'm honest, I think I've missed the bees.'

'And that's my point; even you care more about them than you do us.'

'That's not fair Jem.'

'Isn't it? You haven't once said that you've missed us; in fact, you haven't even kept in contact since you left, have you.'

'We both know why that was, don't we.'

'Well neither of us have got him now have we.'

I looked at her in disbelief. 'I'm going for a walk.'

'Connie I....' She moved towards me.

'Not now Jemmie.'

Despite the temptation to slam the kitchen door, I closed it gently behind me. The freshness of the day caught me, and I pulled my cardigan around my shoulders, wishing there had been time to get my coat. I couldn't go back inside now; at least not yet. The kitchen door exited the house mainly to the east and caught a good deal of the sun; but there was still a bite of cold in the air. I looked around the large garden, which was looking somewhat unloved. I turned right and walked along the path to come around to the rear of the house which faced south, where the low midwinter Rhododendrons were beginning to bloom with rose purple flowers which had started to brighten the garden. The tall, later flowering bushes had grown to at least twenty feet high and looked absolutely stunning. I was reminded of how beautiful Meadowsweet could be at this time of the year.

I wandered across the garden toward the south-east corner and the meadow, and within a few minutes I had arrived at the large white gate. I didn't open it but leaned over the top, wrapping my hands in the sleeves of my cardigan. I could see the hives from where I stood. Memories of magical journeys into the meadow came flooding back; and I hadn't looked to see if the bucket was still in the same place in the kitchen. It wasn't yet time to collect the honey and prepare the jars. That would be later in the year. Who was going to do that this year? And what about the coming years? As much as I had tried to forget the bees, along with everything else, I found it hard to imagine that there might not be any bees at Meadowsweet.

They had been such a big part of our lives growing up; especially during the summer months. There were so many stories; going back to way before we were born. Mummy had told us about Aunt Katherine and the Rossi family in Italy, and the many summers they had spent there. She had always said that Aunt Katherine hadn't liked the bees so much, but she had loved Mummy. They were inseparable. It would have been nice if Jemima and I could have had that kind of relationship. I tried to remember Aunt Katherine; images of picnics in the garden and days out by Colne brook flashed into my mind. but I felt that I knew her more through Mummy's stories, and because of that I missed her, and if I was honest I missed my sister. We should have been so happy; most of the time we had been; so what went wrong? In truth, I knew the answer to that question. Was I hoping for too much to try and find some kind of peace with Jemima?

For a moment I wished I was back home in Milan. But this had been my home, and it wasn't fair that I had been forced to leave; that I had had to spend so many years of my life looking for another place to call home. But, more than anything else, standing here now at the gate to the meadow, and listening to the soft hum of the bees, I knew that for all those years I had missed everything that Meadowsweet had stood for. And now I was being told that we might lose it all.

∞ ∞ ∞

When I came back downstairs to the kitchen Jemima had already prepared a tray of lunch for Mummy. A light ham salad with cheese. I had spent the rest of the morning in my room; trying to pick over the broken pieces of our relationships to see if any would fit back together. I hadn't had much success.

She smiled softly; as if everything in the world was right. 'That's perfect timing Connie. I was about to take Mummy some lunch. Perhaps you could do it?'

'Yes, I would love to. Have you put some honey...? Yes of course you have; you know her better than me.'

'Would you like me to get you some lunch now?' she asked.

'Thanks, but I'm not hungry right now. I don't tend to do lunch really. Never enough time when I'm working.'

'Okay.... Listen Connie,' she said. 'I thought that perhaps we could have a talk later; that is, if you don't mind.'

I took the tray, and we stood facing each other for several seconds. 'I don't mind, but could we make it tomorrow? My head is spinning right now.'

'Great.' Jemima's eyes brightened with the prospect. 'Oh, and if Mummy is sleeping, it would be good to wake her. She'll need to eat to keep up her strength, and I've put a piece of her favourite cheese with the salad. I remind her that it's her favourite, and she always says, 'Is it dear'?' We shared a momentary laugh.

I carried the tray up the stairs, and along the long wide landing, and I stopped outside my mother's room, the first of five bedrooms, each with its own bathroom. I tapped quietly on the bedroom door and entered. The bed was empty. Placing the tray on the side table, I walked over to the open French doors leading out onto the balcony to find Mummy sitting at the small iron table to one side; she was reading. The balcony looked out over the gardens, and it had been set back into the house so that it would shelter one from the crosswinds, but would also catch the arc of the sun for most of the day. Mummy had always had a book in her hand, even when she was working, and I remembered that she used to say, *there are more books than I will ever have time to read.*

I stood watching her; absorbed in her task; a smile travelled across her face as she turned the page. I used to watch her as a young child, and even back then I could see that there always seemed to be something in her life that had prevented her from being truly happy; some unknown memory playing on the lines of her face. But for this moment; this polaroid of time, she seemed truly at peace. I almost envied her. I must have sighed, because she turned at the sound. 'Hello dear; I was just reading a favourite book.' She gave a slight laugh. 'At least I think it was a favourite of mine.'

'What are you reading?'

She looked down and turned to the front cover. 'The Wind in the Willows. Yes, I have read it before, I'm sure.' She pushed her bookmark in between the pages and closed the book. 'It truly is a beguiling book Constance.' She looked out cross the gardens, and I saw her shiver. 'So many memories.'

'I should read it,' I said.

'It was set right here you know. Well not just here, but not too many miles away. On the banks of the river....' She frowned and placed her fingers on her chin.

'The Thames? I said.

'So, you have read it?'

'No Mummy, but I will, I promise. I've brought you some lunch.'

She rose from her chair. 'Goodness, is it that time already?'

'I thought that after you've eaten we could go for a walk.... if you feel able, of course.'

'That sounds lovely. Shall we sit in the bedroom?'

The room was large enough to fit a small dining table in the corner, and we both sat there. I watched in silence as she ate. I wanted to tell her so much; to tell her about my life; about Gabriel. How he was such a kind man, and how he was always happy, and would say the wisest of things. At thirty-six, he was two years younger than me, but in maturity he seemed so much older. I wanted her to meet him; I wanted her to tell me that he was the right one for me. Maybe it was too late for that. I knew that I would have to make that decision for myself.

'Jemima reminded me that the Murianengo is your favourite cheese.'

Mummy didn't reply, but concentrated on cutting herself a slice of the cheese, which she held up and said, 'it so reminds me of Italy. It has such a fine delicate odour.' She examined the blue veins running through the cheese. 'They make me think of the Lake. Do you remember Connie?'

I picked up a small piece of the cheese and placed it in my mouth, and I remembered; I saw the long summers we spent in Serralunga d'Alba, in the hilltops of Barolo. Warm summer days at Lake Maggiore, and cool nights playing in the gardens with the Rossi family on their vineyard estate. I remembered that we were laughing most of the time; and I wished we were back there.

'Yes, I do Mummy; wonderful times. You remember then?'

'I miss Cesare[1] you know.' Before I could reply she continued. 'Where do you live Connie?'

'Milan mummy.'

'Oh of course you do; how silly of me.' She finished the last of her meal and saved a small piece of the cheese until the end. She poured the tea into her cup and put a teaspoon of honey into the mixture. Then she rubbed the piece of cheese on the honey coated spoon and placed it in her mouth. Her eyes closed, and a warm smile crept across her face as she chewed. Just then a shadow came across the room and we looked through the French doors in disappointment as the sky began to cloud over. 'It doesn't look like we will get to go on that walk now does it,' she said.

'Never mind Mummy,' I replied. 'We can talk for a while, if you want to.'

She lifted the cup and saucer, took a sip of her tea and placed it back onto the tray, and without looking up she spoke. 'I know why you have come you know.' I waited for her to continue. 'I know that I'm dying.' She quickly put her hand on mine. 'But it's alright; I'm at peace; at least I will be when I know that you're happy.'

'But I am happy Mummy.'

She smiled at me. 'But you're not. You see, the one thing I can be is honest. I know a terrible thing happened; between you and...'

'Jemima.'

'Yes; and I would like you both to be happy. My two girls.'

She looked out through the French doors, as if she were searching for a past memory. 'I did it for Katherine you know.' She paused, frowned, and stared into space. 'I know I could help you Constance; if I could just remember.' I could feel the burning of tears, and I tried to force them back, and Mummy squeezed my hand, and

---

[1] pronounced Chesaray.

it was like squeezing a sponge full of water. 'It's okay my darling, really it is,' she said. She took another sip of her tea and carefully placed the bone china cup back onto the saucer. 'Have you met the Doctor?'

'Yes, just this morning. He seems like a nice man.'

'I remember things when.... when I go to visit my bees.'

'Yes, he did mention that.'

'But what he doesn't know, is that the bees are looking after something for me.'

'What do you mean?'

'The bees, my babies.... they have my memories.'

'But Mummy,' I protested. 'I know that you believe they listen, but....'

'Please.... let me explain,' She interrupted, and scooped another teaspoon of honey and poured it into the cup before emptying the rest of the teapot. 'After you left, I made it very clear to....to your sister. I made it clear that you were to have a life. And I'm sure that you have. Then a short while ago, I was told that I have this heart thing.... whatever it is. But before things worsened, I knew that there were things.... from the past; my past; things that would perhaps help you to understand; things that I can't remember. I may have lost so much Connie, my Connie, but I have always wanted to make sure that my life; our life, was not forgotten.'

'By telling the bees?'

'By asking them to look after my memories.' She swallowed the last of her tea. 'My diaries.'

As dusk was falling, I made my way out to the meadow.

Chapter 3

I did my best to make sure Jemima wasn't in the kitchen before bringing the package into the house, and I placed the bucket onto the kitchen table. I wasn't sure why, but Mummy had asked that it just be our secret for now. I took her hat off and placed the package discreetly behind it, and I made my way through the hallway and up the stairs. Wearing the hat had felt as if I were taking over the role of chief beekeeper; a role I didn't want or need in my life, and I couldn't help but wonder what Jemima would say if she saw me. I tapped gently on the door of my mother's room and entered, and I found her sitting on the balcony. She wasn't reading; just staring out into the garden.

'Hello Mummy, are you ok?' I wandered onto the balcony, and she turned in surprise.

'Oh, hello dear. Yes, I'm fine. But I thought I saw my mother in the meadow. Is she collecting honey?' She pointed to the package I was carrying. 'And what do you have there?'

'The diaries Mummy. You asked me to get them for you.'

'Did I? Whose diaries are they?'

Ignoring her confusion, I placed the package on the table in front of her. 'I tell you what; why don't you open them. In the meantime, I'll leave you in peace, and maybe later you can tell me all about them.'

'Yes, of course dear. That sounds lovely.'

'You look tired Connie.' Jemima placed a mug of tea in front of me. 'You really didn't need to get up this early. I checked on Mummy and she's sleeping soundly.'

'I thought maybe I would wake her a bit earlier today. See if I can get her to move around a bit. Maybe take her out to the bees.' I had slept very little during the night, having been plagued by old memories. Every time I had closed my eyes, vivid ideas of what might be in the diaries had kept me awake. I had often wondered what

Mummy's life had been like, but when I had left home, the past was something I had spent more than half my life trying to forget. I had dreamt of Gabriel too. He was smiling at me as he turned and kissed Jemima; I had been screaming at them both, but they just carried on smiling. I had woken up crying.

When I had taken a tray up to Mummy the previous evening, she was avidly reading the diaries, and as I had placed the tray in front of her I could see that there were tears in her eyes. When I had asked her if she was alright, she didn't look up from her reading and had dismissed me with a wave of her hand, so I had thought it best to leave her to her reading.

'Would it be a good idea to wait until the Doctor has been?' Jemima woke me from my wanderings.

'She's not going to get any better Jem. I was thinking that maybe he doesn't really need to come so often. Now I'm here...'

'Are you saying that I can't cope? Because I've done very well without you all this time.'

I pursed my lips and looked down at the table. 'You called me Jem. I was thinking more in terms of sharing the burden.'

'Yes, I'm sorry. I know that you're only trying to help.'

'So...if you don't mind, I'll go up and see her now.' I waited for her response, and she just smiled sweetly. I didn't want to tell her that I was also eager to talk to Mummy about her diaries.

I tapped gently on the bedroom door and entered without waiting for a reply. I found Mummy sitting at the side table with a book in her hand. She continued to read for some time before she carefully placed her bookmark in the page and closed it. I took that as my cue to sit down. She looked up at me and smiled.

'How are you this morning dear?'

'I'm fine Mummy. Was that the diary you were reading?' I asked her.

'Well, that is what I want to talk to you about.' She took both of my hands and squeezed them. 'I'm going to tell you all about them.' I must have hesitated for she gently pulled my arms toward her. 'It's alright you know. Reading the diaries is bringing things back to me. So, I will read them to you; and I will tell you the story of my life.' She let go of me, and picked up the first diary. 'And we will start right away.'

Chapter 4

Diary; July 20th 1962

Today is my last day at school. I can't tell you how excited I am this morning, in spite of that, I stretch and yawn and then pull the pillow over my head in response to my mother's calls to, *get out of that bed young lady.* I always laugh at my mother's attempts at sounding threatening, which never really work; her voice is just too soft and warm. What does make me jump out of bed is the smell of bacon wafting up from the kitchen, and I pull on my dressing gown and follow the aroma to its place of origin.

Walking down the stairs at Meadowsweet always fills me with a sense of wonder. Whenever I run my hand along the polished oak banister I feel an overwhelming urge to climb on it and slide to the bottom; something I had done only once before, and I wince at the memory of reaching the volute, as Mummy calls the ornate twist at the end of the handrail. Today I manage to resist the urge, and instead say good morning to my grandparents on my way down, as I do every morning.

Their portraits smile back at me; along with the one of my mother, which she said had been painted on her eleventh birthday. My grandparents have splashes of grey hair in the paintings. Had they truly been happy when they sat for the artist, or had he just presented them that way? My grandparents had pretty much given up on the prospect of having any children, until their darling Constance had come along, and Mummy had been adored by them. It would be nice to have them around.

Mummy had been nagging me for years to have my portrait done, but I had so far avoided it; feeling as if it were the height of vanity. I fight the urge to sit for a while on the bottom step, as I often do, and I make my way along the hall to the kitchen. The aroma that greets me promises a special breakfast.

Mummy is in front of the stove tightening the bow of her floral apron, while at the same time cracking eggs on the griddle plate. When she smiles, I see the young girl in the painting, but Mummy's short, dark hair is in stark contrast to the long golden curls she has in the portrait. Time is cruel; I vow there and then that I will always keep my hair long. 'Well good morning young lady,' she says, 'I was beginning to wonder if you had decided to stay in bed for the day.'

'Don't be silly Mummy; I just had some last-minute things to do.' I kiss her softly on the cheek. 'That smells good.'

She frowns. 'You don't look as if you've been doing much more than sleeping.' I pull a face, and in response she runs the fingers of her left hand softly down the side of my cheek, which she would do at every opportunity.

'Mummy!' I say in vain protest, knowing that she would take little notice.

'Well as it's your last day, I know you will be gallivanting all over the place....' She tries to untangle my long dark black hair. '....and I thought that maybe you might not get the opportunity to eat very well today.'

I sit at the large oak kitchen table and run my hands over the surface. It's still as solid as the day it had been made, and the scrub lines following the grain of the wood just give it even more character. My Grandfather had made the table from oak beams taken from the old barn that used to sit in the meadow. Because of its size, they had had to bring it in through the kitchen by removing the large sash windows, and now it took pride of place in the middle of the kitchen.

I love sitting in this room. The tall ceiling and elegant cabinets, which had been built from the same oak as the table, warm my insides, and I pick up my knife and fork and place them each side of an imaginary plate, and when it arrives I waste no time in beginning the task of devouring the bacon and egg and fried bread and tomatoes and mushrooms placed in front of me. Mummy watches as I open the jar of honey and use the teaspoon to pour some over my bacon. Whenever the jar was opened I would catch Mummy mouthing a silent thank you to the bees in the meadow. She had told me that for her bees to produce a single jar, they would have to travel the equivalent of three times around the world.

She stands patiently beside me for a while as I take another mouthful of bacon. 'What do you think?' she asks cautiously.

I chew slowly and then swallow. 'Delicious,' I reply, but I can see from the look on her face that that was not what she meant.

'I suppose you're talking about College.' I gather up another mouthful of bacon and egg onto my fork and stuff it into my mouth, again chewing slowly as if I have all the time in the world. Mummy moves around to the other side of the table and sits, waiting. I give way after the third mouthful of bacon. 'Camberwell College.'

'Mary! Why on earth do you want to go to Camberwell?'

I really can't wait to be old enough to not have to explain myself to anyone. What must that feel like? To just not answer a question. 'Well.' I reply, continuing with my breakfast. 'Do you remember Katherine?'

'Katherine?'

'You must remember; I used to go to school with her when her family lived in the village.' I finish my last mouthful and carry the empty plate over to the sink, and on the way, I use the last piece of fried bread to mop up the juices.

'Just leave it on the side Mary.' Mummy gestures toward the wooden scrubbed draining board. 'I must confess,' she says, 'I'm still none the wiser.'

I place the plate on the board and pick up a tea towel to wipe my hands, and ignoring another frown I continue. 'Ok....they moved away a few years ago, and I knew her from school and....' I pause as I run my tongue around my teeth and look at Mummy intently as if I have something really important to say. '.... Katherine had a really dishy brother.' She gives me her disapproving look, but I continue regardless. 'Anyway, we bumped into each other a couple of months ago, and we really got on; and well, Katherine is going to Camberwell.'

She moves me out of the way and turns the tap on; the water spits out, as it always does, before settling into a steady flow. 'And that's it? That's the criteria you have used to decide on your education? Despite the fact that it's quite a long way to travel every day, and you may have to stay away from home; have you thought of that?' The lines on her forehead deepen. 'I must say Mary, it doesn't seem to me to be a sound choice.' She holds her fingers under the tap to see if it's hot enough, then picks up the empty plate and runs her dishcloth around it.

'But Mummy it is,' I protest. 'You haven't let me finish. You see, Katherine wants to study art, which as you know is my first choice, so this way we can do it together. There are so few girls at college; it will be so much more fun to have someone of my own age. Besides, I've checked out the journey and I can catch the train from Wraysbury station.'

Mummy is silent. 'So, tell me again, about the family.'

'Well, Katherine has a really dishy brother.'

'Yes, you said that.'

'Did I? Well, all I know is that they moved to Egham, I don't know when.'

'What is their family name Mary?'

'Why so many questions?'

She sighs and turns toward me.

'Hunter, Katherine Hunter.'

As she turns, the plate slips from her hand and crashes violently on the hard-tiled floor, and I jump back, startled at the noise.

We both bend to the floor and immediately begin to pick up the broken pieces, and Mummy looks at me frowning. 'That's annoying; it just slipped out of my hands.' She stands quickly and looks at the kitchen clock. 'My goodness, look at the time Mary, you don't want to be late now do you.'

I throw the broken pieces of the plate into the bin, and after pouring another tea from the pot I make my way back up the stairs to dress for my very last day.

Chapter 5

I dreamed of sunny places and soft sheets. If life could be just one long dream, would it be better than the real thing? I wanted to fly. To float away without any effort. I looked straight ahead, and I could see a bright yellow disc, and I thought that it must be the sun. Looking down I could see I was standing in a pool of swirling colour. I tried to walk toward the yellow disc; and as I moved, the colours swirled around me and became dark and thick. It was only if I stood still that they brightened into the most beautiful array of splendour that I could possibly imagine.

I was woken once again by the brightness of the sun through the bedroom window. I had had a better sleep. Jemima and I had spoken for a while the previous evening; about nothing in particular as it turned out. We had both avoided discussing Meadowsweet. I think we were still feeling wary of each other. I hadn't mentioned the diaries. I knew Jemima was feeling quite vulnerable, and despite the hurt of the past, I had no desire to cause her any more pain, and to be honest, I didn't know what was to come. As far as everyone else was concerned, Constance had always been seen as the sensible one; the wise one. In fact, people had often expressed their surprise in finding that I was not older than my sister.

I was eager to continue my conversation with Mummy from the previous day, and was also hoping that she could recall telling me about the diaries. I rose from the bed, and after I had showered and dressed, I made my way downstairs, hoping to find that the Doctor had not been, as I also wanted to talk to him about Mummy.

Jemima was busy cooking some breakfast. 'Oh hi,' she said. 'I imagined you might be tired, as we had had a late night, so I thought you might want to sleep in.'

'One of the curses of my job,' I replied. 'No matter if we had to attend a business function the night before and entertain clients until the early hours; you had better be at work the next morning on time, or don't bother to come to work ever again.' I sat at the table. 'Do you have any coffee Jem?' I was beginning to miss the Italian pick me up I would have in the morning to start my day.

'I'm pretty sure we have some around here somewhere.' She opened several cupboard doors in succession. 'Ah, here it is. Can I get you to make it? I'm cooking breakfast for the Doctor as well.'

'He's here already?'

'Yes; and buoyed by your visit, I think.' Jemima laid three plates out on the table. 'He sometimes drops hints about breakfast when he comes, but I don't think I could cope with him on my own; but now you're here...'

'Oh thanks,' I said.

'Yes. Sorry about that.'

'I'm sure that will be fine. I want to talk to him anyway. The distraction of breakfast will hopefully allow for doing away with awkward pauses.'

'So, your boss is a bit of a slave driver, is she?'

'Oh, she's not so bad really; and I really do love my job, but she's very self-motivated and extremely driven; it's just that she expects everyone else to keep up. I suppose I don't mind; I'm kind of used to it now. In the early days, the work was a welcome distraction.'

'From what?'

I hesitated, instantly regretting leading myself into a corner. Old memories stirred, and I had no desire to discuss the past; at least not now; not yet.

Just then, the Doctor pushed his head around the door; tapping on it at the same time, and I whispered a silent thank you into the air for his good timing.

'Er, hello; good morning ladies.'

'Hello Doc; I heard that you're having a bit of breakfast with us this morning.' I pointed to a chair on the other side of the table. 'Come and sit down. Would you like some coffee or a cup of tea?'

'Well, tea please; if you're sure that's not too much trouble?'

'Of course not Doctor Sidle. I'm very grateful for all that you have done for Mummy,' I said, as Jemima placed a cup in front of him. 'Please help yourself to the pot.'

He started to twitch, almost imperceptibly. 'I tell you what Doc,' I said, 'why don't you pass me your cup and I'll pour it for you; Sugar and milk?'

He visibly relaxed. 'Ah, thank you; not too strong for me please Miss Swan, and four sugars please.'

'Please, call me Constance,' I said as I counted the sugars into the cup.

'Thank you.... Constance.' He gave me a beaming smile of gratitude that didn't warrant the favour.

'How is Mummy doing?'

'Oh, of course; how rude of me.' He took the cup, and hovered between taking a sip and placing it on the table to cool. He opted for the latter. 'Mary, your mother; she is quite tired this morning, and her blood pressure is up; I think she needs to rest until this afternoon. I'm presuming that she went for a walk yesterday; she couldn't remember whether she did or not.'

'No,' I replied, feeling rather guilty, and also, a little disappointed that she seemed to have forgotten about our time together. 'It started to rain so we didn't get the opportunity.'

'I see.' He rubbed his chin. 'Perhaps the excitement of seeing you has tired her; yes, that must be it.'

It was possible that Mummy might have mentioned the diaries to him. I glanced over at Jemima who was busy finishing off the bacon, and turning to the Doctor, I spoke in a slightly lower voice. 'So, she has no memory of anything from yesterday?'

'It's difficult to say; although she did mention the bees.'

'Those bloody bees. Why can't she forget them and remember us for a change?' Jemima's harsh words made me jump. She must have noticed my reaction. 'I'm sorry; that was rude of me,' she continued.

I wanted to tell her that it wasn't a problem; but that wasn't how I was feeling. Her reaction threw up all sorts of questions. Who would look after the bees if something happened to Mummy? How would my sister cope; with everything? And would we have to sell Meadowsweet?

'I have often thought about keeping bees.' We both looked at the Doctor and smiled at his sudden statement. He didn't appear to have the disposition to be around one bee, let alone a swarm, and I imagined him running screaming from the room flapping his arms above his head, and I gave a small laugh. 'No, really,' he continued. 'I'm a lot sturdier than I look.' He said, as if reading our minds. 'I come from farming stock you know.'

Jemima quickly sat at the table. 'Really; tell us more.'

He picked up his cup and saucer, which shook so much that he immediately placed it back on the table again; then he attempted to continue. 'I grew up on a farm not far from here; my family still own it today; although my older brother runs it now.' I could see his mind wandering, as if lost in old memories, and he picked up his tea spoon and gently stirred his cup as he stared into the contents. 'I loved nothing more than milking the cows or birthing a lamb. I spent many a day with my arm up a cow's....' His face reddened. 'Anyway, because my brother was due to inherit the farm, I decided to become a veterinary surgeon.' He picked up his cup and downed the rest of the hot tea without a thought. 'Somewhere along the line; I'm not really quite sure when, that changed to becoming a doctor. And I love it, I really do.' He looked at both of us in turn with renewed confidence.

'Well, all I can say Doctor Sidle is that you are very good at what you do.'

'Why thank you Miss Swan; Constance. That means a lot.'

Jemima placed a plate of breakfast in front of the Doctor and he tucked in heartily without a moment's hesitation, not waiting for us to begin. Two minutes later his plate was wiped clean with his slice of bread. Maybe that came from the need to eat as and when he could between his busy schedules. Through the silent smiles he glanced at his watch. 'Is that the time? My goodness I really need to get a move on; I have morning surgery in ten minutes.'

After he had left I took Mummy a tray of breakfast. She was awake, and her bright and cheerful demeanour seemed to fly in the face of all he had been saying about her.

'Good morning dear,' she said, her eyes lighting up at the sight of the tray. 'Oh lovely, I was hoping you would be bringing me breakfast this morning. And how is your sister Jemima?'

'She's...okay,' I replied, feeling slightly thrown by Mummy's ebullient mood. I placed the tray on the small table and we both sat down. 'Listen Mummy, I was thinking that perhaps if you were feeling well enough, we could go for a walk in the gardens, and maybe visit the bees.'

She placed her hands together in delight. 'Oh that would be wonderful Connie.' Her smile faded slightly, and she looked over to the window. 'I do miss them you know.'

'Yes, I'm sure you do.' I reached over to touch her hand. 'But we can take care of that today.'

She looked at me, her eyes bright and direct. 'There was a time you know, when I didn't much care for the bees.'

'I find that hard to believe Mummy. You have always had a passion for them; at least as long as I can remember.'

'Yes I have. But this was when I was very young. A lot younger than you are now. In fact, I've been reading about it.'

'I tell you what; why don't you eat you breakfast,' I said, 'and you can read it to me.'

She nodded and picked up her knife and fork.

Chapter 6

Diary; June 18th 1964

I wish I hadn't chosen to sit so near the window in the classroom. The sun is bursting through the glass, and as much as I try to shield myself from the glare, it seems to find its way through. The class is full so there is very little chance of sitting elsewhere, and just when I think I can't bear it any more, the lesson finishes for lunch, ending a forgetful morning.

I make my way to the small tea rooms on Church Street; a place called Annie's, which has become a favourite of the students during the day as they serve up the right amount of sugary foods to satisfy any sweet tooth. I find Katherine sitting in the corner booth; her head buried in a book, and I sit opposite her and wait patiently. She won't speak to me until she has finished reading to the end of the chapter, so I take the opportunity to order a pot of tea for two along with the obligatory jam scones for lunch, as well as a good portion of fresh cream. As the waitress walks away I glance around the room; it seems quieter today. Maybe it's because the sun is shining, and many of the students will be congregating on Camberwell Green. I yawn as Katherine continues her studious devotion to her book.

'What are you reading this time Katie?' I ask. Without looking up She raises the slender fingers of her left hand in taut dismissal and keeps them there whilst reading. My pursed lips tighten as several seconds passed by. As I watch her concentration, I wish that I had the same devotion to my studies. I love looking at art, but writing about it was proving to be so tedious.

Katherine's piercing deep-sea blue eyes seem to dart across the pages whilst her freckled pixie nose twitches in response as she silently mouths each syllable. How does she always manage to put so much energy into everything? Her hand lowers and she slams the book shut. She looks up at me, and brushing her long red hair back with her hand, she breathes out heavily as she beams a smile. 'Oh Mary, he's such a hero.'

'Who is?'

'Edmond Dantes of course.' She leans forward and grabs my hand. 'I'm telling you Mary, you really must read The Count of Monte Cristo. It's never been out of print you know. It's so tragic; his former fiancé, Mercedes, has secretly come to him begging for forgiveness, and she asks the Count to spare her son,' She looks ponderously out of the window, 'I think he'll end up marrying her.'

'No, he doesn't,' I say, somewhat mischievously.

'What?'

'He doesn't marry her. In the end, he falls in love with...'

'No, don't tell me!' Katherine places her hand on the closed book as if to protect whatever secrets it might hold, and she leans over the table and stares into my eyes. 'So, you've read it?'

I laugh and spread the jam on one half of my scone as Katherine fulfills her part of the bargain by pouring the tea. 'It's a favourite book of Mummy's; she reads it all the time. I think I must have read it myself at least half a dozen times over the years.' I take a bite from my scone and lean forward as it crumbles ferociously, whilst Katherine does the same.

'Well I'm working my way through the classics.' She sprays a mouthful of crumbs across the table as she speaks, and mumbles an apology in between sips of her tea. 'I'm going to read Alice in Wonderland next.'

'You mean Alice's Adventures in Wonderland.' I always took some delight in correcting her, but this time she chooses to ignore the comment. 'I think you'll find that quite a different read from Dumas' book.'

'Don't tell me you've read that too?' Katherine sighs as her shoulders droop. 'And please don't tell me what it's about.'

'Mummy likes to read, what can I say? The apple obviously hasn't strayed too far from the tree.' I glance at my watch. Mummy will most likely be with her bees. She visits the meadow every day and talks to them. My babies, she calls them. She can't live without them. It seems daft, but it makes her happy.'

'I wish I could say the same for my Mother,' Katherine replies.

'The same about what?'

'Reading, silly. I don't think I have ever seen her pick up a book. She's too busy preening herself to worry about such trivia.'

'Things still not going too well at home then?'

She shifts uneasily in her chair. 'Not since David started his new job; he's hardly ever home now, and she hates it. Speaking of apples, he's definitely the Orange Pippin in her eye. He only comes home at weekends, and even then, he's off out somewhere most of the time.'

'I think the last time I saw your brother was when I was about thirteen. Are you meeting up with him anytime soon, he was so dreamy?'

Katherine grimaces. 'Disgusting.' Finishing the last of her scone, she brushes the multitude of crumbs from her lap. 'Funny you should ask; he's coming home this weekend. Anyway, he's too old for you.'

'Mature,' I retort.

'Old,' Katherine repeats, but more firmly this time. She stands up and I follow her lead, picking up the uneaten half of my scone and placing it in a napkin for later. 'I tell you what,' she continues, 'if you're so keen to meet him why don't you come and stay?'

'What, you mean for the weekend?' I can feel my face burning at the thought, and lower my head and pull out my purse, as it is my turn to pay. 'I didn't think your mum liked you having anyone to stay?'

'Don't worry about that, with her darling David home I'm sure she won't even notice that you're there.'

As we leave the tea rooms I stop briefly and turn to Katherine. 'Look, there's something else I want to talk to you about.' I hesitate and look around cautiously, as if I'm about to share some awesome secret. 'Will you walk to the Green with me? I'm not going back to lessons this afternoon.'

'Sure, I have a free study period anyway,' she replies. 'We could go back and eat more scones.'

'No I don't think so.' I look backed into the tearooms which suddenly feel very small. 'Let's catch some of the sun on the Green.' Several students from the college are already camped out on the grass, and are taking advantage of the midsummer sun. Camberwell Green had been common grazing land for centuries, and now it stands out in stark contrast to the busy traffic working its way around the island of green carpet and well tendered borders. Nowadays it's a haven for young lovers meeting during their lunchtime work breaks, as well as students wanting to escape the pressures of college life. Following the same student tradition, we find a quiet spot toward the centre of the Green and sit on the grass.

Katherine lays back on the grass and places Alexander Dumas under her head. 'Now this is what I call studying.' She smiles and closes her eyes. 'College life is so tough.'

I sit cross legged beside her, pick a couple of daisies from the grass and begin to slowly dismantle them. 'That's what I want to talk to you about Katie; I don't think I'm coming back next term.'

Katherine's idyll ends abruptly, and she sits up sharply. 'What on earth are you talking about? You can't do that; it's your last year.'

'I've thought about it for some time. It's just not what I want to do.' I pull some more daisies from the grass and continue. 'I can't even remember what my last class was about; now that's pretty awful isn't it.'

She gives me her serious look. 'It's just a phase Mary. Listen, we've got the summer hols coming up in two weeks; you'll probably feel completely different once you've had a break.' She sits quietly for a moment, and then she lets out a growl as she stands up and paces off to the centre of the Green. Grabbing hold of a post with both hands, she gives an almighty scream and at the same time attempts to strangle the post. Several of the students sitting around us clap and cheer as she paces swiftly back and sits down as abruptly as she had stood. We didn't speak for several minutes. Katherine pulls the grass out in large tufts and begins throwing it aggressively to one side. 'What am I going to do Mary? I'll be here on my own.'

'I'm sorry Katie, really I am.' I sit with my head bowed. 'I'm going to miss you too, but the truth is I can't take another year of this.'

She stops her frantic destruction of the grass and looks squarely at me. 'So, what are you going to do? You haven't mentioned anything else.' Before I could reply, Katherine breathes in sharply and puts her hand to her mouth. 'Mary, what is your Mum going to say? Have you told her yet?'

'No, I haven't, and I don't know what she'll say,' I feel a cold pit in my stomach at the thought. 'She probably won't be too pleased, so don't you say anything to anyone, do you understand.' I try my hardest to imitate my mother's best scowl.

'Of course not, but you still haven't said what you want to do?'

'I'm not entirely sure; I have some ideas, but I just don't know how to go about it.'

'And what would that be Mary Swan?'

My mind raced through all the thoughts of the past several months. 'I would love to get into acting.' I wait for the cold derision of laughter to follow.

Katherine's eyes widen at my reply, and then slowly, a big, unexpected smile travels across her face. 'Really? In that case, you need to talk to David.'

I narrow my eyes. 'Why?'

'You do know what his job is? I'm sure I've told you before.'

'No, you haven't Katie.'

'Well in that case I'm not going to tell you now.' She lays on her back again, this time, holding the book close to her face in mock reading. 'I'm afraid you will just have to wait until the weekend to find out.'

Chapter 7

Diary; June 19th 1964

I push the doorbell for a second time. Mummy had driven me to Katherine's house but hadn't wanted to stay. After she had let me out of the car she had driven off more quickly than her normal snail's pace. I had originally arranged to travel with Katherine directly from the college, but Mummy had felt quite unwell in the morning, and so I had decided to stay at home. She hadn't said what was wrong; just that she felt under the weather.

I had offered to call the Doctor, but Mummy had been insistent that she would be fine, and she had recovered enough to offer to drive me, but she was not her usual self. I had been reluctant to accept the offer, as I hated being a passenger in the car with her. I was always saying to her that it was not that she was a bad driver; more that she would drive so slowly that other motorists would become extremely impatient and start to honk their horns. I found it so embarrassing, but she had been very good today; especially considering that it was Friday evening and the traffic was always at its worse then. But we had also been driving from Wraysbury, and most of the traffic had been going in the other direction.

I hadn't been to Katherine's house before, and as I had walked along the path to the front door I had looked back toward the large gated entrance; taking in the pristine borders and the well-manicured lawns. My gaze had run along the path and back up to the white painted house which was immaculately maintained and quite large. I had thought how it made Meadowsweet seem small in comparison, but that was really just an illusion. Looking over the walled borders, I notice that the houses either side are almost identical, and for some strange reason that disappoints me.

After getting no answer I press the doorbell for the third time; and am just beginning to wonder if anyone is home when the door swings open; and I jump back a little.

'I heard you the first time.' A tall lean man steps forward and fills the doorway with his body, glaring intensely at me. 'And who might you be?' he asks as he moves a little closer onto the threshold whilst staring straight into me.

I have to lean back slightly, and I look up and open my mouth to speak, but nothing comes out. Standing in front of me is the most beautiful thing I have ever seen in the world. He is so tall that his head touches the top of the door frame. His golden locks are rebelliously long, and his piercing blue eyes shine intensely, and as he moves, his unbuttoned shirt reveals a golden tanned chest. 'Well, speak up young lady; has the cat got your tongue?' he asks.

I watch his lips move and feel an instinctive urge to kiss them passionately, and I think about Emily Dickinson's poem;

> His feet are shod with gauze,
> His helmet is of gold;
> His breast, a single onyx
> With chrysoprase, inlaid.
> His labour is a chant,
> His idleness a tune;
> Oh, for a bee's experience
> Of clovers and of noon!

Before I can stop myself, I lift my hand and push my hair behind my ears. 'I....I....'

Just when I think that I will collapse from embarrassment, Katherine's voice bursts out from behind him, 'David, will you leave Mary alone you bully; and get out of the way so she can come in.'

'Oh, so you're Mary are you; the budding actress.' He smiles, revealing a line of perfect white teeth, and he offers his hand. 'Pleased to meet you Mary.'

I force myself to look beyond this man called David; this masterpiece of renaissance architecture; this dreamy boy who had become a man, and I glare at Katherine, finding it hard to believe that she would have told her brother about our conversation. Before I can offer my hand in anticipation of feeling his touch, which I know of course will be heaven itself, Katherine pulls her brother out of the doorway. 'David! Mary told me that in confidence,' she hisses, and she grabs my arm. 'Come on, let's get out of the way; he's being insufferable tonight.'

He laughs; and it sounds like cool water trickling softly on a hot summer's day. Katherine leads me quickly into a spacious and elegant hallway and pushes me hurriedly up a wide curving staircase. A flurry of emotions prevents me from taking in the plethora of pictures lining the walls on our swift journey aloft.

'I'll see you at dinner in an hour,' David calls out as we make it onto the landing, and I turn to see him disappearing through a door into an unknown room, and at that moment I experience a surge of despair and disappointment which leaves me feeling unfulfilled and bereft. We stop briefly at the top, and I use the opportunity to take in my surroundings. The only word I can think of to describe my setting is 'graceful'.

Katherine shrugs and pushes the door open to her bedroom to reveal an entirely different world. My eyes widen at the total chaos I see around me; with clothes thrown on every possible surface; folders and papers strewn about the floor, and large posters adorn purple painted walls. Katherine catches my expression and simply says, 'I tidied the room because you were coming.'

We stand in silence for a few seconds, and then we turn to look at each other before bursting into laughter. Through the intermittent hilarity, I offer to help Katherine tidy the room just a little more.

Precisely one hour later Katherine leads the way back down the stairway. This time I take the opportunity to examine the pictures filling the walls. There are a few photographs of Katherine, obviously taken when she was much younger, but there are several of David, and simply loads of a glamorous looking woman in a number of different poses. 'Who is that?' I ask Katherine.

'Oh, that's Mummy,' she says dismissively. 'And the man is Daddy, but we don't talk about him.'

'Why on earth not?' I ask without thinking.

She ignores my question and nudges me further down the staircase. 'Remember what I said Mary,' she warns in a low voice, 'My mother likes to be complimented.'

'Complimented on what?'

'On everything, but more specifically on how she looks,' she replies, breathing out rapidly. 'Weren't you listening to me?' She stops on the stairs and lowers her voice further. 'Look, she's insecure; what can I say. She catches her breath. Why is it that whispering always makes you feel as if you have just stopped running? 'She will have spent the past two hours preening herself, especially because David is home for the weekend, and when I told her at breakfast that you were staying, well, it was almost too much.'

'You mean she doesn't want me here?' I ask in horror.

'No, it's not that, it's just that she has....' Katherine shakes her head from side to side. 'Well, she has insecurities; like I said.' She closes her eyes. 'Look... on her dressing table is a photo of Elizabeth Taylor, and she's with some guy called Rock somebody or another.'

'Oh, you mean Rock Hudson.'

'Yes, that's the one.'

'That would have been from Giant.'

'Giant what?' she asks.

'The film Giant,' I explain. 'Liz and Rock are in the film, and she has short dark, curly hair, and well, she's gorgeous.' Katherine frowns. 'What's the look?' I ask.

'I think that I make her feel old.'

'What do you mean?'

Before she can reply, David appears at the foot of the stairs. 'What are you two whispering about?' he asks accusingly.

'Mind your own,' Katherine replies, and turns me around to continue down the stairs.

∞ ∞ ∞

Katherine's mother is seated and waiting at the table as we come into the room. 'So, Mary, I hear that you are leaving college.' As I sit down I cast a sideways glance at Katherine, who in turn glares at her brother, and he just raises his eyebrows nonchalantly at his sister. It must have been David who had told his mother about my intentions, but I am curiously embarrassed by the public discussion of my private thoughts.

'I haven't entirely decided yet Mrs Hunter.' I reply as I fight to find an answer that might end the conversation without being rude. 'I'm er...considering my options.'

'I see,' she replies.

If all that she is going to say is *I see*, then I am probably getting off lightly, but I still hate it when people say I that. What they really mean is, I don't approve, or, that's a ridiculous idea.

'Have you spoken to your mother about it?' she asks. I'm beginning to worry that this might turn into a full-blown interrogation.

'Mary told me that she is going to talk to her mother after the weekend,' David replies to his mother, 'She asked me if I could give her some advice.' As he speaks to his mother he smiles broadly at me, and without looking away he continues, 'Now where's dinner mother? I'm starving.' Katherine looks at her brother with mild shock, and I fall even more in love with him; this gallant knight who has just come to my rescue. The fact that he caused the problem in the first place is neither here nor there. At that moment, a rather plump woman dressed in black, and wearing a white apron comes through the door with a large dish containing roast lamb edged with steaming vegetables, and the conversation turns to food.

∞ ∞ ∞

I fall backwards with arms outstretched onto Katherine's bed. 'Oh, I'm so full,' I say, and place my hands on my swollen stomach. 'Your mum is an amazing cook.'

'Cook is an amazing cook,' Katherine replies. 'That's the one good thing about staying here. Anyway, I'm surprised that you managed to get any food into your mouth.'

'What do you mean?' I do my best to look puzzled, although I know perfectly well what she's talking about.

Katherine laughs. 'Oh c'mon. You spent the whole time talking to David; and when you weren't talking, your mouth was drooling disgustingly.'

I feel my embarrassment returning, 'Well he's...' I struggle to find the words to describe him.

'He's my brother Philippa Mary Swan.' Katherine only uses my full name when she's annoyed, or angry, or both.

'I was going to say that he's an assistant film producer. Of course I wanted to talk to him. Anyway, wasn't it your idea in the first place?' Katherine remains silent, and I sit up. 'Look....if it makes you happy I won't talk to him again for the rest of the weekend.'

I hold my breath as Katherine paces the room, and then she stops to look at me, her face a picture of concern. 'He's nearly twenty-three you know.' She continues her pacing.

'Yes, and I'm nearly nineteen, that's only four years' difference.... you know,' I reply, mimicking Katherine. 'Oh come on Katherine, don't do this to me, please.'

She stops at the bedroom window and lifts the curtain slightly. I can hear a car leaving.

Katherine!' I throw a pillow at her, 'Are you listening?'

In response she turns to face me. 'Can we be serious for a minute?' She walks over to the bed and sits down. 'Mary, you know we are friends.'

'Of course I do,' I reply.

'I think that you should know that David has just gone out for the evening.'

'And?'

'And he's probably gone to see one of his girlfriends.'

I wince at the thought but try hard not show it.

'One of his many girlfriends; you understand what I'm saying,' she adds.

Chapter 8

How do you forget the past? How do you forgive someone? I have pondered these questions so many times over the years. I wish I could fly away. I don't want to be amongst beautiful colours; they just make me sad. But if I leave, I will go back to a life of looking at the colours of other people's lives. Explaining to the ignorant what the artist was trying to say when he used those colours. Was there really no escape?

'Penny for your thoughts?' Jemima finished clearing the lunchtime debris away and took a seat opposite me at the kitchen table.

'Oh I'm sorry,' I replied, 'I was just thinking about work. What were you saying?'

'It wasn't that important. I was asking whether you knew how long you were able to stay.'

'To be honest, I really don't know. I left in such a hurry that we didn't get time to discuss it. Lucinda did say that I could take as long as I needed; but what she means by that is anyone's guess. Knowing her as I do, she probably means get it sorted and get back; not a second more.'

'Look, if you need to go...'

'Let's cross that bridge when it happens,' I said. 'Besides, it looks like there are issues we need to deal with.'

'Can she manage without you?' she asked.

'Well I'm her personal assistant, but just lately she's been leaving me to do everything. She's courting one of the rival art houses, I think in the hopes of a merger; but that means that she's hardly ever there.'

'So she can't manage without you.' Jemima looked concerned.

I smiled at that thought. 'Lucinda would like nothing more than to make me think that I'm not really needed. She thinks it helps her keep control of her minions; but I know how hard she must be working right now. So it won't do her any harm.'

'It must seem really quiet here,' she said in reply.

'Are you kidding?' I replied. 'It's just so nice to spend some of the day looking at real colours. The gardens never did disappoint. And I don't have to explain to a buyer what the artist was trying to say.'

'Anyway,' she replied. 'It's after one so it would be a good idea to wake Mummy. What if I make her some lunch and you take it up? If she's not already sitting on the balcony reading.'

∞ ∞ ∞

I gave my customary knock on the bedroom door and entered the room. 'I'm reading,' Mummy called from the balcony.

'Hello Mummy; how are you feeling?' I sat by her and could feel the warmth of the afternoon sun.

'Same as yesterday...I'm sure.' She looked thoughtful. 'I have a question Connie.'

'Yes Mummy; what is it?'

'Did we talk about.... well, my memories?'

'I smiled reassuringly at her. 'Yes, we did.' I omitted to say that it was just this morning that we had spoken, and I wondered if taking her for a walk in the gardens would be such a good idea.

She frowned, and then she smiled. 'We did? Oh, that's wonderful.'

I placed my hand on hers; maybe reassuring her was going to become quite important. 'We've been reading about many of your memories.'

'Oh.' She paused in thought for some time. 'Do you think I've done the right thing dear?'

'I'm not sure what you mean Mummy.'

'I wonder?' she said, 'if I should have left my memories with the bees?'

'I can put them back if you would like me to,' I said, and was surprised to find that I felt almost relieved at the thought. 'We need never talk about them again.' I was still unsure about whether I wished to know all that was in the diaries.

Mummy sat in silence, as if looking for the right thoughts. 'No....no this is the right thing. I don't entirely know why; but I know that it's the right thing to do.' She turned to me with a look of resolution on her face. 'We must read them Connie. Katherine would want it that way.'

We sat quietly for a while. 'Mummy?'

'Yes dear?'

'What do you remember about her?'

'She smiled sweetly at me. 'I remember that I loved her; I love her still, and I miss her.' She picked up the diary. 'I don't want to forget her Connie.'

An hour later we were making our way through the kitchen door and into the gardens. Mummy seemed unsure as to which way to go, and so I put her arm in mine and led the way. She moved much more slowly than I had imagined she would, and in a way, that told me more about her condition than the Doctor could ever express. The soft warm breeze was pleasant on the skin, so I relaxed a little. When we reached the white gate, she stopped and looked around her and a smile crossed her face. But then her eyes narrowed, as if something was wrong. 'Are you okay Mummy?' I pulled her arm tight into mine in an attempt to reassure her.

She reached out and held the gate; and then she repeated what I had just said. 'Are you okay Mummy?'

I was unsure what to do. 'I'm fine,' I replied.

Very slowly, the smile returned, and I felt her relax once again. 'That's far enough,' she said as she let go of the gate. 'The bees have worked hard enough today. I don't want to bother them anymore.'

Chapter 9

Diary; June 22nd 1964

Monday morning; it's raining heavily. That's not going to improve my mood. I haven't seen David again, even though he was supposed to be staying for the whole weekend, and I've wasted all my time at Katherine's pining for him to return. I've also tried, unsuccessfully, to compliment Katherine's mother, who it appears, can see right through me. She is not impressed in the slightest. It's probably in my best interests to try and avoid her; for the rest of my life, if that is possible.

After my shower, I make my way down to the kitchen in my dressing gown and make some breakfast. I'm quite sure that it's officially the worst day of my life. I'm going to have to tell Mummy that I'm leaving college, and I am not looking forward to that. I had arrived home late the previous night, and the house was dark, so I had assumed that Mummy had retired to bed, and in my efforts not to make any noise I had banged my toe on the bottom stair and it is still throbbing like mad. I really don't feel like eating my breakfast; I had eaten so much over the weekend; another reason to be depressed.

I glance across to the kitchen and notice the unwashed dishes in the sink. When I think about it, the back door had been unlocked when I had arrived home last night. Perhaps Mummy is still feeling unwell, and had gone to bed early. I can't help thinking that something is missing from the kitchen, but can't put my finger on it, so I leave my empty cup at the table, go back upstairs and gently tap on Mummy's bedroom door and wait; but there's no answer. I tap again, this time a little louder, and call her, but there is still no reply. Perhaps I should have brought her some tea; an even better idea would have been to ask her if I could cook her some breakfast; maybe that would improve her mood, and help soften my bad news. I knock more loudly this time and open the door. 'Mummy, it's me; are you okay?'

My stomach drops cold. The bed is empty.

So many questions shoot through my mind. What is happening? Had she left? Why were the dishes unwashed, and why was the back door still unlocked? I can't make sense of this. And then the realisation hits me. Mummy begins collecting small amounts of honey at this time of year. I run down to the kitchen and stand in the doorway, looking for something. Then I see it. The bucket is missing. The bucket that Mummy uses to collect the honey is gone. I feel cold and sick, and I begin to shake. She could still be in the meadow; with the bees. There is no use getting wild ideas; I have to try and stay calm. I run to the door and open it violently, only to be met with a sheet of rain. I step out into the garden but stop quickly. I need to think. What to do? What to do? Should I call the police? But what if she isn't there? Will they be angry? But if she is, then every second might make a difference. I run back into the house, through the kitchen and into the hallway. I pick the phone up and hesitate as I put my finger into the dialler; then my resolve returns as I dial the first nine. It seems to take forever for the dial to return. I dial the second nine, wait again, and then the third. The sound of the ringing makes me jump, and as I turn I see my reflection in the hall mirror. Looking back is a scared and fragile young girl; and I want to cry.

I turn away from the mirror as a voice cuts in. 'What service please?'

'What?' I reply.

The voice repeats the question, and I stutter a reply. 'My mother is missing, and I think she might be hurt.' The words slap me hard, and I feel the tears burning my cheeks.

The voice speaks again. 'Do you know what is wrong with her?'

'I can't find her,' I reply through the tears. 'I can't find her.'

I hear muffled words on the line, but can't understand what is being said. 'Hello?' I say, afraid that I might have lost the voice.

Then another voice comes on the line. 'Hello.' It's a man; calm; reassuring. 'Hello, my name is Peter. Do you mind if I ask your name?'

'Uh, Philippa, I mean Mary, my name is Mary.'

'Ok, Philippa Mary. 'he says reassuringly. Nobody but Katherine has called me that in such a long time. 'Now; I would like to help you; so just start from the beginning, and then I can send the right people.'

'Thank you, Peter.' I want to know this man. I want to hold on to him; to be comforted by him, and I imagine that he might be my father. Perhaps the man that had left us alone was not really my father. How could he have been? My real father would never have left; he would have been there when we needed him; just as Peter is now.

'Alright young lady, this is what we are going to do,' he says, and I realise that I have explained the whole problem to him. 'An ambulance and a police car are on their way. I'm sure that she is alright, but we are not going to take any chances. So, I don't want you to worry about that. Now this is what I want you to do.'

He speaks to me for a few more minutes, and he gives me clear instructions, saying that somebody will be there very soon. 'Thank you,' I say tearfully, 'Thank you Peter.'

'Now off you go child, and be careful.'

'Thank you,' I say once more and replace the receiver. 'Thank you, Daddy.'

I run up to the landing and open the linen cupboard, where I grab a large blanket as Peter had instructed, and then I run back down the stairs to the kitchen. My coat and boots are near the back door, and I slide the coat on quickly over my dressing gown and run out of the door. Halfway across the garden I realise that I have forgotten the umbrella, but it's too late to go back now. As I reach the gate I can see that it has been opened and has swung back halfway. The wind is cutting across the meadow, driving the rain sideways. I stop and blink the water out of my eyes and peer through the rain. I can see nothing, and so I push the gate fully open and step into the meadow. As I walk forward I see the dark outline of someone lying on the grass next to the hives. I move slowly toward the lifeless shape and stop about five feet away, afraid to go any nearer.

I pull the collar of the coat around me and whisper softly. 'Mummy.' There is no reply, and so I call a little louder. 'Mummy....are you alright.' The outline moves a little, and I breathe out sharply, and then I realised that it isn't Mummy, but bees that are moving. They are covering her entire body and had responded to my voice. I start to shake, wondering if the bees might try to attack, but I need to get to her. I wipe the water from my face and cover my mouth with my hand in an attempt to stop crying. I move forward through the rain, and I can see that she is lying face down. There doesn't appear to be an inch of her body not covered in bees. I'm certain they don't like the rain, so what are they were doing?

'Oh Mummy.' I sigh. 'What have they done to you?'

'Mary?' A soft, barely perceptible voice, that sounds so unlike Mummy, speaks. 'Mary, is that you?'

'Mummy; you're alright! Are you alright?' I can't see her beneath the moving mass. 'The bees; what are they doing?'

'I can't move Mary,' she says in a whisper. 'I fell, and I can't move. They are looking after me.'

'What?' I stop a short distance from her. The bees are moving; writhing like one creature. There are so many of them on her, and those on the top are constantly changing places with the ones underneath. I ask her how long she has been here.

''I don't know.' She sounds so weak. 'What time is it?'

'It's Monday morning.'

'I came here after dinner; Sunday.'

'Oh my goodness, you must be so cold. I need to get the bees off you. What should I do? I don't know what to do.' I begin to shake with the cold. 'An ambulance is coming, and I have a blanket. Shall I cover you over?' I wait for more, but nothing comes. 'What shall I do?'

There is a long pause and then Mummy says, 'ask them to leave Mary....ask them to leave, but thank them.'

'Thank them?' I ask.

She speaks again, but more calmly this time. 'Ask them to leave Mary.'

I look at the scene in front of me, and I can't see how I can cover her with the blanket without the bees leaving, and so I stand up and wait, and then I speak. 'Please, please leave,' I say softly, 'I need to look after Mummy now.' Then I surprise myself. 'But thank you; thank you for looking after her.'

I wait for a while in silence, and then I hear the faint sound of a siren in the distance. The ambulance is coming, and I speak to the bees again. 'They are coming to help her now; she will be alright; you can go now.' I close my eyes, causing tears to roll down my cheeks and mix with the rain. 'Please, let me have her back, please.' I lick the rain, and the tears, from my lips; and I taste honey.

I watch as the bees rise into the air. First just a few; then more as the air becomes filled with the sound of thousands of vibrating wings. The noise increases until it builds into a crescendo, and I close my eyes, afraid of what I might see. The air rushes and spins all around me, taking my breath away. I can feel my wet hair lifting and swirling around my face. The sensation of the rain slowly ceases, only to be replaced by the warmed air of a hundred thousand bees flying around me, and I can't feel my feet, and for just the briefest of moments, it feels as if I am floating through the air. Slowly, very slowly, the sound dies away; and the wind is once again replaced by the awareness of rain, and I can feel the ground again, and hear the wind, and within seconds I am wet again. I feel heavier than I ever have before. I open my eyes slowly to see steam rising from Mummy's body, and her clothes appear to be completely dry. The bees have gone.

On the ground; all around her, are hundreds; possibly thousands of bees, and I know then that these lifeless shapes have given everything to protect her. I quickly kneel beside her, and cover her with the blanket. And as I lean forward I glance up at the hives, and for the second time that morning I say, 'thank you.' And as I lay the blanket over her, I softly recite part of a poem Mummy had said to me so many times.

> What's left to us is only a kiss –
> The kisses bristly like the little bees,
> That die the moment they desert the hive.[2]

---

[2] Persephone's Bees by Osip Mandelstam

∞ ∞ ∞

The cry of a child wakes me from my dream, and I am back in the waiting room of the hospital. I move my body and feel the ache of stillness. The seats are not designed to encourage comfort; the wood is cold and hard. They obviously want people to leave this place as soon as possible to make room for the next group of waiting, and worrying, relatives and friends.

The journey to the hospital in the ambulance had been both scary and loud. How could they stand working in such a thing? They had been wonderful; the way they had taken care of Mummy so well, but they still didn't know what was wrong with her. The nurses had let me go through with her for a while, but her condition had worsened, and now I am cold and tired. I have seen so many people come and go, but it's quieter now; although it's an unpleasant, hollow silence. I'm still wearing my coat, and underneath that, my dressing gown, and my feet are still gracefully shod with oversize wellington boots. I haven't even been able to brush my hair, so I can just imagine what onlookers are thinking; probably that I've escaped from the local asylum. One of the policemen had kindly offered to take me home, but I knew that I wouldn't be able to get back to the hospital, and so I had decided to wait. Now I'm wondering if I had made the right decision.

It crosses my mind to go to the reception desk again to see if they have any news, but after my last attempt I think that they're getting somewhat annoyed. They always seem to be so busy, but busy doing what? Why can't they be busy helping me to find out what's wrong with my mother? And I can't stop thinking about what had happened in the meadow. What exactly had happened? Did I imagine all of it? But I'm here, now, at the hospital, with Mummy. Even the ambulance men had seen all the dead bees, and they had expressed concern that Mummy may have been stung many times over. The truth is, they had not found a single bee sting.

I had persuaded the receptionist to let me call Katherine, who hadn't been at home. I knew that she couldn't do much, but I just needed to talk to someone. I had to leave a message with Katherine's mother, who sounded sympathetic when I told her what had happened, but also seemed somewhat disinterested; distant even. The clock on the wall above the reception desk tells me it is ten to nine. It looks as if I might have to sleep in the waiting room all night.

I hear another baby cry, and as I turn to look, Katherine walks into the waiting room. 'Oh my, thank goodness you've come,' I say as I stand up and waddle across the waiting room and hug her. Tears well up.

'Well it's a miracle we found you; there are several hospitals in this town you know,' she replies.

'Yes, I know that, so...?'

Katherine stands back and holds up her hands. 'So.... you didn't tell Mummy which one you were in. Fortunately, this is only the second one we have tried.'

'Sorry....did you say, we?'

'Yes; someone had to drive.'

'So, who brought you?'

'I did.' I turn toward the golden silky voice to find David standing in the doorway.

The whole weekend, I had dreamed of our next meeting; imaging so many romantic scenarios; most of which involved soft music and ambient lighting, and now this. I'm finding it hard to breathe, and I can hear Katherine asking if I'm okay, but it's as if she's calling to me from the end of a long tunnel. I reach out to grab hold of something, but I'm falling into a deep black hole. The last thing I see is Katherine and David running toward me.

I'm floating on a soft bed; enjoying the feeling of David's cool hand on my face. If I open my eyes I know he will stop, and the moment will be gone. 'Mary.' I can hear Katherine calling, and her voice sounds urgent. 'Can you hear me Mary?' The coolness vanishes, and I slowly open my eyes, only to find that Katherine is not there. There is just a nurse by the side of the bed, and she's rinsing a cloth in a bowl of water. 'Mary. You're back with us again.' She smiles softly and places the cool cloth back on my head.

'Where is he?' I ask with some urgency.

'The doctor will be here soon,' The nurse replies, and I feel too dizzy to argue. Katherine comes into the room and walks around to the other side of the bed. She has a look concern on her face, but smiles softly and looks up as the doctor walks through the door.

'Hello young lady; what have we been up to then?' he asks me.

I notice that in place of my coat and wellingtons, I am wearing a hospital gown. Before I can say a word, Katherine answered for me. 'She has been here since early this morning waiting for news of her mother, Mrs Swan. Can you tell us anything?'

'I tell you what.' He replies. 'Let's have a look at...' He pauses, leans sideways and takes a glance at the clipboard hanging on the end of the bed. '.... Mary; let's have a look at Mary, and then perhaps we'll find out what's going on. How does that sound?'

'Perfect,' Katherine replies. 'So, you're a doctor, are you?'

'Well that's what it says on my badge,' he smiles broadly. 'Doctor Simons. But if you want to know anything special then you should always ask the nurses.' The nurse picks up the bowl and cloth and, after raising her eyes to the sky, wanders off.

'I can tell you what's wrong with her,' Katherine continues. 'She needs to eat something, she's exhausted.'

He smiles patiently. 'That's probably all that it is, but we always like to make sure. So, give me five minutes and then we'll get Mary something to eat.'

'You can do that?' Katherine asks, 'Gosh you must be pretty good at your job.' At first, I thought that she was being sarcastic, that is until I could see look of sheer adoration on her face.

'Well, I can arrange for somebody to do that,' he replies. 'Now, I'm just going to sit you up a little, and then we can check that you're okay.'

After he has lifted the back of the bed, I lean forward and whisper to Katherine. 'Where's David?'

'He's probably on the phone knowing him; cancelling one of his many dates no doubt,' she replies.

'Do you think so?' I begin to feel quite important.

'Well he didn't have to go to the film set today, so he picked me up from college, and brought me home. When we heard what had happened, he offered to drive me wherever I needed to go.'

'Really?' I reply, as the Doctor lifts my wrist, holds it between his fingers and looks at his watch. I can feel my pulse start to quicken, and I glance at him guiltily, then turn to Katherine. 'He must have been so disappointed when he saw me in the waiting room. Is he coming back? How long are you staying?'

With the Doctor's wry smile and one of Katherine's looks, I'm beginning to feel claustrophobic. 'Mary, you are so transparent,' she replies. 'I told you, he has lots of girlfriends, and most of them are older; than him I mean. In fact, I think some of them are even married.'

'You're a fine one to talk,' I reply. 'Look at how you flirted with the Doctor.'

Katherine blushes, glares at me fiercely and glances quickly at the Doctor, who just lowers my wrist and continues his observations. 'Well everything seems fine here,' he says. 'So...I will arrange for something to eat for you.' Picking up the clipboard from the end of the bed, he scribbles quickly on the paper; and without looking up he asks, 'what was your Mother's name again?'

I open my mouth to speak, but Katherine bursts in. 'Swan.... Mrs Swan.'

He turns to look at me for confirmation. 'Constance Swan,' I confirm.

'Thank you. I will go and check on Mrs Swan. In the meantime, I will leave you young ladies to catch up on your love lives.' He smiles first at me, and then at Katherine, and leaves, only to return a short while later with a rather disappointing looking sandwich. I am so hungry I take a large bite without even looking at the contents between the slices of bread. He explains that Mummy is comfortable but sedated, and that they are going to do more tests in the morning. He also tells me, much to my disappointment, that there is nothing more they can do tonight, and that when we are ready we should go home and get a good night's rest.

∞ ∞ ∞

How can being so uncomfortable be such a pleasure. Every time David changes gear in the car he touches my arm. Both Katherine and I are squashed into the front seat of his sports car; in fact, they are the only seats, and although I'm beginning to ache from sitting in such an awkward position, right now I wouldn't want to be anywhere else. Katherine had offered to let me stay with her, and David had returned just in time to be instructed by his sister that he was to take us both back to the house, after first stopping off at my house to pick up some things. She had then gone on to tell him that he would also be bringing us back to the hospital tomorrow, at which point, I had blushed at her directness.

David had smiled softly and slid his jacket on before making his way to the exit. 'Come on then you two.' He had said. 'I'm going to have to ring my boss and give him the bad news.'

When we get back to her house, I find that I'm so tired that I need Katherine to help me walk in a straight line; but that didn't stop my mind from racing in all sorts of directions with conflicting emotions, all vying for position and trying their hardest to overwhelm me.

Chapter 10

Colours splash all over me as I try to make sense of the canvas. The sun once again pours its light into the scene and I'm distracted by its brightness. I try to push the colours away, but my hands sink into them and I can feel myself being sucked into the picture; and I ask myself; is this my opus; my life?

I sat back into the fireside chair and soaked in the heat of the fire; remembering my first night home. It had been quite a few years since I had sat in this room, and I thought about Jake, and I wanted to both smile and cry all at once. He had sat in the chair opposite me, and we had spoken about our future together; where we would live; the travelling we would do, and the children we would make. And I had spent my days back then thinking of nothing else but him. But the very last time we had been in this room together, he had pleaded with me to forgive him; to let him have another chance. But how could there be another chance? He had painted thick black lines over our brightly coloured canvas, and they would always be there to alter the landscape. I took another sip of my chocolate, clinging to the mug for comfort. 'It's been a long time Jem.'

'Seventeen years.' Jemima curled her legs up onto the chair and placed her finished cup of hot chocolate on the side table. 'Why did you never come and see us?' The light of the day had all but gone, leaving the glow of the woodburner to light the side of her face.

'I thought we'd covered that subject,' I replied, as if I was dealing with a PowerPoint presentation; and I changed the subject. 'Did Mummy ever talk to you about...Daddy?'

Jemima looked puzzled, and wiped her sleeve across her eyes. 'Why would you bring that up now?'

'Haven't you ever wondered who he was? I mean, what kind of person he was.' I thought back to the diary entries about David; my father; our father. I wondered how different life might have been if he were here now, and I imagined him sitting opposite me in Jemima's chair, as he most likely would have done. 'We know more about Aunt Katherine than we do Daddy.'

'No, Mummy never spoke about him. She has told me stories about her time in Italy; but she had the gift of talking only of magical things; never the dark stuff. She loved to paint enchanting pictures with her words.' Jemima picked up her empty mug and peered into it; as if she were looking for something. 'I'm not sure I would want to know.'

That took me by surprise. I knew so little about Jemima; at least the Jemima of now. 'What have you been doing with yourself since...?'

'Since you left,' she finished, and she placed her mug back onto the side table. 'Well it feels like I've done so much, but when I really think about it, probably very little really. Bringing up the twins I suppose.'

'There's still time for dreams Jem,' I replied. 'What would you have liked to have done?'

She replied without hesitating. 'I always wanted to be an artist, like Aunt Katherine.' I saw her smile at the thought.

'So, why don't you?'

'What do you mean?'

'Why not have some fun? The workshop is still there. Perhaps when Mummy...' I stopped myself, realising I was discussing the inevitability of our Mother's death.

We sat silently for several minutes.

'Do you like your job?' Jemima asked.

'Yes. Yes, I do; very much so. I sometimes get frustrated with prissy artists who are so far up their own backsides that it's a wonder they can hold a brush, but in all, I get to see some amazing work. It can be truly inspiring at times.'

'Doesn't it make you want to paint?'

'No, not really. I occasionally feel envious of a particular artist and their talent, and I wish that I were able to interpret the world in such a way, but when you talk to them, you realise that they're just like you and me; trying to find the answers to life's problems, but they are just doing it in a different way.' I placed my finished cup down. 'The truth is, when you get to sit quietly with one of these people you find that they are full of doubts and insecurities.' I gave a soft laugh. 'It might surprise you to know that part of my job description is being a counsellor and comforter to troubled artists. I've become quite skilled at it you know.'

'You always were Connie.'

'How do you mean?'

'I could always come to you for advice.'

'Really?' I said in surprise. 'But you've had Mummy, haven't you?'

'I always felt that you understood; whatever the problem. Even boyfriend trouble.'

'Then.... why Jem? Why Jake?'

She was silent for some time. 'Because I was jealous.'

'And that's it? That's the reason?'

'I'm sorry I haven't got a better one. I can never make it okay Connie; and I'm sorry for that. If you only knew how sorry I am.'

'It would have been easier if you'd loved him. Did you ever...love him?

'No.... I'm sorry.'

'I loved him you know. I loved him with all my soul; every part of me. He sat right where you are now, and we spoke about our future. It was as if it had already happened. We even spoke about the children. Our children; my children. The children that you had.'

'I'm so sorry.' Tears poured from Jemima.

I ignored them and continued. 'We even discussed whose eyes they would have....and they both look like him you know. Michael has his eyes.'

'Yes, he does.'

'How could I come home? I couldn't bear to look into his eyes.'

'Oh Connie, I can't bear it.' She sobbed and buried her face in her hands. 'I lost you, and now I'm going to lose Mummy; and when that has happened, I'll lose you again. It's just too much Connie.'

I rose from the chair and went over to her. 'It's alright Jem. I'm here now.' And as I spoke the words, I realised that it didn't hurt so much anymore. But how much would it hurt if I saw him; or at the very least, saw his eyes? I had no doubt that if I stayed long enough that would happen.

Chapter 11

Diary; June 23rd 1964

'Good morning you; time to eat.' I slide my eyes open to find Katherine at the foot of the bed in her dressing gown and carrying a tray. 'Hurry up, this is heavy, and it's going cold.'

I still feel so tired, but I sit up in the bed slowly and pull the hair out my face. 'What time is it?'

'Ten o'clock lazybones, I tried to wake you earlier, but you were having none of it.' The tray of bacon, sausage, eggs, tomatoes and mushrooms she places on the bed make me think of Mummy.

'Have you heard anything from the hospital?' I ask.

'Not a sausage, excuse the....er.'

'Pun?'

'Oh yes. Anyway, what we thought was that, rather than wait, you could call the hospital shortly, and based on what they say, decide what to do.'

'That sounds good to me.... Is David...?'

'He went out very early this morning,' she tells me, much to my disappointment. 'But he said he would be back in time to do whatever.'

I try my hardest not to let Katherine see my reaction, but I suspect she knows me well enough to guess that I'm pleased.

Katherine and her mother stand close by, as I sit in the hallway by the telephone and nervously dial the number to the hospital. I begin to shake when I remember the emergency call I had made just the day before; I try not to think about the meadow, but the images keep flashing into my mind. I can still hear the bees, and feel the soft, warm vibration of their wings. The phone crackles after they put me on hold for several minutes, during which time I look apologetically at Katherine's mother, and then jump nervously when the receptionist comes back on the line.

Once I finish the call I take a deep breath and turn to Katherine. 'They told me that she had had a comfortable night; whatever that means, and that I can visit her after two o'clock.'

'Did they tell you what the problem was?' Katherine's mother asks.

'They said I could talk to the Doctor this afternoon.'

'Well that's not much help is it,' she says abruptly.

'Mother!' Katherine barks. 'That's not helping either. Mary is stressed enough as it is.' Her Mother doesn't reply, but attempts to smile at me as she wanders into the drawing room. I need some time to think, so I collect my jacket from the bedroom and go for a walk along the lane. I try and clear my mind, but can't stop thinking about David; about how kind and gallant he had been, and even though we had barely spoken; I really feel that we have a connection, but I can't help but feel guilty that I'm thinking of him, and not Mummy.

David arrives back just in time for lunch at one o'clock; I'm hoping that we might get an opportunity to talk, but his Mother wants his attention and keeps him busy the whole time. I'm secretly hoping that because David only has a two-seater car, it will be just the two of us on the journey to the hospital, but his mother offers to let us use her car. I am pretty sure that's because she doesn't want us to be alone together. I am grateful at least, that I get to sit in the front on the way there, and Katherine, reluctantly, sits in the back. We all travel in silence for a while, as, ironically, now I have the opportunity to speak to David, I don't know what to say.

'So Mary.... you said that you would like to be in films?' David asks, and I jump awake.

'Well yes, I think I would,' I reply.

'To be an actress?'

'Yes; it's something I've thought about all of my life; every time I watch a film, I have this feeling inside.' I must sound like a teenager. What is he going to think?

'That's great,' he replies.

That's great. He said that's great. I wasn't expecting that, and I sit up in my seat. 'I am so inspired by actresses like Elizabeth Taylor,' I say in a very grown up voice, as I feel Katherine's eyes boring into my back.

'Do you know how much I would love to work on one of her films?' he says excitedly. 'She is just amazing.'

We talk all the way to the hospital, and I almost forget where we are going. As we step out of the car, my elation turns to disappointment when David says that he will pick us up later and promptly drives away without another word.

We make our way to the ward and are ushered to the waiting room, where we are told that the Doctor is with Mummy. Half an hour later a nurse comes to find us, and we are taken into a consulting room. The Doctor sits quietly for some minutes looking through a pile of notes; long enough to feel a coldness in my stomach. Are all those pieces of paper about Mummy? He closes the papers and looks up, smiling. I'm beginning to learn not to trust people when they smile. 'Now.... Constance Swan.' He glances back at the pile of papers. 'Well, young lady,' he says. If another person calls me young lady, I think that I might explode. 'Your mother has had a cerebrovascular accident.'

I am sure that he can see that I look puzzled, and so he continues. 'She has suffered a stroke.' He pauses, and looks as if he's waiting for a reaction. 'We can't say what has caused this, but it seems likely that is was as a result of a thrombosis or blockage. What we can say is that Mrs Swan has lost some of her motor functions.'

I shift uneasily in the chair. 'What does that mean?'

'It's too early to say as some functions do return after a short period of time, but she has very little use of her left arm, and her vision is not as clear as it was previously'.

I want to cry.

'The good news is,' he continues, smiling again, 'that it's entirely possible, as I said, that some of the function will return. In the meantime, we will place Mrs Swan on a program of medication and physiotherapy to help strengthen those areas affected.

I try to imagine that I am Liz Taylor in a hospital melodrama, and that I need answers. 'What's the bad news?' I ask, surprised at my own confidence.

'The bad news is,' he continues, 'that we can't be certain that it's not going to happen again.'

Leaning forward, I hold his gaze, and he looks down and moves the papers around nervously. 'As far as we can tell her memory is fine; she certainly remembers you. But there may be...' He pauses again, '.... occasions. You need to be prepared for this to happen at any time; but we'll go through the details with you when we have a clearer picture of Mrs Swan's full condition.'

I can feel my resolve weakening, and Katherine takes hold of my hand and squeezes it. We both sit silently for some time, and the questions form a disorderly queue in my mind.

Katherine is the first to speak. 'Okay Doc, what do we do now?

He breathes out slowly, possibly thinking that his ordeal is over. But he takes a while to answer, as if he is still gathering his thoughts. 'We need to talk about that, but for the time being, we'll keep Mrs Swan under close observation. Do you have someone to stay with, Miss Swan?' he asks.

Katherine doesn't hesitate in replying. 'She's staying with me Doc.'

He sighs, as if a burden has just lifted that isn't his, and I wonder if I should be grateful that he cares, but in reality, I'm beginning to feel angry at the whole situation, and I wish I had someone to blame. My questions start to become an orderly list, and at the top of the page is the one that asks, *what about me? What about my dreams, my life?* And then another question asks; *how can I be so selfish?*

We leave the Doctor's office and make our way to the ward. I can feel my legs shake as we approach the nurses' desk, and Katherine asks to see Mrs Swan. The nurse has a kindly smile, and she tells us that Mummy has been placed in a private room along the corridor, and points us in the right direction. When we get there, I stop outside. Maybe I should have asked the Doctor more questions. Katherine grabs my hand, pushes the door open and leads me into a softly lit room; it takes some minutes for our eyes to adjust to the light. Mummy is sleeping, and we sit silently for an eternity before she stirs, and I can feel us both holding our breath as she blinks continuously. It takes her a while to notice that we are in the room.

'Hello Mrs Swan,' Katherine says quickly, and I feel both relieved and then angry, thinking that it should have been me.

'Hello Mummy,' I add softly.

Mummy slowly turns towards the direction of our voices. 'Mary, hello; who's that with you darling?'

'It's Katherine Mummy, my friend Katherine.'

'How are you feeling Mrs Swan?' Katherine asks. My head begins to whirl with questions.

'I'm tired dear.' Mummy narrows her eyes in an effort to bring them into focus. 'Mary.'

I sit forward and carefully rest my arms on the bed. 'I'm here Mummy.' I say softly and hold her hand.

'What have the doctors told you?' she asks, and I want to leave, to run away, and I wonder how much I am supposed to say.

'We have just come from the Doctor's office Mrs Swan,' Katherine cut in, 'and he has only told us the same things he told you.'

How does she know just the right things to say?

'Oh, that is a relief,' Mummy replies, I was beginning to worry that I may have to explain it all, and the doctor had used so many big words.' She laughs softly and attempts to raise her left hand. That doesn't work, so she lets go of my hand and, lifting her right arm, runs two fingers jerkily down my cheek. A tear follows her fingers. 'How are the bees Mary?'

We spend the next couple of hours wandering between talking, and sitting in quiet contemplation, but Mummy is looking very tired, so we say our goodbyes and leave the ward. We find David in the waiting room, laying across the seats and looking very uncomfortable; and I'm so pleased to see him. Katherine shakes him gently, and he sits up and runs his hand through his golden hair, but my smile disappears when I see the faint outline of lipstick on his cheek. I turn to Katherine, and she has noticed it too. After giving him a look of disgust, she turns to leave. 'Come on, let's go,' she says indignantly, but he shrugs his shoulders and follows obediently.

The journey home is silent, and I sit in the back with Katherine and I fall asleep from exhaustion, waking with a start when David honks the horn as we pulled into the drive. As he opens his door to get out, I lean forward and grab his shoulder. 'Thank you for today,' I say quietly and quickly kiss his cheek. I can't help but notice that the lipstick marks have gone.

He jumps out of the car and opens the back door for me. 'For you Mary, anything.'

Katherine climbs out the other side and sighs. 'Oh please you two.'

'Come on Katie, you have all been very good,' I say. 'What would I have done without you? What would I have done without David? I add.

'Okay, okay, I get the point,' Katherine says reluctantly. 'Thank you, David.' She turns her head sideways in mock affection. 'We couldn't have done it without you.' Then she plants a kiss on his other cheek.

'Gee, thanks sis,' David grins at Katherine, and then he bounds along the path ahead of us, turning just before the front entrance. 'By the way, I have the rest of week off, if you would like me to take you to the hospital again.'

Katherine looks puzzled. 'But I thought...'

'Oh the studio called me Monday morning to tell me there was no filming this week due to some technical stuff. I won't bore you with the details,' he says, and laughs as he turns and walks into the house.

I grin as Katherine lets go one of her famous screams.

Chapter 12

So many colours swirling together. So much colour. So much brightness. If you mixed them all up, would you just be left with black? The colour never stopped coming. If I could close my eyes; just for a moment. But when I do; there is blackness.

'I was thinking about your father today.'

The statement from Mummy caught me off guard. Doctor Sidle had been this morning and declared that Mummy had improved slightly; but warned us not to expect too much or push things too hard. We had moved into the bedroom, as it had started to rain on the balcony. 'What were you thinking?' I asked.

She looked into the distance. 'I miss him.' I noticed a tear in the corner of her eye.

I placed my cup down and gave her a hug. 'Oh Mummy; I'm sorry, I'm so sorry.'

'It's not your fault dear. It's nobody's fault really. Just something that happened. I may not be right, but.... we are alright.'

'Now that sounds like something the bees might say; if they could talk of course.'

'Oh, but they can.' She took in a deep breath and sat up in her chair. 'How do you think I would have survived all these years without the bees talking to me?'

I laughed, but I knew that she was being serious. I realised that this had become quite a secret, and it had created an unwelcome tension. I felt quite relaxed as Jemima had gone to pick up some groceries. I glanced at my watch.

'Do you have to go somewhere? she asked.

'No, not at all. It's just that Jemima has gone shopping and I was thinking about when she might be back home.'

'Jemima?' she asked.

It occurred to me that she hadn't mentioned any of our names this morning. Jemima your daughter; my sister. Do you remember anything else about Daddy?'

She finished the last of her tea and placed it on the table. 'I have something to show you.' She said, and walked over to the chest of drawers and opened the top drawer, where she lifted out a small envelope, pulled out some photographs, and came back and stood in front of me whilst she looked through them. 'Ah, here we are.' She handed me several of the pictures, and I looked at the first one, and knew instantly that the man standing with my mother was David, my father. I let out a distinctive gasp. 'Yes, he was a beautiful man, wasn't he?' She smiled with noticeable pride. 'And I didn't look too bad either I think.'

'Mummy, you are still stunning.' I held the photograph up again to catch the light. 'And you're right, Daddy was a beautiful man.' For the first time, I felt her loss, and a deep pit of grief threatened to overwhelm me. 'Mummy; however did you cope when he was gone?'

'I never have dear.' That thought cut me sharply, and it forced me to examine my own feelings; about Jake, and Jemima; and mostly about Gabriel. And I wondered if I should send him a message.

Chapter 13

Diary; June 24th 1964

David is taking Katherine and me to the hospital in his mother's car. He promises to take us on Thursday and Friday; probably in his mother's car again. Katherine tells me that she has some coursework to do and won't be able to come, which reminds me that I haven't even spoken to the college about leaving, but that probably doesn't matter much now anyway. I'm full of mixed emotions and questions, but they are crowded out by the thought of spending more time with David. There are questions that don't leave me though. Such as how am I going to look after Mummy? What sort of care is she going to need, and will we be able to stay at Meadowsweet? I feel like I have no choice but to put those kinds of questions on hold; at least until such time as I know what is going to happen.

Diary; June 25th 1964

David does drive me to the hospital again, but this time we go in his car, yes! And we talk the whole way there about films, and directors, and actors. He almost seems to be disappointed to leave me here. 'I'll be back at six o'clock to collect you,' he says with his best Adonis smile. 'I'm sorry it's a bit earlier Mary, but I have to go somewhere tonight. Will that be okay?' Of course it's okay. He's such a gentleman about everything, and so polite. I ramble some words to him about looking forward to continuing our conversation, and give him another kiss on the cheek; and I wonder if it has the same effect on him.

Mummy is making good progress, and it's a surprise to find her sitting up when I come into her room. She looks so concerned when I tell her that I haven't been home, except to collect some clothes, but says nothing more about it. She tires easily, and there are long silences between conversations. She even dozes off several times, and I feel slightly guilty at being so bored. During the quiet times, I think about David, and wonder what he might be doing; I shudder when the image of him with another woman comes into my head.

David arrives an hour later than he said he would, and he apologizes, but doesn't say why. Katherine and her mother have already begun eating when we arrive back at the house. Mrs Hunter smiles at David, but looks disapprovingly at me, assuming, yet again, that I am the one who has made us late.

After we have eaten, Mrs Hunter decides to take me to one side. I'm pretty sure that I am going to receive another lecture, but to my surprise all she says is, 'life will throw a lot of rubbish at you Mary. You just have to keep tidying it up and get on with it.' I watch her walk away; leaving me open mouthed. The woman doesn't say another word, not even to ask how my mother is.

Diary; June 26th 1964

The day begins with another lecture.

Before we leave the bedroom for breakfast Katherine grabs hold of my arm. 'Listen Mary....about you and David.' I attempt to look puzzled. 'I know how you feel about him.' She gives me one of her hard stares. 'Do not trust him; do you understand.' I say nothing, and just give her a hug. To be honest, I really don't know what else to say. I'm beginning to feel that none of this is real anyway; that I'm going to wake up tomorrow only to find that it's all a dream, and as I wander down the stairs I try to remember where I had read that line somewhere; and then it comes to me. *Some beautiful morning, she will wake up and find it is tomorrow, not today but tomorrow. And then things will happen...wonderful things.* Some words from Mummy's favourite book, Anne of Windy Willows. She had read that to me so many times, and it's hard to swallow the lump in my throat.

David is quiet on the drive to the hospital, and he seems distracted. I want to smile at him; instead I just look down at my hands and squeeze them together.

'I'm not all bad you know,' he says suddenly. I give him a quick sideways glance.

'My sister... she thinks I'm a bad person you know.... because I date a lot of girls.' I still don't reply, and we continue our journey in silence for a while. 'Do you think I'm a bad person?' he asks.

His question takes me by surprise. 'No....no I don't,' I reply, 'I think that maybe you're looking for someone.'

'What do you mean, looking for someone?' he asks.

'Why would you care about what I think?' I say, and immediately regret my harshness.

'Because you're a special person Mary.' His answer stuns me, but curiously I don't feel flattered, and I don't respond, and so he persists a bit longer. 'You have to tell me what you mean.' Is it me does he seem unsure of himself? 'I mean.... I would be grateful if you would...' It's a side of him I haven't seen before; and he sounds lost, vulnerable even.

I don't like his awkwardness. 'I think that you must be looking for someone special to love.' He doesn't respond, and so I continue. 'I'm still young enough to dream, and maybe fall in love a thousand times, but I think that maybe it's different for a girl. A man.... a mature man, is probably looking to love someone, not to be in love anymore.' Is he as surprised as I am at my answer? What I am sure of, is that if Katherine were here now, she would most likely be having a fit, and she would probably say something like, 'When did you get to be so wise'?

It's silent again for a while and then he asks, 'What's the difference?'

'You mean between being in love and loving someone.'

'Yes.'

I have to think hard about that question. 'Well I'm no expert, but being in love is all flowery and romantic, you know, dreamy love songs and stuff. But loving someone on the other hand is something you want to do forever. After all, it's a lifetime commitment, isn't it?'

'I think you're right,' His forehead wrinkled in deep thought. But then he confuses me. 'I don't know that I could love someone forever.' He turns to look at me. 'So, what about you?' I look away as I feel my cheeks burning, thinking that even Katherine never asked me these sorts of questions. 'Do you think that you could love someone, you know, for a lifetime?' he asks.

I move awkwardly in my seat. 'I don't know.'

He persists. 'But you're in love with someone though, aren't you?'

How can he how he be so direct? Before I can stop myself, I answer. 'Yes.' Embarrassed by his directness, I open my book and pretend to read. We reach our destination a short while later, and I thank him for the lift, but I can't bring myself to give him a kiss, even on the cheek. He says he will pick me up again at six and drives off. I stand in the entrance of the hospital for some time, feeling lost again;

questions swirling around in my head. What has he just been asking me? Is this some sort of code that I'm supposed to figure out? Or is he just lost himself? Aren't things like this supposed to be wonderful and exciting? So why don't I feel like that now? Have I just learned the difference between being in love and loving someone? I have barely known David for a week, but I want him to come back. Want to tell him that I'm in love with someone; I am in love with him. No.... that's wrong. I'm not just in love with him. I love him.

I make my way inside, and to Mummy's room, and I panic when I find that she's not there; only to be told that she has improved somewhat and has been moved to the ward. The Doctor tells me that she should be able to return home within the week, so I decide to go back to the house during the weekend to organise everything for her return. Sadly I don't see David again after our conversation in the car. And when Mrs Hunter arrives with Katherine to collect me, I don't think to ask why he isn't here. Mrs Hunter is obviously not happy at being inconvenienced and she waits in the car. Even Katherine doesn't mention him, and from the mood I pick up, I sense that something isn't right.

When we get back to the house Katherine tells me that he had called to say that he couldn't make it back, as the film crew had phoned, and he was off to Europe within the next few hours. I can't help but feel a deep sense of loss, and then guilt, when I should be thinking of Mummy.

Chapter 14

I could see colours that might belong to my palette; and if they blended then my greyness might dissolve; and so I stirred them until my arms ached. I was distracted by the constantly changing patterns they made, as one moment they looked so amazingly beautiful, and at another they would distort into conflicting, ugly colours.

Mummy came down for breakfast. I felt a great unease as I still hadn't mentioned the diaries to Jemima, and if Mummy spoke of them there might be awkward questions. Doctor Sidle took the opportunity to stay for another plate of egg and bacon, and he seemed to be more confident than ever.

'So, Miss Constance.' He had taken to calling me Miss Constance of late, and my sister had become Miss Jemima. He sounded like someone out aft a 1950's film. It seemed to make him feel more comfortable around us for some reason. 'How are you coping with the climate here?'

'To be honest, Doc, I've tried not to think about it too much.'

He flushed red. 'Oh; and there's me, reminding you. Oh dear.'

Mummy smiled at his comments, and despite her problems, I could see that she had a handle on the good Doctor. 'How long do you think you are going to continue to visit me Doctor?' she asked him.

'Well I suppose that now both your daughters are here, I can space my visits out somewhat; I can also arrange for the nurse to come and see you for certain days.'

'Now that is a relief,' she replied with a grin. 'I was beginning to think that you had.... intentions.'

He flush turned to a deep crimson, and his hands shook, causing him to place his cup down quickly for fear of spilling it over the table. 'What! Oh no. I mean, not that you aren't an attractive woman.... oh dear, what I mean is....'

'Doctor Sidle.' I interrupt his blustering.

'What, er yes Miss Constance? He said breathlessly.

'I think my Mother is teasing with you.'

'Oh really? Well yes, obviously she is.' It was good to see that she hadn't lost her sense of humour; at least not yet.

'How long do you think I have got Doctor?' She continued.

Her question almost threw him into an apoplexy, and it made my heart jump.

'I think that's enough questions for the poor Doctor today Mummy,' Jemima interrupted. 'I have a much more important question for Doctor Sidle.' The man had almost stopped breathing. 'Can we take Mummy into the town to do a bit of shopping?'

'Well, that's up to your Mother really. If she feels well enough then, I don't see why not?'

'Oh that's wonderful,' Mummy replied. 'What town is it that we'll be visiting?'

'Windsor Mummy,' we both replied with equal patience.

'Excellent. Is David coming?' Mary asked.

I cast Jemima a glance, and she quickly stood and collected the cups from the table in response to the question.

'We can talk about that later.' I said.

'Okay dear. I have some things to tell you anyway. Shall we go then?'

The Doctor announced that he needed to be going, and we all made our way into the hall.

Chapter 15

Diary; September 20th 1966

It's been a long time since I last put pen to paper. Lately my days have been so full that I barely have time to think of writing.

In the two years that have passed since Mummy's stroke, I have become a full-time nurse, and now I spend most of my time at Meadowsweet. Mummy has been finding it increasingly difficult to use her left arm, and her eyesight appears to be deteriorating on a daily basis. I never got around to telling her that I was going to leave college, and as far as she knows, I hadn't gone back because of her stroke. Every time Mummy apologizes for holding me back, I feel a twinge of guilt at not telling her, but then I think about my own dreams; at least the ones in my imagination, as they never really got started, and the guilt evaporates along with them.

Within six months of her stroke, I had learned to drive, as it was the only way we could get around. And I have also become something of a cook, and to my surprise, I quite enjoy it. Despite having little time to myself, I've arranged to meet up with Katherine for the first time in ages. I'm determined to make the most of any free time, especially as Katherine is so busy with college work.

Meadowsweet is a constant worry. Has the house always been this big? Mummy has never spoken about selling the house, but I constantly worry whether we can afford to stay in the house. Mummy doesn't seem to be concerned, so I avoid the subject. We go to the meadow almost every day, and when possible, we collect honey. It seems to be Mummy's way of clinging on to some independence of her own. In fact, she speaks about the bees constantly. She tells me stories about their lives, and how they can be so loving and kind to one another, even sacrificing their own lives for the good of the hive; and then on another occasion she will turn them into selfish, ruthless despots who vie for supremacy in their cutthroat world. Often, I don't know what to believe. I have seen them give their lives to save my Mother. But I also know how they can cause pain. I have, on the occasional visit to the hives, felt the pain.

'There's rain in the air,' I say softly, as I get Mummy ready to take her out to the meadow.

'Do you think we should take our coats?' Mummy asks as we step through the kitchen door. I go back inside and fetch them, and as I pick up the umbrella, I remember that day in the meadow and try to put it out of my mind. We make our way slowly across the garden, and Mummy waits patiently as I push back the bar and open the gate. As we walk across to the hives, I feel the first smatterings of rain.

Mummy never talks about that day in the meadow, but as we arrive at the first hive, she lays her hand gently on the top and whispers, 'Thank you'. There's a soft hum from inside the hive. Today she wishes to take some honey, perhaps the last of the season, and so I've borrowed a long white dress from Mummy's wardrobe. I have adapted a white hat I bought a while ago from a charity shop; the mesh I had sewn around the edge covered my face. 'Hello my babies,' Mummy says, as I lift the lid from the first hive. The bees fly around us excitedly and I pull out the first rack.

∞ ∞ ∞

Diary; September 21st 1966

I am up earlier than usual, as I'm going to meet up with Katherine, and it means leaving Mummy for several hours. You know; she had never complained once in the past two years. She is able to get about quite well on her own, but I've strictly forbidden her to leave the house without me, even to see the bees; and I'm praying that she will listen to me; especially when the events of that awful day flash through my mind. I even suggest that I should cancel the day, but she insists I go and enjoy my time with Katherine. I had turned twenty-one the previous week and Katherine had said that she wanted to take me to lunch; 'to somewhere special.'

I leave reluctantly, but I'm reassured by how well Mummy is looking, and as I open the front door, she says that she has a surprise for me when I return, and I feel like a little girl who wants to know the secret. I haven't been to Katherine's house since Mummy had been in hospital, and it feels somewhat different. The house seems smaller, and I walk up the pathway more confident than I have been in a long time. I knock on the front door, and my stomach jumps with the sudden realisation that David might be there, and that he just might open the door. That feeling proves unfounded when Katherine appears with her coat on, ready to go. I'm concerned when she doesn't return my smile, and quickly have to follow her fast walk back along the path to the car. She jumps in the passenger side, shuts the door loudly and waits for me to get in. I put the keys in the ignition, but hold them there as I look across at her.

'I'll be fine,' is all she says.

'So... what's happened?' I ask sheepishly.

'I've just had a blazing row, that's all,'

'So, you're still not getting along with your Mum?

'No, it wasn't her, it was David.'

'David!' I exclaim rather too loudly. 'He's back?'

'Yes, he's back home again.' Her eyes narrow and then the anger pours out. 'He turns up....out of the blue I might add; and then he just saunters in as if he's never been away....and do you know what he did?' I think that it's best to remain silent and simply raise my eyebrows in response. 'He just basically asked, 'what's for dinner'? Can you believe it? What's for dinner! She gives a muted scream. 'I have been working my backside off trying to be nice to my Mother, and does she appreciate it? No, she doesn't. She has been sulking all the time he's been away; moaning about how he never calls, and how he never lets her know if he's okay, and most of the time she takes it out on me. But David.... her beloved David, wanders in as if everything is fine and what does she do?' I stay quiet. 'She throws her arms around him as if nothing is wrong.'

I start the car, press the accelerator lightly and tap my thumbs on the steering wheel. 'So, where are we going then?' I ask in as cheery a voice as possible.

'Oh Mary, I am so sorry. This is supposed to be a fun day out, and all I'm doing is throwing my troubles on you.'

'That's what friends are for.'

'You're right,' she says. 'C'mon, let's get going; I'm taking you to the most amazing eating place; and then.... well, you'll just have to wait and see what we're doing for the rest of the day, won't you.'

I arrive back home much later than I had planned, and can't help but feel nervous about what I might find. I have had the most wonderful day. Katherine had taken me into London, and we had visited Madam Tussauds and the National Gallery. But I had felt troubled the whole time. Thoughts of David, and Mummy, had filled my mind most of the day. Just when I had come to the conclusion that my feelings for David had only been infatuation, they all surfaced again. I had declined the invitation from Katherine to go in for coffee, and had left as quickly as possible; explaining that I needed to get home to check on Mummy. I drove the car hard and only slowed when I nearly lost it on a sharp bend. When I pull into the drive at Meadowsweet, dusk is beginning to fall, and I go around to the back door. I can see lights on in the kitchen, and breathe a sigh of relief. As I open the door, I am greeted with the sweet smell of Meadowsweet honey.

I stand for several seconds in the doorway, taking in the scene in front of me. Mummy is busily pouring the freshly harvested golden liquid into several jars. When she sees me she just smiles happily, looking very pleased with herself. I slide my coat off and struggle to find a hook as I ask, 'what on earth have you been doing?'

Mummy continues with her task, humming to herself some unknown song. 'Well dear,' she lays the bucket to one side, 'I had finished reading my book, and didn't know what else to do, and so I thought that I would just wander out to the bees and see how they were doing.' She picks up a lid and screws it onto the jar. 'They were so happy to see me, and I think they were quite glad that I took some honey. This is the last of the crop for this year; and as you weren't here....' Her voice fades out as she looks at me, and she lowers her eyes.

I feel completely stunned. Not sure whether the look of guilt on Mummy's face is from going out to the meadow, or because of what she has said. I'm unsure how to react, especially as she looks so happy. 'But what if something had happened?' I blurt out.

'But it didn't dear,' is all she says, and I wonder how I can argue with that. 'Anyway, I'm glad you're home Mary, as I have something to talk to you about.'

She wipes her hands on her apron, and then ushers me to the other end of the table, where she sits down in front of a large folder bulging with papers, and after carefully opening it, she takes the top sheet of paper from the pile and lays it in front of me. 'Sit down Mary.' She scans the page and, obediently, I sit opposite her wondering what is going on. 'Mary,' she begins. 'You turned twenty-one last week.'

'Yes,' I reply.

'Well, I know that we haven't been able to do anything special for you, but I think that this will make up for it.' She holds up a piece of paper. 'What I have here, is the simplified version of all of this.' She points to the folder. 'Now the information in this folder is quite complicated; and that's because my Father, your Grandfather, was a shrewd man. But make no mistake; he was also a frugal man. Not long before he died he made some changes to his will, and to our financial future.' I listen patiently as she continues. 'As a man of business, he understood the implications of passing his house down to his family, and by that, I mean the financial implications. All of this was way beyond my understanding, but suffice to say, he told me that he hadn't worked hard all his life only to see everything he had accomplished, including building this house, taken away from his children. And because of that he made sure that Meadowsweet, and the bees were protected.'

'How do you mean protected?'

'Well, to start with; I think you should know that Meadowsweet has never belonged to me.'

'What does that mean?' I ask impatiently. 'Will we have to move out?'

She reaches across and gently puts her hand on mine, smiling warmly. 'No Mary, it doesn't mean any of those things. My Father, your Grandfather, left the house and the bees in trust....to you.'

That statement makes me sit up wide eyed. 'But, he never knew me.' Then I'm unsure. 'Did he?'

'He died a year after you were born.' I can see that that touches her. Memories can be so cruel. 'In leaving the house in trust, it left us free of any financial burden we might face later,' she continues.

'But what about other relatives; wouldn't they have some claim, or my Father?'

Mummy's smile fades slightly and I can see the pain again. 'I have something else I need to tell you Mary.' It's obvious that this is difficult for her. 'Your Father.' She pauses for several long seconds. 'He was never.... we were never.... married.'

We sit in silence for some time as she waits for me to take in what she has said. She must have known that I would have many questions. The first thing that comes out is more of a statement, in an attempt to place some logic into the memories. 'But I remember him.'

'You remember.... seeing him,' she replies. And so it falls into place. That's all I remember. There are no memories of playing with him, or days out, or bedtime stories, or.... anything else. I just remember seeing him. And then she answers a question that I'm sure I would have asked given time. 'He loved you Mary.'

I sit quietly. There is still one question I have to ask, but I'm not sure if I want to know the answer. 'Is he.... still alive?'

Mummy squeezes my hand and simply says, 'No.'

We spend some time talking about him. She shares some details about how soft and kind he was, and what he looked like. 'But he was not a strong man, emotionally,' she adds. But then she says something quite strange. She says he had been a beautiful man; and I think of David, and wonder if my mother and I are drawn to the same kind of people. I ask if she has any pictures of him, but again she says no; and it's at that point that she seems reluctant to share any more details, and although I kind of understood, I want to know more.

'Mary, I want to explain about the other details here if I may.' And that is the last we speak of my Father. Maybe I will learn more in the future; but for now that's it. She tells me how my grandfather had also left his money in trust for me, and that now it's mine. She is quite animated as we discuss how that will mean we can afford to stay in Meadowsweet, as the money she had inherited has all but run out. 'And besides dear,' she concludes, 'who would look after the bees?'

'What do you mean?' I ask.

'His will stipulates that to stay here you must let the bees know who you are, and you must look after them.'

So, in the space of an hour, I have learned that my mother had never been married to my Father; that I own Meadowsweet, and the bees; and along with that, I have also inherited a considerable sum of money. And yet, somehow, in spite of all of that.... I still feel trapped. Will I would ever find my own dream? Because now it seems even further away.

Chapter 16

Diary; August 27th 1967

Still not finding much time to write.... almost a year since my last entry; it feels like so much has changed and yet very little has.

After that evening in the kitchen our relationship had changed; and as I cook breakfast it becomes obvious to what extent our roles have been reversed. I am now the woman of the house; and then it dawns on me for the first time, that it has been like that for some time; but it has taken until now for me to realise just how much things have changed. I had already been wandering out to the bees alone on the few occasions when Mummy was too tired. She had told me to go around 11 o/clock during the day, as the bees would be busy foraging, and those that were at the hive would be occupied guarding the hive and feeding the young. Mummy had also changed; she didn't seem quite as happy as before. There are questions that I have; questions that might never be answered, and so I slide into a routine. It's the same role that Mummy had occupied when she had become the Lady of the Meadow.

After that day, I had explored the house. I found myself just wandering in and out of rooms and digging into cupboards and wardrobes. I had looked at everything so differently before; and now I feel a strange responsibility toward it all. I had walked along the long corridor on the first floor and looked at each of the white painted six panelled doors in turn before wandering into the rooms. I had found it odd that I had only ever really thought about my room and Mummy's, but when I had wandered into each of the other three bedrooms, it had all felt so large and so extravagant. I wandered back down the stairs and walked through to the dining room on the ground floor and I had seen, for the first time, the elegant dinnerware in the two glass cabinets. Opening one of the cabinets, I had removed a dinner plate and had run my fingers around the rim of the pure white porcelain, feeling the gold embossed band, and I had been surprised to see within the pattern six bees interspersed equally. Mummy had later explained that the plates were quite old and very valuable and had been bought by her Grandmother.

Wandering into the study, I had discovered shelves full of folders containing legal papers and invoices, all carefully filed in order. It was the one room that still felt like it belonged to my mother; and so I had moved on to the drawing room. I had always thought that this was the most elegant room of the house, and had seldom ventured in there. The grand oak fireplace with its woodburner was stunning, and was easily as tall as me. I had run my hands over its intricate carving, thinking of the work my Grandfather had put into such a work of art; and then I had seen it, for the first time. Cut into the top corner of the wooden mantle were the initials of my Grandfather and Grandmother; both wrapped neatly in a heart shape. I had found it so exciting to imagine them as a younger couple, when my Grandfather had just finished building Meadowsweet; and I had pictured them alone in the house, and had wondered whether they had made love in every room. Meadowsweet had a history, a past. Were my journeys around the house a sign that I was searching for something; looking for clues to my own past maybe. Then it occurred to me that what I had really been looking for were clues to my own future.

Diary; May 27th 1968

I had been taking meals to Mummy's room almost every day for some time now. She had been rising and dressing every day, but it was often after lunch, and I hadn't known what one day or the next was going to be like. The routine had been absorbing me, and I had frequently found myself looking outside, only to notice that the light was fading and then trying to remember where the day had gone.

The memory of last night is still so vivid.

I slide on my dressing gown, put my head around the bedroom door and notice that Mummy is still sleeping; so, I wander down to the kitchen and put the kettle on the stove. I pin a reminder on the kitchen notice board that I have to drive to the doctor's surgery today to collect some medication. There would be no point in rousing her too soon. It's while I'm standing over the kettle, and waiting to hear the bubbles start to rise, that I hear the thump. I turn the gas off and run to the stairs; going up to the landing two steps at a time. I open the door quickly and go into the bedroom without waiting to knock. There's no sign of her in the bed; and then I notice the sheets and blankets have also disappeared. I run around to the other side of the bed and find her lying face down on the floor, tangled up in her bed linen.

I quickly, but gently, pull her over onto her back. Her eyes are closed, and she appear to be breathing, but when I call her name, she doesn't answer. Familiar feelings of panic begin to rise. I don't want to go through the same trauma as before. I need to think.

I know that I won't be able to lift her back on to the bed, and so I retrieve the pillows from the bed and slide one of them under her head, and place the other in between her and the dressing table, as I don't want her to hurt herself should she try to move. I had used some of my money to have a telephone installed in the room. Mummy had called it an extravagance, but I had seen several benefits to the exercise; not the least of them being the opportunity to call for an ambulance without leaving her alone. I stand and pick up the telephone from the side of the bed to dial the emergency number.

It is as I am holding the telephone to my ear that I hear the sound that will haunt me for the rest of my life. I see her open her eyes, look straight at me and smiled. As she does so she breathes out quite heavily, but the breath seems to go on for an eternity; and then it stops. She continues smiling and looking at me, and I stand for a time with the receiver still against my ear. I had also stopped breathing, and I jump, as if startled. I take a deep breath in to fill my lungs, and carefully replace the receiver so as not to make a sound. I slowly place the telephone on to the side table and sit on the stool of the dressing table next to her. From this position, I can see that she is no longer looking at me, and I resist the strong urge to go and stand where I can see her eyes.

I softly place my hands on her eyes and close them.

Chapter 17

Colours poured everywhere, over everything. I placed my hands in the eddying, pouring, liquid, but they continued to flow and expand, until I could see nothing; but the swirling kaleidoscope rose around me. The colours rose to my neck and I stood on tiptoe to stop them covering me. As they reached my neck I found that I had stopped breathing. I wanted to cover my face with my hands, but they were covered with the colour. I must breathe.

We arrived back at Meadowsweet much later than intended. Mummy had been enthralled by the many shops in Windsor. It was if she were seeing them for the first time. I could see the changes in her just in the short time that I had been home. I wondered how Jemima must be feeling; what with everything changing so much. Was I being unfair in not sharing the story that Mummy was reading to me? It seemed that I couldn't let go of the past. At least, not yet.

Mummy declined any dinner, and Jemima took her up to bed, and I took on the role of making dinner. I had a strong desire to creep upstairs to the bedroom door and see if I could hear what they were saying. It would be so easy for Mummy to tell Jemima her story. I listened, but I could hear nothing; and realising how silly I was being I continued with the task of preparing the food. I was lost deep in thought when I heard a chair scrape as it was pulled back, and I dropped the knife I was using to cut the vegetables. I turned to find Jemima sitting at the table with her head in her hands. Leaving what I was doing, I went to the other side of the table and sat down.

'What's the matter? I asked.

After a couple of minutes, she replied, 'you know what the matter is Connie.'

I thought that if Mummy had told her about the diaries, I had no excuses, no reasons to give her. She would be totally justified in being angry with me. But deep down I knew that there was a reason; I just didn't know what it was. I decided to remain silent for the time being.

'I saw them.'

My stomach turned as I waited for a barrage of accusations and abuse to come my way. Still I said nothing.

'I saw the pictures.... the photographs of Daddy.'

Relief. I felt utter relief.

'She didn't know who he was Connie. She said that you would know. Have you seen them?' She looked straight at me. 'Why didn't you tell me?'

Relief turned to a spinning head. I had barely escaped one confrontation, only to be faced with another. I knew that I had to lie, but I also knew that in doing so I would begin to dig a hole, one that could end up being very deep indeed. 'I was trying to find the right way to say something Jem. I didn't want to cause you any distress.'

She looked deep into me, as if searching for something, and I held her gaze, a practice I had learned from my time dealing with sensitive artists in Milan. Reassuring them often required a great deal of truth-bending. They would peer into your soul; their gaze cutting and penetrating, and often quite emotional. Jemima lowered her eyes and I breathed. 'He was a beautiful man Connie,' she said.

'Yes.'

'Could you.... connect with him?'

'What do you mean?'

'Did you see.... your father; Daddy?'

'I hadn't thought about it. I don't know. I just now that he's our father; and that's it.'

'Not our father.'

'What does that mean Jem?'

'I don't know; something's missing.

'It's just a photo Jem.'

'I just saw a stranger; and I was scared.' She began to cry.

'I wish I could see more too.' I said. 'we never knew him, did we. Maybe it has something to do with the fact that Mummy couldn't recognize him.'

'Do you think so?'

After all this time I could answer that question. 'Listen. I'll get on with the dinner.'

'I'm not hungry.'

'Come on, you've got to eat something.'

'Just some tea please Connie. I really couldn't eat anything.'

I put the kettle back on the heat. It occurred to me that I had probably drunk more tea since I had arrived home than I had in the past ten years. Why did we always see it as the solution to any problem. 'To be honest, I'm not hungry either,' I admitted. 'Maybe I'll make some tea and head off to bed. It's been a long day for all of us.'

Chapter 18

Diary; June 4th 1968

Standing at the side of this neatly trimmed rectangular hole, I can see how easy it would be to jump in and wait to be covered over by the gravediggers. Katherine is standing silently by my side, holding my arm. It began to rain as soon as we had arrived at the cemetery; kind of a cliché really. And now it is dripping enthusiastically from my hair onto my face, making it hard even for me to tell if I'm crying or just too wet to notice. Until now, I had never really thought about the fact that we were the only family remaining. Besides Katherine, I have no other friends; but I had presumed that perhaps Mummy would have had some friends to come and say goodbye to her; but no one?

One of the attendants had rushed off to find an umbrella, and he arrives back at the grave just as the vicar concludes his eulogy. I thank the man for being so kind, and as I open it I am surprised to find that it's made up of several bright colours, and it looks quite at odds with the black outfits the ushers and the vicar are wearing. We both look up at it and laugh quietly. 'C'mon Mary, it's time to go,' Katherine says softly; and just then a solitary bee flies under the canopy of the umbrella, looking for shelter from the rain. Katherine raises her hand ready to brush it away, and I put my hand on hers and lower it gently. 'She won't stay long Katherine. Let's just wait until the rain eases so that she can find her way home.' I wonder if she might be from my hives.

And that was it; the moment of letting go and moving on. The vicar had spoken about it in his service, and I didn't really understand what he meant. He had also said that it would take time; perhaps a long time, but he had said that it would definitely come. Is it really going to be like this? Does it have something to do with the bees? Would they allow me to let go; because I could still be with Mummy, through them? Are they now my hives; my bees? Meadowsweet had always been mine, although I might not have known it until recently; and my Grandfather had given me money before I could even walk. But the bees are different. They may have been my Grandmother's at some time in the past, but I had only ever known them as belonging to Mummy. Was it really the case that we had all belonged to the bees?

And there it is. If I care for them as my mother had, I will never have truly lost her; and maybe I will find the answers to questions I have about my past, and my future; both of which are after all, part of Meadowsweet. The rain eases, and I hear buzzing as the bee makes out from under the umbrella. It's time for both of us to go home.

Chapter 19

I dreamed of colour. It was everything. It covered my head, and I couldn't breathe. I could feel my chest tighten, and as much as I tried I couldn't reach the top again. I opened my mouth to scream, and it filled with colour. When I could no longer hold my breath, I let the last of the air out of my lungs and breathed in the colours. I could feel my lungs being filled as the colours became part of me.

I slept late the next morning. As I said good morning to my family looking back at me from the wall on my journey down the stairs, I smiled; but I stopped at the portrait of my Grandmother. She looked so happy. I tried to picture her as Mummy had described her in the diary, but all I saw was this smiling, happy young girl who was so much in love with my Grandfather. And now she was gone. I felt her loss almost as much as if I had been there. I had so enjoyed the previous day shopping with Mummy and Jemima. For just a few hours we had not a care in the world. But now this sadness was overwhelming. Walking into the kitchen, I was greeted with three more smiling faces. Doctor Sidle was deep in conversation with Jemima, and sitting opposite them was Mummy, listening intently.

'Good morning,' Mummy said, and she looked up at me and beamed. 'Are you visiting us?'

The question took me by surprise, and I looked over to the Doctor in mild panic. He placed his hand on her arm. 'Mary, this is Constance, your daughter.' It appeared that he was telling her this for the benefit of us both; schooling me.

'Good morning.' I replied. My tummy rumbled with hunger and a cold discomfort slid quietly in.

'Oh hello Constance.' She raised her arm high and pointed across to Jemima. 'This is....'

'Jemima.' Doctor Sidle added.

Mummy smiled for a second, and another look came across her face; and I felt weak. It was there for just a split second; but I saw it. Terror. I sat quickly at the table, next to the doctor. Both he and Jemima stopped talking and turned to me.

'What's going on?' I asked.

The Doctor took the lead in speaking. 'It's nothing to be unduly concerned about; just a bad day. We've been having a chat with your mother, haven't we Mary?' he turned to Mummy and placed his hand on hers again.

'What about?' I could feel myself beginning to shake. The Doctor noticed and quickly poured me some tea. He placed two scoops of sugar into the cup and stirred it vigorously.

Pushing the cup toward me, he continued. 'Drink this miss Constance, it will help. I think Mary is feeling out of sorts today. Jemima called me after she found Mary wandering down the stairs in the early hours of this morning. After our conversation yesterday, I thought it would be a good time to discuss the options ahead of you.'

'Options?' I asked.

'Yes. Regarding the care of Mary.' Again, he looked at Mummy and squeezed her hand. 'She is the most important one to think about; aren't you Mary?'

'If you say so,' she replied obediently.

'I don't understand.' I protested. 'Surely that's a long way off.'

'Yes, it might well be; but....' he chose his words carefully, '.... it's good to cover all eventualities.' He picked up his tea and took a sip; I had not seen him so calm and professional. 'If you remember, when we first met, I mentioned that it was hard to determine the progress of the dementia.'

I was surprised at how comfortable he seemed to be in using the D word in front of Mummy. 'Yes, I remember,' I replied, feeling slightly irritated. 'But I wasn't expecting.... especially after yesterday.'

'Invariably, no one is. It is so difficult, if not impossible to prepare ourselves. But be assured that we are only covering all eventualities, as I said. Think of it as making sure the spare tyre is good before setting off on a journey.'

'How do you feel about this Jem?' I could see the tension in her face.

'I just want it all to work smoothly.' She squeezed her hands together. 'I was scared this morning; and you're not going to be here forever Connie, and I need to know that I can cope with her.'

'Please don't talk about Mummy as if she's not in the room,' I said tersely.

'But I am here dear,' Mummy replied. 'I'm here for all my girls.'

'I'm sorry,' Jemima said, looking at Mummy; and she turned to me. 'But do you know how long you're staying? It would help a lot if I knew.'

'No, I don't.' I spat the words unfairly. It was a question I had been avoiding myself. But it was a question that needed answering. I had been surprised that my boss Lucinda had not asked me the same thing. And then I thought of the one person I wanted to ask me the question; Gabriel. I began to shake again. 'As long as I need to I suppose.' My head started to bang, and all I could see was the image of my Grandmother laying on the bedroom floor with her eyes open.... smiling, and then the image became my mother, and I put my hand on my head. 'Can we talk about this later?'

He stood up. 'You're right Miss Constance. Now isn't really a good time to go into any detail, is it. How about we spend some time thinking about this and meet up again at the beginning of next week, around about the same time.'

Jemima stood and walked to the kitchen door. 'I think that's an excellent idea Doctor. We can talk about it over breakfast.'

Doctor Sidle followed her lead and made his way into the hallway. He stopped in the doorway and turned toward us. 'Until then. Goodbye Mary, I'll see you soon.'

'Goodbye.' Mummy replied, and waved. When they had left the room, she turned to me, her face bright and innocent. 'He seems like a nice man.'

'Yes, he does,' I replied.

Do I know him?' she asked.

'It's Doctor Sidle Mummy.'

She looked across the room toward some imaginary place, as if searching for something that was missing; and then she smiled. 'I'm so looking forward to seeing him again.' She turned to me, the smile gone. 'Is he coming again?' I wasn't expecting this, and I was frightened; unsure of myself, and I wished I was back in Milan, dealing with Lucinda on her worse day. Before I could answer, Mummy stood up and walked into the centre of the kitchen. 'I'm tired.' She turned in a circle, looking lost. 'Will you take me to my Mother's room?'

I took her arm and led her toward the kitchen door.

She stopped and looked at me. 'Constance; why did it have to die?'

'What do you mean Mummy?' I asked. She held up her clasped hands and I noticed that she was carrying a book, and looking closer I could see that it was one of the diaries. I wondered how Jemima and the Doctor had not seen it.

I led her into the hallway where they were still in conversation, and I stopped and turned to them. 'I'm just going to take Mummy to her room.' I didn't wait for their reply and led her towards the stairs. I needed to know what she had read.

Chapter 20

Diary; October 19th 1969

Halfway through my breakfast, I get out of my chair at the end of the long oak table, move my plate to the side and sit down again. I've been alone in the house for sixteen months, and it feels like sixteen years. What word would I use to sum up my disposition? The best I can come up with is disinclined. I feel disinclined to go out there and find something to do; anything. I had thought the other day that maybe I would decorate the house, as it hadn't been touched for several years, but as soon as I went to the store to buy the paint, I had been disinclined. And I had left the house several times to visit the bees, but never made it past the gate. Ironically, the fact that I don't have to work and have this big house to ramble around in doesn't seem to help. It just all feels too late.

After I finish breakfast, I clean the few items I have used and place them in the cabinets in their respective places. Whilst opening the cupboard to put the honey away, I notice that it's the last jar. I hadn't collected honey since Mummy had died, but there is still time to take some more from the bees before they settle down for the winter. I find my boots, slide my coat on and open the back door; but it feels like something is missing. The bucket. But not only is it not in its usual place, but I hadn't noticed it was missing. It shouldn't bother me so much; but it does.

When had I last seen it? The best I can remember is seeing it just before Mummy had died. She had taken it out to the bees then, I was sure of it. After searching the whole of the kitchen, I wander up to Mummy's bedroom. I can't imagine any reason why it should be in there, but I can't think of any other place to look. I stand in the doorway and look around the room. To be honest, I have only been in the room once since she died, and hadn't even cleared away any of her things. I look in all the cupboards and drawers, even those where I know it can't possibly fit. I'm beginning to feel desperate and anxious, and I stand by the bed scratching my chin in the vain hope that it will inspire something.

And then without thinking I go down on my knees, lift the bed valance and peer underneath. And there it is; sitting completely in the middle of the floor underneath the bed. As I reach under the bed and pull it out, I think I understand why she had placed it there. The smell of honey from the bucket is strangely reassuring. All she had wanted was to be close to her bees; and this was the only way she could do it. I carry the bucket down the stairs, glancing first at my smiling grandparents, and then, as I reach the bottom of the stairs, I stop and looked at the little girl smiling back at me; and I see my Mother's smile, the same one she had the last time that I had looked at her, and I burst. The tears flood out and I run into the kitchen and drop the bucket onto the hard oak floor as I fall into the chair and bury my face in my arms; and it feels as if my heart will rip open.

After what seems a lifetime the phone starts to ring. I ignore it, but the sound breaks the cycle of sobbing. After sitting quietly for some minutes, I rub my face with the flat of my hands and try to go out to the bees again. I pick up the bucket from where I'd dropped it; but this time I fetch Mummy's hat with the veil from the bedroom, and I put on the long white dress.

It's warm outside, but there's a strong breeze, and I have to hold the hat on with one hand whilst I carry the bucket with the other. I had been out to the bees on my own before, but I'd always known that Mummy was not too far away, and that I was going to her bees. Would they know what had happened? Will they accept me? I walk through the opening in the trees and reach the gate, and the wind softens as I make my way through the gate and into the shelter of the meadow. As I get closer to the hives I can hear the sound of the bees increasing. I fight the urge to run back to the house, and not because I'm afraid; the presence of the bees is strangely reassuring. I just don't want to do this alone. I pull the gauze on the hat over my face when I to the first hive, and then I place my hands on the lid. The air around me becomes quiet and I can't see a single bee outside of the hive.

Keeping my hands on the lid, I speak softly to them. 'Hello my babies.' And when I say it, I know that she has gone, Mummy isn't here anymore, and I let go of the lid and step back, letting out a single choked gasp. I can hear a deep pulse in the hive, like a lament, and I feel their loss too.

A single bee flies onto me and crawls underneath the gauze surrounding the hat; and I stiffen, unsure what to do as the bee moves onto my face and flaps her wings softly; and it feels like my mother's fingers running across my cheek, and I close my eyes as a tear falls. The bee moves quickly across my face, and stops just below the teardrop; and as it reaches her, I can feel her soft caress as she drinks the salty liquid, as if she is trying to take away the pain.

When the bee is finished, she falls, and I step back as she tumbles through the veil and lands quietly on the grass. I kneel beside her and can see that she is dead; and I speak the soft words of a remembered poem to her.

Take for your joy my present, simple and wild –
Uncomely, shrivelled necklace

Of bees that die transforming honey into sun.[3]

I go back to the house with an empty bucket, but glad that I have been out to the bees; my bees. I jump as the phone rings again, but leave it until it stops. I really don't feel like talking to anyone. I make a start on sorting out Mummy's bedroom. There is still quite a lot of paperwork from the solicitors that has also not been signed, but that can wait. I had put off getting so many things done, but legal papers are not high on my to do list. Maybe it would be a good idea to write a list, just so that I can leave that particular task off.

Moving around the half-packed boxes in the bedroom, I pull the large suitcase from the top of the wardrobe, and I'm instantly covered in dust. I brush it out of my hair and use one of Mummy's old scarves to tie it back. I don't know anyone who might want any of Mummy's clothes, so I fill the case with the intention of taking it to the charity shop in Windsor High Street. I can't bring myself to empty the drawers of her personal items, it's too soon; so once the suitcase is full I drag it downstairs and leave it in the hall. It's nearly dark outside; I must have been upstairs for several hours. I sit on the case to catch my breath, and I can't help but wonder how on earth I'm going to clear the bedroom, as there are several other cases and drawers to deal with.

The front door bell rings, and I nearly fall off the case. I'm not expecting anyone to call, particularly this late in the day, and so I call through the unopened door, 'who is it?'

There's no answer, and so I call a little louder, 'who is it please?'

'It's David,' comes the reply.

I can't believe it. How could this happen? I haven't seen David in such a long time, and now, out of the blue, he's standing on the other side of the door. Why does he always seem to appear when I look a mess? Life is so unfair.

'Are you okay?' he calls back, and I realise that I'd been thinking out loud.

'I...I'm fine,' I reply. 'What do you want? I mean how can I help you?'

I hear him laugh. 'Well...for a start, how about opening the door.'

'Yes...the door. Okay, I'll just be a second.' I pull the suitcase out of the way and turn the latch on the door, opening it wide with a nervous smile. It must have been about four years since I had seen him last, and he has changed. His face looks softer; friendlier; but there is something else about him, although I can't quite figure out what it is.

'You've changed,' he says, almost in response to my thoughts. And then I remember that I still have the scarf tied around my hair, and I quickly grab it and throw it onto the suitcase.

---

[3] Osip Mandelstam

'Hello David, how are you?' I say, smiling foolishly.

'I'm fine Mary. More importantly, how are you, because Katherine has been calling you several times today, and she was quite worried.'

'Oh, so that was Katherine.' I reply, feeling very guilty. 'I...was so busy that I didn't have time to answer the phone.'

'Well she'll be pleased to know that you're alright. She asked me to drop by on my way out.'

'That was very kind of you.'

'So.... you're alright?' He asks again, as he lightly clasps his hands together.

'Yes I'm fine. Oh sorry, would you like to come in?'

Chapter 21

Diary; 17th November 1969

David has not been back since that day, and I haven't heard from him either. He had told me that he was going abroad to work on a film for a while, but he could at least have sent a letter, or something. How could I have been so stupid? My mind is full of questions about that night. Was it me, or did he.... seduce me? I'm trying to remember all the wonderful things he had said to me. Did he say that he loved me, or was it that he could love me? And hadn't he said that he had never met anyone as beautiful as me?

On that night, I had given everything I had so completely to him; and now I so desperately need to talk to him. I want him; want to spend the rest of my life with him; to give so many things to this special man; walk in the rain arm in arm; leave little love notes, and find them too. I want to be woken up with a kiss; and snuggle together under the sheets and talk about the day; and make love on a rug in front of a roaring fire, and walk hand in hand along the beach at sunset, and take photographs of beautiful things together; a butterfly emerging from a cocoon, a flower. I want to cry at a movie together, and laugh, and talk about books, and art, and all sorts of things. I want to argue and then have make up sex; I want to cuddle and hug and not be afraid; I want to look deep into his eyes and see.... all the love, and promise of forever. That's what I want; and what I have to give. Is that too much?

And I want one more thing.... I want him to love honey; to love the bees.

I had fallen out with Katherine, and it was over something so trivial that I can't even remember. I'm not sure if I hadn't done it deliberately to stop her asking so many questions about David's visit. If I ask them, then maybe the bees might tell me what I should do.

Chapter 22

The colour of my skin became red and green and blue and yellow; all colours. But my eyes were black, and when I opened my mouth to scream, a stream of rainbows poured out onto every surface, leaving them changed forever.

I had been carefully schooled in the life that I had had without my Father; Jemima also. I was both angry and sad. I had come to know this beautiful boy, who had become a man. I placed the diary on the side table next to the bed. My eyes were sore. Mummy was sleeping. I had been reading the diary to myself as she slept. Jemima had poked her head around the door, and I smiled reassuringly. She smiled back and closed the door softly.

I should tell her, I knew that; but not now, not yet. I also knew that the further I went into Mummy's world would make it so much more difficult to explain to Jemima what we had been doing. The guilt I felt was somewhat tempered by her betrayal; but I knew that that was not a good enough reason.

I wanted to read on, but I knew this was as much about Mummy's journey as it was mine. Perhaps even more so. I decided to wait until she woke and to see if she could continue, and I placed the diary in the bedside cabinet and went downstairs to have some late breakfast; this time ignoring the pictures of my family. The smell from the kitchen told me that Jem had anticipated my arrival, and right on cue she dished out a welcome plate of eggs, bacon, fried bread and hash browns. I sat at the table with her and dabbed a neat circle of brown sauce close to the side of my eggs. Jem, on the other hand, shook the bottle vigorously until every item was covered in the dark sauce. I breathed in the aroma and filled my lungs in the process. Once full, I let my breath out slowly in an effort to relax. I looked up at Jem before taking my first forkful of breakfast and breathed quietly, 'thank you; thank you.'

'You're welcome,' she replied. 'I knew you hadn't eaten since lunchtime yesterday, so I thought this might be needed.' She looked at me softly. 'I presume Mummy is still sleeping.'

'She is. I can only imagine that she didn't sleep well during the night. Doctor Sidle did say that it wasn't unusual for sleep patterns to be disrupted.'

'Do you think that we should move her into my room? I could keep an eye on her then,' Jemima asked.

I dropped my fork onto the plate at the suggestion. 'No Jem. That's not a good idea,' I said rather too harshly. 'I just think that she needs the reassurance of her surroundings.'

'But she is in her surroundings,' she replied. 'She knows this house better than either of us. She has spent her life here.'

'Yes, that's true; but did you notice that she asked to be taken to her mother's room?'

'But that's her room. When did this happen?'

'When you were in the hall speaking to Doctor Sidle. She must be remembering early times. Her bedroom obviously brings her some comfort. I really don't mind spending the time with her,' I suggested.

'If you think it's best,' she replied, taking my empty plate.

I felt rather guilty, as I knew it was inevitable that she would eventually discover the real reason I wanted to spend this time with Mummy. But I also figured that Mummy would have shared the diaries with Jemima if she had wanted to. I was sure too that, at some point, I would discover the reason why she had decided to read the diaries with me, just me.

Chapter 23

Diary; November 18th 1969

It's raining; it's been raining all night, and the bees won't like it. They would be snuggled into the hive keeping each other warm and dry. I am eager to go out to the hives. Am I expecting too much from the bees, for them to listen to me? When I finish breakfast, I slide my wax coat on, and open the kitchen door and then the umbrella. It's big rain; large noisy drops that thump hard on the canvas of the brolly; dangerous stuff for a bee. I walk steadily across the grass, being careful to avoid the dips that are full of water. When I reach the gate, the music of the rain changes as it falls amongst the trees. I can hear the faint hum of the hives, the sound of thousands of sleeping bees, and as I make my way toward them the buzzing grows louder. They know I am here.

I stop a few feet from the hives and listen. The sound is comforting, restful, but as I take a few more steps forward the noise grows louder. I'm surprised that my legs are shaking, and I pull the collar of the coat tighter. I don't know whether to stay or leave. Very quickly there are several bees around me, and the noise they make is unfamiliar. My first instinct is to wave them away, but that would only annoy them. I take a step back from the hive and more of the bees surrounded me. They are everywhere. One flies close to my ear, and I drop the umbrella. I resist the temptation to run, wondering if I have done something wrong, but aware that I need to trust them.

Perhaps there's a new queen. Mummy had told me many times that the bees would become more aggressive when the old Queen died, and it took some time for the new Queen to acquaint herself with their keeper. They didn't like strangers very much, and they didn't like strange smells. Could that be it? Do I smell differently? And then it dawns on me. It must be the baby; they can smell it. How could I have been so stupid? I say out loud. But how can they possibly know? I knew it was too early to say, but I have felt it inside me for some days. I haven't even brought my hat.

And then I feel it. one of the bees had made its way into the collar of my coat, and once there, she planted her sting. She is prepared to die to protect the hive; as are the other bees. It is like an electric shock, and I twitch in response. But curiously, I feel the bee draw her barb slowly from my neck, and my body tightens in anticipation, waiting for the sensation of the poison to pulse its way through my veins in a split second. But she leaves no venom.

And then the memories come.

The tall white gate of the meadow throws its image into my vision, and the strange sounds of the meadow play into my memory as I wander, for the first time, through this new and forbidding place. I gasp, wanting to mimic the screams of a young child; and I see the pain of relentless stings to my face and body; and I experience the fear; the fear of a child, but as an adult, a grown woman who now understands the implications of that pain. The desire to run, to leave this place, overwhelms me and swallows me whole.

But these are not my memories.

As I attempt to push the energy and willpower I need into my limbs, I see a different scene. This time I am in the meadow again; I had returned from the hospital; but I am holding my Mother's hand; and as we approach the hives she speaks; not to me, but to the bees.

But this hadn't happened to me.

I hear the soft voice; soothing them, explaining gently by the song in her tone that she loves them and will do them no harm; I hear the voice tell them that my child will also love them. and it is my voice. And then I say something very strange. I tell them that the girls will not harm them; and I feel their love; and they know that I love them. And in that moment, I also know something else, something very special. I am going to have two daughters. I am going to have twins.

I sing to the bees a long-remembered poem; using the same tone I had heard from the memories.

> *A maiden in her glory,*
> *Upon her wedding - day,*
> *Must tell her bees the story,*
> *Or else they'll fly away.*
> *Fly away – die away –*
> *Dwindle down and leave you!*
> *But if you don't deceive your Bees,*
> *Your Bees will not deceive you.*[4]

---

[4] The Bee Boys Song; Rudyard Kipling

And when they have listened to me, they reply with their own song. A song of welcome.

Chapter 24

I remembered the pain also. If we knew the inevitability of something, would we try to change it? Maybe there is a value in allowing life to take its course. I preferred to think that I might make my own choices. I didn't deceive the bees. But did they deceive me?

My Mother and I sat against the bed pillows silently for a while; her remembering, and me reading for the first time. Mummy used to sit next to me on my bed and read to me; and I remembered being stung by the bees. When I say remembered; before I had come home I think I had forgotten about the experience completely. Erased it from my memory, so to speak. I had thought about it when I first found the diaries, and it felt quite strange reading about it now. The memory was so faded that I had wondered for a while whether it was me that it had happened to, or my sister. But the detail slowly returned; in such a way for me to be sure that it could not belong to anyone else. But there had been something else; a long-ago resolution on my part to stay away from the bees. Was that the real reason I had run away? The reason why I had never made a connection with this place; with Meadowsweet? I think I knew there was more to it than that. It would be a convenient hook on which to hang my blame; and my guilt.

'I'm sorry Constance.'

She knew me today. 'What for Mummy?' I asked.

'For lots of things my beautiful daughter; but for mostly not protecting you from the bees.' She cried softly.

I placed the diary to one side and laid my hand on hers once again. 'You don't need to be sorry Mummy.'

She sat forward resolutely. 'But I do, and I want you to know it.'

I laughed lightly, and she gave me an angry look that lasted for a few seconds before she too laughed. It was possible, that in reading the diaries, there would be many challenging days; and I hoped I could face them, regardless of how difficult they proved to be.

The bedroom door opened, and Jemima leaned around the edge. 'What are you two laughing at?' she asked.

Mummy answered first. 'Just old memories dear,' she said. 'Have you brought tea? I really could do with a lovely cup of tea.'

'This family does nothing but drink tea; as if it were the answer to every problem.' Jemima sighed and turned to leave. 'I'll bring you a cup.'

'But it is dear,' Mummy replied. 'Why don't you make a pot of tea for all of us and bring it up. I would love to have some time with my girls.' My sister left with a smile on her face; but it was the wink that my Mother gave me that told me she most definitely did not want to share the diaries with Jemima. Not at this time at least.

Chapter 25

Diary; November 30th 1969

David had asked me to marry him, and I had said yes straight away. We exchanged rings eight days later. His mother didn't come to the wedding. She had made it very clear that she disapproved of the whole thing. And now, sitting alone with my lunch; I was finding it hard to believe that David had only actually slept at the house on two occasions, and it was the first time he stayed that had led to me getting pregnant. I still couldn't tell for sure, but I had told him anyway; and he had believed me; he never questioned it. The second occasion was on our wedding night.

He had left for Italy two days ago. We had spoken only over difficult long-distance phone calls, when he told me that he wouldn't be able to come home for some time due to the busy filming schedule. Would he be there for the birth? There had been a look of shock on his face when I'd told him that we were going to have twins. I do feel a twinge of guilt that I haven't even had my pregnancy confirmed as yet; let alone the advent of twins. But I know the bees won't lie to me.

On the car journey to the hospital several years ago, he had said that he didn't think that he could love someone forever. So, if he does love me, as he had said during that one night of passion, how long would that last? Part of me knows that I should have asked him these questions before. I have spent the past few weeks travelling through a whole raft of emotions. The one question I haven't yet answered was; do I love him? Katherine had asked me the same question the day before we married, and I hadn't given her an answer. As much as she could be a pain, she has also been such a darling; and I know that I can't manage without her. There was a time when I had been convinced that I loved him more than anything or anyone else. But so much had happened since then. Now I am going to have two daughters to think about. Although he had phoned earlier that day, all he seemed to want to talk about was how the filming was going, and his reassurance that he was thinking of me did little to ease my mind. Things don't seem to be going to plan; but in truth, I haven't really had much of a plan. I've been drifting along for some time; wrapped up with Meadowsweet; and the bees. The damn bees. I have only one friend, and no career prospects; and if I am honest.... a husband I barely know. The money that I have been left, means that I will never have to work; but I haven't even discussed those issues with David.

∞ ∞ ∞

Diary; December 3rd 1969

I am exhausted. I haven't slept well for several days. Katherine has come to stay but had already gone to bed, and just as I think I might go to bed early for want of nothing better to do, the phone in the living room rings.

'You'll never guess what has happened today?' Are the first words David utters in answer to my greeting.

'No David, I probably won't,' I reply abruptly.

'I have just had the most amazing news.' His voice is slurred. I can almost see him jumping up and down.

I ignore his enthusiasm. 'David, there's something I'd like to talk to you about.'

'Yes sure, but let me tell you this first.' He sounds just like an excited school boy.

'You're coming home.'

'We just have a few things to wrap up on this section of the film. There have been big changes going on here.' There is silence for a while. I wonder if he is waiting for me to ask him a question. I don't. 'I'm being made assistant director,' he says. There is another long pause. 'Assistant Director,' he repeats, as if he thinks I didn't hear him the first time.

'I thought you were already Assistant Director?'

'Well, yes, I am....an Assistant Director, but now I'm going to be THE assistant director.'

'So, what has happened to THE Assistant Director on the film?'

'He was caught with one of the actor's wives.'

'What do you mean, caught?'

'You know, caught...in a compromising situation; that kind of caught.'

'What has happened to him?' I ask.

'Never mind him; I'm now THE assistant director.'

'You get the sack for that kind of thing, do you?'

'No, not really; it goes on all the time; but you do get the sack for getting caught.'

'And you haven't been caught then?' There is silence on the line for some time. 'David?'

'I'm still here....no of course I haven't been caught.'

'What does that mean?

'Listen Mary, don't you understand how important this to me. I've worked hard to get to this point, and now you're just throwing it in my face.' The line crackles.

I hold the receiver away from my ear in response. 'David, when are you coming home?'

'What.... what did you say?'

'When are you coming home?'

'I've already told you. Listen, I have to go.' I put the receiver back to my ear and can hear voices in the background. The phone hisses, and it sounds like he has covered the mouthpiece. 'I'll be there shortly,' he says.

'Who's that with you?'

'Sorry, what did you say?'

'You were speaking to someone.'

'Oh yes.... we're having a little party to celebrate my promotion. Something you don't seem to be able to do.' The phone crackles again.

'Well maybe I would if we were together.'

'Look I've told you.... oh, never mind. I must go. I'll talk to you when you're in a better mood.'

The line goes dead.

The room feels cold. I listen to the buzz for a while, hoping David will come back. But he doesn't, and so I replace the receiver.

∞ ∞ ∞

Diary; December 4th 1969

I eat breakfast in silence, whilst Katherine is at the sink singing a happy tune. I am sure that she knows something is wrong, but I'm not in the mood for sharing. I have so far resisted any of Katherine's attempts to discuss the topic of David.

'So how is David?' Katherine asks, making me jump slightly.

'What? Oh, he's fine,' I lie. And then I cry. The tears pour out like a broken water pipe. Katherine stops what she is doing and turns around in confusion, and I bury my head in my hands, remembering the last time my friend had seen me cry; which was at my mother's funeral. Then I had shed some silent tears gracefully and with some element of dignity. Now, I might as well be throwing up for all the grace and dignity I have.

'Alright.' Katherine says, 'Tell me all about it.' She waits patiently whilst I continue sobbing for a while longer, and allows the torrent to end its flow. I try to find the words to begin, but my mind is a fog. 'Has he left you already? My goodness. You've not even given birth.'

I pause a while longer; realising that I haven't told her that the pregnancy hasn't been confirmed yet. 'I'm not sure,' is all I could manage between the sobs.

'That bloody brother of mine; I could kill him.'

'That's not helping Katherine.'

'I'm sorry but someone has to say it, he's a bast...'

'And he's also my husband Katie.'

It is silent long enough for Katherine to resume the washing up. 'So, what has he done sis?'

I think about that, and wonder what he has done. I can remember my conversations with him, but struggle to put the whole thing into a string of coherent sentences.

Katherine proves very adept at doing that for me. 'You'll have to forgive me for being blunt Mary, but I'm pretty sure he's thinking that he's made a big mistake. He didn't want to get married, because he wants to live life his way, and you will.... you and the twins will be tying him down. Your excess baggage; you don't contribute to his happiness; he wants to fly; he....'

'Alright Katie, I get the picture. You're not making me feel better.'

'I'm sorry sis. I can't help but tell it like it is.' She dries her hands and walks over to the table. 'I'm only saying these things for your own good.' She squeezes my arm, which hurts almost as much as the pain in my heart.

Chapter 26

A thousand bee stings. No, a million stings, couldn't be greater. Not more than the pain of loss. But what had I lost? For I had never had it in the first place. And there was the dark shadow. The man I had never known. The colours were fading, along with the dreams. What would replace them? Not pain. Please not pain.

Since her episode some two days ago, when she appeared to have forgotten who we were, Mummy had been decidedly lucid. Along with that, she seemed to be really happy. That was in spite of the diary entries that we had read. I wondered at that. In contrast, I couldn't shake off this feeling of melancholy. Knowing that, so early on in their relationship, my Mother and Father had had such problems, made me feel so uncertain about my relationship with Gabriel. I had been hurt and betrayed so badly in my life that I had begun to wonder if it was really possible for anyone to find real happiness. What was to come in the diaries? In my own life?

I had decided to go out for the day on my own. I tried to explain to Jem, but she didn't seem to understand. She almost seemed to fall apart at the thought of looking after Mummy on her own, even though she'd been coping for so many years. It made me realise just how close she had come to cracking; and how much I was needed. I didn't know how much longer I could stay. I was surprised that Lucinda had not tried to contact me yet, and I quickly dismissed the idea of letting her know how things were going. That, I thought, would just make her even more impatient. I think that I was hoping for the out of sight is out of mind response.

After looking around the small groups of shops in Windsor high street I found myself sitting in a small café by the river, overlooking Windsor Bridge. The day was warm with a soft breeze, and the hot chocolate and scones in front of me boded a pleasant experience, and I remembered an afternoon spent with Gabriel by a canal side restaurant in Milan. The preceding days had been hot, and a warm breeze had blown down from the north to cool the afternoon. Gabriel had persuaded me to leave work early; something I rarely did. Instead of scones we had enjoyed a glass of nicely chilled white wine in anticipation of an early dinner. That was some two months ago; and I recalled that particular afternoon because Gabriel had asked me to marry him.

I knew that my reply had hurt him, but he had never shown it. He just smiled back at me and kissed me softy on the cheek. That had made me feel even worse. I hadn't even told him that I would think about it; just that I could never marry. Now; sitting here at the side of the river Thames; I almost wished that he could be here with me. And I wondered what my reply would be right now. I had been so sure then. Perhaps he knew me better than I did myself. Since then he had been no different to how he always was. I took my phone out and brought his number up. I held my finger over the call button for several seconds, and then I quickly placed the phone on the table as if it would burn my fingers.

I finished my the last bit of my scone and decided to wander over to Windsor Bridge. From there I could watch the occasional boat making its way along the Thames. Such a setting was not the place for making decisions, and I leaned on the bridge rail and watched the swans wander aimlessly across the water. A larger boat which appeared to be overflowing with people made its way toward the bridge. Many of the occupants were attempting to dance on the small deck as the excessively loud music added to the noise of shouts and screams. From where I stood I could see there was a mixture of boys and girls. There was no doubt they were in high spirits. As the boat drew nearer, some on the bridge were laughing and cheering them on, whereas others were scowling in annoyance. I couldn't make my mind up how I felt, although the swans seemed not to be amused either, and slid out of the way to find a more peaceful setting. Several of the boat's occupants looked up at the bridge and waved at us. One of the boys held his glass aloft and offered it in mock generosity. As the boat slowly made its way under the bridge he pointed the glass at me. And then I saw his face.

'Jake?' I shouted, as I stood up from the rail.

My stomach turned as he lowered the glass and called back. 'Constance?'

I stepped back from the edge of the bridge and stared out along the river. The boat had disappeared under the bridge and was travelling behind me in the opposite direction. I knew that I should run to the other side of the bridge, but I found I couldn't move. I heard a shout, but I wasn't sure it was meant for me. I kept staring ahead and moved back to the rail, placing my hands firmly on it to steady myself.

There was another shout, but further away this time, and I recognized my name. I still couldn't move, and I could feel my heart beating in my ears. I turned to my left and walked back into the town, but kept one hand on the rail. My head was full of images and questions. What was going on? How could Jake be here? It made no sense. I thought that I would never see him again. But something didn't quite fit. I glanced to my left but could see no sign of the boat. Everything around me was a blur. And then I felt angry. So very angry. How dare he come back into my life, I thought.

Then I heard another shout from behind me; from the bridge. 'Constance!'

Chapter 27

Diary; December 12th 1969

We sprawl out on the sofas in silence. Having spent the past few hours talking about life and family and love; I am surprised when Katherine reveals that she is so very unhappy at home. I haven't seen her this emotional before, and I'm not sure what to do. She explains that she wants to explore some of the arts, and that she is particularly drawn to sculpting, as she has enjoyed crafting several pieces during her time at university. Her Mother is not happy that she wants to use what she has learned in such a practical way. Rather, she expects her to become an art critic, or art historian, or something like that. Katherine scowls at me when I laugh; and I imagine her, telling it like it is, as she rubbishes a Monet, or telling everyone that, Da Vinci can't draw for a toffee. She tells me that her mother has threatened to cut off her allowance if she doesn't follow her advice.

'I know,' I say, climbing up out of my seat. 'Why don't you move in here? Permanently, I mean.'

I wait as she sits quietly thinking, searching for any obstacles to such an enterprise, which she soon finds. 'What about David?' she asks.

'What about David?' I reply. 'We don't even know when he's coming back. And even if he does, look at the size of this place. You can have your pick of the bedrooms, excluding mine of course.' I try to ignore the pain of memories, but it bites me nonetheless.

Katherine continues to think about the possibilities. 'I suppose I can use the garage as a workshop.'

'That won't work; the car is kept in there, along with any other junk. I'll have a workshop built.' I say it before I think about the implications. Katherine stares at me in disbelief. 'It's okay, I can afford it. You can pay me back by helping when the twins are born, and I can try and find some kind work to keep me happy.'

We talk for some time about all of the possibilities, and Katherine pours herself some more wine from the almost empty bottle on the floor beside the sofa.

'Here's to....' Katherine searches for something to drink to, '.... here's to Meadowsweet, a magical place to live.'

I raise my glass of fresh orange. 'Here's to the bees.'

'The bees?' She looks at me quizzically. 'Why the bees?'

'Because....' and I smile at the thought. 'Because if it wasn't for the bees.... there would be no Meadowsweet.'

'Really? Why is that?'

'Have I never told you the story of how Meadowsweet came to be built?'

'No, you haven't. You mean it has a history?'

'Well, of a kind. The house was built by my Grandfather. Both he and my Gran lived in Windsor, and Gran kept bees. They had quite a large garden with their property, and my Grandfather sold it to developers, as Windsor was growing in size. Gran was not happy, because it would mean that she couldn't keep the bees anymore, and she made my Grandfather buy the meadow here in Wraysbury, which at the time had an old barn sitting right in the middle of it. She promptly moved her bees here, and because she spent so much time here, Grandfather bought another piece of land next to the meadow; big enough to build the house on.'

'So why was the house called Meadowsweet? Is it because of the meadow?'

'It's because of the plant. Gran named it after the herb growing in the meadow. And it's where I get my name from.'

'You are named after a plant?'

'Its Latin name anyway. Filipendula Ulmaria, to be precise.'

'That is so amazing. I will never look at this house the same again; or you, or the bees.'

'The bees are special you know. I write about them in my diary. We have a unique relationship.'

'Shouldn't you and David have that kind of relationship?'

I sigh. 'I do want that you know. I want it to be special. But the bees are.... different.'

'How do you mean?'

'I don't know if I can explain. I just know that....'

Our conversation is interrupted by a knock on the front door, and Katherine jumps out of the sofa, and regrets it instantly as her head spins.

'Who on earth is that?' I ask.

We stand there, not knowing what to do. 'Well we won't find out unless you open the door, will we.' Katherine replies.

I walk into the hallway and turn the lights on. 'Who is it?' I ask.

'It's David,' comes the reply. I feel a strong sense of déjà vu. He has come home, and I look a mess. I haven't changed out of the clothes I had worn all day. My first thought is to run upstairs and change, and I look around to see if there is anything that can help, but all I can see are coats. 'Well, are you going to open the door? I don't have a key.'

'Oh, I'm sorry; just a second.' I run back into the living room and grab Katherine by the hand and pull her into the hall. In one breathe, I blurt out to her. 'It's David. Open the door; take him into the living room, and don't let him come upstairs. I'm going to change; he can't see me like this; not after being with beautiful women for all this time…. I'm going.' I make my way upstairs and dash into the bathroom. Slipping off everything, I jump into the shower, and scream as the water hit me, as I hadn't waited for it to heat up properly. I throw several bottles of scented shampoos and creams over myself, and just as quickly wash them off. When I jump out of the shower I realise that I haven't grabbed a towel, and so I pull the hand towel off the rail and dry as much as I can. I peer out of the bedroom door and all is quiet, so I run into the hall and grab a large towel from the cupboard.

Several minutes later, I am dressed and making my way down the stairs. I pause halfway down and catch my breath, smiling back at my grandmother as I do so. At the bottom of the stairs I stop again and listen, but there is silence. And then it occurs to me that David and Katherine don't exactly get on; and with the things that Katherine had said about our marriage, I just might have made a big mistake in leaving them alone together. I pause once more at the living room door, which has been closed, and take a deep breath. I push it open with all the enthusiasm I can muster and walk in confidently. David and Katherine are sitting opposite each other in silence; but at least they are both smiling; and more importantly, as David stands up, I can see that he is holding the biggest bunch of flowers I have ever seen.

'David. I'm sorry, I didn't want you to….'

'It's okay. Katherine explained….and I understand sweetheart.' He steps towards me and holds out the flowers rather awkwardly. 'I just wanted to say I'm sorry.'

'Oh David, they're beautiful. You really didn't have to….'

'I did, really have to. I've treated you very badly.'

I stare up at his big, piercing, sorrowful eyes and I melt. I grab the flowers, throw them on the sofa and fall into his arms. They wrap me up securely, and I feel safe for the first time in such a long while. I turn to say something to Katherine, but she has gone.

Diary; December 13th 1969

I wake to the sound of cups chinking together and the smell of bacon, and I pull my head above the sheets to find David placing a tray on the bed. I slowly sit up and shield my eyes as he opens the curtains. 'What time is it?'

'Around nine o clock,' he replies.

'Oh my goodness, it's so late.'

'It's okay. I have everything sorted.'

Noticing the look of surprise on my face he replies, 'I can make breakfast you know. Well I can now anyway. And what I didn't know Katherine showed me. And Katherine being Katherine, I made sure I learned pretty quickly.' He smiles deeply. 'You look beautiful Mary.'

'You've never said that,' I reply, and regret it as quickly as it is said.

'You're right.... but that's going to change.' Sitting on the bed, he pours the tea. 'I don't know how, but I'm going to work things out. I've got to go back tonight, but you've got to believe me Mary when I say that the intention is there.' David points to the jar of honey. 'Apparently, this is the most important thing to get right.' For the first time in months I feel happy, and I laugh.

We spend the rest of the day together looking around Windsor and standing on the bridge and watching the boats working their way along the Thames go under and out the other side. I had been surprised to find that David was even happy to let Katherine come along with us. It feels as if we have turned a rather large corner. Everything seems to be coming together at last. I can't help but smile for most of the day, and I think that David and Katherine look happy too. The evening comes, and David's smile softens. 'I need to think about going my darling,' he says tenderly.

Chapter 28

They say that the sensations of pain and pleasure are pretty much the same thing. But what if you are experiencing them both all at once? Things lost, now found. Together they are grey.

I stopped walking across the bridge and stood rigid; again, staring straight ahead. I couldn't turn. I felt hot and cold all at once. 'Is that really you?' I knew the sound of his voice; even after twenty years; but something still wasn't quite right. I didn't want this. But I couldn't leave. I wanted so desperately to know what would happen next. He walked around the side of me and turned to directly face me, and I looked into his eyes; Jakes eyes. A thousand memories came flooding back; and we were walking hand in hand together across the bridge, this bridge, pausing halfway to kiss in the moonlight, his strong hands holding me against the rails as his passion grew. 'I suppose I should call you Aunt Constance.'

'What?'

'Well you are my aunt, after all.' He tilted his head in that familiar way. 'Are you alright?'

'Yes, yes I am.' And that was it. Not quite right. Jake's son.

'Well it's lovely to finally meet you Constance; Aunt Constance.'

He held out his hand. I hesitated, and then I took it. There was a familiar strength in his grip. 'It's nice to meet you too...Jake's son.' He laughed; that almost right laugh, and I prickled.

'All my friends call me Jake. It's my middle name. How did you know?' He answered his own question. 'Mum must have told you.' He took a step back and looked straight at me. 'So.... the elusive Aunt Constance.' He smiled again and placed his hand on his chin. 'You're just like your photos you know; only older.'

I ignored his comment. 'What are you doing here?' I asked, a bit too abruptly.

'Ah.... well that's the thing you see. I've skived off uni for a few days.' He walked over to the side of the bridge and, looking over, he waved at friends I couldn't see.

'So, Jemima.... Mum doesn't know.' I took a deep breath and walked over to the side of the bridge to look down at the boat he had been on. His friends waved him down impatiently. One of them whistled.

He raised his hand casually and, ignoring their pleas, he turned to me again. 'Well, no, she doesn't.' He looked at me sheepishly, placing his hands in his pockets, and he shrugged his shoulders and shuffled.

'Well I shan't tell if you don't.' I said, and I smiled at him.

'Really? Oh you're a darling Constance.' He grabbed my shoulders and kissed my cheek. I felt my skin prickle again. I heard some more whistles from the boat. 'Listen,' he said. 'How about we meet for lunch tomorrow? Be on the bridge at twelve.'

I remembered how assertive Jake used to be. I must have appeared reluctant, because he backed off. 'Only if you want to of course,' he continued. 'I don't want to get you into trouble.'

'You don't want to get me into trouble?' I should have said no. Everything inside me told me to say no. 'Yes. Ok. But I'll call you by your first name.'

'Which is?' he asked with a mischievous grin.

'Michael,' I replied.

He laughed again. 'And I'll call you Aunt Constance; out of respect of course.'

Chapter 29

Diary; January 6th 1970

Katherine and I stand hand in hand as we watch the last of the doors being fixed to the opening of the new workshop. I can feel Katherine's excitement, and I can feel my jealousy. We had argued over where to place the workshop, as Katherine had wanted it to be in the meadow; but I had been insistent that that would be out of the question, as it would upset the bees. Katherine's laugh had told me that she still didn't understand what they meant to me. We had compromised, and it was placed in the garden on the west side of the house; well away from the bees, and with easy access to the front entrance. I found that helping Katherine with the project took away the sadness I felt at David not being home. As I watch her smiling, I can't help but feel that I really don't know what I am letting myself in for, and I'm beginning to realise that this is what life is like. You have your dreams and then you negotiate.

I am beginning to feel restless. The days are cold and the nights colder. I had had the heating replaced in Meadowsweet; but it's at night when I am alone that I feel the cold most of all. If David is my soulmate, then I am truly alone. Even the bees don't want to be sociable in this weather. My impatience is beginning to irritate Katherine, and I am thinking that once the twins are born, I might try to find some work whilst David is away. Quite how that will happen, I have no idea.

I am preparing lunch when the phone rings. Katherine answers it with her usual terse hello, and without saying another word, she hands the receiver to me. It's David. 'I'm coming home,' he says. I can hear noisy traffic in the background.

'What? But you're not due for a visit for another week.' I'm sure I must sound rather negative.

'Yes, but my job here is finished. And the good news is....' My heart misses a beat. 'I'm coming home today'.

Chapter 30

I was beginning to understand the dreams. How the colours were so wrapped up with reading the diaries, and with my emotions. The question was...could I control them? How could I? Everyone around me had a brush. And no matter how much colour I added to my canvas, their brushes swirled colours all around me.

I told the taxi driver to let me out at the front gate. The late afternoon sun was settling itself behind the trees at Meadowsweet, and I wanted to walk to the meadow. As I made my way along the drive I looked over to my right at the house. A soft orange glow had spread itself across the timbers, and I stopped for a moment to soak in the view and took in a deep breath. The air was undemanding and quiet, and I let my breath out slowly as a warm smile spread across my lips and worked its way around my face. For the first time since I had been here I felt.... safe.

I swung the gate open to the meadow and glanced into the shade of the trees. I could hear the faint hum of the bees as they were beginning to settle down for the night. After my encounter with, Jake, I needed to tell someone, and I had worked my way through the list of who might understand; a list which began and ended with the bees. I placed my hands in my jacket pockets and walked slowly across the meadow and into the shade, and I stopped at the hive where I had, several days earlier, removed the diaries. I pictured Mummy first coming here to place the diaries into the hive, and I wondered at what point she must have realised that she needed to do so; and I thought about how hard that must have been for her to let them go. And then I understood that she hadn't let them go at all. When she had first mentioned the diaries to me she had spoken of the bees looking after her memories. And what better place could she have put them? For a moment, I wondered if she had secreted other diaries in the hives; an idea that I knew to be ridiculous; but it did cross my mind that I might want to leave my secrets with the bees one day. I hadn't written about my life, or any memory I had had in my life up until today. And that thought made me sad. Maybe it should be compulsory for everyone to record their life for future generations. But, in truth, the lives that most of us led would make for hard reading by those that followed us; as Mummy's diaries were proving to be; and for the first time, I understood the real purpose that the bees had. Of course, they provided us with their farmed produce; and without charge, thank you very much; but their real beauty was in their ability to listen with impartiality, and without malice aforethought; and that they could connect with all humanity; and require no compensation, or exact no judgement. I had already seen what the bees were capable of from my Mother's diary entries; and holding onto that thought, I did feel safe. I had not yet shared my thoughts with them, nor my secrets for that that matter; but I knew that this was not the time. I also knew that whatever would happen, I could come to the bees with my story.

I remembered the Rudyard Kipling poem Mummy had written in the diary.

> A maiden in her glory,
> Upon her wedding day,
> Must tell her bees the story,
> Or else they'll fly away.

Was that really true? If so, then the bees needed us as much as we needed them. They wanted to hear our stories; but they also wanted our honesty. I had wondered how much of my Mother's diary entries were true. And I thought about the rest of the poem.

> Fly away – die away –
> Dwindle down and leave you!
> But if you don't deceive your bees,
> Your bees will not deceive you.

Mummy had no choice but to write the truth. Otherwise the bees would have known; and they were still here.

I stepped closer to the hive and gently placed my hands on the top. Now I was listening, I could hear the hum of their singing. A solitary bee landed on the top of my hand, and although I tensed slightly, I made no attempt to remove it. The bee danced around in circles across the ridges of my hand, and I could feel it softly brushing my skin as it endeavoured to identify me. And, once again, the memory came; but this time, it was my memory. A small child, leaving the security of the house and exploring the meadow; curiosity getting the better of me. A thousand bees all over me. The overwhelming sound shutting out every other sensation. And then the pain; the unbelievable pain as the bees sought to defend their hive from this aggressor. I had confused them. They had wished to welcome me to the hive; to their family; and I had resisted, as any child would. My Mother's memory had become mine.

'I'm sorry.' I heard myself say. I had said it back then, before the screams began, and I said it quietly now. 'I'm so sorry.' One bee became two, and then four, and quickly, very quickly, many more joined them as they explored my hand. The singing of the bees rose into a crescendo of sound, once again shutting out every other sensation, and I wondered if they recognized me. They began to settle all over my body, but I couldn't feel them. I stood perfectly still. This time, I wouldn't panic; I wouldn't be afraid. I could feel their warmth begin to penetrate me; and I heard my Mother's, and my Grandmother's voice. 'Hello my babies.' I said softly. They spent some minutes exploring me. Then they left.

I closed the gate to the meadow behind me and began walking back to the house. I knew that as soon as I stepped into the kitchen Jemima would ask me about my day; and I had no desire to reveal my encounter with Michael, her son. I even pondered the wisdom of mentioning it to Mummy as there was no guarantee that she would keep the information to herself; although she had done a pretty good job with the diaries. As I walked up to the kitchen door, I could see Jem standing at the sink. She smiled and gave me a wave. I pushed open the door and stepped inside, enjoying the sensation of the warm air as it rushed to meet me. I closed the door and slid my jacket off; it felt damp. I hadn't realised how cool it had become since I had walked to the meadow. I shivered, my body shaking off the dampness, and the day, and I thought of Jake, and Michael.

Jemima placed the plate she had been drying on the work top, along with the tea towel. 'Mummy's been hard work today,' she said, before I could speak.

I put my jacket onto a coat hook. 'What's been the problem?' I asked and walked across to the wall cupboard and took two mugs out.

Jem took the mugs from me. 'She's been saying some strange things about memories; her memories.' My heart missed a beat. 'She also asked me when David would be back from filming.'

'Dad?'

'Yes, Dad,' she replied.

'You said memories.'

'She said I wasn't to worry because the bees were looking after her memories, and if I wanted to know anything I should talk to them. What does that mean?' The kettle whistled so Jem pulled it sideways off the heat. 'And when I asked Mummy what she meant, she just kept asking where you were. That you would know. What does she mean Connie?' She tipped a small amount of the water from the kettle into the teapot and swirled it around. Then she placed the kettle back onto the heat again and turned to face me. 'Has she said anything to you?'

I walked over to the table and sat down. So here it was again. If I was going to lie I didn't want to look her in the eye. I was well practiced at bending the truth at the gallery, but this was different. I was sure in my own mind that this still wasn't the time to tell Jemima about the diaries; I needed to read all of them first before I decided what was the best thing to do. She didn't have a connection with the bees; of that I was certain. Did that mean that I did? They were one of the reasons I left; weren't they?

'Have you spoken to the bees?' I asked her.

'Have I what?'

'You said that Mummy spoke about talking to them.'

'Connie, you can't be serious. Mummy has dementia, and the best that she can do right now is suggest talking to the bees. And now you're saying that I should do the same.'

'Maybe there's something in it. even if it's just a way to keep our sanity right now.'

'You've done it haven't you.' She said. 'I saw you walking back from the meadow. Did you talk to them?'

'I... went to see them.'

She turned back toward the kettle which was whistling again, and placing the tea into the pot she poured the boiling water in, then banged the kettle down. 'So, you've been away for all these years, and then you just wander down to the meadow and pick up where you left off.'

'Well, I don't know if it's quite like that, but, for good or bad, they never left Jem; none of you did. I was the one that left. And they hurt me too.'

She stood silently, her back to me. 'You remember that?' she said in a whisper.

'Yes, do you?' I asked.

'Kind of; but I wasn't sure if it was you or...'

'You thought it might have been you?'

'You forgave them?' she asked, avoiding the question.

'I forgave all of you Jem.' I thought about Jake's son.

'I haven't,' she replied.

'You haven't forgiven them?'

'Not them; not Mummy; not Jake; not the bees.' She turned to face me. 'I can't forgive them. I can't forgive myself.'

I stood and went across to her and I took her hand. 'Listen Jem; we have to find a way through this. Yes, I was angry; very angry; but we have to find the reason things turned out the way they did.' At that moment, I could have so easily shared what I had learned from the diaries.

'What makes you think there's a reason?' she replied. 'Life is basically crap. You have your dreams....'

'.... And then you negotiate.' I continued.

'Where did you......?' she asked.

'I think Mummy used to say it.' I squeezed her hand again. 'Jem, I'm sure that it will become clear to us before....'

'Before what?' she asked. 'Before Mummy dies?'

'Before I go back home.'

'You are home Connie.'

'Yes.' It was beginning to feel like I was home again. But with all that was happening I wasn't sure how I felt about that. 'Before I go back to Milan,' I said;

'So, you will go back?'

'It's where I live Jem. It's where I have a life. If I came back here, back home, well....it would mean starting all over again.' I moved away and walked back to the table. 'Anyway, it's too early to say right now. I just think we need to be patient.'

'Easier said than done Connie.'

'We don't really have much choice Jem.' I didn't want to have this conversation. It was too soon. I was sure that if I could continue to read the diaries it would all become clear. 'Did Mummy say anything else?'

'She just kept asking where you were.'

Chapter 31

Diary; January 7th 1970

I am woken by the smell of coffee.

'Good morning sleepy head,' David says as he places a tray on the bed next to me, in the space he has spent the night. As I rouse from my dreams, images flash into my mind of his arrival in the early hours; when he had slid into the bed, his cold naked body had filled me with longing, and we had gently made love with remembered passion.

'What time is it David?'

'Early. But don't think about that darling. Just enjoy this.'

I glance at the clock. 5:45 am. 'Oh David. I'm so tired.'

'I know, but you won't regret this; trust me. Come on sit up old girl.'

'Hey! Old girl? Where did that come from? Anyway, I like a cup of tea in the mornings; and I don't fancy any breakfast.' I feel mildly nauseated this morning, and I sit up slowly trying to open my eyes. I can see that it's still dark outside.

'I know you like your tea, but you have to try this darling.' He pulls the tea towel off the tray to reveal a small loaf of bread. 'Tada!'

I look at the tray suspiciously and run my eyes over the array of treats David has assembled. 'Ok, so what have we got here then?' I ask.

David rubs his hands together. 'Well, to begin with; we have bread; not just any bread mind, but locally made, and by that, I mean Peidmont Italy. Locally made brioche; and.... you have never tasted anything quite like this; filled with cream, I might add. We have strudel di mele, or apple strudel; or if you prefer, a slice of crostata, a local breakfast tart; and these particular pieces are filled with apricot. You are about to enjoy colazione, that is breakfast, Italian style.'

I stare at the tray in speechless amazement. 'How?'

He sits on the bed with the widest grin on his face. 'I know, I'm a genius, aren't I. That's why I've woken you so early. You see, in another couple of hours these won't be worth a salt.'

He can see my obvious reluctance, and so he points to the tray in encouragement. 'And to top it all.... I've put a jar of local honey, that is, local Peidmont honey, right in the middle of the tray. You see, I haven't forgotten.' He carefully lifts up a cup of the coffee and hands it to me. 'Just try a sip, I know you'll like it.' He then sits on the bed next to me and picks up a slice of the crostata and takes a bite. 'Whilst we've been filming I've been staying at a vineyard near Peidmont. The Rossi's. They're like family now.'

He places his hand in mine and I swell at the softness of his touch. 'I've brought some photos and details back with me for you to look at. I was thinking that maybe you and I...'

'We are going to be a family now. Whatever we do, we do as a family.' I wonder why I had said that. Perhaps I'm looking for reassurance.

'Yes, yes. Of course.' He points to the coffee enthusiastically. 'Have a taste.' I take a sip of the coffee and find it sweet to taste, but not unpleasant. I want to join in his excitement, but feel I need time to get over the memories of him not being here; and I don't want him to bring home his life, but want him to enjoy my life, our life. Am I being ungrateful? We finish breakfast as the sun is beginning to rise and make love again, but this time with undemanding affection. I come down to the kitchen just before lunchtime, as I needed to catch up on sleep, and I find David sitting at the kitchen table looking through some paperwork.

'Good morning darling.' He says affectionately.

I smile and sit down next to him. 'What are you doing?'

'I'll tell you about that later. I just wanted to know....' He pauses awkwardly. 'You didn't tell me that Katherine had moved in permanently.'

I struggle to answer him, feeling guilty. 'No.'

'Don't you think that we should have discussed it first? You did say we are a family.'

'I presume Katherine told you.'

'Yes, she did. She's gone out to her workshop; something else you didn't tell me about.'

'How could I?' I say defensively. 'You've not been here.'

'Yes, you're right. I haven't been here. But...as I said, that's going to change.'

'How?'

'What do you mean? He asks.

'How is it going to change?'

He looks puzzled, and I realise that he probably doesn't have any concrete plans, just good intentions. He lifts the papers that he has been looking at. 'First thing we are going to do is go away.'

'Really? When is that going to happen?

'Well, today is Wednesday, so in three days' time.'

I stare at him in amazement, not knowing quite what to say. 'What? Where?'

Chapter 32

I closed my eyes for the first time today. It shut out the light, and the colours;

and the darkness was such sweet relief. I just may never open them again.

I stood in the middle of the bridge and glanced at my watch. 11:55am. The tingle in my stomach was beginning to become a familiar sensation. Lucinda had said that she had it all the time. 'Stress,' she said, 'was good for the soul. It is the life blood of every Italian.' I was never sure whether that was the tenet of every Italian or it just belonged to her. She wouldn't have understood that there was a difference. As I stood on the bridge, familiar memories crept once again into my mind. Cool December evenings snuggling into Jake as we talked about our future. I had shivered then on the bridge, and Jake had placed his hands in the pockets of his long coat and opened it wide so that he could wrap me into it. I remembered snuggling into his warm body and feeling his passion. And it was that passion that I remembered most of all. It never left him. He had wanted to make love to me every second that we were together; but I had wanted that to be something special. When he knew that the only way he could have me was to marry me, he hadn't hesitated in asking me. I had said yes straight away. How could I not wish to be consumed by such passion? What I didn't realise was that his passion was there in spite of me; and he couldn't wait; And Jemima had become consumed by it also.

'Hello Aunt Constance.'

I jumped as his familiar voice bounced through my head. 'Jake; I mean Michael. Hello. How are you.'

He stood directly in front of me. He had tight dark trousers on with a white tee shirt that was also tight on his body. He was holding a light grey jacket over his shoulder, and his bent arm was firmly rounded from time spent working out. A soft whistle came from behind him as two girls walked past. He ignored it.

'Happens all the time.' He said dismissively. 'A little bit fragile after yesterday. Too much wine I think.' He held out his arm and pointed to some tables and chairs outside a small eating place on the riverside. 'Shall we go? I've booked us a small table just down there.' Without a moment's hesitation, he took my hand and walked me to the end of the bridge. I felt the strength and warmth of his hand, and I was with Jake, my Jake. I listened to Jake's voice as Michael spoke, and I looked into Jake's eyes as Michael looked back at me.

I glanced over to the tables and felt overwhelmed with guilt. I was having a secret lunch with Jemima's son, and she had no idea. Is this how she felt when she was out with Jake? Uneasy thoughts crept into my head. I wanted to feel that moment of fulfilment with Jake. To have what Jemima had experienced, and I wished then that I had made love to him. Then at least I would have truly known his passion. And here I was with him; with Jake. But this was Michael. This was my nephew. What was I doing? I stopped and pulled him back. 'I'm not sure that this is such a good idea.' I said.

'What's the problem?' he asked, one eyebrow raising in reply.

'I think we should tell your Mother.'

'You are joking. Please tell me you're joking. Do you know what a shed load of trouble I would be in?'

'Yes, you're right. I'm sorry. Perhaps I should just go.'

'What's worrying you Connie?'

Aunt had gone. It was obvious that he had been saying it just to please me, so I ignored the omission. 'Just old memories.' I replied.

'Look. Mum is home looking after Gran. Yes?'

'Yes.'

'Then what's to worry? I'm just getting to know my long-lost aunt; and a beautiful one at that.'

And there it was. There was the twist that was Jake. He could hold you and drop you all at the same time. Now I remembered how constantly insecure I had felt. Now I remembered why I had never made love to him. I had always known that I could never trust him. And then I knew that what had happened to Jemima would have happened to me. he would have left me. And I felt sorry for the young girls that would have their hearts broken by this version of Jake.

'So, what's on the menu then?' I asked.

He smiled and grabbed my hand again, this time moving me faster, perhaps in the fear that I might change my mind again.

Chapter 33

Diary; January 10th 1970

Katherine is sleeping peacefully in the back of the hired Range Rover. I guess we have travelled around forty miles from Turin airport toward our destination of Serralunga d'Alba, which means we have about another ten or fifteen miles to drive. I had been shocked when David revealed that we were not only going to Italy, but also to the place he had spent most of his time living whilst filming. Despite protestations from both David and Katherine, I had managed to persuade them both that this could be an opportunity for them to improve their relationship. 'After all, we are family now,' I had said in the most convincing voice that I could manage.

We pass a sign for Novello. Apparently, it's not the quickest way, but David had planned the route to get the most out of our journey. The main houses of the town seem to rise to the right in several tiers, whilst the landscape drops away to the left. I see a layby up ahead on the left and ask David if he will pull over. Despite the time of year, it's a warm, bright day, and in the distance, we can see what appears to be a range of mountains. David tells us that they are part of the Alps which surround three sides of the Piedmont region. If this is a taste of what's to come, then I really can't wait to get to our destination. David turns off the engine and we sit for a moment, taking in the tranquillity. I tie a scarf around my hair and wind down the window, feeling the fresh breeze that is rising from the valley and passing us by to be enjoyed by the townsfolk further up the hill.

'Why have we stopped?' Katherine asks as she lets out a yawn. 'Are we there?'

'Not quite Katie; I just thought it would be nice to take in some of the Italian countryside.' I open the car door and step outside, and a pleasant aroma drifts through the air and I close my eyes as I slowly breathe it in. Katherine opens her door and follows me to the edge of the road.

'This is amazing Mary. Truly amazing. I never realised that places like this really existed.'

'So, you're pleased you came then.'

'Oh yes. I am. Look at that view.'

'You're welcome. You took some persuading, but I'm glad you're here.'

She has the biggest grin on her face. 'Let's face it, you couldn't cope without me.'

'I wouldn't go as far as that Madam,' I say as I look out across the vista, and I feel a sense of excitement well up inside; and for a moment, I forget all the reasons why I have come here.

The final part of the journey takes us past Barolo and Muscatel, and the views promise to add to our time here. Twenty-five minutes or so later we arrive in Alba, where row upon row of vines snake along the valley to our left and travel past us to make their way up the rising hills toward the town. Just before we come into the town, we see the sign indicating the Rossi villa. David turns the car right, and we make our way up the long track which winds its way around to the right, and then pull back to the left. Coming over the crest of the rise, the villa reveals itself, sitting toward the front of vast fields of vines; and the valley drops again on the other side of the crest. Several people are waiting as we drive through two large iron gates set onto the biggest brick piers I have seen in my life. It is my guess that they could see us arriving as we drove out of the valley toward the town.

'Is this where we are staying? Katherine asks. 'It's little wonder you didn't want to come home,' she says to David.

'Katie!' I say in protest.

'Sorry.'

A hand comes out from the waiting party and points toward our right, indicating where to park the car, and we pull up beside several vehicles of different ages and size. I climb out of the car feeling slightly nervous, and for the first time I become aware of my small bump. I join David and walk over to where the family are waiting, and Katherine follows behind us.

'*Benvenuti amici*. Welcome.' I am guessing that the man who welcomes us is the patriarch of the family. Then there are several voices all offering a welcome, along with lots of hugs and kisses, as if they had known us for all their lives.

'Okay, okay everyone. Lunch is nearly ready so let us help our guests with their bags.' The patriarch steps forward and takes control of the greetings fair, and several of the party wander over to the car, take every bag we possess and make their way into the villa. He introduces himself as Edoardo, and turning to us he asks. 'Now, which one of you *bella signore* is Maria?' He has a full head of handsomely dark hair, and his age is only given away by softly greying temples.

'That would be me,' I reply. I'm Mary; and this is my sister in law, Katherine.'

A strikingly elegant woman places her hand on Edoardo's shoulder and says, '*Amore mio*, you have seen the photographs that David showed us. It is easy to tell who is who.' She turns toward us, opens her arms wide as a welcome gesture and smiles warmly. '*Ciao*; I am Gaia Rossi, and I am the head of this family.' Her welcome comment brings chimes of soft laughter from the family. 'This is *mia Figlia*; my Daughter, Vittoria.' I can't take my eyes off Gaia's daughter. Her long dark hair and tanned face fill me with envy. 'And this *ragazzo sciocco* , this foolish boy, is my son Nicolo.' looking over to her left toward the house, Gaia nods at a young girl wearing a black dress with a white apron. 'You can meet the rest of the family over dinner.'

A very tall and lean Nicolo steps forward and, taking Katherine's hand, says, '*incantato, bella signorina.*' He raises her hand and kisses it softly. I have never seen her blush before, and take great pleasure in her reaction. He keeps hold of her hand, so Gaia steps forward and taps her son around the back of his head, causing him to raise his hands in protest, and mumble something in Italian under his breath. This is going to be a special time.

Gaia ignores her son and walks across to me, and taking my arm, she walks us toward the house. 'Now where are your *bambini?* I have heard so much about them.'

I am surprised to hear her speaking about the babies. Had David shared so much with them? 'Sadly, they have not yet arrived,' I reply.

Gaia gently places her hands on my small but growing bump. 'Ah, you are still waiting.' She turns to the family. '*Lei è in attesa.*'

They all nod in agreement as they follow her through the wide stone portico of the villa.

The long table on the covered terrace at the rear of the villa is filled with more food than I can imagine they will all eat. There is so much chatter and laughter, and as we all sit down, several other individuals join us. I take in the view, and draw in my breath at the stunning vista. The terrace overlooks the valley, and from here I can see the road we had driven along. I struggle to bring my attention back to the table, and as I look around at this large family and listen to their lively chatter, I have such a warm feeling of being home. David is sitting beside me, and he gently takes hold of my hand. Much to Katherine's embarrassment, she has been placed next to Nicolo, and she's doing her best to fend off his attention. I think he would marry her there and then if he was given the opportunity.

I hear a glass being tapped, and turn to find Edoardo standing at the head of the table waiting for everyone's attention. When all is quiet, he speaks in broken English. 'May I say, on behalf of everyone here, that it is a pleasure to finally welcome the David family. We have all heard from him so much about Mary; and some about Katherine.' There is a soft laugh from Vittoria, causing Gaia to send a scowl in her direction. We also have heard about the *Bambini* and will look forward to seeing them when you visit us many times.' I am surprised to find that David is held in such high regard. On the days when I had felt alone I had imagined him at parties having a good time. This was the last place I would have expected him to be.

Chapter 34

I kept my eyes closed. But I could still hear them; I could hear the colours, and I could feel them; and when I listened to them or I touched them I could tell which colour it was.

I arrived back at Meadowsweet about the middle of the afternoon. This time I went straight to the house. Jemima had not questioned me when I said I was going into town again. My lunch with Michael was.... interesting. He was so much like his father. Memories of our time together flooded through my mind. At times, it felt like yesterday. Michael avoided the subject of his father; it seemed that Jemima had not wanted the twins to have anything to do with Jake. It was obvious though that Michael didn't need the influence of his father; he was like him anyway. What was really curious was that I didn't like him. Oh, he wasn't a bad person; but I just didn't like his manner. It very quickly became irritating. I had asked him about his sister Katie, but he told me they didn't get on and they very seldom saw each other. I was surprised at that. He had wanted to know why I had come home. I lied. His question told me that he probably didn't know the details about Mummy, so I told him that I was just missing home. When I left, I had said that we should meet up again, but I lied about that too. I really had no desire see him again; and at that thought I felt sorry for him.

When I went into the kitchen there was no one around and so I made my way up the stairs. I stopped outside Mummy's room and heard voices, and so I tapped gently on the door and opened it. Jem was sitting with her back to the door and reading from a book. Mummy was listening intently as Jemima read words that had become familiar to me over the past several days. My stomach lurched at the thought that she was reading from one of the diaries. They had not heard me come in and I stood for a moment in the doorway. Listening to Jemima talk about David and Aunt Katherine sounded strange, and I felt left out of the intimacy of my mother's past. I couldn't begin to imagine what Jemima must be thinking as she read the diary and my mind raced at the possible onslaught that might come from her.

Mummy stopped listening and turned to me and smiled. Jemima paused, laid the diary in her lap, and turned to face me. She also smiled, and I was confused. 'Hello Connie. I'm glad you're back. Did you enjoy your lunch with Michael?' I tried desperately to hide the look of horror on my face. 'He phoned me a short while ago to say that he bumped into you in town and apologized for not having time to pop in as he was picking up supplies.' There it was again; the ghost of Jake. unpredictable and not to be trusted. I could think of nothing to say and just nodded. 'I'm sorry Connie,' she said.

'You're sorry?' I asked.

'I should have waited for you to come back.' She stood up and turned toward me. 'It seems that Mummy had a diary.'

'Right,' I said, not sure quite how to respond.

'I began reading it earlier,' She said.

'How?'

'Oh.... well I came into the bedroom earlier and found Mummy reading it. I did wonder at first why she hadn't shared it with us, but then I thought, why would she? Especially now.' She stood and handed me the diary. 'I think you'll find it very interesting reading.'

'Is this everything?' I asked.

'Mummy doesn't seem to know, so I don't know.'

I looked at my mother and she smiled again but said nothing. I didn't know whether I felt more guilty or less. It was obvious that Mummy had not told Jemima about the other diaries; but now that this had piqued her interest, how would I be able to continue to read them? Jemima had clearly not read as much as I had, but if she wanted to talk about it, which seemed inevitable, then how would I know where to begin or end?

Chapter 35

Diary; January 11th 1970

My back is aching, but I have had the most amazing night's sleep. David is still sleeping, so I slide out of the bed, slip on my white silk dressing gown, and go over to the French doors, which are slightly ajar. Pushing them open, I step out onto the first-floor balcony. It had been dark when we had come up to the room, so I'm not ready for the view that confronts me; and it takes my breath away. Our bedroom overlooks the Rossi gardens; and they don't disappoint. They seem to go on for ages; and such an assortment of colours assault my senses I almost want to cry. Oranges and reds and crimsons melt into soft yellows and blues, which are all blanketed in a backdrop of green foliage sprayed intermittently with white and powder blue. All of this is decorated with a myriad winding paths all intersecting at different angles; and some just end without going anywhere. The soft orange glow of the early morning sun just completes the picture, and I stand in silence for several minutes, allowing myself the opportunity to become accustomed to the view.

It's then that I notice the gardener. An old man dressed all in white and wearing a straw hat is wheeling along an old wooden barrow. The barrow is full of the colours I have been enjoying. He moves slowly but with a sense of purpose, pausing occasionally to cut another small clump of colour from the garden; and I wonder what he will be doing with his barrow of colour.

The Meadowsweet bees would move from flower to flower with that same sense of purpose; and I imagine that they would love to spend some time in this garden, enjoying the array of colours and smells. I give a small laugh at the thought of loading them into the back of the Range Rover and bringing them to this place for a vacation. The gardener pauses yet again, and looks toward the villa; trying to determine where the sound has come from. When he sees me he stands erect, lifts his hat from off his head and proffers it to me in greeting, bowing slightly. I wave to him in return, and he replaces his hat and continues with his task.

I feel two hands slide themselves around my waist and stop on my small bump, and I catch the now familiar scent of David as he lowers his head onto my neck and kisses it gently. 'Good morning, my Lady of the Meadow.'

I tense lightly in response. 'Where did you...? You've been talking to Katherine, haven't you?'

He laughs. 'Well I think it's lovely. It might have been nice if you had told me the story.'

I pull away and turned to face him. 'I think you're jealous.'

'Well don't sound so pleased at the prospect.'

'I am pleased that my husband is jealous,' I reply. 'It means that he loves me.' I look at him seriously for a moment. 'Do you love me David?'

'That's a strange question, considering the fact that I married you recently.'

'You didn't answer the question.'

He looks puzzled. 'What was the question again?'

I push him into the bedroom. 'Ooh you...you...beautiful man you.'

He stops. 'That's a strange thing to say.'

'Are you saying that everything I say is strange? Or do you think I'm strange?' I ask jokingly.

'Hmmm; I take your point.'

'You still haven't answered the question.'

'What was the question?

'Do you love me?'

He places his hands on my shoulders and pulls me softly to him. 'Mary; I couldn't love anyone more.' But as he finishes saying the words I see his eyes flicker to the side.

'David!' I exclaim.

'What?'

'There was a 'but'.'

'What do you mean?'

'I couldn't love anyone more...but.' I step back. 'What does that mean?'

Laughing nervously, he says. 'It doesn't mean anything. Listen Mary; I've brought you here. To this place; for us. No one else. Just us. Give us a chance.' He uses his puppy dog eyes; the same ones I had seen him use on his mother; It worked then, and it works now.

'I love you David.'

We lay back on the bed, and I allow the freshness of the morning to fill my senses as we make love once again.

When we eventually go down for breakfast most of the family are already on the veranda enjoying good food and lively conversation. The table is once again filled with an assortment of foods and drinks to suit each and every person who chooses to join them. Everyone gives us a hearty '*ciao*', and there are several '*buongiorno's*'. Katherine is already at the table, sitting with Nicolo; and this time she appears to be much more relaxed than the previous day.

David puts his hand on my waist and whispers in my ear. 'I just have something to do. I'll be with you shortly.'

I sit down, and Gaia joins me. She introduces me to the various cheeses and breads that are on offer, and I'm sure that some of them are the ones that David brought back with him as a foretaste to our adventure, and I realise how shrewd he had been in giving me a taste of things to come.

Gaia tells me about her family, and as I listen I notice that she has the most pleasing eyes I think I have ever seen. Although they are deep and dark, they are also so warm that they invite you into her world with just a look, and for dessert, she would smile with her full lips, which remind me of the sweet orange groves I had seen on the journey here. Gaia asks many questions, and at times I struggle to keep up with her, particularly as she slides in the occasional Italian word. As things quieten down, and some of the family wander off, I notice the gardener wander onto the veranda with his wooden barrow laden with the fruits of his labour. He pushes the barrow to one side, and walking over to a sink located in the corner, he washes his hands. After drying them, he comes over to the table and sits at the other end, next to Edoardo. Gaia spots him and calls a greeting. '*Ciao Papa.*'

'*Ciao bella,*' he calls back and blows her a kiss. And when he sees me, he sends another kiss and says, '*Ah, ciao bella addormentata.*'

Gaia laughs, and explains that he has called me sleeping beauty. In response to my puzzled look Gaia continues. 'That is Edoardo's father. It was his father that planted the first vines on our land.' She looks across to him, and it's obvious that she has great affection for this gardener.

I ask Gaia, 'would you know where David has gone?'

'Our men; they are never too far away; and if they wander, we just need to remember their heart song and sing it to them.'

'Oh Gaia, that is beautiful.'

'*Prego,*' she replies.

'I suppose I should enjoy some of these delights before they're taken.'

'Yes my dear; and I also have some things that I must do, so I will leave you to enjoy.'

Before Gaia rises, she kisses me softly on both cheeks, and then goes back into the villa; and I have a closer look at the assortment of cheeses on offer in front of me. I take a few small chunks of a particularly crumbly cheese from one of the platters; then I find a jar of honey on the table, lift the cloth from off the top, and dip my small spoon into it. Wrapping the honey around the spoon, I let it pour slowly over the cheese. Once the spoon has been all but drained of honey, I hold it close to my nose and take in the aroma. It is sweet and soft; summer fresh. I then take my honey spoon and go over to the wooden barrow left in the corner by Edoardo's father; and kneeling, I bend over the barrow to take in the assortment of aromas and compare them to the smell of the honey on the spoon. The barrow is filled with bougainvillea blossoms, geraniums, irises and lavender. I'm sure the honey is from this locality. Returning to the table, I break off a piece of the honey covered cheese on my plate and put it in my mouth. I am met with an array of flavours that burst onto my palate, and I close my eyes in response.

When I opened them again, the gardener is sitting opposite me. He has taken his hat off and placed it on the table. From where I'm sitting, I can see that he has the most amazing head of grey and white hair, and his beard is short; maybe two or three days old. The curling, shoulder length locks are loosely tied back with what looks like an old piece of string. His face is ruddy but with fewer lines than I would have expected; and his sharp watery blue eyes perfectly reflect the multitude of colours that surround them.

'*Buongiorno Maria.*'

'Good morning; *buongiorno signore.*'

'Cesare, please.'[5]

'Buongiorno Cesare.'

He studies me for several moments before speaking.

'You like the honey?'

'The honey?' It's not the question I'm expecting. 'Oh yes; it's exquisite.'

Maintaining his gaze he lifts his hand to his face and strokes his beard in contemplation. He has strong hands, made rugged from a lifetime of work. 'What do you like about it?'

'Without looking away I reply. 'Well, I see that it's a little foggy; so the pollen hasn't been filtered out. I like that.'

'Why?'

'It is pure Cesare.' I continue, noticing that my heart is beating a little faster. 'There are several layers of flavour, mostly floral, and not at all woody. And it is darker than some. Maybe from the bougainvillea blossoms?' I think I might be guessing now, and that maybe I have said enough.

He continues to hold my gaze and narrows his eyes a little. Then he places both of his hands on the table and raises himself from his seat. '*Seguimi*; follow me.' at that he turns and begins walking in the direction of the gardens he had come from

---

[5] Pronounced Chesaray

earlier. I grab a couple of pieces of the cheese, leave my seat and attempt to catch up with him. Although he appears to be walking at a leisurely pace, I find myself almost running whilst holding onto my slightly rounded belly with one hand and the chees with the other; but I only just manage to maintain the distance between us. Once in the gardens, I become aware of how vast they are, and I'm beginning to tire quickly from the pace. I stuff a piece of the cheese in my mouth just as Cesare disappears behind some large conifers to the south of the gardens, and I stop in my tracks as I lose sight of him. A moment later he re-appears and waves me on impatiently. He waits a few moments until I am close enough to see where he is going and disappears once again. When I arrive at the trees I can see that there is an angled opening in them, and I pop the last piece of cheese in my mouth and step through. When I come out the other side I stop dead; this time, I'm frozen on the spot, and no amount of waving or cajoling would have propelled me forward.

I am open-mouthed as I look at row upon row of hives, all of which are painted in various colours, and it seems that no one hive is the same as another. The air is filled with a sound that is very familiar to me, but multiplied a thousand times over. Cesare appears at my side, and I feel his hand on my shoulder. '*La mia famiglia di api.*' I don't understand much Italian, but enough to know that he has told me that this is his 'family of bees'.

Chapter 36

Diary; January 12th 1970

The day had started with brilliant sunshine, and breakfast had proved to be just as exciting and eventful as the previous day, although several of the family members were absent, including Cesare. I am struck by their ability to successfully run a demanding business, whilst still being able to make time to enjoy their day together.

The beautiful day prompted Katherine and me to sit around the Rossi's pool. Cool lemonade, lounger, and sun. I close my eyes and think over yesterday, and my encounter with Cesare. He had shown me around his hives with obvious pleasure, and had indicated how rare it was for a visitor to see his 'family'. We had both spoken with great enthusiasm of the joys of beekeeping; but I couldn't help but feel guilty at how I had neglected my family; my hives. I hadn't felt inclined to share that with Cesare. As we had walked along each row, he would stop occasionally at a hive and tell me stories about the residents. 'This one...she has a nasty temper. She can be so *arrabbiato* sometimes; so.... angry; and her children...they are *teppisti*, how you say? Er, thugs.' He shook his fist at the hive and we had moved on. A little further on he had stopped at a hive painted in a soft blue colour and had laid his hand on it affectionately. 'Now this *signora*; she is my *favorita*....and her honey,' he had held his fingers to his lips and threw out a kiss into the air. 'It is soft and sweet, just as she is.' I loved the idea of painting the hives different colours. He had turned and smiled at me enthusiastically, and then held his arms wide and said. 'But I love them all. Italian bees; they are like no other. Very *docile*, very docile. Looking at the *teppisti* hive, he had shaken his fist and growled, 'Except for that *donna*.' As we began our journey back to the veranda he had asked me a question. 'Tell me about your bees; you love them *si*?'

'Yes,' I had replied. 'I love them.'

'They change your life?' Memories of my mother laying in the orchard covered by the bees had instantly flashed into my mind, and I had felt the familiar sting of tears in my eyes. Cesare had stopped walking, and he had taken my arm gently. '*Mia figlia*; memories like those cannot be shared with strangers. I have many, many stories also. Maybe, we will be...*spiriti afini*.'

'Kindred spirits?'

'*Si*. He had narrowed his eyes in thought, as he had done at the table. 'Then, we will share the stories of our *famiglia*. Until then, please come and visit my bees whenever you miss your family.' He raised his hand toward the remaining diners at the table. 'I would ask just one thing from you. Even my own family; they do not go in to the bees. *Capisci?*' it was then that I realised what an enormous privilege I had just been given. This man had put his complete trust in me, and had allowed me to step into his world; a world that even his *famiglia*, his own family, could not inhabit. I had felt humbled and honoured all at once.

'*Capisco* Cesare.'

∞ ∞ ∞

'What are you smiling at?'

I open my eyes, look up from the sun lounger and shield my eyes from the late morning sun. Although I can only make out his outline, the voice tells me it was David. 'Hello. Just enjoying relaxing.' I reply, not really wanting to share my encounter with Cesare. 'Where have you been?'

'On the telephone, mainly. work.'

'What work? I thought that had finished.'

David moves out of the light and sits down next to my recliner. 'Oh, that has. But new contracts are on the table, so I have to put my name into the pot.'

I feel a sudden wave of overwhelming disappointment. 'Can't it wait until we get back home?'

'I wish it could darling; but when these things come along you have to move quickly.'

'So.... whereabouts is this contract?'

'Contracts.'

'Okay, where are these contracts?'

'All over the place.'

'Oh stop stalling David and tell her the truth.' Katherine joins in.

'Stay out of this sis.' David replies. He stands up to face her.

'Not a chance. This is my best friend you're talking about; and I'm tired of seeing her hurt.' Katherine also stands up and faces her brother. 'You've probably already got a contract lined up ready to go; so why not just be honest for a change.'

'That's not true. When I do have some work, Mary will be the first to know.'

'So, the leopard has changed his spots has he; I don't think so.'

David turns to walk away.

Katherine steps toward him and grabs his arm. 'Time to walk away again is it? You never could stand confrontation. Mummy's not here to protect you now.'

I climb out of my lounger and push between them. 'Come on you two; we are supposed to be on holiday.' I turn to David. 'I'm sorry I brought it up now. Maybe we can talk about it when you know more.' I hear Katherine sigh behind me, and so I turn around to face her. 'Listen Katie, I really appreciate all the support you have given me, but I, that is, we.... have to work this out ourselves; that's if we....' Just at that moment, I feel a sharp pain in my stomach, my legs go weak and I begin to fall forward.

I feel David grab my arm. 'What on earth is the matter Mary?'

'I need to sit down.' The pain intensifies, and I feel light headed. Both David and Katherine help me back into the chair, and David kneels by my side. I close my eyes and hear him tell Katherine to find one of the Rossi's and get them to call the Doctor. The pain eases a little. 'I'll be alright.' I say rather unconvincingly.

'Go Katherine.' He says somewhat more urgently.

'Yes, yes, of course. I'll be as quick as I can.'

I feel David's hand on my forehead; it's cool to the touch.

'No temperature. That's good, right? He says, as if asking for me reassurance.

'David I'm scared,' I reply.

'Don't worry.' He places his other hand on my arm and lightly squeezes it. 'I'm sure everything is fine.' I can feel the tension in his touch.

Another hand rests on my shoulder; a calm, soothing hand. I peer through half open eyes to find that Gaia is by my side. 'Hello my dear. I am told you are feeling poorly.' She smiles warmly. 'I am sure that it is fine; but just to be sure, Edoardo's brother is on his way.'

I say that they should perhaps call the Doctor; and David replies that he is the Doctor; Edoardo's younger brother, who had also been named Cesare. When he arrives, he checks me over and orders a good dose of bed rest; and no amount of protest on my part will assuage the growing number of concerned family around me, so I spend the rest of the day in bed.

I wake around seven thirty in the evening and I'm surprised at how well rested I feel. The French doors are open, but the air is still warm, so I dress lightly, but place a cotton cardigan over my shoulders. Walking down the wide staircase in the villa, I stop and look more closely at the Rossi family portraits; and I think about Meadowsweet. I promise myself to have a painting done of Katherine, David and myself to place in the hall at home. When I reach the bottom of the stairs I glance to my right at the sound of talking, and I see David in the corner of the dining room. He's having an animated conversation with someone who I can't see because they're hidden behind a cabinet. I catch a hand gesture, but can't recognize who it is; only that she's wearing a distinctive silver bracelet with small rubies dangling like charms around it.

I turn left into the drawing room before he sees me, as I have no wish for another confrontation. I go through the doors and make my way toward the noise of conversation. There I find several members of the Rossi family, along with Katherine and Cesare, the Doctor.

Katherine gives me a beaming smile, and looks quite relieved to find that I'm alright. She throws her arms around me and gives me a long hug. 'I'm so sorry sis.'

When she pulls away I can see tears in her eyes. 'Oh Katie, it's okay. Let's forget about it, shall we?'

'Okay. We will,' she replies.

'*Ciao* everyone,' I say as I look around the table.

It seems that Cesare the Doctor has stayed for dinner, and he walks around the table, offering his hand. He has the same full dark hair as his brother Edoardo, but he is taller and not as stocky. I also notice his deep blue eyes. '*Buonasera Maria.* I trust that you are feeling better this evening.'

'Yes, thank you, I am Doctor.'

'Please, call me Cesare.'

Yes, but that's going to be so confusing you know.'

He looks puzzled for a moment. 'Oh, yes. My father. In that case, you must call me as the others do... Anatra.' It's my turn to look puzzled, and he laughs. 'It is my family's *soprannome* for me. He turned to his brother for help.

'His nickname. Edoardo says.

'Si, my nickname; and it is Italian for duck. But please do not ask me to explain; it is a long story relating to me being a doctor. Enough to say that I believe that you sometimes call a doctor a.... quack.' Several of the older family members chuckle and cast knowing glances around the table, while at the same time making duck noises.

I laugh along with them. 'Well.... Anatra, I'm feeling somewhat rested thank you. And I'm also rather hungry.

'Ah, please excuse my manners *Signora*.' He moves to one side and pulls a chair out for me.

Chapter 37

Red for anger, or was it passion? Blue for melancholy, or maybe serenity.
Green.... with envy? Green with freshness. Black.... heart; night; silence. The
colours were so confusing. What did they all mean?

Was it strange that I had ended up living in Italy? Something had drawn me there. I
was grateful for a little time out, and I pulled the chair in my room over to the open
window and listened to the early evening light rain. The air was warm, and I
imagined walking out to the bees in my mother's hat again. I longed for the smells
of the meadow as they mingled with the damp air. And I wished that I were one of
the bees. I wished that we all were bees, and our only pursuit was to travel from
flower to flower and to wallow in the softness of the petals as we took our many
colours and flavours back to the hive. To have a life of such purpose would surely be
better than the uncertainty that we now faced.

My mother, and the other Swan women, must have enjoyed such musings. Was
that why they each gave a lifetime to the bees. Was that why they had all loved them
so much? Was that why Cesare chose to live with his bees rather than with his
family? I thought of Anatra; Doctor Anatra. He was like....an uncle? Yes, an uncle. He
was a good man. A lovely man; I remembered that much; but I couldn't remember
why we had stopped going to the Rossi farm; or when for that matter. I hoped the
diaries might tell me that.

Jemima hadn't spoken about the diaries again. It was almost as if she had
forgotten the whole thing. She was becoming increasingly dependent on me taking
care of Mummy, and I was worried that she was becoming too dependent on me.
when I had arrived, Mummy seemed to be coping really well, but just the past few
days I began to notice that the routine things of life seemed to be slipping away.

Doctor Sidle had called in earlier in the day. I asked him about that, and he said
we should expect the worst and hope for the best. There would be times, he said,
when she was doing all the things most people do; and then at other times she
would be like a child, a baby even. I wondered how Jemima felt about that. In the
nearly twenty years I had been in Milan, I had hardly found the need to become too

domesticated. I had been expecting the doctor to take up the conversation again about Mummy going into care, but he had said nothing about that this morning. In all honesty, I think he picked up the feeling that none of us wanted to have that conversation just yet.

My phone buzzed, indicating a message. The first one I had received since I'd been here. I left it on the bedside cabinet. It could be Lucinda. When are you coming back? Or maybe Gabriel was missing me. When are you coming back? Either way, I couldn't answer their question. The phone buzzed again. Why did it always sound more urgent the second time? I walked over to the cabinet and picked it up. Gabriel. *Mia Madre ti manca.* My mother is missing you. Your mother misses me? How about you Gabriel? Do you miss me? The phone buzzed again. *Ma non tanto quanto faccio.'* But not as much as I do. That's more like it. What could I say? I did miss him; but did I miss him that much? If I was being honest, I wasn't sure, and I didn't want to think about it. I hadn't had time to think about it. The light was beginning to fade outside. A cool breeze travelled into the room and I felt a shiver. I walked back over to the window and pulled it closed; then I turned the table lamp on and lay on the bed. I closed my eyes and tried to picture Gabriel next to me. what did I feel? I wasn't sure; and that bothered me. You would know, right? You would be sure; you would be telling everyone, wouldn't you? I sent a text back; *miss you too x.*

Chapter 38

Diary; January 14th 1970

My eyes wander over the breakfast table as I try to decide what to eat. David and Katherine seem to have fallen into a comfortable routine, but I feel bothered and restless. David puts it down to being pregnant, which I know to be untrue, but a convenient peg to hang my symptoms on. Katherine sits with Nicolo every morning; and she looks particularly excited this morning as he has told her that he's going to take her horse riding across the estate. I feel quite envious. David had declined to go, saying he had things to do. In the end, I settle for a spoonful of honey, and decide that I will perhaps go and see the bees.

As I wander across the gardens toward the entrance I pick up the sound of the hives, and when I reached the tall hedge, I find it necessary to walk along it for several feet before I discover the concealed entrance, so cleverly is it placed. Stepping through the entrance, I'm once again filled with a sense of wonder. The bees seem more subdued today; perhaps they are busy foraging early flowers for nectar; but the plethora of colours still brings excitement to my senses; and I think about the idea of painting the hives at Meadowsweet. Is it cold back home? I imagine the bees snuggling into the centre of the hive, sharing the heat of their bodies, the ones on the outside changing places with those nearer the centre as they lose their body heat; the cycle continuing over and over.

On my first visit to the hives, I had noticed a very old, but large wooden hut in the corner to the left, and I wondered whether that was where Cesare processed the honey. So I wander over to the hut and lift the latch on the door, and the hinges creak loudly as I swing it open, and I stepped forward into the cool and darkened shade of the interior.

'*Buongiorno,*' comes a voice from inside. As my eyes adjust to the shade I can see Cesare sitting in a very old sofa chair in the corner. He has an apple in his hand, which he carefully cuts a slice from and puts into his mouth. One side of the hut contains a small kitchen area with a stove set between two cabinets. Above the cabinets are shelves filled with various utensils and assorted plates and cups. The whole thing is very organized and quite unusually tidy. To the left of the kitchen is another chair, and behind that a large bench which contains various bits of equipment for processing the honey.

'Oh, I'm sorry Cesare, I didn't mean to....'

'E 'bello vederti *Maria*. You are welcome to come in. I am just finishing my breakfast.'

'Thank you.'

'Please, sit down.' He points to the other equally old sofa chair in the opposite corner. 'I presume you have had your breakfast? he asks.

'Yes, I have thanks. The bees are very quiet this morning?'

'It is because they know I do not like to be disturbed when I am eating my breakfast.' he replies. 'At my age, I like my day to start more slowly.'

'I can come back later,' I say, feeling guilty.

'Not at all Maria. You are welcome always. I have said so, *si*?' He cuts another slice of the apple. 'My family moves a little faster and with a great deal more noise than me. I join them when I know that I am needed.' He looks at me through half closed eyes again as if studying me. 'You are well now?'

'I am well enough, thank you. Just a little tired; but your son has reassured me that all is well.'

He nods. 'That is good; that is good,' he repeats, and then he looks at me thoughtfully again. 'But not all is well; is it?'

'How do you mean?' I ask, unsure of his question.

He sits in silence for several moments while he thinks about his words.

'You had your dreams *si*?'

'Si; yes.'

'But in truth you do not have your dreams. You still...how you say?'

'Negotiate,' I interrupt.

'Si. *Negoziare*.'

'That's what I say,' I reply enthusiastically, 'I mean, that's my saying.... You have your dreams, and then you negotiate.'

'I understand you, my daughter.'

I feel tears. No man had ever called me his daughter. Not ever. Not even my own father.

'*Maria*.' He places his knife on a small table beside him and sits forward. 'There are those dreams that will happen, and those that you will never see; but remember this always; even when you are an old, old lady; they are still your dreams.'

I relax back into the old chair. my old chair.

∞ ∞ ∞

It isn't until after lunch that David returns. I think about my conversation with Cesare, and try to reassure myself that all will be well. 'I have something to show you,' David says excitedly. 'Can you come up to the room?' Once in the bedroom he sits down on the sofa placed at the end of the bed. 'Now, close your eyes; and promise me you won't open them until I say so.'

'I promise,'

At least a minute goes by before he speaks again. 'Okay, you can open them now.'

I open my eyes to find him standing in front of me holding a dress, which more closely resembles a ball gown. I rise from the sofa and walk over to him. Up close, I can see that the powder blue dress is subtly overlaid with fine lace and beautifully decorated with small flowers cascading down one side. It has full length transparent lace sleeves which are finely cut with a vee shape at the cuff. There is a small raised collar to the back of the neck which disappears as it travels to the front and falls into a soft plunge.

'David; it's beautiful. I don't know what to say; except, it's not what I expected.'

'Just say that you'll try it on; please.'

'But...how will it fit...?'

'Just...try it on.' He hands the dress to me and I lay it on the bed and unbuttoned my dress. As I slide my dress off, I'm aware that David is watching me, and I feel a familiar tingle. I can see his eyes go down to my bump and I wondered what he's thinking. I pick up the gown and undo the concealed zip, which has been beautifully machined. Holding the dress as carefully as I can step into it, and pull it up slowly around my waist, and then more confidently, to my shoulders. David walks behind me and starts to pull the zip up. It's only then that I notice that the waist has been carefully sewn to accommodate my bump. Once he has finished I gently smooth the dress down with my hands and then step in front of the mirror. I let out a small gasp. The lacework has been shaped to almost disguise the bump and makes the whole dress flow seamlessly.

'David, I don't know what to say.' I turn to face him, and he smiles approvingly. 'But...?'

'You want to know what it's for?' he interrupts.

'Yes.'

'We...are going to a Rossi wedding.'

David had known about the wedding for some time, but he had asked them to keep it as a surprise. As the sun begins to go down the veranda takes on a whole new feeling. The air is still warm, and everyone is excitedly talking about the coming weekend. He had told me that he ordered the dress before we had left England; and had even bought a dress for Katherine. I had found it slightly amusing to see the confused look on her face when he gave it to her. It must have been so hard for them all to keep the event a secret.

We are going to the city of Asti, some twenty-five miles away, where the daughter of Edoardo's cousin is going to marry a certain wealthy businessman. The family all adore the cousin and they are pulling out all the stops to make it a day to remember.

Chapter 39

Diary; January 16th 1970

As David drives the Range Rover through the gates of the elegant historic villa located in the hilly countryside of Monferrato, Katherine lets out a small gasp. The driveway of the hotel travels each side of a long stretch of water which has fountains of varying heights along its length. It is a beautifully bright day and the sun reflects off the spray causing a plethora of colours to travel across the moving waters. The vast stretches of verdant lawns are broken by informal borders that reflect muted colours; all waiting for spring to begin. David drives the car under a long portico and stops at the front entrance, where porters are busy offloading cases and ushering guests into the reception area. The head porter is attempting to keep a semblance of order and calm amid the chaos of people and baggage. If these are all wedding guests, then it's going to be a grand affair. And before we can step out of the car, our doors are opened by the porters, and within seconds the cases are loaded onto a trolley and disappear into the hotel. David takes my arm and leads me into the elegant hotel, followed closely by Katherine.

The interior proves to be as elegant and lavish as the outside, and the porters wait patiently as the guests take in their surroundings. Within ten minutes we are in our rooms and enjoying the complimentary cocktails.

'David?' I sit on the end of the plump, elegant bed and slide my shoes off, breathing a sigh of relief as I do.

David opens the tall French doors, allowing the midday sun to pour into the room. 'Yes darling.' I stand up and walk over to him, and as he turns around, the sunlight catches his face, and I am reminded of the first time I saw him; and for a moment, I become lost in him. 'What is it Mary?'

'Do you remember when we first met?' I expect him to smile; instead, he returns a sideways glance, as if he doesn't trust me.

'Yes.... I do. What about it?'

'Did you know how I felt about you from that first moment?' I lean on the doors and placed my hand on his chest. Did you know that you made me think of a poem?'

'You and your poems.' He looks into my eyes. 'Do you know how lucky you are?'

'What do you mean?'

'To be so romantic about things.'

'So...you're not? Romantic, that is.'

'Not really. I wish I could be.'

I drop my hand. 'Then I'm not so lucky.'

'Why do you say that?'

'Because romance takes two.'

David puts the palm of his hand on my cheek. 'I suppose it does. I'm sorry.'

'For what?'

'For not being romantic. I know it means a lot to you.'

We stand in silent thought for several moments. 'Tell me what you want David.'

He continues out onto the balcony. The room overlooks the gardens at the back of the hotel, and they are almost as stunning as the Rossi gardens. Several of the guests are already enjoying a walk around the meandering pathways, and some are finding shaded seating areas to escape from the heat of the midday sun. He doesn't answer. 'This should be the happiest time of our lives David,' I continue.

He turns back to me; a look of frustration on his face. 'Don't you think I know that Mary?' he replies as he steps back toward me and grabs my arms. 'Don't you think that I don't wake up every day and wish that I could make you; make us, happy?'

I can see tears starting to form in his eyes. 'Oh David. I'm so sorry. I didn't mean to upset you.' I throw my arms around him and pull his head into my shoulder. 'We want the same things; can't you see that?' Instead of replying, he puts his arms around me and holds me tight. My first thought is to protect the babies; and then I think about him; this vulnerable boy, who just wants to be loved. I remember back to the times I saw him at home, and the way that his mother had demanded that love, without returning it. Is it possible that she had ruined him for anyone else who came along; that she had left him so confused and conflicted, that it would take a lifetime to help him. I want to help him; to give him that lifetime; if he will just let me. I take his hand and lead him back into the room and onto the bed, and we make soft love and sleep for the afternoon.

In the warm breeze of the early evening we leave the hotel and join the wedding party in a convoy of vehicles as they drive around the city. The cars honk their horns continuously, and the rest of the party generally make as much noise as they possibly can. Can you imagine the reaction we would receive if we were driving through the backstreets of Windsor right now? I can't think of anything that would annoy the residents more. To my surprise, everyone around seems so excited to see and hear the convoy. People in the streets shout and cheer at us whilst waving enthusiastically, and any passing cars add to the noise by also honking their horns. It is impossible not to get caught up in the excitement of the moment.

I tire quickly, and although I am determined to continue, David suggests that we should think about going back to the hotel. I'm too tired to go to the pre-wedding party that had been arranged that evening at the hotel, and tell David and Katherine to go without me. Although I am exhausted, sleep doesn't come easily, and when it does, I dream of Mummy, and the bees.

Chapter 40

Diary; January 17th 1970

The morning sun breaks through the windows of the hotel suite and bursts onto the small dining table; and I sit alone with the breakfast I had ordered for the room. I pick up a piece of toast and, dipping the teaspoon into the jar of honey, I spread it carefully, making sure I push it right to the edges. Imagining the day ahead, I think back to my own wedding day. I had had so many romantic notions about what that day should be like; and today would have been it. The love and attention and splendour and romance that is being lavished on this day, is the day that I had wished for. Today is the day that David should have given me. Instead, we had gathered in a small registry office on Windsor high street, and performed what felt like a hurried legal process that had allowed us to call each other husband and wife. He had never asked me how I felt about that. He had just fitted the day into his busy schedule; a schedule that I was a part of; and then he had left the following day.

In spite of the beautiful dress that David had bought me, and in spite of the conversation we had had the previous afternoon, I really didn't want to be reminded, for every second of this day, of what I had missed out on. When I had woken, I had found him in the shower. He wanted to go down to join the wedding party for breakfast, but I had decided to have breakfast in the room. Just as I take a bite of my toast there's a knock on the door; and I find Katherine standing in the hallway with two Italian coffees.

'I would have preferred tea.' I say as she carefully carries the cups across the room and places them on the table.

'Philippa Mary, I do believe that one day I will leave you for someone else,' Katherine replies, her voice somewhat gravelly.

I sit back down at the table and look at her. She closes her eyes for a moment and sways slightly.

'Are you feeling okay?' I ask.

'I will be,' she replies.

'What have you been up to?

She smiles and opens her eyes and I see something; a glow; a reflection in her eyes of the night past. 'You've met someone.' I sit forward with eager interest and fix my gaze on her. 'I know you Katie. You have, haven't you?'

She responded by picking up her teaspoon and playing with the coffee. 'What if I have?'

'Tell me more Katie.'

'You don't have the monopoly on good looking men you know.'

'This is sounding interesting. So, did you sit next to him at breakfast?'

She looks out across the gardens. 'Not exactly.'

'You mean, last night? You met him last night and you didn't come and tell me? I can't believe you.'

'Okay. Calm down; and please don't shout. I'm telling you now aren't I.'

'Yes, but only because I guessed; and I'm not shouting.'

'That's not true; you didn't guess, I mean. Anyway, do you want me to tell you or not?'

'Well of course I do.'

She takes a mouthful of her coffee and continues. 'Well, last night, whilst I was talking to some of the guests, I was introduced to Adriano Lavezzo and his wife.'

'You met a married man? Katie is that a good idea?' I say with some concern.

She gave me a look of disgust. 'Have I finished the story Mary? Well, have I?' I apologize and beg her to continue. 'Well, Signore Lavezzo is a wealthy businessman from South Tyrol, and he knows the groom very well.' She rubs the side of her face with her hand, and I can see she looks tired. 'Anyway, while we were talking with Signore Lavezzo...and his wife; a friend of his came and joined in the conversation. I have to tell you Mary; I have never seen such a gorgeous man. He's from the same area as Mr.... that is Signore Lavezzo.' She plays with her hands nervously. 'So, we got to talking and....' Her voice trails off.

'Katie!' I say accusingly. 'You didn't.'

'What was I supposed to do?' She can see my obvious displeasure. 'Well actually, we didn't. Anyway; you're a fine one to talk.'

'What's that supposed to mean?'

'Well.... you and my brother.'

'That's different.'

'How so?' She asks.

'Never mind.' I reply. 'You had better tell me more Katherine Hunter, or I shall have these babies right here and now.'

'Alright, alright.' She rubs her forehead again. 'His name is Alexander von Treffen; although he told me that he doesn't use that title back in Austria; and he was born in.... South Tyrol, I think he said. Anyway, he's a businessman; and very wealthy from the way he was dressed, and also from the fact that he has the penthouse suite.

'You went to his room?

'Yes, but he was a perfect gentleman, and...'

'I'm not sure about this Katie,' I reply.

'Like I said, you can't talk.'

'The thing is Katie, I knew who David was, and I could answer important questions; like for instance...is he married?'

'No, of course he isn't. At least...I don't think so.'

'Okay. What about family? Does he have any children?'

'I'm sure he doesn't otherwise he would have said....' Her voice trails off again, and she stands up and strolls shakily over to the balcony. 'He has asked if he can see me again.'

'So, he has an appetite; what does that prove? Does David know him?'

Katherine spins to face me. 'You've got to be joking. I'm not talking to David about this; and even if he does know him, you had better not say anything to him. Besides, He's not in any position to say anything.'

'That's all in the past Katie.'

She diverts her eyes away from me. 'Yes, of course it is.'

'What's that supposed to mean?'

'Nothing at all. I'm just being...me.' She shrugs her shoulders and tilts her head.

David chooses that moment to come into the room. He stops halfway through the door. 'What are you two up to?' he asks.

'Just girl talk.' Katherine replies, and at the same time gives me a look which says, don't say a word to David, otherwise I will kill you. in reply he gives a low grunt and disappears into the bathroom.

'I want to meet him later.' I say in a low voice and give Katherine my best stare; and she agrees to introduce me on the condition that I don't interrogate him. As she leaves I call to her. Katherine stops with the door halfway open. 'Katie, be careful.'

After I finish my breakfast, I take a shower and begin the process of getting ready for the day. When I have finished adjusting the dress around my lump, I call to David to come and zip me up. As he does so, I can't help but wonder when I had become so cynical.

I sit at the table in the elegant hall watching all the couples dancing. Stunning dresses swirling to the graceful sound of violins; the men holding their partners with slender arms aloft, as they seem to float around them. I turn to look at David, who appears to be looking at each gorgeous woman in the room in turn. How beautiful he looks in in his dark jacket and crisp white shirt and black bow tie; I try to think of some words, some poetry or something. Something that will touch my heart; and maybe his. But there's nothing. I had told him that I felt too tired to dance; and he had said that was okay, and I curse myself for that, wishing that he had just ignored me and swept me off my feet. Had I said it just to test him? I did wonder.

A familiar voice interrupts my thoughts. 'And why do you not dance today sleeping beauty?' Cesare asks as he stood next to me. The gardener is nowhere to be seen. Instead an elegant, eccentric, beautifully dressed man stands by the table. His soft powder blue jacket covers a waistcoat of diamond shaped colours of blues and yellows and crimsons, amongst others, and all are interspersed with gold thread that sparkles as he moves. The string hairband is gone too, only to be replaced by a piece of gold cloth tied around his long hair. I pat my bump in explanation, and he smiles knowingly. 'I would dance too,' he says, 'but I do not want them to feel...*insufficiente*.' He lifts his arm aloft, sways his hand in mock deference to the dancing party, and spins elegantly in a full circle on one foot.

I'm amazed at his deftness and laugh; and I feel all at once lighter in his presence. 'They do look beautiful though, don't you think?'

He sits at the empty seat to one side of me and narrows his eyes again, and I know that he is thinking over some story. I enjoy the anticipation of the things he might share with me. 'Have you ever watched your bees dance Maria?' he asks.

'Yes, I have,' I reply.

He looks around at the dancing crowd and raises his hand toward them. 'When they dance with each other, what do you think they are trying to say?'

I look round at David, but he seems lost in his own thoughts. 'Oh, I don't know,' I reply. 'I suppose they're saying lots of different things. Come, follow me; I love you; I'm happy; perhaps they're saying that they want to be happy.'

'*Si*. You are right. They are saying many things, and some of the time, maybe nothing. But when the bees dance they know what they are saying. I have found food, do come with me. And when a bee finds a bush loaded with flowers, or a tree covered with blossoms, they will dance to their family, and that dance will tell the family where they need to go; and within a short while they will be joined by the rest of their family in gathering the nectar they need to feed on.' Once again, he looks around at the dancing. 'Whether we dance, or whether we choose not to dance....it is possibly of no real.... *conseguenza*. But, for our bees, it means to live; to stay alive.'

'I can see that,' I reply.

'Do you Maria?' This time he looks across to David, who has left the table and is standing a short distance away, and is in conversation with Nicolo and Vittoria. 'Whether you dance with your family, or you do not. What you must do is live. Find what it is you want that will make you live, and dance that dance; for then you will live a life that is full.' We sit silently, looking around the room, and then he takes a deep breath. 'Now.... I must eat; so I go to my room.' He stands slowly and bows lightly to me. 'As you know, I do not like to be disturbed when I eat; so, I will bid you a good evening.'

I sit for some time watching the dancing; and it seems to take on a whole new meaning. I watch each couple in turn as I try to guess what they might be saying to one another with their dance; and I realise that the world is a lot bigger than I had imagined. And then a thought occurs to me. My bees may live in a small community, but when they dance.... They can see the world. I say a silent thank you to Cesare.

'It is good to see you smiling again.' I turn this time to find Anatra standing by the table. 'I see my father has had a positive influence on you.'

'He is a wonderful man. You must have had an amazing childhood.'

He smiles; but there is something; something dark? underneath the expression. 'Si.... he was a busy man, but he always made time for us.'

'Anatra. May I ask you something?'

'Si, but on one condition Maria.'

'And what would that be?' I ask.

'That you would do me the honour of dancing with me.' I had told David I didn't want to dance, but Anatra persists. 'I will move very slowly Maria. I will dance like a doctor. It will not harm your *bambini*.'

I look across to where David had been talking, but he has gone. Why do I feel so guilty all the time? I remember what Cesare had said. 'Okay Anatra, I will dance with you, although I can't guarantee that I will be as graceful as you would expect.' We move slowly onto the dance floor, and I feel a buzz of exhilaration as Anatra takes my hand. Without hesitation, he moves me across the floor, falling effortlessly into the rhythm of the slow waltz. The softness of his movements and the light flow of air as we brush past the other couples dancing is immediately hypnotic. Anatra is taller than his father, and the eyes are different; perhaps his mother's; and as he looks at me, they absorbed every colour around them with each move we make.

Several minutes pass before we speak, and as we dance I become less aware of my surroundings, almost feeling as if we are alone on the dance floor. Anatra's soft, low voice eases me back to reality. 'So, Maria. You have a question for me.'

I think for several seconds; recalling what I wished to ask him. 'You have seen my friend Katherine, David's sister, with Von Treffen?' I ask, thinking about my promise to Katherine not to ask any prying questions. 'Do you know him?'

His eyes narrow. 'Si, I know of him. Why do you ask?'

'Oh, I don't know; just a feeling really. Katherine seems to be really taken with him.'

'He has taken her?'

I smile. 'I mean, she has met him and seems to like him.'

He waits for a while before speaking. 'I understand. I am afraid that I cannot tell you many things about him.'

'Oh. That is a shame.'

'Forgive me. I do not wish to give you worry. It is probably better that I do not say.

'No please, it's better that I know.'

'I can tell you that he is a very wealthy man.'

'Yes, Katherine mentioned that.'

'That has also made him a powerful man. As you will know, my family are a large part of wine production in the Piemonte region. The consortium we are part of; it is there to protect the.... *autenticità* of the wine; that is what I can say. Signore Von Treffen has a great many business interests here in Piemonte. Our *famiglia*, we no longer have business with this man.'

'Should I be worried?'

'I do not know; but would your friend have business?'

'No, no nothing like that. More.... Romantic.'

'Ah, romantic. Then I cannot advise; for I do not know this. In business is different.'

'Yes, I understand.'

'But this is not a suitable subject for a wedding. Perhaps you would like to stop now? I do not wish to tire you greatly.'

'Thank you,' I reply. Anatra walks me back to the table, where we find Katherine deep in conversation with the man I presume to be Alexander von Treffen.

Anatra stops before we reach the table and takes my hand. Giving me a light bow, he raises my hand and kisses it gently, and I feel a guilty pulse of electricity flow through me. 'I would like to thank you Maria for the pleasure of *la danza*. I hope that you enjoy the rest of the day.' I watch as he turns toward Katherine and Von Treffen. When he catches their attention, he bows politely. Von Treffen immediately stands and returns the bow.

'Thank you Anatra. It was most...*piacevole*,' I reply.

He laughs lightly. 'Ah, I see you have been practicing you Italian. Indeed, it was most...enjoyable.' As he walks away, I am left with that familiar feeling of emptiness, and I turn toward Katherine to find von Treffen still standing in anticipation.

'Mary, this is Alexander von Treffen.' Katherine says.

He steps around the table and offers his hand; and as I take it, he looks into my eyes. He is tall, but not a big man, and his fair skin seems to glow with an unusual brightness. He is immaculately dressed in a light blue suit that accentuates the deep blue colour of his eyes. He bows lightly and lowers his eyes for a second, but instantly returns to look deeper into me. He has a presence like nothing I had felt before; and I feel a shiver run through me; but this time, it's more confusing. Not at all like David; or Anatra. I force myself to reply. 'It is a pleasure to meet you Senior von Treffen.'

'Please, call me Alexander.' He replies; and holds out his arm toward the table. His voice carries something with it; something I couldn't immediately understand, but the confusion I had first felt now stirred my insides; and I had the almost insatiable urge to be kissed by him. And then I felt something else; something so important, that our lives depended on it.

The bees are angry. With him? Me? I don't know.

'Please, will you join us Mary?' His cool voice interrupts my thoughts.

I'm surprised to notice that his accent sounds more Italian than anything else. 'Katherine tells me that you are from Austria.'

'My family is from northern Italy. South Tyrol. My father was Austrian, but my mother was Italian. It is a long story.' He waits until I am sitting before he sits himself. 'Katherine tells me you are with child. I would offer my congratulations; you must be very excited.'

'Yes,' Katherine interrupts. 'Mary is having twins.'

Von Treffen's eyes widened. 'Twins? How delightful. When are they expected?'

I am surprised at his level of interest; expecting some deference from him. 'August,' I reply.

'Well I am sure that you and your husband must be looking forward to the event very much.'

For the first time, as I think about the birth, I wonder if David will actually be there; and I wish he were here now. 'Do you know the bride and groom very well?' I ask.

'To be honest, I do not know them at all.' He looks around the hall, as if searching for them. 'I have business interests here. That often leads to invitations to social occasions such as this.' He turns to Katherine. 'But it also allows me the opportunity to meet such beautiful women as yourselves.' I can see Katherine blushing, and I feel strangely angry with this man; or is it jealousy? 'So where do you live in England?' he asks.

'We live in a beautiful part of the country,' Katherine replies. 'Wraysbury, near Windsor. And we keep bees.' I look at her in shock. Katherine had never expressed an interest in the bees, and had, in effect voiced her disdain for them. If she is trying to impress Von Treffen it seems to be failing, because he had a distinct look of unease on his face.

'Ah, that would be a problem for me,' he replies. 'I have a bee allergy.'

Katherine's face drops. 'Well, it's not exactly me who keeps the bees. They're Mary's really.'

He looks puzzled. 'So, you ladies live in the same house?'

'Yes,' I reply.

'David is away a lot of the time; so I live there.' Katherine adds.

'Is your studio at the house also?' He asks.

Katherine glances across at me and shifts nervously in her chair.

He catches her look at turns to me. 'Katherine told me last night that she was an artist; but she did not say that you were too.

'Oh no, I'm not. I am married. It's just Katherine who has the studio.'

He turns back to Katherine. 'You do not want to marry and have children, like your friend here?' he asks.

I have never seen Katherine so flustered. I think about changing the subject to help her out, but I'm becoming curiously drawn to the conversation. 'I.... I would love to.... get married, that is,' Katherine replies, 'and maybe have children. Why? Do you want to get married? In general, that is. Not necessarily to me.... although that would be okay. Not that I'm asking.... though. Anyway, are you married?' with that she picks up her glass of wine and gulps down a mouthful of white wine.

Von Treffen smiles and looks directly at Katherine. 'No. I am not married. I do not presently have children; although I will one day have a son; to continue the Von Treffen family name.' Katherine's face relaxes at his explanation.

I'm sure that I feel my bump move. 'If you will both excuse me,' I say. 'I think that I will go and find David.' I leave them to their conversation and wander around the reception hall and eventually find David sitting alone in the conservatory. It is a large room that has absorbed the heat of the afternoon sun, and as the warmth of the room soaks into me, and it feels pleasing to the bones. I stand to one side watching him, as he is sitting deep in thought; and I see the David that I had first met. After a few minutes, I wander over to the sofa, and bending over him, I kiss him gently on the cheek, and then sit next to him. 'A penny for them?' I say.

'Sorry?'

'I just wondered what you were thinking.'

'Oh, nothing really; just work,' he replies.

He hadn't told me anything more about the progress he's making regarding another contract, and after the last upset I had been reluctant to question him further. 'How is it going?' I ask.

'We don't have to talk about that now, do we?'

'Alright.' I reply, and sit down and put my arm through his. 'Have you met the man Katherine is with?' I ask.

'What she gets up to is none of my business,' he replies. 'She stays out of my life, and I do the same for her.'

'But David, she's your sister; shouldn't you be worried, or at least, interested?'

He laughs. 'My sister can take care of herself Mary. You of all people should know that.'

'Katherine is more vulnerable than you know.'

'I find that hard to believe,' he replies. She's spent her life giving me a hard time.' We sit in silence for several minutes. 'So, who is she with?' he asks eventually.

'Alexander Von Treffen. Do you know him?'

'I met him...once.'

'What did you think of him?' I ask.

'I didn't like him. Too sure of himself.' He looks straight at me. 'What did you think of him?'

I avoid his eyes, afraid that I might look guilty. 'There's something about him....'

'I'll give you that, he's an attractive man, but....'

'No, I mean, something else.' I took his hand and slide my fingers through his. 'Can I ask you something David?' He doesn't reply. 'Please will you keep an eye out for Katherine?'

'I've told you; she won't listen to me. In fact, she's more likely to do the opposite of anything I might say.'

'Can't you just watch out for her. She doesn't have to know.'

He stands up quickly. 'It's getting too hot in here. I'll have a word with the Rossi's. They will no doubt have some idea about him.'

'I've already spoken to Anatra.'

He sits down again. 'You have? When was this?'

'A short while ago; when I danced with him....' My voice trails off.

'When you danced with...Anatra.'

'Yes.' Now I do feel guilty.

'I see.' I wait for more to come; but that is it. That is all he says; I see. I want more. I want him to tell me that he's jealous; that he loves me so much he can't bear the thought of me in the arms of another man. I want him to say that he's angry, and to demand an explanation. That way, maybe we can talk about the things that are wrong, the problems that need to be solved. But nothing. 'I'll go and speak to them now,' he says, and kisses me gently on the cheek before he leaves.

I close my eyes and lay my head back on the sofa. The desire to sleep overwhelms me, so I hurry to leave the hall and go to our room, eager not to speak to anyone else. Undoing the zip of the dress proves to be a challenge, and I wonder if I should call room service; and then picture a nervous looking bell boy trying to perform the task whilst averting his eyes. At least the thought brings a smile to my face. Maybe if I was to go the bees for help, they might be able to collectively carry out the job; but I know there are some things that are beyond even them. After eventually managing to remove myself from the dress I quickly climb into bed, eager to fall asleep and shut out the day.

Chapter 41

I ran as fast as I could. I knew I was dreaming. The black darkness became white light; black silence turned into white noise.

I woke with a start. Was that a scream? I listened in the dark; what time was it? I checked my watch; 3:20am. It was quiet; and grey. I had grown up here, but after living in Milan for so long I couldn't get used to the dark. I turned on my table lamp when I heard it again; it was Mummy. I couldn't hear what she was saying, but she was calling out. Jemima had said that she would wake in the night, but this was the first time I had heard her. I slid out of the bed, pulled on my dressing gown, quietly opened the bedroom door and walked out into the corridor. Jemima always left the light on in the hall and I squinted at the brightness. My room was the next one along to Mummy's, and I crept along the hall and stopped outside her room. There was silence again. I turned the handle on her door as quietly as I could and eased the door open. Through the darkness I could see that the bed was empty, and I remembered the diary entries about my grandmother.

'Is that you David?' I heard Mummy say. I walked further into the room and saw her standing on the balcony. I pushed her door closed, becoming once again lost in the darkness, and I went as quickly as I could to the French doors. 'Mummy, what are you doing out there? You'll catch your death.' I bit my lip as I said it, and took her arm and gently walked her into the room. As my eyes adjusted to the darkness I could see that she was wearing her white dress; the one she always wore when she went to the hives. 'Why are you dressed?' I asked.

'I must look my best; for David,' she replied. 'Is he here yet?'

'Not yet Mummy,' I said, unsure of what to say. 'I don't think he's coming until morning; shall we get some sleep until then?'

'I need to ask Cesare,' she said, her eyes darted around the room, as if she were looking for him. 'He will know what to do.'

'Yes, I believe he will. And do you know what I think he would say right now?'

'What would that be?'

'He would say that you can think better when you've had a good night's sleep.'

'Yes; yes, he would.' Mummy waked back to the bed and sat down. 'Would you help me out of this dress?' she asked. 'David had this made especially for me you know,' I said nothing and helped her to slide the dress off, and she sat on the bed and looked up at me. Are you my mother? she asked. I swallowed hard.

'Shall we talk about that in the morning? I replied. 'Now let me tuck you in the bed.'

She pulled the sheets back and climbed in obediently. 'Will you stay with me? I don't want to be alone,' she said as she laid back and pulled the sheets around her. I walked round to the other side of the bed and lay down beside her. She turned to look at me. 'Do you live here?' she asked.

I looked into her eyes as she laid barely a foot away from me. 'Do you know you're my mother?' I asked.

'Yes,' she said.

'You do?'

'Yes.'

'A while ago you asked if I was your mother.'

'Well, you look like my mother.' She replied.

'I look like your mother? I asked.

'Yes.'

'I'm saying that you're my mother.'

'I'm your mother?'

'Now, do you think that I would lay here with just anyone?'

'No.... I think you would have to love them to lay down with them.'

'Yes, you would have to love them.' She said.

'I love you Mummy.'

'And I love you.'

'But you.... do you know who I am?'

'Yes.'

'Who?' I asked.

'Constance.' She smiled and touched the side of my face, and she ran her fingers softly down my cheek. 'And I love Constance.'

'Yes Mummy. Yes, you do.'

'And didn't I name you Constance?'

'Yes, you did.'

'Well I love you Constance.'

'And I love you too Mummy,' I said; and I saw her for the first time since I had returned. I saw Mary. 'Shall we read the diaries?' I asked.

She wiped the tears from my eyes.

Chapter 42

Diary; January 18th 1970

I can hear the rain. I slide quietly out of the bed and wander over to the windows. It's just getting light outside. David is still sleeping. I don't remember him come to bed the previous night, but I did go up to bed early. I go through to the lounge area, close the dividing doors between the rooms and dial room service. I ask them to bring up some breakfast, and also some more honey. I sit quietly at the small table in the corner of the room and think over the conversations with both the young and old Cesare, and I wonder if Katherine had succumbed to the dance of her new love interest. There's a light tap on the door and I open it expecting room service; only to find Katherine standing in the hallway.

'Have you had breakfast? I ask her.

She peers through half opened eyes and shakes her head. 'Is David awake?

'No; it's early.'

'Is it?' she asks. 'I thought it was late.' She makes her way into the room and sits quickly at the small table. 'Do you have some water?'

She is still wearing the clothes she had on the previous night, although they appear somewhat dishevelled.

'And maybe some painkillers. Several, in fact, would go down quite well.'

'What....'

'Don't ask.' Katherine interrupts, and she leans on the table and places her head in her hands. 'Oh, alright. Ask.'

I sit opposite. 'Have you and....?'

Katherine looks up at me, still holding her head. 'Me and....?' She moves her head slowly from side to side. I thought at first that she was indicating no, but then realise that she is attempting to clear her head. 'Painkillers?'

'Ah yes. Sorry.' I jump out of my chair, knocking the table, and she groans. 'Sorry,' I say again. 'I think we have some in the bathroom.' I return with two tablets and a glass of water, which she swallows with some difficulty, and then proceeds to screw up her face in disgust.

'When will they learn to make these things taste better? Anyway; what was the question?'

'Where have you been Katie?'

'I've been asleep in bed.'

'Really?' I ask.

There's another tap on the door. I open it this time to a waiter carrying a tray full of breakfast products, along with a jar of honey. He places the tray on the table. Katherine takes one look at the food and promptly throws her hand to her mouth and runs to the bathroom. 'Is the signorina alright? The waiter asks.

'*Si grazie.* Just too much wine.' I tip my hand up to her mouth to indicate drinking.

'Ah, Si. Would the signorina like me to bring *tavoletta?*'

I frown, trying to understand his meaning. 'Ah, si; tablet. *No grazie.* I have *tavoletta.*'

'Is there anything else I can help with signorina?'

'*No Grazie.* This is fine. This is *buono.*'

Once the waiter has gone, I butter my toast and waited for Katherine to return. The rain has stopped, and the sky is beginning to lighten. I take the teaspoon and pour some of the honey onto my toast, and then place a spoonful into the tea. As I bite into the toast, I think of the bees, and I miss them. I wander over to the desk, toast in hand, and take my diary from the drawer. The diary that no one has seen; the diary that keeps me sane; alive. When I read back over the events of the past few days, I can't help but feel how it all seems so surreal. I know that this is not how I thought things would turn out. And I'm so aware that the only constant in my life; and yet the thing I write about the least, is the bees.

When I'm with the bees, all the people that I miss; all of the people I want to be with, are with me then. And those that scare me, or make me feel lost or alone, can't harm me. Why that is so, I don't yet understand; but that's how I feel when I'm with them; safe. But even though I know that somehow, they will keep me safe, I have a strange sense of foreboding. Is it David? or Von Treffen? Maybe even Anatra; though why I should be afraid of Anatra I'm not sure. I just don't know.

Katherine returns from the bathroom with a bit more colour to her face, and I return the diary to the drawer and join her at the table. 'Are you feeling any better?' I ask.

'I think so. A bit too much vino, I think.'

'So....'

'What can I say?'

'Well you can start by telling me where you slept last night.'

'Well, the truth is, I didn't.'

'Didn't what?'

'Sleep last night.'

'You mean to tell that you've been up all-night partying?'

'Well, not exactly.' She gets up from the table and opens the French doors. 'Do you mind if we let some air in?'

'No, that's fine. So, where were you?'

'Okay.' She whirls around to face me. 'I spent the night with Alexander.'

I stare at her wide eyed. 'You slept with Alexander?'

'Well, we didn't exactly sleep.'

'You know what I mean Katherine.'

She sits at the table, her face bright and clear; all traces of any hangover gone. 'Mary, he is the most amazing man I have ever met.' He's so interesting; there's nowhere in the world that he hasn't been.' She gets up from the table again and walks quickly around the room. 'And last night; he was amazing.'

'You said that.'

'No, I mean, the way he made me feel. The way he made love....'

'Katherine, please.'

'Sorry.' She sits down at the table. Her face loses its colour again. 'Is that honey?'

'Yes, it is. Would you like some?'

'Will it help?' she asks.

'To ease your conscience?'

'You know what I mean,' she replies.

'I'm sure it will.' I take a clean teaspoon and fill it with the amber liquid. 'Here, try this.'

She takes the spoon of honey and, leaning forward places it in her mouth.

'What do you think? I have another slice of toast, how about trying that with some honey? I'm sure it will settle your tummy.'

She screws up her face. 'Why not. This isn't half bad. Maybe there's something to these bees after all.'

'So....' I continue, ignoring her comment. 'Are you going to see him again?'

She carefully balances the honey laden toast to try and prevent it from running off the sides. 'I must say Mary; you do seem a tad jealous.'

I redden slightly at her comment. 'Not jealous; just.... concerned, that's all.'

'But you don't know the man Mary. How can you be so judgemental?'

'You haven't answered my question.' I sip my honeyed tea. 'You must want me to know.'

'Why do you say that?' Katherine asks.

'Because you could have gone straight to your room Katie Hunter.'

'Ok; so you got me there.' She places the last piece of toast in her mouth. 'Thish really doesh help you know,' she says as she chews enthusiastically and swallows. 'I just want you to be pleased for me.' She wipes her mouth with her napkin and stands up, swaying slightly. 'Will you.... be happy for me, that is?'

'Katie.' I stand up and follow her to the door. 'I love you very much. You're like my sister. Hey, you are my sister. And it's because I love you that I worry for you. But you're right; I will try Katie, I promise.'

Chapter 43

Diary; January 23rd 1970

The breakfast table at the Rossi house is especially busy this morning. David had announced the previous evening that we were going back to England. He told everyone that he had secured a new contract and they would need to depart before the weekend. It seems that every member of the Rossi household has come to say goodbye, although I can't see Cesare.

It has been an eventful couple of weeks, that's for sure. David had brought me to this place so that we could draw closer together; at least that's what I thought. Now I'm not so sure. Katherine is not at the table either; mainly because she had disappeared two days after the wedding when she had received a telegram to say that a car would be collecting her and taking her to Von Treffen. My protestations were met with anger from Katherine, and we had not parted on the best of terms. She had said that she was a big girl and would find her own way home. David had told me that if Katherine didn't return, we would leave without her, and we had argued also. He has become even more withdrawn and quiet, and I wonder if it might have been because of my dance with Anatra, but I know that it runs deeper than that.

I leave the table halfway through breakfast and wander through the gardens toward the beehives. As I get closer, I hear the familiar sound of the bees, although they are quieter than usual. I had become quite comfortable with wandering around the hives, and I take the opportunity to walk along each row in turn, occasionally stopping to examine one of the hives. Once I have walked along the rows, I make my way to the shed in the corner. The door is slightly ajar, and I tap on it lightly, hoping to get a response. I'm pleased when I hear the gravelled voice of Cesare.

'*Buongiorno* sleeping beauty. Please come.'

I pull the door open and step inside the now familiar surroundings. '*Buongiorno* Cesare,' I say.

He looks up from his breakfast and holds out his hand toward the other chair. I sit quietly, watching him while he finishes eating; and I try to imagine how he might have looked when he was my age; and I see a rugged, handsome man, with thick, dark hair. I imagine that he wore similar dark trousers, with a full white shirt, and braces akin to the ones he is wearing now. I think about what his wife might have looked like, and as I look more closely around the room, I see, for the first time, a photograph on the shelf next to Cesare. What surprises me is that the woman in the picture is not the dark-haired beauty that I would have expected to see. Rather, there in the frame, is a soft and demure young blonde girl; who could just as easily have been my own mother.

Cesare must have seen me looking at the picture, and he reaches up, takes it off the shelf and hands me the frame. 'We were together for.... many years.' I look closely at the woman. 'She was the love of my life,' he says. 'I loved her even more than the bees.' We sit quietly for some minutes before he continues. 'It was Annalise who taught me the beekeeping.'

'You must miss her very much.'

'Every day I think of her.' I hand the frame back to Cesare and he holds it gently, then he kisses the picture, before placing it gently back on the shelf. 'We have breakfast together still,' he says. 'And when I am with the bees; then I am with her.'

I smile at him, knowing that any words would not be enough.

'So, my sleeping beauty. I hear that you are to return to your home.'

'Yes Cesare, we leave in the morning,' I reply.

'And you are happy to go?'

'No, not really.' I sit forward in the chair. 'I'm looking forward to seeing my bees, but I honestly don't know how I'm going to cope on my own.'

'But you will not be alone Maria. Your bees will look after you.' He sits forward too and takes my hands. 'I know that they will not let you come to harm, if it is in their power to do so. But you must trust them Maria.'

I can feel the emotion welling inside me and I struggle to fight back the tears. 'Cesare; what should I do about David?' I know in my heart that he can't answer that question, but I can't help but ask.

Sitting back into the chair, he strokes his beard. 'What I will tell you, is not what you will want to hear.'

'Probably not,' I reply. 'But it will be the truth; and that's what I need right now.'

'Forgive me for what I say Maria.' Taking a deep breath, he lets it out in a low rumble. 'I have been watching David. He is not a man to get close to. He is a man who is.... *agitato*.'

'Troubled.'

'Si, troubled.' He smiles softly at me. 'He loves you Maria. I see him watching you sometimes, and his *guardare*...his, how you say.... his look, tells me that he wants to love you.' I redden at his frankness. 'But, my dear Maria; you must be prepared for him to leave.'

The tears come; I can hold them back no longer. Cesare sits forward and takes me in his arms, and I lower my head into him. His warmth and comfort assuage the tears, but I need to let go of the emotion.

Chapter 44

Diary; January 24th 1970

David takes the last of the bags downstairs. Once he has gone, I go over to the desk and remove the diary. I tuck it into the side of my bag and zip it closed. A tap on the door is followed by a soft, 'hello.'

I open the door to find Anatra waiting in the hallway. He looks down the hall and back to me. 'I wanted you to know that I have sent word around to my colleagues to look out for Katherine.'

'Oh, thank you Anatra, that's much appreciated.'

'You are welcome. I know how you must be worrying.'

'Yes, I am.... very much. And David; well...he's being David.'

'Si; I think I understand. But please do not be concerned. I will do whatever is necessary. Si?'

'Thank you.' I step forward and give him a hug. 'I will miss you Anatra.'

'And I too will miss you Maria.' He steps back and looks once again down the hallway. Turning back to me, he smiles. 'More than you will know.' And he leaves me standing at the door to the bedroom.

Saying goodbye to the Rossi family is more painful than I could have imagined, and as we drive away from the house, the sun dips behind a bank of clouds in protest. They had implored us to stay longer; and at the very least, to come back and see them as soon as possible. The journey to the airport is quiet. Curiously, I don't seem to mind as it gives me an opportunity to think. And I think back to my last conversation with Cesare, and when my tears had all but gone, we had spoken for some time. He hadn't burdened me with mountains of wisdom, but had simply said that he was there; and so were the bees. And he had also told me to come back soon.

Once we are settled on the plane I hold David's hand, but I feel none of the warmth we had on the journey out to Italy; and so I sleep most of the way home. The journey in from the airport to the house is equally as quiet, and the cold rain doesn't ease off. By the time that we arrive back at Meadowsweet it's too dark to even see the meadow; so I leave David to unpack the bags and go straight up to bed.

Diary; February 9th 1970

I load the sink with the breakfast dishes, run some hot water on them, go to the kitchen door and slide my boots on. It has been two full weeks since David left for his new contract. He hadn't unpacked his bags when we had arrived back home, and he was gone before I woke up. I had found the letter the following morning. He had placed it in the drawer where I kept this diary. He didn't say whether he had read it, but there were a lot of sorry's in the excuses. I was angry that he hadn't been able to tell me to my face; but I knew that it was over; particularly since he hadn't even told me where he was going, and had left no contact details either.

It's an unusually warm and breezy day, and as I make my way across the garden, I can see that the clouds are moving quickly, and so the warm sunshine comes and goes. I take the letter with me and go through the gate to the meadow, comforted by the familiar sound of the bees. I sit down on the damp grass and lay back against one of the hives, wrapping my cardigan around me. Several bees settle on me and I smile and close my eyes. It is good to be home. 'Hello my babies,' I whisper softly. I feel a soft flutter in my womb and place my hands on my bump. 'Oh, hello to you two.' I say.

I feel as if I can sit here forever and then I stop breathing, as I hear the faint ringing of the telephone. Damn!

Diary; February 12th 1970

I open the envelope and place its contents on the kitchen table. Rubbing my eyes, I try to focus on the details. I hadn't really slept much since the long-distance telephone call two days ago. Anatra had sounded so far away on the line, and I had found it hard to resist the urge to shout my replies. He had told me that Katherine had been seen briefly by a business colleague, who had recognized her from the wedding, and he had confirmed that she was with Von Treffen and had been seen climbing into a car with him, but there had been nothing since then. Although he told me the location, I had found it difficult to understand what he was saying. When he had asked how David was, I had broken.

It was then that I had heard the faltering in his voice. 'I am so sorry Maria,' he had said. 'Please let me help you.'

I pick up the papers from the table. The top sheet consists of an itinerary of taxis, airport transport and hotels; all booked and paid for. Pinned to the back of the sheet is an airline ticket. The whole journey ending at the Rossi villa.

Anatra had insisted that I shouldn't be alone. When I had protested, saying that I needed to care for the bees, he knew enough about them to tell me that I was just making excuses. What surprised me most was his anger. He had expressed, in no uncertain terms, how he felt about David, and I was certain that he also felt the same way about Katherine, but was being more sensitive for my sake. The ticket told me that I was to leave in a few days. If I were to go, then I had a lot to do. As it was, I had barely unpacked from the previous trip.

Diary; February 19th 1970

As the plane taxis along the runway, it occurs to me that David will have no way of knowing where I am; and then I think about his letter. Had we only been together for just three months? I kept going over the first conversation about love we had ever had. Did he not love me? I had wondered if I had given up too easily, because I hadn't been able to get rid of the feeling that I hadn't put up much of a fight.

It was while I had been tidying the kitchen that I had come across an envelope that David had left behind, and I had sat at the kitchen table to look through its contents. There were several photographs of him at the villa with the Rossi family, along with some people I didn't recognize. I had browsed through the other photographs and found one of David standing in front of some large cameras, behind which was what looked like a film set. He stood with his arm around a stunning female who I had recognized instantly; Vittoria Rossi. Looking more closely at the picture, I had also recognised the distinctive silver bracelet on Vittoria's wrist, and I had thought back to the moment I had seen David in conversation at the Rossi villa with a woman wearing the same bracelet, with the same ruby charms, just like the ones I could see in the photograph. She was also looking at David with such adoring eyes. The words that he had said to me several years ago, had come back into my mind. 'I don't know if I could love someone forever.'

I had known then that I would love him forever; but it was only now, as the plane is leaving the runway on its journey to Italy, that I make the decision that if I can I will fight for him.

Chapter 45

Diary; March 27th 1970

I wake up to the sound of singing. Shafts of sunlight force their way around the edges of the closed curtains, and I slowly sit up in the bed and look around. Although I've been at the Rossi villa for over a month now, I follow the same routine of disorientation every morning, and eventually I walk over to the curtains and pull them open to reveal a bright spring day. I walk out onto the balcony and the singing stops; then a voice bellows up from below, '*Ciao Bella addormentata.*' I'm quite sure that Cesare has been given the task of waking me, for he hasn't missed a morning since I had arrived.

It's only at this particular moment of the day that I wish to be nowhere else.

'Good morning Cesare,' I call down.

'*Come stai?*' he asks.

'I am.... fine thank you.' I'm not fine. I am a long way from fine, as I haven't heard from either Katherine or David in the time that I have been at the villa.

'I have something for you today Bella.' Cesare gives me a huge grin. 'Come to my hives *per favore.*' He lifts his barrow and walks away, and then stops, lowers the barrow and turns to face me again. 'Before *colazione*; before.... breakfast.' He smiles again and blows a gentle kiss before going on his way.

I return his kiss and smile back. Then I wander into the bedroom and sit on the end of the bed. Coming here had been the right thing to do; I know that now. The whole family had looked after me so well. In the short time I had known them, I had come to love them very much; but my feelings are mixed. A nagging thought in the back of my mind asks me if David and I would still be together if he had never come here. And one of the reasons for that doubt is because when I had arrived I had found out that Vittoria Rossi had also gone missing.

As I wander down the stairs, I stop in the hallway and glance to my right. Just a few short weeks ago, I had seen David in conversation with a mysterious female, who I now know to be Vittoria; and I wonder what had been going through his mind back then. I am certain that he had regretted marrying me, and although I had resolved in my heart to fight for him, I am beginning to doubt my chances of success; and if he is with Vittoria, then his heart may have already gone to someone else.

'Maria.' A familiar voice greets me.

I turn to find Anatra walking from the dining area. '*Buongiorno* Anatra.'

'Are you alright,' he asks. 'You seem.... lost.' He comes to me and takes my hand.

I feel tears forming, but know that I won't cry. I had done all of my crying when I had first arrived. 'Just thinking,' I say.

'I understand.' He stands closer and looks directly into my eyes. 'You know I am here for you, *amore mio*.'

I still find it difficult to be comfortable with his familiarity, but I know that it is his way; the Italian way. 'I am grateful to you Anatra. I don't know what I would have done without you.'

'We are all here for you Maria.' Keeping hold of my hand, he turns and begins walking back through the dining room toward the veranda. He stops again halfway across the floor. Turning to me once more he continues. 'This is your home; for as long as you wish it.' I smile softly, but say nothing, as I know that words can express no sentiments strong enough to satisfy. I also know that, without Anatra I would be sitting alone in the kitchen at Meadowsweet; and as much as I miss the house, and the bees, I have no desire to be alone; I had tasted too much of that. Since my arrival, Anatra had been staying at the house. There had been knowing smiles from some of the family when he had sat at the table with me for every meal, but rightly or wrongly, I had welcomed the attention.

'Your father has asked me to join him before breakfast this morning. It seems that he has something he wishes to share with me,' I tell him.

'Ah, so I have some competition for your attention today.'

'I don't suppose....?

'I am sorry Maria, but there is still no news,' he replies.

'I'm sorry Anatra. I ask too much of you.'

'My dear Maria, whatever you ask is never too much.' He walks over to the table and takes a small spoon. 'Now, best not to keep my father waiting.' He places the spoon in my hand and clasps his hands around mine. 'You will need this, I am sure.'

∞ ∞ ∞

I tap on the door of Cesare's hut and enter without waiting. There is always a strong smell of honey, but this morning it is exceptional; and I can see the reason why. On the bench, by the side of Cesare's honey extractor, lay several pieces of comb honey. He is not in the hut, so I wander over to the bench and pick up a medium sized piece of the comb. It still contains several pieces of hexagonal beeswax cells; the love and attention the bees have lavished on these beautiful structures always amazes me, and I feel a tinge of regret at their destruction. Cesare would place the frames containing the honeycomb into the honey extractor; the large metal container that sat on the end of the bench. The frames would then be spun to extract the honey from the combs. Although it was much larger than the one my mother would use to extract our honey, I am familiar with the design. I had tasted comb honey before, but as we had only six hives there was not always a great deal left over. Cesare, on the other hand, had more than enough hives to be generous with the comb; and I am glad of that.

The door of the hut opens and throws the morning sun across the bench. 'Buongiorno Maria, I see that you have discovered your treat.'

I place the comb back on the table, feeling slightly guilty. 'I'm sorry Cesare, I hope I didn't spoil your surprise.'

'No, no, no. not a surprise bella, just something for you to enjoy.' He holds out his hand toward the honeycomb. 'Please.... taste.'

I turn back to the table and pick up the comb again. After examining it quietly for some time, I take a careful bite from the edge. I am not disappointed. As I chew on it, the comb delivers a profusion of sweetness and flavour that sends a warm tingle through my whole body. Old images of Meadowsweet flash into my mind. I am sitting at the kitchen table with my mother; we both have a piece of comb that she has divided for each of us. I feel the soft touch of her hand as she brushes it gently down the side of my cheek. And now, as I lift my hand to my face I feel the wetness of my tears.

Cesare walks over to me and takes me in his arms; the way a father would comfort his daughter; 'It is alright to cry my child,' he says gently, 'because you have those who will catch your tears.' I sob, and I can feel the movement of the babies as they protest at my emotion. I am reminded of the last time he had comforted me; just before I had returned to England; and as much as I want to be home, I also want to stay. I want this to be my home. As if he can read my mind, Cesare answers. 'This is your home right now bella. You have no need to go anywhere; for as long as you need.'

'Thank you,' I reply.'

'The comb is sweet si?'

'Yes, it is sweet. Sweeter than any I have tasted.'

'That is because it is from the blue hive.'

'The soft and sweet bees.'

'*Si*. As long as you live Maria, you will never taste honey as sweet. They only find the sweetest pollen.'

'It is lovely.'

He places his hand softly under my chin and looks deep into me. 'I will not always be here *bella*. My bees, they will live forever. Should you ever need my help, the blue hive will give you the sweetness to satisfy you. You or your *bambini*.'

Chapter 46

Diary; May 16th 1970

I have put off buying baby clothes in the hope that David will return, but there's a possibility that the babies will come early, so I can't leave it any longer. Gaia has kindly offered to take me shopping, and Anatra is keen to act as our chauffer for the day. The day had begun with glorious sunshine lighting up the countryside on our journey into the city, but as we drive back from Asti darker clouds are running across the sky, bringing the threat of rain. I shiver at the thought. Gaia must have seen me, and so she leans forward to touch Anatra on the shoulder while saying something quickly in Italian that I didn't recognize. He takes one hand from the wheel and moves the heater controls. Within seconds I can feel hot air blowing into the back of the car.

Gaia treats me as a daughter, and I enjoy the feeling of closeness she offers, but I also wonder, rather guiltily, how Gaia is coping with Vittoria's continued absence. I had sat with Gaia at breakfast for most mornings, and she had taken great delight in helping me to improve my Italian. We had had many conversations about our families, and Gaia had told me of their history in the hills of Alba, and their struggle to establish the vines. Some of the stories she had shared had been heart-breaking, and I understood why the Rossi's viewed the world as they did. I had been surprised to learn that Gaia had a sister who had died when she was just three years old. My time with her had been a welcome distraction from the endless days with no news of either David or Katherine. How could two people just disappear like that?

In spite of everything that was happening, it's been an enjoyable day. Anatra had even joined in with the shopping; taking great delight in holding up colourful baby clothes to show us. I had blushed quite heavily when one shop assistant had referred to Anatra as my 'marito', my husband. Anatra, on the other hand, had grinned from ear to ear at the comment.

As we pull into the long drive and up to the villa, there seems to be a lot of activity at the front entrance. When we stop, I negotiate my way out of the car and can see Edoardo standing at the entrance. He is waving his arms furiously at someone; and then as he moves I can see Vittoria facing him. She is equally animated and looks as if she is crying. Gaia once again speaks quickly to Anatra in Italian, and then walks swiftly toward them.

Anatra walks around the car and puts his arm around me. 'Shall we go inside?' he asks softly. 'I will send someone for the bags.' He leads me across the drive toward the back of the garden. at that moment the skies decide to open, and the dark clouds let go of their watery load. Anatra quickly runs back to the car and returns with an umbrella. I take the opportunity to walk toward Edoardo and Vittoria, but Anatra gently but firmly places his hands on my shoulders and guides me away and toward the rear of the house. As we turn the corner I look back to see a very wet Vittoria still arguing with her father. I then see Gaia take her daughter into her arms and lead her into the house, leaving Edoardo standing in the rain with his arms outstretched.

I sit on the end of the bed drying my hair. On the instructions of Anatra, I have had a hot shower and have put on a dressing gown. I hear a soft tap on the bedroom door and know that it will be Anatra bringing me a promised cup of hot cocoa. 'May I come in?' he asks as he stands in the doorway holding two cups.

I stand to one side. 'Please.' I say, as I hold out my hand to take the drink, and Anatra hands it to me and comes into the room.

He walks over to the French doors and peers out at the rain. 'We have not had a storm like this in some time,' he says.

I gently blow the hot drink and take a sip as I walk over to join him. 'Even the heavens need to let go of their tears sometimes,' I reply.

He smiles softly. 'You have become quite the philosopher Maria.'

I laugh. 'I believe that may be the influence of your father.'

We stand in silence for several minutes; both deep in thought.

Anatra is the first to speak. 'She has not been with David.'

It's some time before I reply. 'I value your friendship Anatra.'

He smiles at that.

'More than anything else,' I continue, 'I want to be your friend. Do you understand?'

He lowers his eyes. 'I understand my dear sweet Maria.' He looks up and touches my cheek. 'And I respect your feelings. I will love you like no one will ever love you. Not even.... If there is ever a time when you need more than friendship, then I will be there.'

I feel the tears again. '*Grazie* Anatra.'

'She wants to talk to you Maria.' He takes my empty cup. 'But not now; not tonight. Will that be right?'

'Do you mind if I have dinner in my room?' I ask in reply. 'I think I would like to spend some time alone.'

'I will arrange it.' he walks to the door. 'I will call for you in the morning, and if you are.... That is, if you wish to, I will accompany you to breakfast.'

I walk to him and standing on tip toe, kiss him on the cheek. 'A friend indeed,' I say.

Diary; May 17th 1970

Sunday morning comes gently into the room, as the sunlight reflects off the bedroom walls. I hadn't closed the curtains. During the night, the rain had turned into a storm, and I had drawn a curious comfort from the rumbling explosions, followed by magnificent flashes that lit up the room, and I found that I had been disappointed when the storm had ended.

I open the French doors and the freshness of the damp air reminds me of home, and the bees. After I have dressed I sit on the balcony taking in the morning, and I think of Katherine. If she's with Von Treffen, then it's unlikely that she has been thinking of me. With all that had been happening it had become easy to be distracted. As it is, I find it hard to believe that I will be a mother in about a month. I'm surprised that I haven't seen Cesare yet. Perhaps he is aware of what had happened and hadn't wish to disturb me. I think about Anatra's comments regarding Vittoria. What did he mean by saying, she hasn't been with David? Then why had she left at the same time? And, in that case, where had she been? And does she know where David is?

The tap on the bedroom door makes me start. I walk across the room and open the door, but instead of Anatra, I find Vittoria standing in the hallway. 'Ah,' is all I say.

'*Buongiorno* Maria. How are the *bambini?* she asks.

'*Buongiorno* Vittoria, and how is David?' I reply.

'*Mi dispiace*; I am sorry Maria, but I do not know, really I do not.' She stands awkwardly in the doorway, and when I don't reply Vittoria turns to leave. '*Mi dispiace*, I should not have disturbed you.'

'Wait,' I call, and open the bedroom door wide. 'Please, come in.'

She walks into the room and as I close the door I say, 'shall we go onto the balcony? The day seems to be brightening.'

We sit opposite each other at the small table. I feel the babies move and get a sharp pain in my left side.

'I can see the *bambino*. He is moving,' Vittoria says excitedly.

'She,' I say sharply.

Vittoria looks at me quizzically. 'You know this?' she asks.

I place my hand on my side and feel the limb pushing against me. I guess it's a foot, and as I rub it gently I feel it relax. 'My bees told me.'

She smiles knowingly. 'Ah, my Nonno, he speaks of such things. Then it must be a girl,' she says. 'And what of the other, also a girl?'

'Yes; both girls.'

Vittoria loses her smile. 'I...I wish for you to know some things. Will that be alright?'

'I also wish to know,' I reply, 'so I would be grateful if you would tell me.' I look intently at Vittoria. 'And please tell me the truth.'

'I will Maria. That I promise.'

$$\infty \quad \infty \quad \infty$$

I walk as quickly as I can manage across the gardens toward Cesare's hives. The day has brightened even more, and the air is fresh and still. The storm has done a great job of lowering the humidity, and the sun has crept to its highest point of the day as midday approaches. As I draw closer to the concealed opening in the hedge I can smell the honey, and my stomach rumbles in protest. I hadn't eaten breakfast, and had spent the past three hours talking with Vittoria. I need to think.

I slide through the entrance to the hives and slow. Cesare will most likely be in the hut, but I want to be alone; just not entirely; so, I wander over to the hives and walk between the rows, and I begin to feel safe again; but I don't know whether to feel happy or sad. I'm certainly scared; I know that. The first question I had asked Vittoria is why had she been talking secretly with David.

'Your dress,' Vittoria had replied.

'What do you mean?'

David asked me to choose a dress for you Maria,' she had said. 'He told me that it had to be special, whatever it cost; and that it had to fit around your....'

'Bump.'

'*Si.*'

So, that was why he had so perfectly arranged the whole thing.

'Are you telling me that you and David....' Vittoria had looked at me in shocked surprise. She had explained that she adored David, but her heart belonged to another; and that was the reason she had left. 'How can I believe you?' I had asked.

'Because of Katherine,'

'Katherine? What has she got to do with this?'

'She has stolen his heart.'

'David?'

'No....no not David. Alexander.'

'I don't understand.'

'Who do you think invited Alexander to the wedding?'

The pieces had started to fall into place. Now, walking amongst the bees, I understand. Vittoria had explained that she had invited Von Treffen to the wedding with the intention of introducing him to her parents. Instead, he had become enamoured with Katherine, while at the same time ignoring Vittoria. When Katherine had left with him, she had known where they might be. She had said that it had taken these past few months to find them. At first, she had gone to confront them, but when she found them she had watched them for several days. So, she had been able to trace them, where others had failed. But what Vittoria had found had both shocked and frightened her.

'Alexander is keeping Katherine a prisoner in the house,' Vittoria had told me. 'She is unable to leave the house unless he is with her.' It appeared that he had personnel who looked after him, but they also seemed to be watching her as well. And Vittoria also thought that she seemed to be deeply unhappy. Vittoria had told me that she had returned because she had become aware that Katherine was in danger.

'But why would you think that I was with David?' Vittoria had asked me. 'Wasn't he with you?' She had been equally shocked to find that David had left me. 'I am so sorry Maria.' She had placed her hands on mine and smiled gently. 'If I had known that you felt this way I would have spoken to you earlier.' I was becoming uncomfortably familiar with the feelings of jealously and hate; and now I am finding it hard to let them go.

Walking among the hives now, I know that I need to speak to the family. I want my friend back, and I will do whatever is necessary to make that happen. I'm not sure what the Rossi family can do to help me, but I have discovered that they resourceful. For now, I need to clear my head. I stop along the row and rest my hand on the hive. Almost immediately I feel the sting, and I draw my hand back in surprise and annoyance. It's then that I notice that I have paused at the *arrabbiato* bees; the angry hive.

∞ ∞ ∞

As I walk back through the hedge I see Anatra pacing along the gardens toward me. When he reached me he was breathing heavily?

'I have been waiting for you Maria,' he gushes out. 'We need to talk urgently.'

'Why didn't you come and get me?' I ask.

Looking across to the hedge, he replies, 'Because I thought that you were still in your room.'

'Has Vittoria told you what has happened?' I ask.

'She has....and we need to move quickly.'

'Yes, but what will we do Anatra?'

'We will talk on the way.' He takes my hand and leads me back toward the house.

'On the way where?

'Everyone, they are in the cars.'

'But, I need to....'

'We have packed a bag for you,' he interrupts. 'It is also in the car.'

'I need to eat....'

'My mother has also prepared some food for you to eat on the way.'

'Where are we going Anatra?'

'We are going for Katherine. I will tell you on the way also.'

I pull at his hand and stop halfway across the garden. 'Wait.... please, wait for a minute.'

Anatra lets go of my hand and turns to face me, and his forehead creases in annoyance. '*Mi dispiace Maria*,' he asks. 'What is it that you wish to ask that cannot wait until we are in the cars and on our way?'

'Where is Cesare?'

'He is speaking with Vittoria.'

'So he knows?'

'Si, he will know.'

'Then I need to speak with him first.'

Diary; May 18th 1970

I wake to the sound of coughing. It is still dark outside and I can't see what the time is. I turn awkwardly in the bed and feel another body beside me. I remember that Gaia had shared the bed with me the previous evening. It had been late afternoon when we had stopped at a house that seemed to be in the middle of nowhere. I had been introduced to Edoardo's cousin and his family, and after we had all eaten we had gone straight to bed. The house was a great deal smaller than the Rossi villa, so we had had to double up in the beds.

I see a light go on under the crack of the door and I can make out the shape of Vittoria in the room. It's her that I had hear coughing. She has offered to sleep on the floor and now she's sitting up.

'Are you okay Vittoria? I ask through the darkness.

'Si,' she replies. 'I need a drink of water. Do you wish for some?'

'What time is it?'

I can see Vittoria looking at her wrist. 'It is 5:30.' She coughs again. 'I think they will all be rising now. We are to leave soon.'

Although the table is smaller, the conversation around it is just as large. I'm surprised at the number of people around the table. There are some that I hadn't met the previous evening.

'We have many cousins.' Vittoria leans across and speaks in my ear as if she has read my mind and she points to two huge boys standing on the other side of the table. Both have arms as thick as my waist and look at least twice my height, and they are both tucking into large crusty loaves stuffed with meats.

'Franco and Roberto will be coming with us,' Vittoria continues. 'That is why we make a *deviazione*.'

I place my drink down on the table. 'May I ask you a question Vittoria?'

'Si Maria.'

'How was it that you were able to find Von Treffen when the family couldn't?'

'That is because he has many properties; so he would be hard to find if you do not know where to look.'

'How would you know this?'

Vittoria turns to face me. 'I feel that this is my fault Maria.'

'Why would you think that?'

'Because Katherine would never have met him if it wasn't for me.'

'How is that?'

'I have been many times with him. Without the knowing of *mi padre*.'

'We are each responsible for our own actions. Von Treffen must take responsibility for what he is doing now.'

'I am scared Maria.' Vittoria's face darkens. 'This could have been me.'

'But it wasn't you,' a comforting voice from behind them replies. Anatra kneels to talk to the two of us. 'We must be grateful of that; for we might never have found you. At least now, thanks to you, we know where to go.' Looking at me, he says, 'we will get your friend back. I promise you with my life.'

'Thank you Anatra. I am grateful to you.'

'We are family Maria. And we will do this with either brute force...' He looks up at the two boys, 'or by cleverness.' He looks back to me and smiles. 'But most likely both.'

'What do you know about him Anatra?' I ask. You must have found out more whilst you were looking for him.'

He places his hands on the chairs to steady himself and leans forward. Speaking in a lowered voice he continues. 'I have spoken to many friends. What I know now.... I almost feel sorry for him. He has had.... an unfortunate past. His family are Austrian, and his father was a ruthless and domineering man who subjected Von Treffen to strict discipline. His mother, on this other hand, will try to smother him with love to compensate for his father.'

'How sad,' I say.

'Si, but we know now that he can be also dangerous. I think that maybe has an illness of the mind, and he has also inherited *tanto ricchezza* to give to that illness.'

'So why can we not just tell the *polizia*?' Vittoria asks.

'What laws has he broken?'

'Couldn't they just speak to Katherine? I add.

'Si. They could. And it is most possible that she would tell them that everything is fine. It may be that she is in fear for her life, but it is also possible that she is happy and contented; although I doubt it much.'

That thought sucks the breath from me, and I close my eyes and breathe it back in. 'Where is it exactly that we are going?' I ask.

'Trento. It is the capital of Trentino. I have been able to find out from a family friend who is working for the administration there that the farm where they are staying is registered to his uncle, who is no longer alive. We need to leave soon as we have a journey of three hours ahead of us.

I shift uncomfortably in the back seat of the car. I am in the lead car with Gaia and Anatra, who is driving, and Vittoria is in the front seat. In the car behind us are Edoardo, Nicolo and the two boys, and the two vehicles behind them contain several men that I don't recognize. 'They are family,' I have been told. If I had felt nervous before, I feel positively sick now, and I am worried for the babies. There have been protestations from some of the family when they discover that I am to come with them, but they also realise that it might be necessary. If the need arises, Katherine will want to know that she is safe. I can't help but feel that I'm caught up in some surreal movie. All I need is David sitting to one side shouting, 'cut'. In all the excitement, I haven't thought about him for several hours. Just why I'm feeling guilty at that I don't know; but working out that side of my life will have to wait for another time.

'How far is it now?' Gaia asks.

'We are about thirty minutes away, and then we have to find the house,' Anatra replies.

'I am sure that Vittoria can guide us there,' Gaia says.

'Si. Once we are on the outside of the city,' Vittoria adds, 'I will know where to go.'

As we draw closer to Trento, Vittoria gives Anatra directions. They speak in fast, often heated Italian, interspersed with arm waving and shouting. If the situation wasn't so serious, I might find the whole scene amusing. As it is, I can feel the tension in the car as we get closer to our destination.

'There; over there.' Vittoria shouts and points to the right, and as the car brakes suddenly, I hear a squeal of tyres behind us.

'So, that is the farm?' Gaia asks.

'*Si, si*, it is the farm.'

Anatra pulls the car over to the side of the road to take in the surroundings. From where I'm sitting I can see that the large house sits squarely in the middle of large fields of vines and is several hundred metres from the road. Behind it are a number of barns and storage buildings. The house is separated from the other properties around it, so we might possibly be seen approaching, which will take away any element of surprise. Anatra drives further along the road, doubles back, stops the car and turns off the engine. He stops where there is a low hedge along the boundary which should keep us from being seen. There's a tap on the window, Anatra winds it down, and the early morning heat pours into the car. Edoardo and Nicolo stand by the side of the car.

'Now we wait,' Anatra says to them.

'We will need a distraction,' Edoardo says to his brother as he bends down and leans on the open window. 'Do you have any ideas?'

Anatra sits thinking and then says to his brother. 'I have my doctor's bag with me. You will drive me up to the house. I can say that I am checking on the patient and give a false name.'

'That will not get you into the house,' Edoardo replies. 'You will have to give Katherine's name. Once we have gone that far, there will be no turning back anyway.'

'I'm coming with you,' I interrupt, and both Anatra and Edoardo look at me as if I had insulted their mother.

'I think now that it is too dangerous,' Anatra says. 'I cannot allow it.'

Gaia lays one hand on my shoulder and looks at Anatra and her husband. 'Anatra, I will drive a little way behind you to the house, and Maria will be with us.'

Edoardo opens his mouth to speak, but she holds her other hand up and continues. 'if Katherine is in the house, there will be no time to reassure her, and she may not leave the house if Maria is not there. Then all of this will be for nothing.'

With that Edoardo and Nicolo go back to their car, and we all sit in silence; waiting. Anatra asks us to close our windows and leaves the engine running to blow cool air around the car, but he has to turn it off after a short while as the temperature gauge rises too high, so we wind the windows down again to allow some air in.

Twenty minutes later, and an old truck rumbles past and pulls up in front of the convoy. From where I sit I can see a large canvas draped over an object in the back of the open truck. I smile when Cesare steps out of the vehicle. They had listened to my idea. Edoardo and the other men walk back to our car, Anatra gets out to join them and I sit forward to lean on the front seat, eager to catch any conversation. Cesare waits at the back of the truck, choosing not to stand with the men. I take in a sharp breath when I see one of them remove a pistol from his jacket.

Edoardo looks across at the house, shielding his eyes from the early sun. They speak in Italian, and Gaia translates what she can hear. 'The rest of you will need to go on foot,' Edoardo says as he looks at his watch. 'We will wait for ten minutes for you to get close to the house.'

He points back along the road. 'If you walk back a hundred metres you can make your way across the field through the vines. They should be tall enough to shield you.' They nod quietly and begin their journey along the road.

Nicolo shouts softly after them. 'Wait, I will come with you.' The burly men look at each other, laugh and beckon him toward them.

'Nicolo.' His father calls after him, and he stops with a look of disappointment on his face. 'If you are spotted,' he continues, 'then fire off a shot.' Edoardo pulls a pistol from his jacket and gives it to his son. 'At least then we will know what is happening.' Nicolo smiles and runs after the others who have made their way along the road and are disappearing into the field.

Anatra turns his attention back to us. 'Gaia, you will drive behind us up to the house, and wait in this car with Maria and Vittoria. You do not get out of the car; do you understand? When we come out you must be prepared to drive fast and hard until I signal to stop. Is that clear?'

'Si Anatra,' she replies. 'We will be ready.'

In spite of the heat outside, I feel cold and afraid, and as the others change places in the car, Cesare walks over to the window.

'*Buongiorno Maria.*' I smile at him. 'I have brought some friends with me,' he continues. 'You can relax now.' I blow him a small kiss and lay back into the seat; where I can be shaded from the sun, and the others sit quietly, not knowing what to say to each other in this strange scene. The morning heat pours around the car, and I listen to the soft chirping of birds as they welcome the day, and I wish, for a moment, my life were as simple. I can feel my eyes growing heavy as the quietness envelopes me.

I wake with a start as the car jerks forward, and look across to Gaia, who is in the driver's seat. She leans into the steering wheel and turns it frantically. Vittoria is now in the back of the car with me, and we roll to the right as the car spins in the road. Gaia slows the car and looks in the rear-view mirror.

'What's happening?' I ask.

'We are going to the house Maria.' She replies, keeping her eyes on the car in front.

I can see Edoardo's car ahead of us; Anatra must be with him. I look behind me and see the truck with Cesare following a short distance behind. We reach the entrance to the farm and Edoardo's car turn into the driveway; seconds later we follow him. I look behind and the truck has stopped at the entrance to the drive. As we draw closer to the house I begin to feel sick, and I look at Vittoria. The colour has drained from her face, only to be replaced by a look of fear. She looks back at me, and I try to smile to reassure her, but the muscles in my face refuse to cooperate. She grabs my hand so tightly that I let out a small gasp.

The car in front turns a full circle as it reaches the house. I look to my left and I can see Nicolo and Roberto peering out from the vines. The others must be close by. Gaia swings the car around to stop by the side of Edoardo, and I see Anatra get out of their car and quickly make his way to the door. Edoardo follows him and stands to one side. For a moment, our car rocks lightly; and I realise that the men have used the cover of the cars to get closer to the house.

The door opens, and a man is standing in the entrance. Anatra is talking to him. It's not Alexander. Is he in there? The man appears relaxed. Suddenly he begins to close the door. The opportunity looks lost. Edoardo moves into the doorway and pushes the man inside, into the dark, followed by Anatra. We can't see them, and I hear Gaia breathe in sharply.

There are loud noises around us as the men begin to move away from our cars and begin shouting instructions to each other and pointing furiously. Nicolo runs toward the house, closely followed by Roberto and Franco, and they all disappear inside. I look out of the back of the car and the other men are spreading out across the drive. Beyond them are two men coming toward them. Suddenly the men stop and run back the way they came. I wind my window down and I can hear the two men shouting. One of Edoardo's men runs past our car and back toward the way we came in, and begins waving his arms.

There is screaming from the house and I look across and see Franco and Roberto run back out. they are followed by Anatra, who stops just outside the door. A few moments later Nicolo appears in the doorway. There is more screaming. It's Katherine, I know it is. I open my door, and Gaia shouts at me. no Maria, no!

I ignore her and climb out of the car. As I stand up, Nicolo stumbles out of the door holding Katherine's arm. She comes out into the sunlight with Edoardo holding her other arm.

She is struggling Hysterically and screaming. I shout. 'Katherine, Katherine! It's alright.' She stops for a moment, spinning her head from one side to the other looking for the voice. I move to the side of the cars, so she can see me clearly. 'Here Katherine, here.' She sees me.

She begins to fall. Nicolo and Edoardo move forward to catch her weight. They lift her and carry her to the car. I hear shouting. I look to my left. The two men are returning, this time with more men. Possibly twenty or so.

'Get back in the car!' I turn toward the voice. It's Anatra. 'Maria, l'auto, l'auto!'

I move back to the door and climb into the car. As I shut the door I can see Nicolo getting into their car and helping Katherine into the back. Whilst Anatra climbs into the front of the car, Edoardo closes the doors and runs to join the other men. Anatra's car lurches forward, and I see Nicolo and Katherine fall back into their seats. Gaia crunches into the gears and leans forward, holding the steering wheel firmly. Both Vittoria and I push back into the seat as we wait for our car to do the same. Gaia does not disappoint, and we jump forward and accelerate along the drive. Halfway along the drive we suddenly swerve to one side, and for a moment I catch a glimpse of Cesare's truck as it speeds by us.

We reach the end of the drive, but Gaia doesn't slow as we shoot out onto the road. I can hear the car wheels squealing in protest as they try hard to grip the road. Within seconds we are travelling at speed through the Trentino countryside. Both Vittoria and I sit forward and watch the other car spin around the bends, and we try to anticipate the roll of the car as Gaia attempts to keep pace with them.

We drive at speed for around twenty minutes, then without warning, the car immediately in front of us makes a left turn. I feel a sharp pain in my side and I have to sit back. Vittoria keeps her eyes on the road.

'Keep going, keep going,' Vittoria shouts, and Gaia keeps going.

A few minutes later Gaia looks in the rear-view mirror and slows the car. Vittoria sits back, but looks ahead. My pain has gone. We travel in silence. The twins are silent. Too silent. I don't recognize any of the road signs, but I notice that sometimes the sun is on our left, and then in front of us.

I must have fallen asleep, because when I wake the light is beginning to fade. I wake to the same questions that had filled my head when I had laid back into the seat. Where have they taken Katherine? Is she alright? Are they all okay? And what has happened to Cesare? And are the twins alright. They are still quiet. I look out at the fields as we slide into the shadow of the fading sun, and I'm sure I recognize where we are. Minutes later Gaia guides the car into the familiar drive of the villa. We are home.

I open the car door, and placing my hand into the small of my back, I ease myself sideways and work my way out of the car; my bones ache. Gaia and Vittoria follow, and we all walk around to the front of the car. The air is quiet. I breathe deeply. I lean against the car and place my hands protectively on my tummy. So quiet. I press softly, and then a little firmer when there is still nothing.

Suddenly the noise of a car spinning into the drive erupts in front of us, and I jump in surprise. Then I feel the pain as one of the twins kicks me; and then the other. Relief.

Edoardo is the first to get out of the car. 'We have her,' he says. Vittoria turns and throws her arms around me. I feel the twins again, and the relief tumbles from me now in cascades of tears, and I pull Vittoria close in response. 'But she is not here,' he continues.

Gaia looks across to me and asks, as if on my behalf, 'where have they taken her?'

'Anatra has taken her to the hospital.'

'The hospital?' I respond. 'Is she okay?'

Nicolo, who had been in Anatra's car, walks to his father and nods to him. Two men I don't recognise get out of the car, and Edoardo looks around at the small group. 'We had best go inside.'

We make our way into the villa and through to the kitchen. Kettles are put on the range and pots filled with water in readiness for cooking as we each sit around the kitchen table. I think of Meadowsweet, and wish that we could be sitting at my table. I can see Edoardo talking briefly to Gaia and she quickly goes to a cupboard and brings out a bottle containing a dark liquid. She then opens a drawer and pulls out several cloths and places them on the table.

Edoardo sits at the table, full of silent bodies, and picks up one of the cloths. He draws in a breath and speaks. 'Katherine is fine.' I feel some of the tension leave me. 'As we were leaving the property Anatra shouted briefly to me that he would be taking her to his place. And so we all made our way there.'

'And by that he meant ....?' someone asks.

'He meant the hospital... because of her condition.'

'So, she's not fine. Did you see her?' I ask.

'No we did not see her. We left her there with Anatra.' Edoardo lowers his eyes and plays with the cloth. 'She is with child.'

'Mio Diol,' Gaia says under her breath. The large kettle whistles on the range, and Gaia fills the percolators with coffee, and Vittoria loads cups and saucers onto the scrubbed oak table top. Just then several more of the men walk into the kitchen. Many of them have cuts to their faces.

Edoardo stands and moves away from the table, where he removes his shirt. His tanned and muscular frame is tarnished by dozens of red weal's beginning to form all over his body. As he turns into the light I can also see several similar marks on his face. Numerous striped lifeless balls fall to the floor around him, and it becomes apparent that he has been stung many times over, and I can see the discomfort beginning to form on his face. Gaia places the steaming pots of coffee on the table, and Vittoria begins to pour the coffee into mugs. Gaia moves around to where

Edoardo is standing. She takes the rag from him and places the palm of her hand on his chest. I watch as she stands directly in front of him and looks him squarely in the eyes. Without removing her gaze, or her hand, she kisses him. Then she stands back and takes the bottle from the table and, opening it, she pours some of the liquid onto the rag. Continuing to watch him, she places the rag on the first bee sting. I see Edoardo tense and flinch briefly, but he never speaks as Gaia makes her way around each sting on his body and face. Finally, when she finishes, Gaia leans forward again and kisses him. This time she holds the kiss, and I see a small tear trickle down the side of her face. Edoardo breaths in deeply, collects his shirt, and leaves the room.

'So, Cesare released the bees then?' Vittoria asks.

Nicolo is the first to speak. 'I made it back to the car before he did so, but papa...he was not so er...*fortunato*.'

'What about the others?'

'I speak with Roberto at the hospital and we speak *brevemente* about what happened.' Nicolo continued. When Nonno pushed the hive from the truck, there were people running all over the place after that. Roberto said that once the bees started to attack everyone, they all ran into the fields and back towards the car. The farm workers, as well as the men who came from the house, just ran around in circles, so the bees concentrated on them. He leans forward onto the table and begins waving his arms excitedly. 'I wish I had been there to see it,' he laughs, 'I've never....'

'Nicolo.' His mother says sternly as she sits back at the table.

'Mi dispiace,' he replies. 'Anyway, when the hive hit the ground it broke into several pieces, and the bees were....'

'*Arrabbiato*,' I add.

'Si,' he said. '*Arrabbiato*; angry.'

'I strongly suspect that they were already angry before they arrived,' I reply.

'You know of these bees?' asks Gaia.

'I do,' I reply. 'And I'm quite sure that Cesare will be glad to be rid of them.'

The door swings open and Franco and Roberto walk into the kitchen.

Nicolo gets up from the table and walks around to where the two giants stand in the doorway of the kitchen. Franco has a dark ring around his eye. And Roberto has his arm in a bloodied sling. They also appear to be covered in bee stings.

'Von Treffen's men must have put up some fight,' I say.

Franco speaks to Nicolo in Italian, and Nicolo laughs. As Franco continues, Nicolo's laughter grows louder, and this time even Gaia and the others around the table join in.

'What happened Nicolo?' I ask.

'Well,' he begins; and then he bursts into laughter again.

'Nicolo!' I say.

He returns to the table whilst Gaia stands and once again retrieves the bottle and rags for the boys. There is a gasp from Vittoria as they remove their shirts.

'They are your cousins Vittoria.' Gaia glances sideways at her daughter.

'Si Mamma.' Vittoria gives the boys one more sideways look as she turns away from them to listen to Nicolo repeat the story to me of how, once Anatra had gone through the front door, they had both followed him in; only to be confronted by Katherine in the kitchen wielding a knife. As Roberto had attempted to take the knife from her she had slashed at him, taking a lump from his arm as she did so. Franco had managed to knock the knife from her grasp, only to be hit squarely in the face by her clenched fist. I found it hard not to laugh at the picture of Katherine fearlessly fighting off the two boys. What had Von Treffen done to Katherine that had allowed him to keep her a prisoner?

It seemed that Cesare had driven furiously along the drive and, once outside the house, had pushed the hive out of the back of the truck, causing it to smash open on the ground and release the bees. Several men had come running from the fields to confront them with pitchforks and knives, and Edoardo's men, who had travelled with them in the other cars, had formed a barrier between Anatra and the others as they made their escape. Anatra had decided to stay at the hospital with Katherine because of her *condizione*. He had kept two of the men with him, but he did not want any of the others to remain.

Franco lets out a squeal as Gaia applies some of the ointment to his stings, and she mumbles something in Italian under her breath and slaps his arm. When I ask if any of them had seen Von Treffen, they all seem to be of the same opinion; that he didn't appear to be at the house. I secretly wish that he had been there as I know that he has an allergy to the bees. I know what the consequences of that might have been, but right now I wish great harm upon the man.

'He's going to be angry when he finds out that Katherine's gone,' I say.

'We can talk about that tomorrow,' Gaia replies. 'I think that now we should eat and then go to our beds.' She pushes Franco out of the way and beckons Roberto toward her. He reluctantly steps forward with a look of fear on his face. 'Ah mamma mia; such boys,' she snaps.

Chapter 48

Should I step through the black door? The white door, looked more pleasing.
Why did it matter? A door is a door. The black door just might lead to what I
was looking for.

Jemima woke me with a start. 'What time is it?' I asked.

'It's 11:30 in the morning. Sorry to wake you; I just wanted to make sure you were okay.'

'Yes I'm fine; at least I will be when I come round. Mummy woke me last night.'

'Really? I didn't hear a thing.' Jemima replied.

'No, I got to her pretty quickly I think. Is she awake?'

'She's still sleeping. I brought you some tea.' Jemima sat on the bed. 'Connie. I had a call from someone this morning.'

'Who?'

She hesitated. 'Jake,' she replied with a guilty look on her face.

'What?' I pulled myself up in the bed. 'What did he want? I thought you didn't have anything to do with him.'

'I don't. The last time I heard from him was about ten years ago.

'What did he want?'

'He wants to come and see me.'

'About what?'

'I don't know Connie. Honestly I don't.' The colour drained from her face. 'What should I do?'

'Tell him you don't want to see him.'

'I can't.'

'Why not?' I asked.

'Because I've already said yes,'

I did my best to glare at her. 'Why? I mean really; why?'

'It's not my fault Connie, you know what he's like.' She stood up and walked over to the open window, where she stood with her back to me.

'No, I don't know what he's like,' I replied. I did know; he had been hard to say no to, but that had been a long time ago. Did he still have that same hold over her? Over me? I shuddered at the thought.

'Can't you call him back? Tell him that it's not a good time?'

'He knows you're here.'

'How? Did you tell him?'

'I don't think so.' She turned back to face me, and I could see a look of almost terror on her face. 'I'm not sure. Connie; I need your help.'

'Me? I don't think so.' I got out of the bed and pulled my dressing gown on. 'I'll have to leave.'

'Please Connie,' she begged.

'I can fly home for a few days. I'll come back when he's gone.'

'How can you just leave like that?

'Because....' I knew all the reasons, but I struggled to put them into words. 'Because he hurt me; and so did you.'

'I thought we had put that behind us.'

'We did; but not if he comes back. The past becomes the present. Can't you see?'

'Yes; you're right, and I'm sorry.'

We stood facing each other for some time before I asked, 'When is this happening?'

'Tomorrow,' she replied.

I closed my eyes. 'Okay. But don't expect me to say and do all the right things. Okay?'

She gave a small smile. 'Maybe it will help to finally end this.'

'I thought we already had,' I said.

Chapter 49

Diary; May 18th 1970

I rise early. I had dreamt of Katherine. A swirling mix of emotions and thoughts had stolen my sleep. I put my dressing gown on and wander down to the kitchen, only to find that everyone else is sleeping; and I remember that I had slept for some time whilst the others were busy either rescuing Katherine or driving for several hours. I make some coffee, wishing that I had thought to bring some tea from home, and I walk onto the veranda with my drink and watch the early mist roll across the garden waiting for the warm Italian sun to melt it away. The mist brings with it an eerie silence to the house, and I continue my journey across the garden, feeling the cool, damp grass under my naked feet. I go through the hedge and into the beehives, where the continuing quiet tells me that even the bees have not yet stirred.

Wandering through the rows of muted colours of the hive boxes, I can feel the hollow emptiness; but it's more than the empty space where the angry beehive had been, or the quiet of the early hour. Maybe others wouldn't notice it, but it's as if the bees are mourning. I pull a piece of paper from my dressing gown. During the early hours when I had been unable to sleep I had written a poem for the bees, and now I read it out to them.

> *Awake you slumbering bees,*
> *For morning calls, 'it's time to rise',*
> *Off to work if you please,*
> *Wipe the teardrops from your eyes.*
>
> *Shake off the night,*
> *Collect the golden dust away,*
> *For it is your right,*
> *To take such sweet riches each day.*

Soon the keepers of time and life,
Will come visit you to see,
Just how your days of endless strife,
Deal death as the final referee.

So taste your moment with no fear,
For soon your time is gone,
But taste, taste that you are still here,
And through you your tribe lives on.

I cannot, must not mourn for you,
Though sorrow is in my heart,
For you have much work to do,
And I am grateful for your part.

'Grazie Bella.' I turn to find Cesare standing in the doorway of the hut, his gravelled voice echoing through the mist. 'I miss them,' he says.

'They were such *teppisti* bees,' I reply.

'*Si*; and they give me pain many days.' He walks over to the hives, swaying slightly. His hair isn't tied back, and he looks dishevelled and wild. 'But they were my bees,' he says.

I feel such a wave of guilt slide over me for having asked him to take the bees. 'I'm sorry Cesare. It's all my fault.'

'No *Bella*, it is the fault of this man who has a *cuore nero*, a black heart.' He reaches into his jacket and pulls out a large hunting knife. I step back and breathe in sharply. 'There was a time many years gone, when I cut out the heart of such a man.' He looks off into the distance, recalling old memories and long-gone adversaries. For just a brief second, I see something dark and cold. He looks at me with sadness in his eyes. 'She loved me without questions *Bella*; and for that I give her these.' He opens his arms toward the hives, and I catch the aroma of whisky. He places the knife back in his jacket and stands silently. 'The *teppisti* bees... they were never mine; she made them. I just cared for them; as I did her.'

'For Annalise?' I'm beginning to understand the full impact of what Cesare had done when he had let the bees go.

'She waited for me,' he continues. 'They take ten years of my life.... when I take his heart; and she waited for me; but I do it for her; for what he had done to her.' He places his hand on the hive nearest him, and several bees immediately land on the top of his hand and busily run around the rugged surface, their antennae taking in his aroma. He ignores them. 'He took her light, and he left darkness for her.' He steps toward me and stumbles slightly, and I catch his arm. 'And I will tell you this Bella; never did she speak of it.'

'Cesare, you need to sleep.' I slide my arm into his and I guide him back toward the hut.

'Do not let that happen to your friend.' He stops again. 'You must not.'

I urge him on again. 'Come on, I'll make you some coffee.'

He stops suddenly. 'No!' he growls. 'No coffee. Did you ever see me drink coffee?' He looks at me and raises his eyebrows. 'No, you did not see me drink coffee. And I will tell you why.' He waves his finger at me as the whisky takes hold, and I lead him toward the hut again as he continues, 'I hate coffee. And that is why you will never see me drink coffee.'

'Then you must be the only Italian who doesn't; that's all I can say.'

'I am not.' He pulls his arm away from me, and swaying slightly he says, 'because she did not like coffee. And if she did not like coffee, then I did not like...'

'Okay Cesare. I get the picture.' I interrupt.

'Get the picture; what is this get the picture?'

'Never mind.... Tell me; what do you drink? Besides whisky, that is.'

'Tea.'

'What?'

'I drink tea; and I will tell you why....'

'Because she drank tea.' I reply.

'*Si*. How you know this?'

'So, you have tea in your hut?' I ask, ignoring his question.

'Si.'

'Then I will make you.... make us some tea.'

I sit opposite Cesare watching him as he sleeps in his chair. He murmurs under his breath as he moves. What is he dreaming about? Without Cesare, I would not have come through this. Soon there will be two new lives in my world; and if the news about Katherine is true, then there will also be another to care for.

Cesare is snoring, so I finish the last of my tea, gently place the cup on the table and pull both me and my load ungraciously out of the chair. I slip out of the hut and find that the sun is just high enough to share some of its warmth, although the grass is still moist under my feet as I begin my journey back to the house. Voices echo across the gardens from the veranda, telling me that the family are awake and having breakfast, and I hear the familiar sound of Anatra talking. I quicken my pace, eager to see if he has brought Katherine with him.

'Ah Maria. I have been waiting for you,' Anatra says as I walk up onto the veranda. 'I should have guessed that you would be with the bees.' He pulls out a chair from the long table. 'Please, join us.'

'Buongiorno,' I reply. Is Katherine with you?' I look around the table and smile. 'Buongiorno,' I say to them all. When I see Gaia sitting at the other end of the table I blow her a kiss.

'She is presently still at the hospital.'

'Is she okay? Is she coming to the house?

'Please, take a seat, and I will share with you all that she has told me.'

I sit down and pour some fresh orange. 'She is okay?'

Anatra sits beside me. 'She is well Maria; and she is *ansioso*...er....'

'Anxious,' Nicolo says from the other side of the table.

'*Si*,' Anatra replies. 'She is anxious to see you.'

'Anatra...is it true?' I ask.

'If by true, you mean, is she with child, then yes, it is true.'

'Is it Von Treffen....?'

'You will have many questions Maria, so I will tell what Katherine has asked me to tell.' Anatra pours himself some fresh orange, and as he does so, it's obvious that he is very tired. To have done all of this, and to be here now, means that he has most likely not slept. He takes a long drink from his glass and continues. 'Katherine will indeed be having a child, and as a guess, we think that it will be some time in October.'

'Oh my goodness,' I reply, a thousand thoughts swirling around my head.

'She is healthy; despite her ordeal. And *si*, she has been kept as a prisoner by him.'

'Do you know why?' I ask.

'Katherine does not seem to know, but her guess would be the child.'

'How do you mean?'

'He has no child, no... *erede*, how you say....'

'No heir?'

'*Si, grazie*.' He takes another mouthful of orange and then rubs his face with his hands. 'Please forgive me, I am a little tired.'

'Maybe we can continue this later.' Although I want to know more, I can see that it would be unfair to press Anatra further.

'Grazie. First, I must sleep *un poco*; then I will be travelling to the hospital this afternoon. I have yet to see what Katherine would like to do next.'

'Surely she will want to come back here.' I look around the table. 'If that's okay.'

'Yes, Maria. But it was not the time to ask of her anything. I am sure that we can do so this afternoon.'

'In that case, may I come with you?' I ask.

'Are you sure it will not be too much travel? I do not wish to exhaust you further.'

'I will be fine,' I say, placing my hands on my tummy. 'Maybe we can talk on the way.'

Chapter 50

I turned the wheel of the honey extractor, and as it spun, the colours rose around the sides and spilled over the top. I could feel them splashing over my face and I closed my eyes. I knew that I should stop spinning the wheel, but I continued to turn it faster and faster.

I sat quietly as Mummy ate her lunch. I was becoming quite familiar with the balcony in her bedroom, and I wondered if my great grandparents would have sat here on a sunny day or a balmy evening, just listening to the birds or catching the hum of wandering bees. The soft breeze cooled the afternoon sun just enough to warrant a cardigan or wrap; but we had neither, so I wandered back into the bedroom, leaving Mummy to continue with her lunch. I opened the drawers and found two woollen wraps that would be suitable. When I closed the drawer, I stopped and looked around the room. My apartment in Milan was so sparse in comparison; cold even; but right now, I wanted to be there. Mummy was really good one day, and really bad the next; and gigolo Jake was coming tomorrow, and I was tired, really tired.

I went back out to the balcony and slid a wrap over Mummy's shoulders. She didn't respond, but continued eating. 'Is that better?' I asked. No reply. She seemed to have wandered into a place I couldn't go today. I sat down and placed my arm around her.

She turned and looked at me. 'Hello dear,' she said. 'The babies are fine.'

'Are they?' I replied.

Her face creased in fear. 'I'm not sure,' she said.

I squeezed her shoulder. 'It's alright.'

'But I must remember,' she continued. 'They need to know.'

'Who needs to know?' I asked her.

'I'm not sure. Do you know?'

'I tell you what; how about we read some more of the diary; maybe that will tell us.'

She relaxed at that suggestion. 'Yes, yes; let's read the diary.'

I returned to the bedroom and went straight to the drawer containing the second of the three diaries, and I took it back to the balcony and sat with Mummy. She placed her tray onto the side table and turned toward me in anticipation. It always surprised me to see how the diaries seemed to focus her mind; to centre her. She even appeared to know who I was during that time. I didn't really feel like reading the diary. What I really wanted, was to talk to her about Jake; and ask her advice on what I should say or do. But I knew that was impossible now, just as I had been unable to talk to her about Gabriel.

I hadn't heard from him, and I was surprised at how much it bothered me. I would just have to figure things out for myself. I couldn't help feeling that tomorrow was going to be a disaster. I had to keep hoping that reading the diaries would give me some answers; not just to the past, but now.

Chapter 51

Diary; May 18th 1970

The front seat of the car is so uncomfortable, and I shift awkwardly. 'Are you going to be okay Maria?' Anatra asks.

'How much further is it?' I respond. 'I really need to....'

'We are not far away.' He frowns at me. 'Did you not go before we left?'

'You sound like my father, well, what my father would have sounded like if I had ever met him.'

'You never knew your father?' he asks.

'No; and now it looks like my girls won't know their father either.' It seems to me that David has no intention of being part of our lives; and I need to think about the future. 'Anyway, what else can you tell me about Katherine?'

'She is confused and dazed with all that has happened; and I am suspecting that she is feeling very guilty. I am speaking to a colleague at the hospital last night, and she is telling me that Katherine will be dealing with very many feelings, and we would need to give her time to settle. The most important of things would be to make her feel secure.'

'How can I do that Anatra? I hardly feel that way myself.'

'We will help Maria. I promise that you will not be alone,' he replies as he pulls into the hospital car park. He drives the car to an area for hospital staff and quickly finds a space. 'I am meaning what I said Maria.' He turns to face me. 'You have no need to worry.'

'Thank you Anatra.' I smile at him, not knowing quite what to say. It's too soon to think about things that complicate my life even more. I trade my smile for a grimace. 'But right now, I need to....'

'Si.' he quickly gets out of the car. 'There is a *gabinetto* in reception.' I don't know what a *gabinetto* is, but as I pull myself out of the car I hope that it will fill my need.

∞ ∞ ∞

I waddle nervously outside the door of the hospital ward waiting for Anatra to return. I'd been told to wait there by him until he knew what was happening. 'But she will want to see me,' I had protested. 'She will need me.'

Anatra had slipped effortlessly into the role of doctor and had placed his hand on my arm, while at the same time leading me to the waiting room seats. 'I am sure that is the case Maria, but I will need to make sure that there have been no complications since yesterday.' I had sat down obediently expecting to see them return within minutes. An hour had now passed, and I can't get the thought out of my mind that Katherine doesn't want to see me. Just then the doors to the ward swing open, and both Anatra and Katherine walk through. Katherine stops outside the doors and smiles at me.

'Hi Kat,' I say, returning her smile. 'How are you?'

'Mary,' she replies. 'Mary.' Soft tears creep down her face.

'Oh Kat.' I walk across and gently place my hands on her face. 'I've missed you so much.' She leans her head forward, and I pull her into my arms; and we stay like that for several minutes. 'Let's go home,' I say eventually. 'But first....' I lift Katherine's head up. 'I need to pee.' She laughs softly through the tears, and Anatra steps forward and takes her arm.

'I will look after her, whilst you....'

'Thank you,' I say.'

As we walk back to the car I can feel the babies pressing down, and have to stop a couple of times as the pain becomes almost unbearable. 'I swear these girls don't want to stay in there anymore.' Anatra stands in front of me and places his hand on my bump. I blush at his touch and wait for Katherine to make a remark of some kind, but she remains silent.

'I think that they are just being active.' He says with an air of seriousness. 'I am sure that you will be fine. You will know that twins; *spesso arrivano presto*; they early arrive.'

'You did say that.' I reply, and I turn to Katherine. 'At least you're only having the one.' The ashen look on her face is not the reaction I'm expecting. 'Oh Kat, I'm so sorry.' I reach out and take her arm. 'That was so thoughtless of me.'

'That's okay,' she replies. 'It's not your fault.'

'Do you want to talk about it?'

'Maybe later; can we go home now? I'm very tired.'

'Anatra takes Katherine's arm and leads her toward the car. I stand still for a moment and watch her walk away, and I wonder what is to come; for both of us.

We make the journey home in silence. I sit in the back of the car with Katherine, and she falls asleep on my shoulder. When David had driven us back from the hospital after visiting Mummy, I had fought tooth and nail to sit in the front; and it was then that I had fallen in love with him. That couldn't, mustn't happen with Anatra, for so many reasons; not the least of them being that I'm newly married and about to give birth. I'm surprised at how concerned I've become about his feelings. But all I can see ahead is a life alone. I try very hard to dismiss the feelings of despair I have, that threatened to overwhelm me.

Katherine wakes as the car comes to a halt outside the Rossi villa. 'Oh my goodness,' she says, 'have I slept the whole way?'

'You obviously needed it,' I reply, and we sit quietly; our situation uniting us in a common purpose.

Anatra turns to face us. 'I must leave you now *signore*. I have neglected my work for too long already. We have spoken as a *famiglia*, and as we have said before, we want you to stay here, at the house, for as long as you wish.'

'Thank you Anatra,' I reply. 'You don't know how much that means.'

He looks directly at me. 'You cannot travel anyway Maria. It is possible for you to er...give your *bambini* to us at any time now.' I smile. 'When I am left, you must call if there are any problems.'

Chapter 52

I let go of the handle, and the honey extractor slowed, and the colours took on a life of their own as they continued to spill over the sides and across the floor; filling the room. I moved away from them as I tried to not let them touch me.

I envied my mother; having Cesare to talk to when she needed advice; and I wished I could go back and sit with him in his hut, and talk over a cup of tea. I really wasn't looking forward to seeing Jake again; old memories surfaced as I thought about all the reasons I had left, but part of me wondered what my life would have been like if he hadn't cheated on me; if he hadn't slept with my sister; if I hadn't rejected his advances. I thought that I had answered that question. But I suppose the real question was, would I want to go back and change it? and the truth is, right now I don't know. No, I wasn't looking forward to seeing him; but I needed to draw a line under this; for all our sakes.

Chapter 53

Diary; May 19th 1970

There's an early mist again, and I pull my cardigan around my neck. I hadn't seen Cesare since the previous day, when he had appeared looking rather dishevelled. I'm tired, but I enjoy the quiet of the early mornings. At Katherine's request, I had stayed with her in her room until she slept, which hadn't come for several hours. Even then, her sleep had been fitful and disturbed. What had Von Treffen done to her? I tap on the door of Cesare's hut before entering. It's unusually dark this morning and I squint as I peer through the gloom.

I call softly. A low grunting noise comes from over in the corner, and I walk across to the bench and look beyond it to the storage area. Sitting on a small stool, and leaning against a steel shelf, is Cesare. I make my way around the bench and kneel beside him. He's asleep, and I touch his arm gently. He lets out another low grunt and stirs.

'*Buongiorno* Cesare.'

He slowly opens his eyes, and in them I see Edoardo. I've never actually seen Cesare come into the villa. Only onto the veranda; and I wonder why?

'*Buongiorno Bella.*' His low gravelly voice echoes in the quiet of the hut. His eyes close, and he begins to snore.

I stand up and go back in front of the bench and over to the worktop, and I shake the kettle to check if it has water and place it on the stove. When I find the matches and light the stove, I breath in the aroma of the spent match. I hear movement from beyond the bench, and Cesare appears, his crumpled shirt hanging low around his equally creased trousers. His hair looks so much greyer this morning as he wanders past me without speaking and slumps into his chair and closes his eyes.

I stand in silence as the kettle begins to make encouraging noises; and I pull two mismatched cups from the shelf above and check that they are clean. I pour a small amount of nearly boiling water from the kettle into the teapot and place it back on the heat. The soft pink rose pattern around the glazed ridges of the white teapot runs easily across my fingers. Perhaps it had belonged to Annalise. The swirling water of the teapot throws its heat into my face, and I feel the china warm in my hands. It feels good; and I empty the water into the sink and then move the cups to one side of the tray to make room for the pot, along with the sugar and the milk. Then I scoop three spoons of leaves into the pot. Cesare is watching me, and I can see him smiling. It's one of those old memory smiles; you know the kind I mean. I take the tea towel and wrap it around the handle of the kettle, then lifting it from the stove as it begins to boil, I slowly pour the water into the teapot, watching the leaves of tea dance in pleasure.

I carry the completed tray to the low table placed between the chairs and sit it down. Sitting back in the chair opposite Cesare, I take in a deep breath and let it out slowly.

'*Grazie Bella*,' he says.

'No, *grazie* Cesare,' I reply.

'For what?' he asks and sits forward.

I sit forward with him and look straight into his watery blue eyes. 'What you have done, for me and for Katherine, is more than I should have asked.' He sits back again and waves his hand in dismissal. 'No Cesare, you can't dismiss it as nothing. I have seen, can see, your pain. And I'm sure that you knew it would hurt; but you did it anyway. So *grazie*, thank you.'

'*Prego*.' He sits forward. 'Now I will pour the tea; and *si*, the pot did belong to her. The leaves have enjoyed the warmth of the pot for long enough, now they can pass on their *vita* to us.

'One spoon of honey please,' I say, as I stand up and wander back through to the steel shelving; back past where I had found Cesare sitting and sleeping. Beyond the shelves, I had noticed a door when I had gone to wake him. Allowing my eyes to focus in the dim light, I step forward and try the handle; it opens easily. I step into a room softly lit by the early morning sun, and I take in a sharp breath.

All around the walls are countless picture frames, each of them containing a photo of Annalise. They are in the most beautiful frames; not one of them the same; and they allow the light to bounce around the room in every direction. The bed is the most ornate I have ever seen, and the soft white linen sheets are immaculately folded. There are several other pieces of sumptuous furniture in the room, and the top of each one is filled with ornaments; some carved, and others painstakingly sculpted from clay and beautifully glazed. Many of them are figurines depicting the same woman. I turn to my left and carefully lift a piece from a curved chest of drawers. The attention to detail is stunning, and I turn the sculpture over and see the initials. C.R. Cesare Rossi. As I hold the figure a single tear drops onto the glaze, and I pick up several more of the pieces close to the door, only to find that each one is embellished with the same initials.

I have intruded on Cesare's private world, and I turn to leave. Cesare is standing silently just behind me, and I jump in surprise.

'So, now you know my secret,' he says.

'I... I'm sorry Cesare, I had no right...'

Taking my hand to silence, he says, 'It is *bellisimo si*?

I look around the room again, taking in the softness and enjoying the warmth and brightness. I can't imagine a more perfect place to be. Now I understand why I had found him sleeping outside the room.

'Come; sit with me, and we will drink our tea and I will tell you about my life.'

I quietly tap on my own bedroom door and open it slowly with one hand while balancing the tray with the other hand. Katherine is still sleeping, and so I place the tray with its two cups on the bedside table and pull up a chair. I don't want to disturb her by sitting on the bed. I had expected to find her awake and hungry, but despite the late hour of the morning, she has most of her head covered by the sheets and blankets and is in a deep sleep.

I pick up my hot cup from the tray and place my hands around it, drawing some comfort from its warmth. I had come straight from Cesare's hut to find that all the breakfast things had been cleared away and the house was quiet. I sit quietly now, enjoying the peace, in contrast to the few hours I had spent listening to Cesare tell me about his life. He had explained that he had not been into the villa from the day that Annalise had died. And then he had spoken about his childhood; from the very first time he had set eyes on Annalise, through to his time in the war, and the difficulties and trials they had had with the vines, and his love, and sometimes hatred, of the bees; and he made me feel like I wanted to be there. He had spoken of love and triumph and death and tragedy, but in spite of all that he had been through, he had made it all sound so wonderful and magical; and as he spoke of Annalise his eyes shone, as if the love he had inside was a glowing furnace that needed somewhere to escape. And with every word he spoke I had fallen in love with Annalise with that same love, and my heart ached with the loss. And as he continued I thought of my own life, and my love, and my loss, and my bees; and despite all that had happened, and all that was yet to happen, I knew then that my life would also be one of magic and wonder, and I miss David.

Just a short while ago I had stood with him on the same balcony and we had spoken of love. I place my hands on my roundness and feel a soft response as the evidence of that love moves inside me. Very soon now I will need to give all that love to new life; two new lives.

I watch Katherine sleep; and her coffee goes cold. I'm worried about her. I want so much to reassure her; to tell her how much I love her, and that she's safe. I can't begin to imagine what she has been through. The Rossi family have been amazing, but they can't be expected to look after us forever, even with Anatra's reassurances that he will do all he can to help and protect us. The time will come when we will have to return home, But before then I will need to find out what else has been discovered; it may help in deciding what to do next.

There's a soft tap on the door, and I look over to Katherine, but she doesn't stir. I sit my cup down and creep over to the door, opening it a fraction as if to signal that no one can enter. Vittoria peers through the gap from the hallway. 'Hello Maria.' She says softly. 'I just wanted to see if Katherine is well.'

'She's still sleeping.' I reply, and I slide out of the room into the hall, closing the door softly behind me. 'Shall we go to the kitchen and leave her to sleep for a while?'

We make our way down the stairs to the kitchen and sit at the large oak table. The kettle is on the stove, but no one is around.

We sit quietly for some time before she speaks. 'I still love him Maria.' Her voice shakes.

I remain silent.

'He is a wild horse,' she continues. 'A man untamed.'

What I want to say to her is, how can you still love him after what he has done, not just to Katherine, but to me as well. I want to tell her that he's a psychopath, that he's evil, and there is no telling what he might do to get his own way. Instead I say nothing and wait.

'I know what he has done is bad,' she says, 'but I cannot change how I feel. I want to know if there is some good in him. And if there is, I want to help him find it.'

I can no longer stay silent, and so I stand, pushing my seat back as I do so. 'Are you mad Vittoria? Are you absolutely crazy? Can you not see what this man has done?'

She recoils as if she has been slapped, but says nothing, and I take a deep breathe in and continue. 'My friend; my best friend in the whole world is laying in the bed upstairs, and I don't yet know what is left of her.'

Vittoria places her head in her hands. 'I'm sorry, I'm so sorry.'

I pace around to the other side of the table. 'I curse the day he ever came into our lives. Do you realise the damage he has caused?' Steam pours out of the kettle and spins and swirls around me. As it whistles I push it aggressively off the heat and immediately the steam evaporates; and I feel some my anger dissolve into the air.

Vittoria stands and walks around to me. 'Can you ever forgive me?' she asks.

I see such pain in her eyes that it makes my heart ache; and I open my arms and pull her to me, saying nothing.

The kitchen door swings open and Katherine walks through into the kitchen; she is still in her pyjamas and dressing gown. 'Is everything okay down here? I heard shouting. I think my room must be directly above here.'

Her hair is a tangled mess of red and her eyes are heavy. 'Is there water in that kettle?' she asks. 'I could do with a drink. Someone brought me up a cold cup of coffee.'

I open my mouth to explain and then think better of it. I let go of Vittoria and push the kettle back onto the heat of the Aga.

'I will get some cups.' Vittoria says.

How are you feeling Katie?' I ask.

'Well, the last time I felt this sick was when I got a little drunk at the wedding.'

'I think that may have passed by now.' I say.

'Well it hasn't. I'm beginning to wonder if it's the same hangover.'

I lighten at the thought that she still has some sense of humour and hope it's a good sign.

'Katerina.' Vittoria says. She hesitates; struggling to find more to say.'

Katherine comes to the table and sits down slowly. 'Listen Vittoria, let's get one thing really clear.' I watch Vittoria recoil once more, expecting another onslaught, and I wonder where this is going. When she settles herself, she continues, 'Anatra has told me everything.' She swallows hard and looks across to me. 'How's that coffee coming along?'

The kettle whistles again, as if on cue, and I spin around and pull it from the Aga and prepare the coffee.

Katherine continues. 'I don't blame you Vittoria. I'm a big girl and I make my own decisions.' Vittoria blinks rapidly to stop the tears, but they come anyway. I start placing the cups and saucers on the table, following that with the coffee, milk and sugar, then I sit down to the side of Katherine.

Vittoria stands. 'I'll get the spoons.'

I place my hand on Katherine's and squeeze it lightly, smiling warmly at her. Katherine breathes in deeply and steadies herself again. 'I'm here for you Katie. I want you to know that.'

'I do. Really I do.' She replies. 'But please can I ask one thing.' I wait. 'Please don't fuss. You know what I mean.'

'Yes, I understand.' I reply, and Vittoria sits down at the table.

'It is how it is.' Katherine continues. 'For all of us. None of us have come out of this well. But it's up to us to get on with it now.'

'Vittoria still loves him.' I say, and immediately regret it.

Vittoria lowers her eyes, and Katherine looks across to her but says nothing for some time, as if choosing her words carefully. 'He doesn't love you Vittoria.' She says it softly, with no malice or anger; and then she continues. 'He doesn't love me either.'

At that Vittoria looks up at Katherine, her eyes wide with astonishment. 'But he has kept you there, with him all this time. And he has made you with child.'

'And that's why he kept me; because he wants the child, not me.' I push a cup of coffee toward Katherine and she picks it up immediately, wrapping her hands around its warmth. 'And the second he discovered that I was pregnant he never came near me again.' We sit quietly again, each buried in our own thoughts. Katherine takes a sip of the hot coffee and closes her eyes. 'Listen Vittoria.' She opens them again and looks across at her. 'I understand that you love him. I even find myself battling with those feelings now; in spite of the way he is. But I promise you this. He will hurt you; more than you could ever imagine. I cannot believe that I've been rescued. And I'm aware that I have you to thank for that also. You and your family; but most of all, I have the love of my beautiful friend to be grateful for; along with a good amount of luck. Do you honestly think that you could be that lucky a second time?

I feel the twins move and what feels like a foot pushes hard against me. I wince with the pain. 'You okay?' Katherine asks.

'They're practicing I think.'

'Practicing?' Vittoria asks.

'For when they decide to come out.' I shift in my chair and the twins go quiet.

'Have you heard anything from David?' Katherine asks, eager to change the subject.

'No. and I don't expect to.'

'What do you mean? Is he on another contract?'

'I'm sure he is...somewhere. But he hasn't told me where.' I stand with my empty cup and take it to the large butler sink. With my back to her I said, 'I had a letter.'

'What did it say?' Katherine asks.

'Basically, that he wouldn't be coming back.' I can feel the emotion of that thought returning and I place my cup down on the drainer and turn back to her. 'But I have you back Katie, and that's far more important to me right now.'

Chapter 54

I tried moving further away from the colours, but they moved faster than me, and once again I was caught, Rainbow coloured bees flew all around me and I waved my arms to push them away, but every time I hit one, it turned black.

My heart was beating out of my chest and I felt like a foolish schoolgirl waiting for her first ever date to arrive. Jake was due to arrive in the next hour, but he might as well have been walking through the door right this second. Jemima finished filling the teapot with hot water and placed it on the tray, and I rearranged the cups for the third time.

'Are you sure that she doesn't want any breakfast?' she asked me for the third time. I think that she was also looking for anything to distract her from thinking about his visit, as I was.

'That's what she said Jem.'

'What about if I make her some toast, just in case?'

'We ate quite late last night, I think that's probably the reason.' I picked the tray up, eager to carry it to the safety of Mummy's room. 'Let me know when he's here.'

'You mean you're not coming straight down?'

The look of horror on her face told me that was not a good idea. 'Well just let me check that she's okay. Does Mummy know that he's coming?'

Well, I did tell her, but who knows.'

'I'll mention it again and see what response I get.' I carried the tray to the kitchen door.

'Connie,' Jemima called.

I stopped at the door and turned back to face her.

'I do appreciate this; I know it must be hard,' she said.

I couldn't think what to say so I just shrugged my shoulders and continued my journey. At the top of the stairs I relaxed a little and walked to Mummy's bedroom door. I tapped lightly before entering. She was reading on the balcony. It seemed to be her favourite place to go lately. I couldn't help but feel jealous as I thought about her in her own private world, where she had the power to shut out anyone she didn't want to intrude. She turned when she heard me, and the look of concern on her face as she tried to figure out who I was took away any feeling of envy I might have.

'Hello Mummy, it's Constance,' I said a little too loudly.

She smiled. 'Oh hello.' She looked at the tray. 'What time is it?' she asked.

'Time for a nice cup of tea,' I said as I placed the tray on the small table. I sat down and picked up the teapot, eager to pour before it stewed. I wondered how I could broach the subject of Jake. I should have asked Jem how Mummy had reacted when she spoke about him.

'When is that young man coming?' she asked, beating me to it.

'You mean Jake?'

'Yes, that's the one.' She picked up her spoon and dipped it into the honey. 'Are you sure about him?' she asked.

'What do you mean, sure?' I asked, not quite knowing what she meant.

'Well, I don't want to upset you darling, but I'm not sure he's right for you.'

Now I knew what I was dealing with. 'Mummy, I think you need to know that he was married to Jemima.'

At first, she seemed unfazed by my comment, and she continued to stir the honey into her tea. Then she frowned and looked up at me. 'Why didn't you tell me about this. I have a right to know what's going on in my own house.'

I didn't know what to say, so I said the first thing that came into my head. 'I'm sorry Mummy, I thought you knew.'

'Why would I know?' she asked.

I could see that this had the potential to get out of hand. 'Why don't you come down stairs? Then you can meet him.'

'Why would I want to meet him? I don't like him.'

'Why don't you like him Mummy?' I asked.

'Because he's not nice to you,' she replied, and her frown deepened as she tried to make sense of the situation. 'And he doesn't like the bees.'

She looked straight at me. 'He doesn't like our bees Connie; he doesn't like our bees.' She stood and walked to the edge of the balcony, looking out over the meadow. 'Just that,' she said pointing to the meadow. 'Just that.'

And there it was. My memories came flooding back. Memories of how he used to laugh every time Mummy went out in her white dress and hat to collect some honey. All the times he used to talk of putting the meadow to better use by building houses on the land; and how he had cursed so much when a bee stung him, vowing that he would never set foot in Meadowsweet again.

But he had come back. He had come back to ask me to marry him. And now I saw it. He had wanted the land; wanted what we had, but not for the same reasons. He had his own dreams. And when he realised that he wouldn't get what he wanted from me, he had used Jemima; just as Von Treffen had used aunt Katherine. So, what did he want now?

I felt angry, emboldened even. I couldn't wait for Jake to arrive. I wanted to hear him try to talk his way into the family. I had to be strong, even if no one else was.

Chapter 55

Diary; June 27th 1970

Since she has returned to the villa, Katherine and I spend a lot of time together; taking solace in each other's company. The days have lengthened as the summer has well and truly returned. Katherine has moved into a room of her own as the Rossi family constantly reassure us that they wish us to stay as long as we like. They could not make us more welcome.

As early summer flowers open their buds toward the sun, the soft palette of spring past deepens into a rich tapestry of vibrant reds, blissful yellows, and soulful blues. Birdsong fills the early mornings, and Cesare once again appears each day at the foot of the balcony to my bedroom. He's beginning to look like his old self, and I blow him a kiss every morning, and he greets me with the title *bella addormentata*; sleeping beauty.

I spend many hours with Katherine in the gardens, and we charge ourselves with the task of collecting the most pretty and colourful flowers to grace the veranda table, and the family begin to look forward to our arrangements. I still wander into the hives, but less frequently, as when I have Katherine with me I don't wish to disrespect Cesare's wishes that no others are to come into the hive garden. I find it increasingly difficult to get around as my bump grows to a ridiculous size. Katherine's bump, on the other hand, barely grows. So much so that Anatra insists that they keep a close eye on her and subjects her to several regular checks. He comes to the conclusion that there are no complications and that the baby is naturally small. When Vittoria is with us we try not to talk too much about the babies as we can often see the sadness in her eyes.

Diary; June 28th 1970

I come down to breakfast to find the family talking in hushed tones which stops as they see me. Katherine is already at the table, as is Vittoria, and they both look ashen. 'What's the matter?' I ask.

Anatra who is standing slightly away from the table, is the first to speak. 'It is Von Treffen.' He says. He has disappeared.'

'What do you mean, disappeared? Isn't that a good thing?'

'Apparently not.' Katherine replies. 'It seems that all the while we've been relaxing Edoardo has had people keeping an eye on him.'

I look across at Edoardo. 'You don't mean that you have done something...?' I struggle to find the right words.

Edoardo, who is sitting at the head of the table, stands and rests the palm of his hands on the table. 'This is a family of honour Maria. It has always protected those who belong to the family and those who become part of our family. But we also value life, every life.'

'I'm sorry Edoardo, I didn't mean to imply...'

'You have no need to apologize Maria; but make no mistake, we will also place the lives of this family above any others, and we will defend them *alla morte.*'

The rest of the family raises whatever glass or cup they have, and say as one. '*Alla morte.*'

Anatra, moves to his brother's side and raises his glass. 'To the death.' He says in English, most likely for the benefit of Katherine and me.

I feel the babies move, and I wonder if they can feel my tension. Rescuing Katherine had been enough excitement for any mother to be, and we were all still struggling with the effects of that. Now I find myself wondering what this news means and, more importantly, how it will affect us.

Anatra moves around the table and places his hand on my shoulder. I still find it hard to feel comfortable with his familiarity, but in spite of that, I warm to his touch; a touch I know should be coming from David. 'How are you feeling Maria?' He asks softly, taking care not to interrupt the discussion that is going on.

'Ready to burst I think.'

'I will be happy to examine you later.' He kneels by my side and takes my wrist, holding his thumb lightly on the inside to take my pulse. 'It would be good to check your blood pressure, especially in view of these activities.'

I feel my pulse rise to the coolness of his hand, and I wonder how that will affect his reading. 'What do you think all of this means Anatra?' I ask.

'I think it means that they will talk for some time about all of this, but in the end my brother will do what he thinks is right.' He stands again and touches the side of my face, brushing a wisp of hair over my shoulder. 'But you must not worry my sweet Maria. My brother is a good man, and I trust him. I have some visits to make this morning, but I will back for lunch, so I will see you then.' He places his hand on my shoulder again. 'Listen to him carefully Maria. He will do what is best for you and Katerina.' I have been trying to avoid his eyes, and as I look up at him, he smiles, and I know that he has taken a piece of my heart. Anatra turns to the table and raises his hand. '*Ciao*,' is all he says and leaves.

Edoardo pauses to wave to Anatra, then continues. 'I have asked the boys to come and stay with us for the summer. They will work on the vines, but they will be here to protect you.' He looks at Katherine and then me in turn. Please feel free to call on them should you have any concerns. That includes you Vittoria.' Edoardo looks at his daughter, who seems surprised to be included in the arrangement, but I think it is more in the way of warning her to stay away from Von Treffen; and it's clear then that they will also act as chaperones to her. It seems that Vittoria's father knows her better than she realises.

Anatra is true to his word and returns at lunchtime. I have spent the morning resting in my room. I had wanted to go and see Cesare and the bees, but the discomfort had increased, and so I thought it best to do nothing. Katherine had wandered in to speak to me but had become irritated and restless when I mentioned Von Treffen. It seemed that she wished to avoid the subject altogether, which was also beginning to irritate me, particularly as she would also throw in questions about David. How can we ever plan a future if neither of us want to talk about it? It seems to me that we are not yet ready to face up to the situation, and I'm beginning to feel anxious about how we will cope; as we can't stay at the Rossi's forever. Perhaps I'm more concerned than Katherine because I am closer to having the babies. Franco and Roberto, the boys who had accompanied us on the rescue mission, sit at the other end of the table. Will they really be able to keep us safe in a crisis? I think about Anatra's words of reassurance regarding his brother and wonder if they are really here for our benefit, to distract them; and I guess that behind the scenes Edoardo probably has other things going on; things that he wouldn't want us to know about; things that will keep us safe. It all feels quite surreal.

It's a million miles away from the quiet life of Meadowsweet, where on a summer day such as this I might wander to the meadow and check that the bees are doing well and talk to them. I would tell them about my day; not that there would be much to tell, and how I miss Mummy. And I miss home more than ever; I miss the bees.

It occurs to me that Katherine has never really had the chance to use the workshop. If she does come home with me, what then? The questions and thoughts once again start to spiral out of control. A kick from one of the babies brings me back to the table. I feel the familiar touch of Anatra as he places his hand on my shoulder, and I see the look of concern on his face, and I realise that he has been watching me.

'You must not worry so Maria.' He says softly. 'You are safe here. Remember, I made a promise to you.' He smiles, and I see the warmth in his eyes, and I breathe it in, and it lifts me.

'Where would you like to examine me Doctor Rossi?' I ask, and return his warm smile.

He laughs and replies. 'I think perhaps that your room would be a good place. I will get my bag and meet you there shortly.'

$$\infty \quad \infty \quad \infty$$

'How is Katherine doing?' I ask as I sit on the bed.

Anatra pulls up a chair as he sits his bag next to me. 'Can you roll up your sleeve please?' he says, and pulls out his blood pressure monitor and untangles the tubes. 'I was concerned as the baby seemed to be very small, but she is healthy, despite her ordeal.' He places the bag around my arm and gently secures it in place. I am in awe of just how tender he is, and I can see why he favoured the profession of a doctor over the tough world of business. And then his face creases in concern. 'She does have plenty of time to go home before she has the bambino.'

'Do you think she will?' I ask him, having been unable to glean an answer from Katherine herself.

'She has expressed a desire to do so.' He replies, his face still looking uneasy.

'You don't look too happy about that idea.'

'I am not. As I would not be happy if you leave us.'

I blush. 'Why?'

'Because I cannot protect you; we cannot protect you, once you are gone.'

'But we can't stay here forever Anatra.' The pressure builds in my arm as Anatra pumps up the bag. He places the stethoscope in his ears and plants it on the inner part of my elbow and I take that as a cue to remain silent. I can feel the blood pumping through my arm, and it's somehow comforting. The twins would hear the beat of my heart every second of the day. Is it any wonder that they would protest when it lost its familiar rhythm? The muffled sounds that they would hear from other places would be incidental to the deep and steady beat that was their world. The pressure decreases, and the sensation disappears, leaving me to face my world.

Anatra removes the stethoscope and begins to unwind the bag from my arm. 'I want you to lie back on the bed please.' As I do so he takes the blanket that is draped across the end of the bed and lays it over my legs and waist. Without being asked, I reach underneath the blanket and pull my soft cotton dress up above my waist. Anatra then pulls the blanket down far enough to reveal my bump. The skin is tight and hard, and he places his stethoscope back in his ears and breathes on the end of it before planting it on my side. I still feel its coldness and twitch slightly in response. '*Scusa*,' he says.'

As he moves the instrument around he speaks. 'I want you to think about something Maria.' I remain silent. 'I do not know the life you have in England. I can only be guessing. But I do know the life you can have here.' He stops and looks up at me. He opens his mouth to speak and hesitates. 'This is not the time to discuss. May I speak with you this evening?' I nod, and Anatra continues in silence. Once he has finished his examination he stands and places the tools of his profession neatly and methodically in his bag. 'I can tell you that all seems well enough.' Again, he hesitates.

'What is it Anatra?'

'It is probably not a thing.' He looks to one side and his face creases in concern again. 'The heartbeats are regular. But I am not sure.'

'Not sure about what?'

'With two heartbeats to listen to it can be difficult. But I would like for us to go to the hospital tomorrow.'

I feel my tension returning. 'What for?' I ask. 'Is there something wrong?'

'I think not,' he replies. 'But I wish to be *certo*. I would like to be sure.'

'Please tell me something Anatra, at the very least.'

'*Scusa*. I would say that...one of the heartbeats is a little fainter; but that could be perfectly a normal thing. And I am being overly *prudente*. How you say?'

'Cautious?'

'*Si*, Cautious. But in the meantime, I would ask that you rest. Are you happy to do so?'

'Yes; I am a little tired anyway.' I pull my dress down and remove the blanket.

Kevin Carey

Sleep doesn't come. I lay on the bed with my eyes closed and the french doors open. There are so many things to think about, one of them being that there could be something wrong with the twins. Anatra had said it was probably nothing. but still the thought bothers me. And he wants to talk with me tonight. I can guess what he wants to say; and I have no answer. How can I? Not only is there too much going on, but it's too soon, much too soon, to make any kind of decision, and I haven't given any time to thinking about how I feel about anything.

There's a soft tap on the door, and I open my eyes. The light is fading already, and I wonder if I have in fact slept and the afternoon has slipped away. I try to rise but the weight of my mound stops me. The door taps again, only slightly more loudly this time, and I wonder if Anatra has come to wake me. 'Come in.' I call, unable to move quickly enough. I try rolling sideways to get a grip on the side of the bed.

The door opens slightly, and Katherine slides her head around the side. 'Hello sis. I just thought I'd see how you're doing.'

'I'll be fine.' I reply. 'Just as soon as I can get off this bed.' Katherine comes in to the room and walks quickly to the bed.

'Let me give you a hand.' She stands in front of me, slides her arm under mine and pulls backwards as I push myself up. With the momentum, I almost come off the bed.

'Whoa there sis.' Katherine says, and she laughs. 'I think that you're stronger than you know. It must be all that hive lifting you do back home.'

'Hive lifting?'

'What, is there a technical name for it?'

'Yes, hive lifting.'

'Well, there you go.' She sits next to me on the bed, and we just sit, shoulders touching, looking down at the floor, for several minutes. 'Will you just look at us two,' she says finally. 'Who would have thought it eh?'

'Yes; who would have? I should have stayed in college with you I think.'

'You see; I told you. If you'd stuck with me then it would have been fine.'

'Well you haven't done so well yourself. Have you?'

'Don't suppose I have really.' She puts her arm around me. 'Well we're stuck with each other now aren't we.'

'I suppose we are. What do you propose we do?'

'That's what I've come to talk to you about. She stands and begins to pace the room. She sounds more like the Katherine I know and love. 'I had a chat with Anatra this afternoon; about us; about me and you.'

'And what did he say?'

'I'll come to that. First I just want to say thanks.'

'For what?' I ask.

218

'You know; for everything. If it wasn't for you...'

'Now don't start that.' I interrupt. 'I'm having trouble holding it together as it is.'

'Yes, you're right.' She stops pacing, turns to face me, and clasps her hands together. 'Okay, how about this? I'm grateful.'

'That'll do.'

'Okay, we'll settle for that.' She starts pacing again, keeping her hands clasped. 'Now, let's look at the facts.' She stops again. 'You okay looking at the facts?'

'No.'

'Oh.'

'But we don't have much choice, do we.'

'Not really.'

'So how about you tell it like it is and I just listen?'

'Sounds like a plan.' She begins pacing again.

'But be kind Katie.'

Yes.' She paces back and forth quietly for some minutes. 'Okay.' She says, stopping once more. 'These are the facts. I can go home, and you can't. well not yet anyway.'

'But you heard the family Katie, it's not safe.'

'Yes, I was coming to that. So now will you let me speak?'

'Sorry. Yes, please carry on.'

'Okay. Now those may be the facts but, as you rightly said,' She purses her lips and shakes her head. 'It's not safe. We don't know how safe or unsafe it is, but I suppose we must assume that it's not safe. Or do we?'

'Yes, we do.' I say impatiently.

'Right. Then let's assume that. But what if I were to take someone with me?'

'Where are you going with this Katie?'

'Okay, just hear me out.' She wanders over to the french doors and I struggle to turn on the bed to see her. 'Nicolo has offered to come with me.'

'What?'

'Nicolo has offered...'

'I heard you Katie. Are you mad?'

'Give me one good reason why that's not a good idea.'

'Okay. Well first of all the family, especially Edoardo, who would never agree to it. Secondly, you have no right to put him in any danger; and last but not least of all, he's just a boy.'

'He's older than me.'

'I seriously doubt it. Alright Katie; let's suppose you overcome all those objections. Why do you want to go home? And where would you go?

'I miss home Mary. I don't want to stay here, and.... I'm scared.' She catches a sob and holds her hand to her mouth. 'I'm scared Mary.'

'Oh Katie.' I climb off the bed and make my way over to her. 'I didn't mean to be so hard on you,' I say, putting my arms around her. 'I'm scared too. But this is the best, the safest place to be. Can you think of a better family to look after us?'

'No.'

'Neither can I, and I miss home; I miss my bees, and believe it or not, I miss the weather.' She laughs as light tears trickle down her face. 'I know you have a choice Katie, and if you decide to go home, I won't stop you. But please think it through carefully. And please, please don't do anything to hurt the family. They have already been so gracious to us, and they have never judged us.'

'That's true.'

'And Meadowsweet is still your home, so I'll give you the keys; but Katie.' I put my hands on her shoulders and hold her out. 'If he is still looking for you, and I don't doubt that he is. Then he will find you.'

'We're never going to be safe, are we.'

'I don't believe that; and neither must you.'

'But we can't stay here forever.'

'We can for now; and that's what matters. Now how about we go and find some good old English tea to cheer us up?'

'I'm pretty sure they don't have any of that here.'

I pull the french doors closed as the air is beginning to cool. 'And I'm pretty sure I know where to find some.'

∞ ∞ ∞

The light outside has all but gone when Anatra finds us laughing in the kitchen, sitting at the table surrounded by the soft glow of several candles. 'What are you two so happy about?' He asks.

'Just talking over old times,' I reply.

'You are hardly old enough to have old times.'

'Why Anatra.' Katherine says, winking at me. 'I do believe that you, how do you say in Italian? That you *flirtare* with my friend.'

'And I do believe Katerina that Nicolo has been teaching you all of the wrong Italian words.' We both laugh and look at each other as if sharing a secret. 'Are you sure that it is just tea that you have been drinking and not my brother's vino? That would not be good for the *bambini*.'

'How could you accuse us of such a thing?' I ask in mock indignation.

'You are right. *Mi dispiace.*'

'Oh Anatra, don't be so serious.' Katie says. 'We were just trying to lighten the mood.'

'And that is a good thing.' He walks over to the table. 'That is why I must apologise again for making your mood heavy.'

We sit up. 'What is the matter?' I ask. 'What has happened.'

He holds out an envelope toward Katherine.

'What's that?' she asks.

'It is a letter, from Von Treffen,' he replies, and I put my hand over my mouth, as Katherine sits paralyzed. 'It has not been opened.'

'When did it come?' I ask.

'Within the last ten minutes or so.'

'Who delivered it?' Katherine stands quickly, ignoring the envelope, and walks over to the window, but all she sees is her own reflection. 'Was it him? Did he come to the house?'

Anatra goes to her and takes her shoulders. 'Please, sit down and I will tell you.'

She shakes him off. 'Just tell me, was it him?'

'No, it was not Von Treffen.' He holds out his hand toward the table. 'Please.'

She walks back unsteadily to the table and Anatra follows her. When we are all sitting, he continues. 'The letter was delivered by his men. There were two of them. The boys stopped them approaching the house, but they were not happy. They said that their instructions were to deliver the letter into your hands and to no one else.'

'So what happened?' I ask.

'The boys would not let them pass, and so one of them pulled a gun.'

'Oh my God,' I say. I can see that Katherine is beginning to shake.

'It is okay. Fortunately, Edoardo had seen them, and he came out of the house with his shotgun. They were not too keen on that, and so they left the letter with the boys and told them to pass it on to you.'

'I am sorry sweet one.' He speaks directly to Katherine. 'But this means that he knows where you are.'

'I suppose that was inevitable really,' I say. 'He only had to put two and two together.'

'Si, you are right, but we thought that it would take him a while longer.' He turns to look at Katherine. 'I would not normally ask this of a *signorina*, but it is important that you read the letter soon. And I must also ask that you tell us what the letter speaks of.'

'I...I'm not sure.' She turns to me. 'What do you think?'

'It could be important Katie. People's lives are involved.'

'Yes. Yes, you're right.' She turns back to Anatra. 'Can you give me a while?'

'Of course, sweet one.' Anatra replies. This is obviously a shock. My brother is busy making calls right now. I will go and help him and return in say, thirty minutes?'

I stand. 'Yes. That will be fine. I'll look after her.' I walk to the kitchen door and speak to Anatra quietly. 'This is serious, isn't it?'

'*Si*,' he replies, equally as quiet, and he watches Katherine turning the envelope around in her hands as he speaks. 'The people that my brother is contacting; they will be coming here tonight. You will see many men. Most of them are not men that I like, but they are *necesarrio. Capisci?*'

'I understand.'

He takes my hand. 'Maria. I had a great wish that I would speak with you tonight.'

'Yes, I know you did.'

'That must wait. Will you wait?'

I'm not entirely sure what he means, but I replied anyway. 'Yes Anatra, I will wait.' He smiles, and the part of my heart that he has taken misses a beat; and he touches my cheek with the side of his hand so softly that I barely feel it, and then he kisses me just as softly on the same spot; then he leaves.

∞ ∞ ∞

My darling Katherine

How can you ever forgive me for not being there when they took you?

I am sure that you must be quite distressed, being held captive as you are, But I wish you to know how much I care for you and for our child. They will try to tell you that you were held a prisoner by me, but that is not true. Sadly, because of my name and my wealth, there are those who would wish great harm on me, and they will use the things I care about to get to me. and that is why I needed to protect you, and my child.

Please be assured that I will always know where you are. Always. There is no place on earth that they can hide you. You can draw great comfort from the fact that I will be able to find you and my son. Yes, I am sure that you have my son growing inside you. And if it is a daughter, then she will be a good and obedient sister to the son that we will have.

Can you imagine what a joy it will be when he is born. That day is not too far away my darling. We will call him Bernhard, which means strong. It was my Father's name. He was a great man. A strong man. I want you to be strong.

Be strong. I am coming for you.

Alexander

Anatra folds the letter and gives it back to Katherine. Everyone sits without speaking for some time. Edoardo and Gaia have joined us in the kitchen and Gaia is the first to speak. 'As a young girl, my Mother would always say to me, 'beware of the wolf offering you a sheepskin coat'.' She turns to Edoardo. 'And so, I married a lion instead.' She wraps her arm through his and smiles.

'How are you feeling Katerina?' Anatra asks. Katherine opens the letter and silently reads it through once again, her eyes red from crying.

Gaia rises and goes to the stove. 'I will make coffee. It is going to be a long night.'

Katherine remains silent.

'Can we speak to the police? I ask.

'Can you see anything in the letter that they will take notice of?' Edoardo replies. 'It is more likely that they will take an interest in us; and they may go as far as removing Katerina from our care.'

I take her hand, and Gaia wanders back to the table and places her hands-on Katherine's shoulders. 'We will not let that happen.' She turns to Edoardo. 'Are the men here?'

'They arrived an hour ago,' Edoardo replies. 'They are guarding the gate already.'

'Someone should tell them what time the postman arrives. I do not want the poor man to die of fright. He has a bad heart already.'

'The fool should have retired years ago,' Edoardo says.

'And you only wish that so that he can spend more time playing backgammon with you,' Gaia says.

'What should I do?' Katherine asks.

Gaia returns to the stove as the kettle begins to whistle.

'We are happy for you to stay here if you wish,' Anatra says.

'I mean, should I go back to him? It would be easier, for everyone.'

I open my mouth to speak but Anatra raises his hand to silence me.

'Is that what you want Katerina?' he asks. 'For we will be happy to do what you wish.' Anatra can see the look of concern on my face, and he raises his finger slightly as an indication to be patient.

Katherine is quiet for several minutes, her face creased in concentration. Gaia brings fresh cups to the table but says nothing. Edoardo speaks. 'I will go and check on the men. Gaia, would you make more coffees for the men? I will send one of them in to take it.

'*Si amore mio.*' She replies and returns to the stove.

'Katerina.' Anatra says quietly. 'What do you wish to do?'

I sit waiting anxiously for her reply. How can Anatra put that responsibility into Katherine's hands. What if she says that she wants to go back to him? Surely, they can't let that happen. I look up and see that Anatra is watching me instead of Katherine. He stares deep into me; and I realise that he is trying to reassure me. To tell me that everything is okay. That this is the right thing to do. And when I think about it, then it becomes obvious that Katherine has to decide for herself. She mustn't feel trapped between one set of captors or another. She has to feel free. Free to make her own decisions, her own choices. I smile back at Anatra to show that I understand.

'I want to stay here.' Katherine says eventually, and she looks up at Anatra. 'Can I stay here?'

Gaia moves quickly from the stove and, bending over Katherine, she puts her arms around her. 'My sweet Katerina. This is your home for as long as you wish it.'

Katherine holds on to Gaia's arm and lowers her head. 'I'm so tired. Do you mind if I go to bed?'

'I will take you up.' Gaia says. 'Maria, would you mind making the coffee?

'Yes, I don't think I could sleep anyway.' I reply.

'I will help you.' Anatra says, and as he stands, the others follow. I hug Katherine, and Gaia walks her out of the kitchen.

The kettle whistles once again. I have to stand sideways onto the kitchen worktop as I lift it from the stove, while Anatra prepares the coffee. 'You were right to do what you did. Thank you,' I say. 'You're a doctor in so many ways.'

'I am Anatra.' He says, and smiles.

I laugh. 'Oh yes, I had forgotten. Well I think it's a great compliment. You are so much more than just a doctor.'

'You are very kind Maria. I am reminded of my days in the *Scuola di medicina*. My *professore* was keen to impress upon me the meaning of being a doctor. He taught me that the true origin of the word doctor was from the Medieval Latin, meaning advisor or scholar. And I learned from him that my calling was not just to heal, but to teach; and to help others to learn how to heal themselves.

'Well I am grateful to him and to you, my young Cesare.'

The kitchen door opens and a huge man wearing a long black coat and a fedora walks in. His chin seems larger than his face and his nose is equally large but almost flat against his face. He appears to have a natural scowl that almost hides his dark eyes under his brow. Under any other circumstances, I would have been terrified of such a sight, but this night is different. I somehow draw comfort from his presence. He says something to Anatra in Italian far too quickly for me to understand, and Anatra replies in like manner, pointing to me as he does so. The man gives me a beaming smile that softens his features into an almost lovable cartoon character. He holds out his hand. 'I am pleased to...' he turns to Anatra for help.

'Meet you.' Anatra says.

'I am pleased...to meet you Maria.' He says something else to me in Italian, then takes my hand, which seems like a child's in his grasp, and kisses it gently. '*Sono incantato dalla tua belleza.*'

'Hey.' Anatra says to him as he thumps his arm. '*Lei è la mia belleza.*'

I feel my heart melt a little as I understand enough Italian to know that they are arguing over whose '*belleza*', whose beauty I am.

'Hey.' I interrupt them. '*Io sono la mia belleza.* I am my beauty.' They look at me and then at each other and laugh; and I'm sure that the room vibrates with the big man's deep and heavy rumbles. He takes the tray and makes his way out of the kitchen, bending his head to clear the doorway; still rumbling as he goes, and it's quiet again. I take a cup of the coffee and wander back over to the table, and as I sit I say to Anatra. 'This must all be costing the family a great deal. How can we ever repay you?'

'There is no cost,' he replies. 'We are all family in one way or another. And we are Italian; so, there is good wine and good food; and that is enough.'

I feel the twins move; but this time it's soft and pleasant. Can they feel my mood? In spite of all that is happening around me, I feel safe. There were other times in my life when terrible things had happened, and it was often during those moments that we had a chance to make good things happen. I stay in the kitchen with Anatra most of the night, and we talk until the early hours.

Chapter 56

The black bees began to fly in a circle around me. were they trying to hurt me or protect me. I wasn't sure. They flew faster and faster, until they looked as if they were one bee.

Jemima came quickly into Mummy's room sounding slightly out of breath and looking flustered. 'A car has just pulled up in the drive; I think he's here.'

I turned to look at Mummy and was met with a quizzical look. 'Who's here?'

'Jake is here Mummy. Would you like to come down stairs?' I replied.

She placed her hand on the teapot. 'No, I think that I will just sit here thank you.'

I stood up and placed my hands together. 'Okay, call if you need us. Let's go Jem.' I said boldly. I took her hand and walked out of the bedroom along the hall and down the stairs. Just as I reached the bottom step the front door opened, and I stopped abruptly. Jemima bumped into me.

I felt my stomach churn as Jemima's daughter, Katie came into the hall. She was tall, and she had vivid blue eyes that looked deep into you, and I thought about Mummy's description of Von Treffen in the diary.

'What are you doing here?' Jemima asked.

Katie looked first at me and then at her mother. I couldn't tell whether she was pleased to see me or not.

'Well that's a great way to greet your only daughter. I haven't been home for several months and all I get....'

'It's just that you never let me know, and....'

'Dad's coming; yes, I know.'

'You know. How?' Jemima asked.

Katie looked at me and smiled; but it was a polite smile you give to a stranger; which I suppose I was. I hadn't seen her since she was a child after all.

'Aunt Constance,' she said, as the smile evaporated.

Why did that greeting make me feel old? 'Hello Katie. It's good to see you. it's been a long time.'

'Why are you here?' she asked abruptly, looking directly at me.

'Katie!' Jemima replied, and I put my hand on my sister's arm.

'I came to see your nan, as she has....'

'Nonna,' she interrupted.

'My mother,' I replied. 'As she has been rather poorly.'

'Well, if that's what it takes,' She said.

Jemima stepped forward. 'Katie, I've told you before; if you're going to be rude....'

'Is dad here yet?' she asked, and walked past Jemima and into the kitchen.

Jemima and I followed her. 'How do you know about that?' Jemima asked again.

'We talk.'

'You talk? I thought you had nothing to do with him.'

'What gave you that impression? He's my father, isn't he?' Katie stopped at the kitchen table and turned to face us. 'He is, isn't he?'

'What does that mean?' Jemima began to shake.

'Ask aunt Constance. I'm sure she remembers what you did. How do I know whether that was a one off?'

Jemima stumbled slightly and grabbed hold of a kitchen chair. I stepped forward and put my arm around her. 'That was a long time ago Katie. We are sisters, and that's all that matters.' She looked at each one of us in turn, and it felt as if we were holding our breath for her next decision on what to say. 'Why are you here Katie?' I asked.

She walked over to the kitchen worktop and picked up one of the tins, and she opened it and pulled out a biscuit. She turned and leant against the worktop before taking a bite from the biscuit. 'I live here; Constance.' She said with a mouth still full of biscuit. 'Where do you live?'

I thought about my first ever meeting with Lucinda. I had decided at that first moment that I would never ever work for her. She had completely demolished me; she had eaten me for breakfast, as the saying goes. I'm sure I even cried afterwards. But in less than an hour she had called me and had asked me to come back and see her immediately. Every instinct had told me to say then that I wasn't interested; that there wasn't a chance that I would want to spend every day of my life being insulted by that woman. But I was curious; and that curiosity had led me to spend several years doing just that. And I stood here now questioning why. What had made me decide to ignore my instincts then, and every day that had followed; and get up and spend almost every day in her company? The challenge. And that was it. I wanted to be challenged; to feel that I was alive; to know that I meant enough to someone, that they would want to challenge me.

'Do you like our bees Katie.' I said in reply to her question.

She frowned, and her smooth features distorted into an ugly caricature of well-practiced lines. 'What does that mean?'

'Have you ever been out to the bees?'

'No. why would I want to do that?'

'You mean to say that you haven't told them that you live here?'

'Well that's just stupid.'

'Did you know that Meadowsweet was built for the bees.'

Katie looked at her mother.

'Yes, it was Katie.' Jemima said. 'Your Great Great Grandfather built the house for them.'

'So, you see Katie,' I continued, 'we are only tenants; lodgers if you like. It's written in my grandfather's will that whoever lives in the house must let the bees know; and they have to look after them.'

Her eyes dropped to the floor. 'I can't see that being legal,' she replied.

'Should it matter Katie. Wouldn't you want to honour the memory of your Great Great Grandfather?'

There was the sound of a car pulling up outside the window. Katie went to the window, and I saw a look of relief on her face. 'Dad's here.'

$$\infty \quad \infty \quad \infty$$

Jemima and I went into the hall, and I watched as Jake walked into the hall. He turned his head back to face the door. 'Come on in,' he said to someone on the porch, 'I'll show you around.' Beyond that I could see a large red sports car in the drive.

'Don't you think you should knock first,' a woman's voice answered back.

'My kids live here,' he said in reply.

I stood in front of Jemima, and so I walked along the hall to meet him. 'Jake.'

His head whirled around. He stared at me with no expression on his face, and I looked back into familiar eyes; they still had that deep blue colour that drew you in effortlessly. His hair was shorter, and he had splashes of grey around his temples. He smiled, and I had that familiar tingle that would leave you defenceless. I tried to focus. The silence seemed to go on forever, and he looked me up and down in that familiar way, and then he spoke.

'Connie. Wow, you look amazing.'

I could feel the heat building in my face.

'Hello Jake,' I replied, as Jemima came up behind me.

His eyes moved quickly to her and then back to me. 'Hello Jem. How are you?' he asked.

I felt Jemima draw in breath to reply but he continued before she could speak. 'How long has it been Connie?'

I stayed silent, and a soft cough came from behind him. He stepped sideways. 'Oh sorry,' he said. 'This is Lydia.'

A slim and attractive girl stepped forward nervously. She looked about twenty. 'Still like them young?' I asked, and Jemima nudged me in the back.

'What?' he said. 'Oh no, this is my daughter; Lydia's my daughter.'

I could see her blushing, and I felt sorry for her. I stepped forward and held out my hand. 'Hello Lydia,' I smiled. 'Welcome to Meadowsweet.'

'Thank you,' she replied, with the sweetest, most angelic voice I had ever heard. She took my hand and gripped it gently. Her touch was soft and cool.

My mind was working overtime. If Lydia was Jake's daughter....

'How old are you Lydia?' I asked.

'I'm nineteen,' she replied. Her eyes were large and round, not a bit like Jake's; but they had that same ability to pull you in with one look.

I turned to look at Jake, still smiling, and still trying to work things out.

'Where's your wife Jake?' I asked.

He put his hand up to his mouth and coughed lightly. 'We never err.... married. I'm just spending some quality time with Lydia.'

The look on Lydia's face told me that she didn't feel the same.

'The old place hasn't changed a bit,' Jake said, to change the subject.

'We have decorated since you ran out on me,' Jemima replied.

Jake stepped forward, ignoring Jem's comment. 'I thought I'd show Lydia around the place; you know, see where the rest of her family lives.'

'Jake,' Lydia replied. 'I really don't think....'

'Nonsense, you'll love it,' he interrupted, taking her arm.

So, if Lydia was calling him Jake, they obviously weren't that close.

'Let's go into the kitchen,' I said quickly, stepping into his path. 'And we can.... talk.' I saw the look of relief on Lydia's face and she smiled warmly at me.

I took her hand again and walked into the kitchen. I watched as her eyes explored the room. She saw Katie, who looked dispassionately at her. Lydia looked back at the old oak table and ran her hand along the side. I remembered Mummy's description of the kitchen in the diaries.

'My Great Grandfather made that table Lydia; when he built the house. It's made from the trees in the meadow.' I imagined him standing here now, watching over us, and I began to feel stronger.

'Oh wow; that's so cool. He was obviously very clever.'

I began to warm to her. She spoke with her eyes; but unlike Jake, you could see what she was thinking.

'Hello Katie,' Jake said with almost no emotion. He either presumed that she would be here, or he had planned for the event.

I walked over to the Aga and picked up the kettle; it had already been filled, so I placed it over the hot plate. I turned to find Jake and Jemima standing awkwardly next to each other.

I held out my hands. 'So, why don't you all sit down and....'

'Why are you here Jake?' Jemima suddenly asked.

Jake walked around to the other side of the table and sat down. He still had that smile on his face. Lydia sat at the end of the table, away from Jake. It was obvious she didn't want to get in the middle of this. Katie took another biscuit from the tin.

Jemima sat opposite him; she repeated her question. 'So, tell me why you are here.'

'Just looking out for my kids Jem,' he replied.

'You mean the kids that you have never paid a penny to since they were born.'

'Well, things have changed. I've changed.'

I took several cups out of the cabinet and placed them on a tray. 'Does everyone want tea?' I asked.

'Coffee, black please.' Jake replied without taking his eyes off Jemima.

Jemima didn't reply.

'Lydia?' I asked.

'Oh, er tea please; if that's okay,' she replied.

I looked at Katie, who just shook her head.

I opened the cabinet and reached for the cafetiere I had bought in Windsor, but grabbed the instant coffee instead. That would be good enough for Jake. I carried the tray to the table and placed it in the middle; then sat down next to Jem.

'So, Lydia, where do you live?'

She opened her mouth to speak, but Jemima got there first. 'What do you want Jake?'

'It's been a long time Jem; can't we put the past behind us?'

'That depends,' she replied.

'On what?'

'On what you want.'

I poured the teas, unsure whether to join in the discussion or just let Jem run with it. I decided on the latter.

He smiled. 'I don't expect you to trust me.'

'Good. At least we know where we stand.'

'Jake; why don't just tell us the purpose for your visit,' I interrupted, ignoring my decision, 'then we can talk.'

'I'm only here for the twins Connie.'

'Perhaps you could elaborate.' I said looking up at Katie, who was munching on a biscuit.

'Alright, I'll get to the point.' He leant forward and placed his elbows on the table. 'I know that Mary is ill.'

'How do you know that?' Jemima asked.

'Michael told me.'

'You've seen Michael? When was this?'

'We keep in touch.'

Jemima looked at me. 'Why didn't he say?'

'I don't know Jem,' I replied. 'He must have had his reasons.'

'It seems that both my children have been keeping things from me,' she said looking over to Katie. 'What has Mummy being ill got to do with anything?' she asked.

'Well, should anything happen to her, not that I would wish that, but if anything should; then the tax implications for the family would be devastating. That would mean that Michael and Katie's inheritance would be wiped out.'

'And you don't think that you can trust us enough to take care of that,' Jemima replied.

'I'm just offering to help, that's all.'

'So.... what if it is a problem? What are you suggesting?' Jemima said.

Chapter 57

Diary; June 29th 1970

I wake to the sound of soft singing, and realise that I have fallen asleep at the table with my head in my arms. I feel the stiffness in my muscles as I sit up slowly.

'Good morning Maria.' Gaia says brightly. 'I am trusting that you slept well.' Edoardo, who is at her side laughs, and he places a hot cup of coffee in front of me.

'Where is Anatra?' I ask.

'He left here a short while ago. He has many calls to make.' Gaia says.

'But he hasn't had any sleep. He'll be exhausted.'

'Oh, he is used to such hours. It is his work Maria,' she replies. 'He said to tell you that he would be back this afternoon to take you to the hospital.'

I had forgotten all about that. I can feel the twins stretching; they're waking up. 'How is Katherine?' I ask.

'She is still sleeping. I sat with her most of the night. We will be preparing breakfast soon Maria. Why don't you go and sit on the veranda? The sun is shining, and that will be good for you and the bambini.'

The veranda is quiet, apart from two of Edoardo's men sitting at the far end of the table talking. I put coffee down and sit at the table, and they both raise their glasses. '*Buongiorno Maria, mia belleza.*'

I'm surprised that they know my name; it sounds as if the big man has told all of his companions about me. '*Buongiorno,*' I reply.

I soak in the early morning sun as it warms my face and arms. It's probably a cool autumn day back home, and I am glad to be here. Here is all I have at the moment. I'm struck by the realisation that I've never been able to have a clear direction about my future. Marrying David should have given that to me, but the truth is, it had made my life even more uncertain. Some things are immutable; set in stone. Such as the fact that I will have two babies; and very soon now. And that that will also be the lot of my friend. What follows though, is as clear a mud. Not only can

I see no way forward, but I'm beginning to slip into the same mind set I had when Mummy had died. I didn't want to think about it then, and I remember the word I had used back then to describe my situation; disinclined. But at least this time I'm not alone. I sit back and lift my head to take in the warmth. The twins move, and I let out a small gasp. The men stop talking and look across in concern.

'*Stai bene?*' one of them asks.

'*Si,*' I reply. '*Mi bambini.*'

'*Bambini?*' he asks again, sounding surprised. '*Si hanno due?*'

'Yes, I have two, *Si due.*'

'*Ah, complimenti.*' He holds up his glass again, along with his companion, who also shouts down the table.

'*Complimenti Signora.*'

'*Grazie.*' I reply as the girls move again, hoping that this won't last much longer.

I don't see Katherine for the rest of the morning. Anatra arrives back early and comes directly to see me. 'Maria. Are you able to leave soon?' he asks. When you are ready I will take you to the hospital. Is that okay?' I'm not expecting to leave before lunch and his apparent urgency unsettles me. He must notice my concern for he adds. 'It is my work. I am to help in an operation this evening, and so I must be ready.' I relax in the knowledge that it's something else, or someone else that he's concerned about. 'I will have Mama prepare something for us to eat on the way.'

I haven't left the villa in some time and look forward to the thought of a few hours of freedom, although I can hardly call spending time being prodded and examined, freedom.

We leave half an hour later, but not before I check in on Katherine, only to find that she's still sleeping. The strain of the situation is taking its toll on her, and I can't help but feel concerned. The journey is quiet, as I'm lost in my thoughts; trying to find answers; but whatever roads I go down, they all end nowhere. I notice Anatra frequently looking in the rear-view mirror; and it's only when we arrive at the hospital that I realise that we have been followed by another car from the villa. It parks behind us and two men I don't recognize get out of the car, but they don't follow us in.

Anatra takes me straight to the maternity ward, where he speaks at length to the sister in charge. She looks across to me and smiles reassuringly. When he has finished, he comes over. 'You will find that many of the nurses and doctors here speak English quite well. But I will be here when you need me, so it will not be a problem.' I spend the rest of the afternoon being checked and prodded, albeit with great care. When we leave, I feel reassured that I'm going to be well cared for during my stay.

Anatra waits until we are travelling back home before he talks to me about the results. 'The *bambini* seem to be quite healthy Maria.'

'Well that's good news, isn't it?' I lean forward so that I can see into the wing mirror. The car that had followed us to the hospital is behind us.

'*Si.*' He replies. 'But the tests confirmed what I had said to you before. The heartbeat of one of the *bambini* is er.... *Un po' irregolare*; not regular. That may not be a problem, but it is something that we will need to look at; mostly when the *bambini* are born.'

'Were you able to tell whether they were boys or girls?' I ask.

Anatra smiles. 'Maria. Both you and I know that you are *convinto* that they are girls. You tell me yourself that your *api*, your bees let you know.'

'Yes, I know.' I reply. 'But I didn't think that you believed in that kind of thing.'

'Why? Because my Father keeps his bees to him? What makes you think that I do not go to see them?'

'I just presumed....'

'Si; and I know the times when he is not there, and when I can I visit.'

'He doesn't know?'

'In truth, I think that he does. But it is a kind of game we play. I have even been into his hut.' I look at him with wide eyes. '*è una sorpresa per te?*' he asks. 'She was my mother too.'

It does surprise me. It had never occurred to me to think of Cesare's loss as belonging to anyone else. But Anatra is right; when Annalise died, it would have echoed through the whole family. 'There is something else I say of the *bambini*,' he continues. 'You must know that we discuss the possibility of you staying at the hospital.'

I'm surprised by that. 'What made your mind up?' I ask.

He pauses as we swing into the drive and stops in front of two men who check who is in the car before they allow us to continue. 'The fact that we are not too far from the hospital, and that you are surrounded by many people at the villa; so we are to expect that you will get more *attenzione* here.' He brings the car to a halt, switches off the engine and turns to face me. 'But that can change if at any time, I feel that you must go. *Capisci?*'

I warm to his concern and take comfort from his control. '*Capisco* Anatra.'

Chapter 58

I had dreamt this. The bees were lifting me, carrying me away to safety. There was a storm all around me, but I felt warm and safe. We flew higher and higher, until I could see both Meadowsweet and the Rossi villa. Where should I go?

I looked across at Lydia. She smiled softly. I could see that she didn't want to be here.

Jake picked up his coffee and took a sip. He jerked his head back as the hot liquid touched his lips, but he kept hold of the cup. 'It seems obvious to me that there are a lot of advantages in letting the twins have their inheritance now.' He took another sip of the coffee.

We all sat in silence for what seemed like an eternity. My eyes went to Katie, who was looking out of the window with apparent indifference. So that's why she was here.

'I spoke first. 'What inheritance is this Jake?'

'Well, once Mary.... you know, leaves this mortal realm and all that; once that happens; it's just you and Jem. And if anything should happen to you then....' His voice trailed off.

Again, there was silence.

'Let me get this straight Jake.' Jemima said. 'On the basis of Mummy dying, then me popping my clogs, you think that Michael and Katie should have money now.'

'It makes sense. That is, if you understood the tax laws it would make sense.' He took a larger gulp of the coffee. 'I'm just asking you to trust me.'

Jemima let out a laugh. 'So, you think that there's a pot of gold waiting to be dished out each time one of us, what was it you said? Leaves this mortal realm.'

'Of course not Jem, of course not. But assets; that's a difficult area. Assets.'

'You mean Meadowsweet,' I said.

'Well, yes that would count,' Jake said.

'That's the only asset we have Jake,' Jem added.

'Right, well there you have it; Meadowsweet could be taken out from under you.'

'What should we do then?' I asked.

'Why don't you offload some of Meadowsweet onto one of the twins now? That way it would reduce the impact.'

'And that's the only solution?' I asked.

'I don't see that you have much choice.' He finished the last of his coffee.

'Some of Meadowsweet? What part exactly?' I continued.

'Well, I had a look at that, and the only viable option is the meadow.'

'The meadow.' I looked across at Katie again. She was doing her best to avoid our gaze.

'Yes; as I said, I've looked at that and it would considerably reduce your liability.' He pulled out some folded papers from his jacket and laid them out on the table. The top page consisted of an ordnance survey map of the house and surrounding land. Meadowsweet had been outlined in blue, and a smaller outline of red followed the boundaries of the meadow.

At the bottom of the page was a provision for some signatures.

'I had my solicitor look into this, and he's drawn up the necessary papers to make it as simple as possible.'

'So, we just put our signatures at the bottom of the page there?' I asked.

'Yes,' he said enthusiastically. He placed a pen on top of the papers and slid them across the table toward me.

I picked up the pen and placed it on the paper, as if to sign it.

'What are you doing?' Jemima said loudly, a look of concern spreading over her face.

'You don't think we should sign it then?' I replied.

'No, I don't; he just wants it for himself.'

I sat with the pen in my hand and looked at Jake. 'What do you think we should do Katie?' I asked, without taking my eyes off him.

'I think it makes sense,' was all she said.

'What do you think the bees would say Katie?'

'What's that got to do with anything?' Jake asked.

'Ask Katie,' I replied, still watching Jake. he looked across at his daughter.

'It's something to do with telling the bees,' she said with a shrug.

'Lydia, what do you think we should do?' I asked.

She quickly looked at Jake, who shook his head. Then she turned to me and smiled. 'I don't think you should sign it.'

I smiled back at her and placed the pen back down. I saw the look of disappointment on Jake's face. 'I won't sign Jem; for two reasons. The first being that I wouldn't want that cheating, lying scoundrel to get his hands on Meadowsweet. Secondly, the signatures would be worthless.'

'Why's that?' Jake asked, sounding as if he felt he still had an argument.

'Because Meadowsweet doesn't belong to us.'

He looked shocked. 'You mean to say that you haven't taken power of attorney on. That's madness, considering your mother's condition.'

'What condition is that?' a voice said from the hallway door. I looked across to see Mummy standing in the doorway. She wandered over to the table with her tray, and I stood and took it from her and placed it on the table. I remained standing. 'What condition is that Jake?' she repeated.

He sat, open mouthed, obviously not expecting to see her. 'I thought....'

'What did you think young man? That I was at death's door? I can tell you that the rumours of my passing have been greatly exaggerated.' I couldn't help but let out a small laugh. I looked across at Lydia and she was smiling broadly. Her nervousness seemed to have vanished, to be replaced by a bright-eyed enthusiasm for what might come next.

Mummy had also noticed her, and she walked around the table. 'And who is this delightful looking creature?' she asked, as she stopped next to Lydia's chair.

'That, Mummy, is Lydia; Jakes daughter,' Jemima said. 'And she is nineteen.'

Mummy took Lydia's hand and held it between hers. I could see her mind working. 'So, Jake was sowing this young lady whilst he was still living here. Hmmm.' She squeezed Lydia's hand. 'Well I am delighted to meet you Lydia; and I am sorry that you have had to endure this, well.... him, on your journey through life.'

'But I haven't,' Lydia replied. 'Had to endure him, I mean.' She smiled up at Mummy, who looked slightly disappointed. 'You see, I met him for the first time a week ago; he turned up out of the blue. He promised to take me out and show me the world. I had no idea he was coming here; just five miles down the road.'

'I see.' Mummy replied with renewed enthusiasm. 'Well I hope that you're not too disappointed with us.'

'Oh no; this is amazing.' Her eyes shone with excitement. 'Obviously, it's not the same for you guys; but Mummy is so going to enjoy hearing about this.' The look of dismay on Jake's face would have been worthy of a framed picture. 'And I am having the most amazing time. You're such lovely people.'

'Well, you are lovely too young lady,' Mummy replied. 'You are welcome to come here any time you like.' She looked across at Jake and her countenance dropped. 'Present company excepted.'

'I am just trying to help you people, and this is the thanks I get.' He grabbed the papers back and shoved them in his jacket pocket. Then he hesitated and took them out again. 'I'll leave them here for you to think about. In case you change your minds and see sense.' He stood up and looked across at Jemima. 'I'm just thinking about the twins you know. I know I haven't been there for them, but I'd like to make up for that.'

Jemima said nothing.

Jake looked at Lydia. 'We're leaving,' he said and walked into the hall, and I followed him to the front door. I could hear Mummy and Jemima talking to Lydia.

'Jake?' He turned to look at me. 'You've had three women in your life that I know of. Did you love any of them?' I asked.

He turned to face me. 'All of them Connie; all of them.'

'And there's your problem.'

He looked at me and creased his brow. 'Problem?'

'You should have loved just one.'

The creased brow remained, and I realised then that he didn't understand the concept. 'I'll be in the car,' he said, and closed the door behind him.

Chapter 59

Diary; July 20th 1970

The morning mist brings an unusual chill to the garden, and I sit slowly at the table on the veranda. I had grown used to sitting sideways to reach anything, and had become accustomed to the crowded table, as I had found that I enjoyed the sound of so many voices talking and laughing. They had all seemed unfazed by the situation, and I had decided to take my cue from the family. But I had risen early this morning; and for now, the table is quiet as I sit alone. Well, nearly alone. I exchange greetings with the now familiar faces of the two men sitting at the other end of the table, and I pick up the glass of orange juice that I had brought from the kitchen. The table had been laid for breakfast the night before, so I remove the flower from my plate and lay it to the side. Cesare would have left it there for me; my gardener. I haven't been to see him since the men had arrived. After my experience with the Meadowsweet bees I can't be sure how Cesare's bees might react to my changed situation.

Since Edoardo has organized our bodyguards into a rota, there doesn't appear to be so many of them. He has explained that those that are here will be staying for one week a month, so that there will always be at least half a dozen men at the villa at any one time. It has been almost a month since this had all started, but surely even Edoardo can't keep this up indefinitely. For the present time, he has refused to discuss any other options, but very soon things will change. I am one week off going full term, and Anatra is concerned that I haven't yet given birth. He has been monitoring me closely, daily in fact; and he is constantly discussing the option of taking me into the hospital, but has so far avoided doing so.

The twins move again, only this time they kick harder than they have before. I must have let out a tiny scream, for the men stop talking and turn in alarm. I can see them watching me as I try to get comfortable, and as I move sideways I feel a warm sensation down my legs. And then there is a tightness as my body responds. I push back in the chair in response and yell out. Both men jump out of their seats and instinctively reach for the weapons concealed in their jackets. This is not the kind of emergency that they have been trained for. 'Get Anatra,' I shout. They respond by gabbling something in Italian and waving their arms about. I take their gestures to mean that he is not at the house. 'Gaia,' I scream. 'Get Gaia, Gaia!'

'Si, Gaia, si.' They both shout, and the two of them run off like errant schoolboys into the house, all the time gabbling loudly.

I am alone at the table. A table that any other time would be filled with people and noise and laughter. I look around and absorb the unnerving silence that solitude brings, which at certain moments in life can be welcoming. But right now, I need Anatra and Gaia and Katherine and my mother, but most of all; I need my bees.

Gaia appears within a few minutes, and the two bodyguards also return, the looks of concern still etched on their faces. 'So, it is time Maria. Then we will begin our journey.' Gaia says. I look at her with a frown. 'Le tue acque sono rotte,' she responds with a beaming smile.

'Yes, yes, my waters are broken.' I reply with a smile.

I attempt to stand but Gaia places her hand on my shoulder. 'Dear sweet Maria. Wait a moment if you will. In this house, we do things the easy way.' Vittoria appears on the veranda holding a cup and saucer containing a hot drink. 'Please sit and enjoy this. Gaia takes the cup from her daughter and places it on the table in front of me. I tense as I feel a dull ache growing in my belly. It starts to pulse though my body, and as it travels to my back I arch in response and grab the sides of the chair. Feelings of panic race through me, and I look at Gaia for comfort, who smiles in understanding. 'Your body is practicing Maria; preparing for its final performance. Go with it my sweetness.'

As quickly as it comes, the feeling fades, and I am left feeling unfulfilled. How could one wish for such a feeling to return but dread it coming at the same time? 'What is the drink?' I ask.

'It is a mixture of mild herbs, suffused with lemon; il più piacevole; most pleasing.' Gaia put her hand gently on my bump. 'It is one that the twins will enjoy, and prescritta by Anatra. It will help relax you for the journey ahead.'

We all sit for a while; me, Gaia, Vittoria, and the two bodyguards; during which time Katherine joins us; followed eventually by every other member of the family. Even the rest of the men come to see how I am progressing. The next sensation takes about twenty minutes to return, and this time I try to follow Gaia's advice and attempt to ride the wave of tension. Shortly after the second contraction Anatra arrives. After checking my pulse and feeling the babies, he listens to them with his stethoscope; after which he arranges for me to be transferred to the car. I try to walk but Gaia calls two of the men over and they lift each side of my chair effortlessly and carry me to the waiting vehicle. One of the men is the flat-nosed giant I had first met in the kitchen, and I smile when he gives me a deep throated chuckle.

As they placed the chair down next to the car his companion holds out his hand. Flat-nose places his hand on the man's chest and pushes him aside, mumbling something quickly in Italian; and then he offers his hand to me. As I take it he moves his other hand under my arm and softly supports me as I rise out of the chair.

'*Grazie*,' I say to him and kiss him tenderly on the cheek. He grins widely, resuming his cartoon face as I ease sideways into the back seat of the car. Flat-nose closes the door and I wind the window down and looked out at a sea of faces. 'Grazie, grazie,' I say as I blow them all a kiss. Gaia walks around to the other side of the car and gets in the back with me, and Anatra climbs in the front along with Vittoria.

'Wait.' A voice cries just as Anatra starts the engine. 'Wait.' Katherine appears at the window and leans down to peer in. She smiles warmly, and I can see that she's crying. 'I love you sis.'

'I love you to Katie,' I reply.

'I wanted to come with you.'

'I know. But it's important that you're safe.'

'*Dobbiamo andare*; we have to go,' Anatra says.

Katherine pushes her head through the window and we hold each other. I can feel the sensation returning and Katherine releases me and steps back, blowing me a kiss as the car pulls away. I sink back into the seat and through the pain I can hear the cheering crowd receding, and as we accelerate out of the drive I let out a scream.

Chapter 60

I could feel the pain. Was it my pain? I was falling. Had the bees let go of me?

I walked back into the kitchen after waving goodbye to Lydia, hoping that we would see her again.

Jemima and Mummy were talking. 'I don't know dear,' Mummy said.

'What's up Jem?' I asked.

'I was just asking Mummy if I should set up a power of attorney. You know, just in case.'

'In case of what?' Mummy asked.

'Jem, maybe it's too soon after Jake coming here.' I say, as I look across at Katie, who is still in the kitchen.

'What if he's right? What if we were in danger of losing Meadowsweet? The situation could be right under our nose, and we don't even realise it.'

I couldn't believe what I was hearing. 'So, you think we should give the meadow away now?' I sat down opposite them.

'He seemed to know what he was talking about,' Jemima replied.

'That's just Jake. He's very good at that remember.'

'Yes, I know but....' Her voice trailed off, and we sat silently for a few minutes. 'Mummy, what do you think?' Jemima asked. She looked up at Jemima, very obviously lost in her own world again. 'Should we let the children have the meadow now?'

She looked at Jemima for several seconds before answering. 'You mean my meadow? My bees? Granny's bees, and your great Grandmother's bees?'

I felt her shock, and the very thought of losing the bees filled me with horror. I reached across and took Mummy's hand. 'It's okay Mummy, I won't let that happen.' Then I realised why Mummy had shared the diaries with me and not with Jemima. She had never loved them as Mummy did; as our Grandparents did. I knew how Katie felt; and probably Michael also. I hadn't even been sure how I felt about them, until now.

Mummy must have known that, because she turned to look at me and smiled, her face slowly relaxing. 'I know you won't,' she said. 'We need the bees as much as they need us.' She looked into the distance, her mind taking her off somewhere; and her hand went to her mouth. 'Cesare?' she said, and I knew that she was grabbing hold of one of the memories from the diaries.

'We may not have a choice,' Jemima said, lost in her own thoughts. 'Better for the land to go to family than to be sold off to strangers.'

'You don't know that Jem. Better we get a professional to come in and advise us on the implications. And besides, it's not just land, it's our past and our future.'

'That won't be necessary,' Mummy said, and we both turned to face her. 'My Grandfather set everything up to take care of all that.' Our puzzled looks caused her to continue. 'It's all with the bank. You just have to call them, and they will tell you all of the details.' She thought for a second, looking puzzled. 'Although I can't quite remember their name.'

'If that is the case,' I said, 'then we may not have to do anything.'

'But if it isn't the case?' Jemima asked.

Then we'll cross that bridge when we come to it. but we're not going to rush into anything.'

'Is it time for some tea yet?' Mummy asked with a beaming smile.

Chapter 61

Diary; July 23rd 1970

Gaia gently rocks the baby in her arms as she walks across the floor of the hospital room for the hundredth time. I sit up in the bed holding her sister, Constance, who is sleeping soundly, seemingly unaware of the commotion. I had known right away that that would be her name as soon as I had seen her; she is so much like my mother. Gaia's charge had been born ten minutes earlier than the sleeping beauty in my arms; but she is smaller than her sister, and she had only just ended several hours of crying. They look nothing alike. If this is an indication of things to come, then it will be easy to tell them apart just from the commotion she's making. I really don't know what to call her. My first thought is Katherine, but I think it will be Jemima, like my Grandmother. When I had first held her, I had felt a hint of sadness when I could see David's eyes attempting to open and look at me.

I can only describe their birth as the most traumatic experience of my life, second only to the death of my mother. I wish she could have been here now. It would have been lovely for her to be holding Jemima, but Gaia had been wonderful, staying with me right through the labour, and she had not left my side since then. There had been some concern when Jemima was first showing herself to the world. Anatra, along with the midwife, had been monitoring the babies, and they had noticed that she was becoming quite distressed. Anatra's fears regarding the irregular heartbeat had been confirmed, and it had become urgent to get her born as quickly as possible. They had taken her away as soon as she was born, leaving me somewhat concerned, but I had had to concentrate on bringing Constance into the world.

There are some messages from Katherine sending me congratulations, but she would want to be here, most likely as much as I also want her with me. I am worried that she might begin to feel a prisoner, and I need to speak to either Gaia or Anatra about it, as they might possibly be more understanding than Edoardo, who had been very firm about the whole situation. The room is quiet, as it often is when Gaia is holding Jemima. I wish I had her touch.

∞ ∞ ∞

When Anatra returns, I don't like the look in his eyes. His innocent face always shows how he's feeling. Mostly I love that about him, but this time it's disconcerting. 'I must talk with you Maria,' he says quietly.

'You look worried.' I reply.

He smiles then, but it's a smile to reassure, a smile of consolation.

'Should I be worried?' I ask. Anatra looks across to Gaia, and she takes Jemima into the hall.

'Maria. There is a problem with the heart. With Jemima's heart.'

Constance murmurs, and I realise that I had tightened my grip. 'What is it Anatra? Please tell me.'

'We will need to do more tests Maria, but it is possible that Jemima has some abnormal muscle fibres in her heart.'

'What does that mean?'

It is something called cardiomyopathy, and it shows itself by abnormal heart rhythms.'

'How serious is it Anatra?'

'This is a difficult question to answer. Jemima cannot talk to us, so we do not have a way to know how she is feeling, apart from her crying that is.'

'Is that why she cries? Is she in pain?' I ask.

'We don't know yet. But she has many symptoms that she will find...*difficile*. Shortness of breath, difficulty feeding. She is not as big as her sister.'

I look into the hall but can't see Gaia. 'Where is she Anatra?'

'Gaia is with her Maria, and she will go with the nurse. You must not worry; Gaia will look after her,' Anatra places his hand on mine, and I look at him with wide eyes, and my breathing becomes rapid. 'Maria.' His voice is firm. 'Constance is going to need you.'

Chapter 62

But Mole stood still a moment, held in thought. As one wakened suddenly from a beautiful dream, who struggles to recall it, but can recapture nothing but a dim sense of the beauty in it, the beauty! Till that, too, fades away in its turn, and the dreamer bitterly accepts the hard, cold waking and all its penalties.

Mummy placed her book in her lap and stared at the pages for some time without moving.

'Is that Wind in the Willows?' I asked.

She picked the book up from off her lap. 'Do you think that mole too was.... lost?' She stopped; lost in her own thoughts.

'Are you ok?' I asked.

'Just reading,' she replied.

The morning sun began to warm the balcony; where we had sat through most of the night reading the diaries. Mummy looked as fresh as the day. I was tired.

It had been two days since Jake had been. I had made an appointment to see the bank, and had drafted a letter which I had Mummy sign, giving Jemima and me permission to discuss her accounts along with any other details.

I leant forward and took her free hand. She jumped at my touch. She hovered between placing her book on the table and continuing to read; she opted to turn the book over to look at the front page. A look of relief settled across her face.

'I'm here Mummy.' I said in reassurance, and squeezed her hand gently.

'Where's David?' She asked. 'I need to see David. he has a dress for me to try on.'

'He's not here Mummy.'

'But I must see him. If I don't try on the dress, he'll leave; he'll go; and that will be that.' I didn't know what to say. I could feel her beginning to shake. 'David,' she called again. 'David; love me until I'm no more.'

And there it was. My mother's pain. I knelt down beside her and took the book from her and placed it on the table, and gently pulled her to me and held her. She began to cry, and as the cry became a sob, it turned into a long low deep moan that seemed to last forever. I could feel her chest beating heavily. He had broken her heart; and now it was breaking all over again. I had read how my father had left, but how could I know how she really felt? And what else did she know about the past that wasn't in the diaries?

'I'm sorry,' she said between the sobs. 'I'm so sorry.'

'There's nothing to be sorry for,' I said, trying to sound confident. But the truth was that I still didn't know the whole story; and what other secrets the diaries held. I knew now that I wanted, I needed, to keep turning the pages. I knew that however painful it was, I might at least understand what Mummy went through, and then I might be able to help her. And I just might know what it was that we should do.

'Shall we read the diaries?' I asked her. I wandered into the bedroom and opened the top drawer. There I found the one we were reading wrapped in paper. I could only hope that whatever happened would help us understand what we should do now; but it felt as if things were moving fast, too fast.

Chapter 63

Diary; July 25th 1970

I wake in the darkness, not sure where I am; and then I hear the soft beeping sound of a monitor. As my eyes grow accustomed to the dim light of the hospital room I can make out the small cot in the corner. Although Constance has been checked over and has been given a clean bill of health, Anatra has arranged for her to be monitored just to be sure. I have only seen Jemima briefly since Gaia had taken her from the room. She is in intensive care and being monitored under supervision. Anatra has done his best to reassure me, but I feel scared and alone. David should be here; he should be holding me; comforting me, and I hate him for that; for leaving me to face this alone. Anatra has tried to fill that void in his own way, and I am so grateful for his care and for all that he has done, both for me and for Katherine. There is no getting away from the fact that we wouldn't have been able to survive this ordeal if it hadn't been for him.

I hear a faint noise coming from the cot monitors and strain my eyes to see in the dim light. A shadow next to the cot moves and then stands. I gasp at the unexpected movement, and a voice whispers in the darkness. 'Are you awake Maria?'

'Anatra, is that you?'

'*Si*, it is.'

'What are you doing here?' I ask.

'I could not sleep, and so I am here.'

'Is Constance...?'

'She is sleeping. How do you feel?' he whispers.

'Tired,'

'*Si.*'

'How is Jemima?' I ask cautiously.

He is quiet for several seconds. 'There is no change, and she is...comfortable.' He leans over the cot and places his hand on Constance. 'We can talk in the morning.'

His shadow shrinks into the corner as he sits back in the armchair. 'For now, you must sleep.'

'It is hard Anatra.' I feel a tear run down my face and onto the pillow.

'*Si.... Mi Dispiace*; I am sorry that I could not do more.'

'You have already done so much.'

'Please, you must sleep *amore mio*. You will need your energy.'

'Yes, and thankyou; *grazie* Anatra.' I close my eyes and feel a mist of tiredness overwhelm me, and the greyness of the room slowly darkens until it is almost black.

∞ ∞ ∞

'*Buongiorno Signora* Hunter.' I open my eyes to find a short, and rather round Italian nurse standing by the side of my bed holding a clipboard. She smiles, and her eyes widen as she nods enthusiastically. '*Buongiorno*,' she repeats.

'Oh, good morning, *buongiorno*.'

'*Come stai oggi?* 'Her eyes widen again. 'How are you today?' She nods her head again; as if prompting me to reply.

I yawn and pull myself up, and I can feel the discomfort of giving birth to two baby girls. She places her board down momentarily and leans over to pull my pillows up.

'*Così è meglio?* So it is better?' she asks.

'Thank you,' I reply, as I lean back into them.

'*Prego, prego.*' She says and goes back to her clipboard. 'I am Maria,' she nods, wide eyed. 'I see that you are also Maria. Such a name we should share, *si?*' She laughs, and once again nods her head, her eyes widening in anticipation of a reply.

Although I smile back, I'm beginning to feel mildly irritated. Anatra is nowhere to be seen; had he really been in the room the previous night, or if I had dreamed it?

'So, *come stanno le tue bambine?*' she asks.

'I was hoping you could tell me.' I reply.

She takes a look at the clipboard. 'Jemima, she is one of your *bambini, si?*

'Yes,' I say more firmly. 'Is she okay?'

'Jemima?' she asked, pointing to the small cot in the corner.

I can hear sounds coming from the cot, telling me that Constance is waking up. 'No, that is Constance. Jemima is not here.' With great effort, I pull myself fully upright. She looks at me quizzically.

At that moment another nurse comes into the room. She is a much taller, rather elegant woman; and very slim. She has a darker uniform on. 'Ah, *buongiorno* Maria,' She says with a singular soft nod of her head.

'*Buongiorno*,' both Nurse Maria and I say in reply.

The tall nurse looks at Nurse Maria and speaks to her in Italian. It's much too fast for me to understand, and Nurse Maria nods several times, her eyes still wide, but with no smile. When the other nurse is finished, she places the clipboard on the bed, and smiling at me, she quickly leaves. The other nurse comes closer to the bed and retrieves the board. 'Good morning Mary,' she says in perfect English. 'You are well?' she asks.

'I am worried,' I reply.

'It's a difficult time; I understand.' She places her hand on mine. 'I believe Doctor Rossi is with Jemima.'

'Really. Will he be able to tell me what is happening?'

'I'm sure that he will be coming to see you as soon as he has some news. He's been here all night you know.' She walks over to the cot and places her hand on Constance. 'In the meantime, it would be a good idea to feed this little one I think.' She gently lifts my little girl out of the cot and brings her to me.

Chapter 64

How can I do this? Two are becoming one. I was dreaming so many dreams. Were they mine? Or did they belong to others? It was all blending into one colour. Yesterday and today.

The morning was cold and damp. Was it really the middle of July? This weather was depressing. I wasn't sure if what I was reading in the diary was making me feel worse, or whether it was the stress of Mummy being ill, or Jake's visit. Maybe it was all of it. I finished the last of my breakfast and took the tray over to the sink. Jemima was upstairs with Mummy and I was nervous. Because we were going to the bank; because Jemima had become set on the idea of giving the land to the twins, and we had argued. And because I was beginning to forget that I had spent the past several years of my life in Milan, not caring; and I had started to care about this place. I knew all about change. It was inevitable, I knew that. I had changed my life many times in the past to solve problems, or to try to make things better. But this was different. It felt different.

I thought about calling Gabriel. Maybe asking him to come over. But in truth, even after being away from him for several days, I still wasn't sure that I wanted him to be a part of this. Where was that connection? Mummy had had it with David; and it had been so deep. But look at the pain it had caused her.

I went to the kitchen door and called up. Time was getting tight. 'We've still got time, we'll be about ten minutes,' Jemima called back. 'Remember we're not in Italy now.' She was right, it would only take half the time here to get to town, but I knew that their ten minutes would still be twenty.

'I'll be outside,' I shouted up.

I slid my coat on and wandered out to the car and started to pace around the drive, which felt worse than pacing around the kitchen. I looked over the tops of the trees along the meadow and could see a patch of blue sky making its way toward us, so I put the car keys in my pocket and wandered across the grass toward the meadow. I stopped at the gate and leant across the top. It was cooler in the shade and I longed for the heat of Milan. Now there was a good reason to go back. Why didn't I just leave them to it and return to my job? If I still had a job, that is. The patch of blue sky broke over the trees and threw a sliver of warmth down, and I grabbed at it and breathed it in. The shaded meadow came alive with streams of light dancing through the branches and leaves, and the hives seemed to move across their soft green carpet. I stopped breathing, and listened, and I heard the sweet music of the bees humming as they journeyed in and out of the hives. I stood off the gate and took hold of the iron latch, and then hesitated, wondering if going into the meadow was a good idea.

I ignored the thought and slid the bar across and pushed the gate open. The sound of the bees instantly grew louder. I placed my hands in my pockets, feeling safer for doing so, and began my journey into the meadow.

Chapter 65

Diary; July 25th 1970

I stare out of the hospital window into the cold darkness; and although my room is warm, I pull my cardigan around my shoulders and lean on the wall to the side of the window. I'm feeling less tired, but I still ache. I had had several visitors throughout the day, including Gaia and Edoardo, but there had been no sign of Anatra. He had sent a nurse to tell me that Jemima was doing well, whatever that meant, and that they were still carrying out tests. Gaia had said that Edoardo had insisted Katherine remain at the villa, as they had had a visit from Von Treffen and his men. When I had tried to question Edoardo about the details he had been reluctant to talk about the visit, although he did say that he had arranged for more men to come to the villa. Vittoria had stayed for the whole afternoon, also helping when Constance needed feeding. It appears to me that Vittoria is still feeling guilty over what had happened to Katherine; and with Von Treffen still harassing Katherine, things are not going to get any easier, especially when Katherine's baby is born. What I really want to do is put the whole thing behind us, but that just doesn't look possible.

Vittoria told me that she had seen Von Treffen, and that she had even spoken to him briefly. I shiver when I remember meeting him at the wedding; and I feel slightly embarrassed with myself to think that I had felt attracted to him.

Vittoria went on to recount how Von Treffen had stood in front of her papa, totally calm, and with a confident danger in his manner. He had handed Edoardo some kind of document, which she had not seen, and after a few brief words, he had walked away. What Vittoria could tell me was that von Treffen wanted Katherine's baby, regardless of the cost; and she had said that she now believed that that was all that he had ever wanted; an heir to continue the Von Treffen name. it was his singular ambition, no matter what devastation he caused to the lives of those around him.

'How are you Maria?' Anatra's question brings me back to the room.

I turn from the darkness of the window, relieved to finally see him, and smile. 'Hello Anatra. How is she?'

'*Stabile* Maria. She is *stabile*.' He looks tired; very tired.

'When is the last time you slept?' I ask.

'I am okay. I will sleep soon.'

I need to know more. 'What are we facing Anatra? Please be honest with me.'

'As you know, it is her heart.' He walks across the room sit in the armchair and wipes his hands across his face. 'She has such a tiny heart Maria.' He leans forward and buries his face in his hands and I watch as his shoulders begin to shake softly, and so I go to him and place my hand on his shoulder, and then he lets go. I pull him to me as the shaking becomes more intense. I can't help but think that he should be comforting me, but I understand his pain, and that is enough. Eventually the sobbing slows, and he lifts his head to look straight into my eyes. 'I am sorry Maria,' he says, almost in a whisper. 'I wish that I could do more.'

'I know that you are doing all that you can, and that's all I can ask of you.' A last single tear runs down is cheek; and I know then that I love this man. Not in the way I loved David, but I love him deeply, and without reserve. And I know that the bees will love him too, and I resolve to tell them all about him when I return home. I just hope that it will be with both of my girls. I kiss him gently on the cheek. 'You are a good man.'

He smiles and leans forward, softly kissing my smiling lips, and it feels both comforting and warm. I place my hand on the side of his face and lean into him again, and I touch his lips with mine, and he stays with me as I feel the warmth pulse through me. We slowly pull apart. 'Anatra I....'

He places his finger on my lips. 'You do not need to say Maria. It is a moment that we need. But now you must think about the girls, and Katherine. And...' he lowers his eyes, 'you have David.'

What I want to say is, David is gone. I'm alone and I need someone. Someone I can trust. I need you. I can't think about the girls on my own, and how can I help Katherine when I can't help myself? Instead I say. 'Yes, you are right.' And I place my hands on his. 'But promise me that you will be there for me; please.'

'Always Maria, always.' He takes my hands and slowly stands up with me.' But now I must tell you what we know.' He moves away from the chair and gestures for me to sit. 'Please.'

'I would prefer to stand,' I reply. 'I feel stronger when I stand.'

'Si.' He walks over to the window and after staring out into the darkness, he turns back to me. 'I have met with my colleagues many times during the day, and the heart specialist has spent many hours with Jemima. He has come to the er.... the *conclusione* that her heart muscles are too weak to support her.'

I feel my legs weaken and grab the side of the cot. 'Oh Anatra, my baby.'

'*Mi dispiace Maria.*' We are both silent for some time. 'What we must try to do is to keep her going and hope that she will grow stronger.

Chapter 66

How do I make sense of the past? I don't know. It all feels like too much; too many colours. But once told, we can't forget. You can't wash all the colour off a canvas. You can only cover it with more colour.

Patches of Meadowsweet flowers peered around the sides of the trees as I walked across the meadow, jumping out in surprise, as if they were hiding from me. I breathed in their sweet aroma, and I tasted honey. I smiled; in spite of my fear. And I smiled again because of it. Several bees flew around my head, and I breathed in deeply as I ran through the images in my head. Warm beaches and soft sand; the cool marble interiors of the gallery; sweet wine; and Gabriel's smile. I loved his smile. It was honest and unaffected, and I could trust it. and I missed him. But I missed here. This, right now. I wanted this. I wanted Gabriel and I wanted this. I couldn't let Meadowsweet go. As much as I wished for it all to be no part of my life; I couldn't let it go.

We wandered into the bank a few minutes before our appointment. I hated cutting it that fine, but Jemima seemed unfazed, and Mummy was oblivious. We were ushered into the manager's office almost immediately, and that threw me too. I needed time; to do what exactly, I wasn't sure. He ushered us into three waiting chairs and then went around to his side of the desk. He held his tie against his chest as he sat down. I hated it when men did that. There was a stack of folders to one side of him, and I wondered if that was his work for the day, or if it all belonged to Mummy.

'So, it's nice to welcome you ladies. As you explained the situation in brief on the telephone I have taken the opportunity of having what we need to hand.' He spread his fingers wide and laid the flat of his hand on the stack. I had a feeling that this was going to take a while.

Chapter 67

Diary; August 4th 1970

The journey back to the Rossi villa is proving to be harder than I thought; for all sorts of reasons. The most important of them being that I had anticipated taking two babies with me. Instead, as Anatra drives slowly through the Italian countryside, I have only Constance in the back of the car.

'Are you okay?' he asks.

'Yes, we're doing fine thank you.'

'It is not too *turbolento*?'

'No.... Really, you're the perfect driver.'

'As long as you are okay.'

'Yes, yes, we're doing fine.' I look out at the passing countryside. Anatra is driving slow enough for me to take in the beauty of the area. 'How is Katherine doing? I ask.

'She has been staying in her room for a great amount of time. I am not sure if it is the heat, or the worry that she has.'

A short while later we pull up at the gates to the Rossi villa, which are now firmly shut. The tall, thick brick pillars each side of the gates send an imposing message to all unwelcome visitors. One of the gates opens slightly and two large men step through the gap, rifles slung over their shoulders. An even more forceful message to any who would dare to venture through without an invitation. I instantly recognise one of the two men as flat-nose, and he grins as soon as he sees me. He pushes his colleague and shouts some orders at him, and the man immediately turns and disappears inside the gates. He then wanders over to my window and places his big hands on the door. '*Ciao bella, come stai?*'

'*Sto bene,*' I reply.

He peers into the car to see Constance asleep in her basket. '*Solo uno?*' he asks.

'*Si,*' I reply. '*Solo uno; il mio bambino è malato.*'

His face crumples into one resembling a giant teddy, and he puts his hands together. '*Pregherò per lei Maria, pregherò per lei.*'

'He says he will pray for her.' Anatra says as he turns his head to look. He then speaks to flat-nose in fast Italian, explaining the problem.

Flat-nose turns again to me. '*Mi dispiace.*' He says, and he blows me a kiss as he moves away from the car.

I kiss my fingers and place them on his cheek. '*Grazie* flat-nose.' I say without thinking.

'*Scusa, che cosa hai detto?*' he asks.

'*Naso piatto.*' Anatra adds, pointing to his nose and laughing.

As the big man stands, he places his hand on the front of his face and feels the shape of his nose, then laughs. It's a low rumbling sound, and he blows me another kiss as he walks toward the gates, his rifle bouncing off his back as his shoulders jump up and down. As we drive through the gates, a car that is parked across the drive slides slowly out of the way, allowing us to travel past and stop at the front of the villa.

The sun is now edging toward the back of the villa, and Edoardo steps silently out of the shadows and opens the door. '*Buongiorno* Maria. We are pleased to have you back here with us. The family are all in the house waiting for you to present you *bambina* to them.'

The first time I had come here all the family had stood confidently outside to welcome us. Now they are in the villa because of the threat from Von Treffen. And I hate him more than I have ever hated anyone. I hate what he has done to the Rossi family, to my family, and to Katherine. I step out of the car, and I turn as I hear the car door open to see Anatra taking the crib from the back seat. I smile proudly at him, feeling determined to enjoy this, and to find happiness in spite of the difficult time we have ahead of us.

Chapter 68

We are always left with just one thing. Hope. Dare I give my heart to this;
knowing that the colours are already painted on the canvas? To give my
heart, is to give my life.

I wandered into the drawing room and sank into one of the armchairs, being careful
not to spill my glass. Jemima had already frowned when I had poured myself some
white wine in the kitchen.

'It's the middle of the day Connie,' she had said, trying to sound official.

'Since when have you ever seen me drink during the day?' I had replied. 'In fact,
I think it's the first drop of alcohol I've had since I've been here. So....' I had raised
my glass to her and left the room.

I did wonder if my choice of liquid refreshment had been motivated by the
memories I had had in the meadow, or whether the trip to the bank had been
motivation enough. I imagined it was a bit of both. The meeting with the manager
had not gone as I had anticipated. In fact, with what he had to say, I wasn't sure that
we would be able to keep any of Meadowsweet, let alone the meadow.

There were still some funds left. My Great Grandfather had been a shrewd man;
but we were no longer living in a shrewd market, and he wasn't here to protect his
interests. If we did nothing then we could perhaps survive for another five years; but
after that, something would have to go. The manager offered several financial
packages that would help, but that would hand control over to the bank, and none of
us wanted that. In truth, I didn't know what we would do. Jemima had spent the
journey back home arguing about the meadow. I asked her to stop when Mummy had
become distressed. She looked very tired, so I had taken her to her room to lie down,
and she had fallen asleep almost immediately. I took a mouthful of my wine and held
on to the taste before swallowing. I thought back to the funeral I had been at in
Milan, when I had received my sisters message. Before then, I hadn't thought about
home for some time. Now, I found myself right in the middle of a family crisis, and I
couldn't see any way out.

There was a tap on the door, and Jemima wandered in. She had a glass of wine in her hand. 'If you can't beat them....' she said, in response to my glare.

'Can we talk?' she asked.

The room was on the north side of the house and the coolness of the day didn't help. I shivered as Jemima sat down, and slid my feet up onto the armchair in the hopes of feeling more cosy. 'No guessing what you want to talk about.'

'We do need to talk Connie. It's not as if we can ignore the problem.'

'No, I don't suppose we can.' I took another mouthful of wine. 'But we're not giving the land away. You know that Jake will get his hands on it.'

'You can say that now Connie, but you've not been the one who has had to try and keep everything going all these years.'

'That wasn't my fault,' I replied. 'Anyway, let's not get into that now.'

'No, you're right. I'm sorry.' Jemima said as she pulled her legs up onto her chair. 'He caused us a lot of pain, I know that.' I saw her shiver too, and a hundred memories flashed through my mind. 'But he's changed you know.'

'You can't believe that,' I replied, looking into my glass, feeling even colder.

'He regrets a lot of the things he's done.'

I looked across at her. 'You've been talking to him.' Her guilty look told me the answer. 'When did he call you? She didn't answer but looked down at the floor. 'You called him?' I asked. 'When did this happen?'

'I called him last night.'

'But why? Why would you do that?'

'I could give you a hundred reasons Connie, but none of them would make sense.'

'Just give me one Jem.'

'I'm lonely, and scared, and worried for the future; and I'm confused about the past. Are they good enough reasons?'

'Don't you think we all feel like that?'

'Yes, but you have a life to go home to. I'm here all on my own; and if anything happens to Mummy....' Her voice trailed off.

I knew I should call Gabriel. I was angry that Jemima made me feel guilty. 'This isn't really getting us anywhere. What have you said to Jake?'

'Just that I'll think about it.'

'You mean, that we'll think about it.'

'I've had to make all the decisions for us for so many years Connie; and now it comes to the most important one I feel like I'm being side-lined.'

'No Jem, I'm not doing that, but Meadowsweet is too important for that. It has; we have too much history here just to find the easy way out.'

'But who says it's the easy way? It could be the right way.'

'It could be, but it's not.'

'So you say.'

'So says Mummy, and Nanny and our Great Grandparents; and so say the bees. There are a lot of reasons why we need to think about this carefully; some I don't fully understand.... yet.'

'What does that mean?'

'Just give me, give us, some time Jem. You heard the bank manager. We should have enough funds to last another five years, so a couple more months isn't going to make much of a difference.'

'What do you know that you're not telling me?'

I knew how easy it would be to tell Jemima the whole story; about Mummy's past, and about the fact that she wanted just me to know what had happened. Instead I said, 'Something feels missing; something important. Can you just give me some time to find it?'

So, there's nothing. You have nothing?'

'Not yet. But I'm sure it's there. Just give it time.'

'So, you're staying.'

'Yes; well for now.... I'm staying. I'll contact my boss and explain, and if she wants to fire me then she'll just have to. I can't leave while things are like this.'

Chapter 69

Diary; September 10th 1970

'Ow!' Katherine exclaims as she moves awkwardly in her chair.

'What is it?' I ask quietly.

'This little one is protesting. I don't think she wants to stay in much longer.'

'You think it's a girl?

'For some strange reason, yes I do. And I hope it is too.'

'Why?'

'Because maybe Alexander will lose interest.'

I rock Constance softly as her eyes begin to close. She has been a model baby so far, and she would go to anyone, which has made it easier for us to travel to the hospital over the past few months. Jemima's condition hasn't improved, and she has been placed on several drugs. They are also concerned that she hasn't grown. There's been nothing I can do but just sit and wait.

I have tried to spend some time alone with her; and I have had the chance to hold her on a few occasions, but she felt so tiny. I would place my finger near her hand, and she would find it, and hold it tight. I want so desperately for her to be with her sister. They had spent the first part of their lives so closely together, and from the moment they had been born, it felt as if they had been torn apart. I have managed to persuade the nurses to let Constance lie with her, and it's at those times that Jemima seems to come alive.

I feel so guilty at turning the lives of the Rossi family upside down, but they continue to be wonderful to both me and Katherine, who says that there is little to gain from constantly talking about it, and that we would do better to get on with things.

Anatra has made detailed arrangements to get Katherine from the villa to the hospital, and has even hired private detectives to be there from the moment she arrives. He says that he wants to make sure that everything is legal; especially now that Von Treffen has served legal documents stating that he wants custody of the baby on the grounds that Katherine is unfit to act as a guardian. I have promised Katherine that I will use every penny I have to fight him, but we all know that it will take more than money to beat him; and I'm unsure whether she has the stamina for this.

I ask if I can read the documents and I take them to my room, and I sit at the small table on the balcony to look at them. Memories of David flood into my head, and I close my eyes, waiting for him to come behind me and close his arms around me. I breathe in deeply, and when the moment doesn't come, I open my eyes again. I look across the gardens for Cesare, and realise that he will be busy with his bees at this time of the day. I need to talk to him.

I scan through the documents looking for details of Von Treffen's address, but all I find are details of the lawyers handling the case, along with the court assigned to hear it, so I make notes of all the details I need. Later that afternoon I make my way across the gardens and slip through the gap in the hedge. The bright sun reflects a myriad of colours from the hives, and since my last visit Cesare has re-painted several of them. I wander over to the first row and warm to the singing of the bees as they go about their business. The sound is softer now that the *teppisti* bees are no longer here. Cesare has left the gap where the hive used to sit, and I feel another twinge of sadness for their loss, and I'm sure that he is hurting too. I look over to the hut and see him leaning on the door post, and I wave. He smiles, lifts his hand in response and disappears inside. If I'm lucky he'll be making some tea. I look around at the hives. 'Can you tell my bees that I miss them?' I ask. I know that's impossible, but the idea softens my troubled mind. For now I will have to take solace from my time here, and I close my eyes again and imagine myself back at Meadowsweet, and I breathe in the sweet aroma of honey. Although the smells are different, it still brings a smile to my face. 'Hello my babies,' I say, 'And how are you today?'

I wander over to the hut and tap softly on the door. *'Ciao Cesare. Come stai?'*

'Ciao Maria.' I hear the water being poured into the teapot as I wander into the grey of the room. As always, it takes a while for my eyes to become accustomed to the contrast from the bright sun, and I make my way to my chair and sink slowly into its softness. Cesare places a cup on the small table to one side of me and sits in his chair, and we both sit there quietly for several minutes, enjoying the opportunity to contemplate in silence.

'I'm going to see him,' I say finally.

'Si,' he replied.

'You don't think it's a good idea?'

'Si,' he says again.

'What, you agree it's not a good idea, or si, you think it is.... a good idea that is.'

He smiles. *'Si,* I think you must do what is to be done. *Si,* there are times in life when to get to your destination you must first travel the road.' He takes a sip from his cup. 'Aah, I love to drink my tea when it is too hot. Annalise; now she would wait until her tea was almost cold; and I would scold her for that, and say that it was disgusting. And she would say that I was a fool. That one day I would burn my lips, and that I would be left with a scar, and then I would not be able to feel her soft kisses.' He placed his cup back down and sat forward. 'And if you look closely, then you will see that I have just such a scar.'

'And you got that from drinking your hot tea?'

He laughs. 'No. I got that from Annalise. She bit my lip when I made her angry.' He sits back again and picking up his cup, he continues. 'It is the things that you think will do you no harm that often hurt you the most. We cannot always know. And I still drink my tea when it is too hot.'

There's nothing more I can ask of Cesare.

Chapter 70

It's the things that you think will do you no harm that often hurt you the most.

I hadn't been able to get those words out of my mind all night. All those years ago, I never thought that Jake would hurt me. I thought the pain had gone, but as I remembered it now, it hurt, and it was sharp. I had always consoled myself with thinking that I was lucky that it happened before we had married, but now I didn't feel so lucky. I wished that I had had Cesare to sit and talk to. I'm sure that I remember him, as a young girl, but the memories were of sitting on his knee. And when I thought about it more, the memory was of him smelling of honey.

Would Gabriel hurt me like that? He was different; from Jake that is, but could I be sure? My hand shook as I pressed the button on my phone to call him. It was dark outside, and quiet.

'*Amore mio,*' his soft voice warmed me. '*Mi sei mancata.*'

'Gabriel. I've missed you too.'

'*Stai bene?*'

'I'm well, but in English Gabriel. It feels like I've been away for a lifetime.'

'*Mi dispiace,* I am sorry *amore mio.* How are things going there?'

'Hard.' I felt the tears coming. 'I miss home,' I said.

'You are home,' he said simply.

'Am I?' I asked. 'I'm not sure I know where I belong anymore.' I wondered if he might tell me that I belonged with him. That would have been the kind of thing Jake would have said.

'Where do you want to belong *amore mio? segui il tuo cuore.* Follow your heart.'

I told him about the diaries, and we spoke for some time.

'I want to meet Cesare,' he said.

And it occurred to me that I didn't know what had happened to him, and I hadn't asked Mummy. Would I find out from the diaries?

'You are my Cesare,' I told him.

'Why do you not go back to see the Rossi family? I think that you will find your answers there.'

'Yes, I will; but I must finish the diaries first. Will you come and stay?'

The line stayed silent for several seconds, and I was beginning to regret asking him.

'You must see this through Connie. I miss you so much, but I will only distract you.' I knew he was right, but it didn't make me feel any better. 'Now go and read your diaries; and go to Alba, to the Rossi's. I am sure that you will find what you are looking for.'

'Do you think so?'

'I am sure of it.'

We said our goodbyes, and I went to Mummy's room. She was sitting up in bed reading. It seemed to be the only thing that brought her any form of relief, or pleasure. I did wonder how much longer that would continue.

'Hello Mummy,' I said, and walked straight to the drawer and took out the diary I had been reading. I came back to the bed and pulled up the chair and sat down. Mummy placed her book on the bed and laid back ready to listen. I prayed that Gabriel was right.

Chapter 71

Diary; September 11th 1970

I had asked Vittoria to come to my room. When she arrives I waste no time in showing her the details I have taken and outline what I want her to do. We go through the details several times, and she reluctantly agrees to help me. That requires us to go to Edoardo's office to use the telephone, which Vittoria is not happy about, and I keep a look out while Vittoria dials the number for the courthouse. When the call is answered, Vittoria holds the phone away from her and begins to shake. When she hears the voice on the line say *Buongiorno*, she quickly puts the phone down and stands there with her hands on her mouth.

'What's wrong?' I ask.

'I cannot do this,' she replies. 'I cannot.'

I go to her and place my hands firmly on her shoulders. 'I understand Vittoria; really I do. I would do it myself, but you know I can't speak enough Italian to get by. If we don't at least try, then Katherine could lose her baby to that man.' I squeeze her shoulders gently. 'Can you at least give it a try. No one will know it's you; I promise.'

She takes in a deep breath. 'Okay, I will try.' I go back to the door and once again open it slightly to peer down the hall. I look back and nod to Vittoria, and she picks up the receiver and dials the number again, which is quickly answered by the courthouse switchboard. She carefully follows the script I have given her, and as she is put through to the right department she turns the paper over and speaks in Italian. *'Good afternoon. I am calling from Baldacci law practice. We are handling the case of Von Treffen versus Hunter. Would you like a reference number?'*

'Yes please,' a woman's voice replies.

After providing the details, Vittoria is put on hold. The voice returns less than a minute later. *'How can I help you?'* she asks.

'It is a small thing. Our client has several addresses, and we believe that we may have registered the incorrect address as his current place of residence.' Vittoria pauses for several seconds, and I turn to see what is happening. I open my eyes wide and nod enthusiastically, remembering the nurse with the clipboard.

Vittoria holds her hand up and then turned her back to face the desk. The woman speaks again. *'What is it that you want?'*

Vittoria takes a deep breath and replies. *'Can you tell me what you have there?'*

The line goes silent again. *'I am sorry, but I cannot give you that information over the phone.'*

I see, well…. how about I tell you tell you what I have in our documents and then you can tell me if that is correct?'

'I am not sure….'

'Listen…if I have made a mistake on this, then the case could be delayed, and my boss is going to be very upset…with me.' She switches the phone to her other ear and begins to gesture wildly as she speaks. *'This job was so hard to find. You know what it is like. The men give us such a hard time as it is.'*

There is silence.

'Please can you help me?'

'I do not want you to lose your job,' comes the reluctant reply, *'but I do not want to lose mine either. I will read out the address I have here only once, and then I must go.'*

'I understand; thank you.' Vittoria writes furiously without speaking, and when she has finished she begins to thank the woman, but the line goes dead.

She places the phone down, turns to face me, takes in a deep breath and closes her eyes. 'Have you got it?' I ask.

'Yes, yes. I have it. Now please can we go before my papa returns.'

We go to my room where Vittoria gives me the paper containing Von Treffen's address. 'Thankyou Vittoria. Thankyou; thank you.' I say, knowing that the most difficult part of my plan lays ahead.

Chapter 72

Pause to think; an artist's greatest enemy. Courage and heart; his greatest friends. Once committed, the brush will give life to your courage and decision to your heart. What looked back at you was the canvas of your life.

I went down to the kitchen. It was still dark. The clock told me it was 4:35 a.m. My mind had been racing and I couldn't sleep. I found some herbal tea in the cupboard. I thought that might help. What had my mother been up to? I needed to understand what she had been doing; then maybe I would know what I should do. I had this sudden urge to go out to the bees. But that was mad; wasn't it? I still wasn't sure I could trust them. What had Cesare said? *It's the things that you think will do you no harm that often hurt you the most.* And they could hurt you.

I looked through the kitchen window. The sky was beginning to reflect the early morning light, so I opened the door to the garden quietly to find that the air was cool. I slid the wellies on next to the door. Then I remembered the story of Mummy going out to find Nanny, and my heart leapt.

I quietly closed the kitchen door, pulled my dressing gown around me, and walked across the garden. The stillness brought a silence with it, and every step in the soft grass seemed to echo around me. I reached the gate and paused before I slid the bar open as quietly as I could. The sweet smells from the meadow were comforting, but in spite of that I stood watching for some minutes, and I went back to the gate several times before I finally, slowly made my way to the first hive. Again I stood in front of the hive for quite a while, my hands tucked firmly into the pockets of my gown, without moving. there were a few bees venturing out, and I tensed when each of them flew close to me. I remembered Gabriel's words; *Segui il tuo cuore;* follow you heart. I needed to know; needed to find out where my heart belonged.

I placed my right hand on the top of the hive, and I could feel the soft hum of the bees as they vibrated their wings. It was a reassuring sound, and I wanted to feel the security of them; their oneness.

I wandered around each hive in turn, placing my hand on the top; and for the first time I began feel their distinct vibrations. I could hear a different sound from each of them. I placed my hand on the fourth hive, where I had removed the diaries; and I thought about how the bees had looked after them. Had they felt a sense of loss when I took them? I knew it to be fanciful, but I even wondered if they knew what was in them, and if they understood them. I continued my journey around the meadow; my eyes had become accustomed to the soft light, and I reached the sixth and final hive in the far corner of the meadow. It was beginning to look sadly neglected, and I thought about Cesare's painted hives. I placed my hand on the side of the hive and the paint flaked off onto the platform it stood on. As a thin shaft of light was catching the side of the hive I noticed that the flakes seemed to vary in shade. I picked a slightly darker flake up and held it under the shaft of light. It was a soft shade of blue. At some point in the past Mummy must have painted this hive. Cesare had spoken many times about the blue painted hive, and I tried to recall some of the things he had said. The sweetness of the honey. Yes, that was it. he had spoken to Mummy about how sweet the honey was from the blue hive, and he had shared some of the comb with her. What else had he told her? There was something, but I couldn't remember what it was. I was sure that whatever it was, was in the second diary.

I left the meadow and went as quickly as I could back to the house. It was still too early for anyone to be awake, and I climbed the stairs and quietly crept into Mummy's room. She was still sleeping soundly. I retrieved the second diary and took it to my room, where I searched through the pages until I came to the piece I was looking for. And there it was. Cesare and Mummy had just shared the comb from the blue hive; from the *soft and sweet bees*, he had called them. Then I read aloud what he had said to her.

'*I will not always be here bella. My bees, they will live forever. Should you ever need my help, the blue hive will give you the sweetness to satisfy you. You or your bambini.*'

I needed to finish reading the rest of the diary. I was sure more than ever that the answers lay there; and if I needed to, I would go back to the Rossi villa; to the blue hive.

Chapter 73

Diary; September 15th 1970

I read through the address once again and pick up the map to look at the circle I had drawn in red around my destination. It had taken me three hours to drive around 190km to the outskirts of Bolzano, as I had had to stop several times to check the route. The city sits in a valley, with a mountain range to the north, so it is sheltered from cool winds during the day. I wind the window down while I sit in the layby, and turn the engine off. Apart from the occasional car travelling past, the air is warm and quiet. It had been difficult to persuade the driver who had been taking me to the hospital every day that I wanted to drive myself that morning; particularly as he had spoken little English. I had had to lie to him, and I felt bad, not only for that, but because I wouldn't see Jemima, but I had no choice. The past few weeks had constantly been a case of deciding each day who I would give the most time to, and I had settled on one day at the hospital and the following at the villa with Constance. Katherine had been able to help on a few occasions, but not only is she ready to give birth herself, but she has also become increasingly withdrawn since receiving the court papers. I am still in awe of the Rossi family and all that they have done and continue to do for both me and Katherine. We can never repay them for the time and love that they have been prepared to give us. Anatra has been simply amazing, and that makes what I'm doing now even harder. He is going to be very hurt that I didn't confide in him, but had he known, he would have stopped me immediately.

Looking more closely at the map, I can see that I'm less than 3km from my destination. I have no idea whether Von Treffen is living at the house, or even whether he will be there; but I know that I have to try, for Katherine's sake. And that will be my reason, when others wiser than me berate me later. I put the car into gear and pull out of the layby with a lurch forward as I lift my foot from the clutch.

Several minutes later I drive past a large pair of solid wooden gates to my left and I see the name I am looking for on one side of the high brick wall surrounding the property. My stomach tightens as I brake and reverse back to the gates and then turn toward them. The brick walls to each side of the gates curve in to allow a car to drive completely off the road whilst they are still closed. As I pull up close to them I notice an intercom to my left, and I wind down the window, take a deep breath and press the small green button below the speaker. I'm praying that no one is home.

There's no answer, he's not here; so I put the car into reverse and jerk backwards.

Instead of turning, I press the brakes hard just before the back tyres touch the road. Then I just sit there, gripping the steering wheel and staring at the gate. I have to try again. I can't come this far and give up now. That means that he wins, and we lose.

I select first gear again and lift the clutch slowly, feeling my calf muscle tense under the strain. The car rolls slowly forward and I press the clutch and brake gently. The car stops back where I need it to be.

I press the small square green button again; this time holding it down for several seconds. Nothing. I press the small square green button, that has 'press' stamped into it, once more, holding it down with no intention of stopping. A voice cuts in, causing me to jump, and my finger slides off the button. 'How may I help you?' a man's voice asks. I say nothing. 'How may I help you?' he asks again, this time more agitated. Is it Von Treffen? I can't be sure. I can't tell whether the man speaking is Austrian or Italian, or maybe even a bit of both. I don't think it's him.

'I wish to speak with Alexander Von Treffen.'

'There is no one here by that name,' the man says.

I think quickly. 'Tell him that Mary Hunter, a friend of Katherine's, oh, and her sister-in-law, wishes to speak to him.'

There is silence. Then. 'Just one moment please.' Silence again.

Several minutes pass, then another man's voice says, 'please wait.' I wait for another few minutes, and there is a loud buzzing noise, and then a click. The buzz turns into a whirring sound as at first one gate begins to open, and then the second one follows a few feet behind. I sit upright, press the clutch down to the floor and push the stick into first gear. The car lurches forward with a sense of urgency, and once through the gates, I drive along a completely smooth tarmacadam road that seems to stretch on into the distance forever. Either side of the road is lined with tall, elegant poplar trees, and I feel as if I'm being paraded past a line of military soldiers. When the trees stop, I stare out at a vista spreading for miles each side of the long road. At any other time and place I would have been persuaded to stop and enjoy my surroundings, but now I look ahead of me, intent on getting to my destination, and I can just begin to pick out another large group of trees. As I approach them I can see that they surround a property, and the drive starts to wind softly, causing me to slow the car. In front of the house is a lake of some considerable size, which is being fed by a river that runs off to the left and right of the lake.

The road runs either side of the lake, and for no reason in particular, I chose the road to the left. A heavy curved wooden bridge with four ornate stone carvings of angels on all of the corners takes me across the river, and I wonder if the carvings are the same on the bridge to the right. I begin to feel lost in the beauty of this place, and to understand how Katherine may have fallen under the spell of this man. Once over the bridge I drive through formal pristine gardens, full of colour, leading to the house some several hundred yards ahead. Until now, the beauty of this country had been captured by the gardens of the Rossi villa, but this is beyond anything I could have imagined. How was it possible for such a place to exist outside of heaven? Is this a product of Von Treffen's imagination, or has his vast wealth commanded the best of the world's talent to create this? It's hard to reconcile what I think of him with what is around me.

The smooth tarmac road ends and becomes gravel, and I steer the car around a stone fountain, again with several angels looking out onto their surroundings; and as I stop outside the front entrance of the house the wheels dig in noisily. I turn the engine off. There is silence; and not a person in sight. It's all quite unsettling, and I wait for my heart to slow. As I stare out at the façade of the house I begin to see the Von Treffen I had imagined. Built from large chunks of rectangular stone, It's height and attention to detail have been cleverly designed to diminish any onlookers; and I know instinctively that this is what he would want; to diminish you, to intimidate you. It looks as if there are three floors, possibly four; and there are too many windows to count easily.

The sound of footsteps in the gravel brings me back, and I look around but can see no one. Suddenly, the car door is pulled open, and I let out a gasp. 'Forgive me Madam. I did not mean to startle you.' A man in his thirties, dressed in a mid-blue two-piece suit, crisp white shirt and dark blue silk tie, stands by the car. 'Please Madam,' he says as he holds out his hand. I reach out to take it instinctively, and as I step out of the car he lifts my hand gently. He lets go as soon as I am standing, and I place the flat of my hands awkwardly onto my dress and attempt to avoid his eyes. Out of the shade of the car I become aware of the heat of the sun. How can this man bear to wear a suit? 'Does madam have any bags?' he asks.

'No I don't; just me.' I reply, and suddenly feel foolish.

He doesn't react. 'Then will madam please follow me,' he says, and he turns and walks quickly toward the house.

I follow him, and have to turn suddenly when I realise that we aren't going to the main entrance with its wide stone steps and Corinthian pillars; but instead he makes his way to the end of the main façade and turns the corner where the left wing of the house is set back some ten feet or so. There's a large yellow door tucked into the corner. It's a door that on any other house would most likely be the front entrance, but on this house, it feels more like the servant's entrance. Does Von Treffen not deem me worthy enough to come in through the main entrance? Or is he playing mind games? Perhaps everyone uses this door, including Von Treffen. The blue suited man stops at the door, places his hand on the large handle and waits for me. When I reach him, he opens the door and steps through, where he turns and holds the door open, indicating with his other hand for me to walk through. If there is a moment that I am going to change my mind, then this is it. Once I step through that door I know that it will be too late. Maybe it is already too late? I quickly look around me, but there is no one else in sight. The blue suited man waits patiently, showing no reaction to my hesitation. I step through the door.

I am led along several wide corridors, each one lined with framed paintings begging me to stop and look at them before we arrive at our destination; but he moves too quickly for me to grant their wish. He stops again beside a door to his left, opens it, and stands to one side. Again he holds out his hand to indicate that I should walk through. Once in the room he closes the door, leaving me alone.

The room is vast, but this is no ordinary room. Every wall is lined with books, and every book sits in a handsomely ornate carved oak bookcase. Looking more closely, I can see many faces carved into the oak; and not one of them looks the same. In the centre of the room is a long oak table with several chairs around it. The middle of the table has been cut out to accommodate a highly polished oak column. It is one of five columns which rises to the centre of the vaulted ceiling and supports the roof. I walk slowly around the room, examining the contents of the shelves; and I'm tempted to pull several of the books from their place and open their pages. By the antiquated look of many of the books, along with their obscure titles, I'm guessing that they are possibly quite rare, which would most likely mean that they are valuable. Did he collect them more for that reason, than for reading them?

I stop at a small side table in front of one of the bookcases as I spy a book I recognize laying on the top. I can't resist the temptation to pick it up, and I open the book to the front leaf and read its title out loud. 'The Wind in The Willows.' The date of publication is 1908. I leaf through the pages to find that there are no illustrations; it looks as if it might be a first edition. I have no idea of its value, although that estimation increases when I turn back to the front page to find that it has been signed by the author Kenneth Graham.

'It's a beautiful story, don't you think Mary.' The voice startles me and I drop the book onto the oak floor, sending an echo through the room.

'I'm sorry I...' I bend down to retrieve the book.

'That is perfectly alright Mary.' Von Treffen is standing in the centre of the room, and I'm annoyed that I hadn't heard him enter, How long has he been standing there? 'Do you like the story?' he asks.

'It's one of my favourite books.' I reply as tersely as I can manage.

'Really; how interesting.' He takes a couple of steps closer and stands with his hands behind his back. 'Now let me guess. I would say that you like it either for its mysticism, or perhaps because of its many tales of morality.' He is dressed in an almost identical suit to the man who escorted me into the room. He raises his right hand and points his finger into the air. 'No...it is neither of those, is it Mary.' I stay silent and hold the book tightly shut. 'You love the story because of the camaraderie. Yes, that is it. That element, that characteristic of human nature that compels one to help another in a moment of crisis; regardless the cost.'

He takes another step forward and holds out his hand, and I step back in response and hold the book against my chest with both hands. 'Please.' He gestures with his hand, and I realise that he wishes to take the book from me; and I feel foolish. I relax my grip and hold the book out in front of me, and he takes it gently. 'It is a first edition; you are quite correct. And it is valuable, or should I say irreplaceable. For on the last page you will find a personal message from the author to my mother.' He opens the book to that page and places the palm of his left hand on it. 'Yes; quite irreplaceable.' He says nothing more for several seconds, as if lost in thought. Then without warning, he slams the book shut, causing me to jump. 'But all things of value eventually become just a memory. Don't you think miss Swan?'

'It's Mrs Hunter actually.' I reply.

'Yes, of course. Forgive me.' He bows slightly. 'You must be devastated that David has left you.'

I can't hide my shock. How can he know that? And in that case, what else does he know?

'Which brings us back to our conversation Mary. Mrs Hunter is just a memory. For me to call you that would be, well.... uncivilized, painful even. And so I will call you Mary, for that is who you have always been, and who you will always be. And you may call me Alexander. He places the book on the centre table and keeps his hand on it. 'As for this, it too is a painful memory; for it will always contain the message to my mother. Unless, of course, I were to tear the page from the book. But would that not remind me even more of my loss?' He takes his hand from the book and looks up. 'I am sure that you of all people can see my dilemma Miss...' He pauses and smiles politely. 'Mary.' Then he stares straight into me, the way he had looked at me when we first met at the wedding, and I go cold. 'So, Mary. Here you are, in my house. And you wish to tear some pages from my book.'

'I just wish you to leave Katherine alone. That is all.'

'That is all.... that is all. He begins to walk slowly around the perimeter of the room and places his hand on several books as he passed them. Yes. But that is not all, is it Mary. You are an intriguing woman, but I fear you have misjudged me.'

I step closer to the table, feeling somehow safer nearer the book. 'I think I have judged you very well.' I reply.

'I do understand why you would think that Mary. But surely even you would not expect me to just agree to your request; at least, not without hearing my side of the story.'

'You'll agree to my request?' I ask hopefully.

He laughs and stops at a protruding section of bookcase that also houses a stone fire surround. He reaches onto the side and presses his finger onto an invisible button. 'Mary, you do me a disservice to think that I would acquiesce so easily. I will...consider your request; if you will agree to one of mine.'

I breathe in deeply before answering. 'What is your request?'

A clock on the mantle strikes one chime and then falls silent. 'I would ask simply.... that you join me for lunch.'

'Do I have a choice?' I ask.

He turns to face me. 'I can arrange for you to be escorted to your car and we will speak no more of this.' He holds out his arms. 'You are free to go Miss Swan.... or you may stay Mary. His play on words cuts deeply, but I know that I will stay.

I sit at what I consider to be a small table in comparison to the one at villa Rossi, and I am surprised to find that it disappoints me. Von Treffen sits several feet away from me at the other end of the table. Numerous dishes are brought in by two silent staff, both men; and they offer each dish in turn, first to me, then to Von Treffen. The men then stand at each end of the table, one to the side of Von Treffen and the other to my side. The meat dishes consist of small, lean cuts and the vegetables are cooked lightly. He eats for several minutes, then he dabs the sides of his mouth with a napkin before speaking again. 'Mary, you have done a very brave thing today; and for that I respect you.'

'I am only trying to help my friend.' I reply.

'Your friend, and your sister in law; but sadly in name only.' I wince at yet another dig at David's absence. He knows how to pain. 'How are you managing.... with the twins?'

'Well enough.'

'I am deeply sorry to hear that Jemima is poorly. The love for a child is like no other love. Would you not agree?'

'Yes.'

'Then you will understand why I wish to have my son with me.'

'You don't know that it's a boy.' I reply.

'That is of no matter. What is important, is that I can give the child whatever it needs.'

'Except for a mother's love.'

'That is true; that is true.' He places the last piece of meat from his plate in his mouth and chews it slowly. When he has finished, he places his cutlery together and dabs the sides of his mouth again. I have been so busy watching Von Treffen that I haven't finished my meal, but I lay my cutlery together anyway, and the two silent men step forward and immediately remove the plates and take them out of the room. 'You are not blind though, are you Mary? You can see the kind of life I can give my child.'

'And you can see the kind of love that Katherine can give her child.'

One of the men comes back into the room carrying a tray of desserts. He comes first to me and lowers the tray for me to select one. Von Treffen clicks his fingers, and before I can take anything from the tray the man stands and walks out of the room carrying the tray with him. Whatever is in the desserts won't be sampled by either of us today.

'The courts here are interested in the welfare of the child over and above any other consideration, and they consider the financial security of the child to be high on the list of priorities. And.... I'm afraid Katherine has no security to offer the child, other than the charity of others.'

'She has a home with me.'

'As I said, charity, not security.' He waves his hand in dismissal. 'But we argue semantics Mary. Such things cannot be decided at the dinner table.'

'So why ask me to stay.... Alexander?' I begin to feel bolder.

'Because.... maybe there are other ways that we can.... come to an agreement.'

'Other ways?' I ask.

'Let me ask you a question Mary.' He picks up his napkin and again dabs his lips. 'What do you know of my family?'

'I know very little.'

He stands up from the table and walks over to a long cabinet. Above the cabinet is a large mirror, and Von Treffen leans forward and grins into the mirror to check his teeth. When he has finished, he steps back and opens a drawer, where he lifts out an envelope and brings it across to me; placing it on the table in front of me. 'Feel free to take the items out of the envelope.' I give him a puzzled look. 'To answer your question; yes, I knew that you were coming. The girl, by the way. She will no longer be working at the courthouse, and I would say that she will find it impossible to obtain a job, in this country at least, possibly for the rest of her life.' He holds out his hand. 'But please, continue. These things are trivia.

My hands begin to shake, and I feel sick at the thought of what I have done; what he has done. I open the flap and pull out two black and white photographs. The first one is a picture of a young couple; a man and a woman, the man could easily be Alexander. The woman appears to have dark curls; but her most striking feature is her soft, round eyes. They are quite beautiful. She is smiling, but she looks sad.

'That is the only photograph I have of my mother,' he says. 'And the second of only two memories I have. The picture and the book. Not much to leave behind for a boy of seven, don't you think. But we had five happy years together.' I look up at him; puzzled. 'My biological mother died when I was barely two years old.'

'I'm sorry,' I reply.

'My father told me that she was always a sickly woman. I never really knew her, and so I feel nothing.' He touches the face of the woman in the picture. 'My father re-married shortly after she died. This is the woman I came to know as my mother. the only woman I ever loved.'

'But not your real mother.'

'My real mother in every other way.'

'But to have lost two mothers in one lifetime.'

'I tell you this not to elicit your sympathy Miss Swan.' His curt reply reminds me that he is still a dangerous man. 'It is merely to help you to understand.'

'Why would you want me to understand?'

He continues without answering my question. 'The man is very obviously, my father. You will notice the resemblance.' He walks to the other end of the table and sits down again, and I look back at the photograph. He is indeed strikingly handsome, and also distinguished, and his demeanour is one of supreme confidence. Something that I had seen quite clearly in Von Treffen.

I place the photograph to the side and look at the second one. What I see both intrigues and shocks me. It is a photograph of Von Treffen's father, and he is wearing the uniform of an officer in the German army. I know very little of such things, but enough to see that he had been an officer in the SS. The man in the uniform carries the same confident, almost threatening gaze as his son. I pick the photograph up from the table and hold it, moving it from side to side. Wherever I place it he is looking straight into me, and a familiar shiver runs through me. He has a strange smile, and I catch his sadness; his desperate loneliness that can never be satisfied. And I know that I need to do whatever it takes to protect my friend and her baby.

'He was a great man,' Von Treffen says.

'He was a German SS officer,' I reply.

'Not all of them were bad.'

'He chose to wear that uniform.'

'He had to protect his family; he had to stay alive, at any cost. Is that not what you are trying to do Mary? Protect your family?'

I look down at the picture of his father again. 'Where are your family from Alexander?'

'So.... you do wish to know more about me?' he smiles. 'A true adversary should know his opponent well. Just as I know you well. And I do know you, and your family. Or did you think that I would allow just any woman to provide me with a child?'

'What do you mean?' I ask, as my heart begins to beat faster.

'First...I would like to tell you more.... about my family.' He stands up from the table again and walks back over to the cabinet, where he picks up a picture frame. 'It may be hard for you to imagine, but I was once a child.' He walks across to me and hands me the frame, and I look at the smiling face of a young boy standing by a river wearing only shorts. 'That picture was taken here when I was six. And as you can see, I was a very happy young boy. He returns the picture to the cabinet and goes back to his chair. 'My father was Austrian. He spent his childhood living in South Tyrol, the home of my ancestors. He grew up to be a clever and resourceful man. It was my father who came up with the idea of dressing Adolf Eichmann in a South Tyrolean costume to enable him to flee Germany at the end of the war. And he also helped many others do the same by providing the necessary documents to hundreds who were looking for a new life in Italy or elsewhere.'

'What you're saying is that he profited from the misfortune of others. And I suppose that is where all of this came from.' I look around the room.

'My family wealth and titles go back many generations. He chose to help others who would otherwise have been shot or imprisoned unjustly.'

'How could he know that?' I argue. 'Surely that should have been for the courts to decide.'

'Mary.... Mary. I cannot expect you to understand what it was like back then. There was a different moral code. The fate of another's life could be decided on the flip of a coin. My father simply chose to survive, and to do so, he had to weigh the odds in his favour. Is that so wrong? And if it were not for that desire in all of us to survive against the odds, then you would not be sitting here talking to me.'

'But how many had to die, so that you could be here?'

'Again Mary, I tell you these things not to gain your approval, but merely to furnish you with the knowledge I think you need.'

Once again, I look down at the German officer. 'When did he die?'

'He died before his time. In this house some twelve years ago. At twenty-seven I became the sole heir to the Von Treffen name, and to his business empire.'

'So why have you chosen to.... how did you put it? ....to furnish me with the knowledge you think I need? There must be a reason.'

He smiles at me, but I can still see his sadness. 'I believe that you alone Mary will understand.'

'I think it's because you want an heir. that's why you held Katherine against her will.' I stare into his eyes, no longer afraid. 'You don't want the Von Treffen name to be forgotten. Otherwise, all that your father did; all the sacrifices he made.... including her life,' I point at the photograph of the couple. 'will have been a waste.'

I see his eyes flicker; and then the smile returns. 'I knew that you would not disappoint me Mary.' He leans forward and takes a glass candle holder from the table. 'Neither Katherine, nor the Rossi girl, nor any of those before, could see what you see.' He pulls the candle out, places the candle holder back down and begins to roll to candle in his fingers. 'But you are going to have to do better than that Mary.'

'Why?' I ask. 'Why do you want me to know?'

'Because you are the only one who can change my mind.'

I am surprised by that, and for a reason I don't understand, it fills me once again with fear. 'But first Mary; I need to know how strong you really are. How much.... pain you are capable of bearing.'

My heart begins to race. Has he lured me here to hurt me? to kill me? What was he capable of? 'You are scaring me Alexander.' I say as my voice begins to shake. 'I think that maybe I should leave.'

He smiles again. 'I give you my word that you are in no physical danger; and you may leave any time you wish.'

'How do I know I can trust you?'

He laughs. 'I merely wish to acquaint you with all of the facts as I know them, and then you will be in a position to consider my offer.' He places the candle on the table and raises both of his hands. 'Now please, leave if you must.' I sit staring at him, every sense in my body telling me to stand up and walk out. But I know that the moment I do that then all is lost. And Katherine, my dearest friend, will lose her baby. I wait.

He lowers his hands. 'And that is why I have chosen to tell you these things. For you are strong Mary. And strength is something I prize very highly.' He sits back and once again picks up the candle to begin rolling it between his fingers. 'My step mother.... the woman in the picture. She was a strong woman. You may well think that it was my father who gave me my strength; and yes, he played a part; but it was her who taught me how to survive against the odds. How to live when those around me were stronger.'

'Until she died.'

He looks at me without smiling, then snaps the candle in half, before placing the pieces onto the table. 'Mary, will you come back to the library with me?' He stands and walks to the door, and I follow him, bringing the photographs with me. In the library, he walks across to the far side and makes his way along the shelf of the bookcase. He stops about half way and places his hand on a book and pulls on it. I hear a soft click as he holds the side of the bookcase and begins to pull it out. The entire unit swings open to reveal a small, circular room, which is also lined with shelves filled with books. In the centre of the room is a high, round table. He steps back and holds out his hand. 'Please Mary.' I hesitate before I walk through into the room, and Von Treffen follows me through.

'This is where I keep my most.... precious possessions.' He goes to one wall, places his hand on the side of a large oil painting and swings it open to reveal a safe.

After tapping out a long code, he turns the handle and pulls the heavy door open. He then lifts several files from the safe and places them on the console table underneath the safe.

Taking out from the pile a thick green file, he opens it and takes from amongst the papers a brown leather folder. I notice several German symbols stamped into the folder. He opens that and takes out all the documents, and before placing them on the table, he pauses and looks at me. 'Once again, I want to reassure you Mary that in showing you these documents, I merely wish for you to understand.'

He takes the documents to the round table and lifts the first paper from the top of the pile and offers it to me. I take it and begin reading the details. A few seconds later I stop reading and look at Von Treffen. 'This is her death certificate. The woman in the photograph.'

'Yes. But please.... read the details.'

I turn back to the paper and begin to read out loud. 'Agnese Von Treffen; born May 20th 1913; died August 10th 1944. That means that she was only thirty-one when she died.'

'Three years younger than I am now.' He adds.

I continue reading. 'Spouse, Bernhard Von Treffen; your father I presume.' He nods. 'Witness; Adolf Eichmann? He was...'

'A friend of the family. Eichmann's father had a mining company that did some business with my father. The company had some difficult financial problems that, if it became public knowledge, could have ruined them. My father dealt with it. They became friends.'

He hands me another sheet of paper, and I read the details. 'Their marriage certificate. March 21st 1939.'

'Six months before the start of the war.' He says.

'Bernhard Von Treffen; marries Agnese Ariella Tsayid.' I read through the details again. 'Agnese Tsayid. That sounds.... Jewish?'

'Yes.'

'Your stepmother was Jewish?'

'Yes, she was.'

'And your father was a member of the SS?'

'He loved her.'

'How did they meet? I mean, how could they possibly have met?'

'She was his housekeeper. She spent several years looking after my mother, before she died.'

'But, her death certificate; it was signed by....'

'By Eichmann.'

'Did he.... have her killed?'

'Quite the opposite.' He places the papers carefully back into the pile. 'Please, let me show you something else.' He walks over to the other side of the room and takes a book from the shelf. There is a small piece of paper sticking out of the top of the book, and he opens it on that page. Coming back to the table, he holds his finger on one line and shows it to me. I read it out.

'Tsayid; Hebrew; meaning, hunting; hunter. I don't understand.'

He picks up another document from the pile. 'This was registered in England on November 2nd 1944, less than three months after her death was registered.' He gives the document to me.

'Application for change of name. Current....' I read the details with disbelief. 'Current: Agnese Ariella von Treffen. New name: Elizabeth Hunter.' I stand frozen to the spot, and stare at the document for some time. 'Is this true?'

He takes out a small photograph from the pile and lays it on the table facing me. I recognize the woman in the picture instantly. David had the very same photograph in his wallet; and he proudly showed it to everyone he met. It is a picture of his mother. I look again at the photograph of the young couple, and I see the woman for the first time as she truly is. Elizabeth Hunter; formerly Agnese von Treffen; formerly Agnese Tsayid.

'No doubt,' Von Treffen says, 'you will have many questions.'

'Such as.... the death certificate was a forgery?'

'Of course.'

'But it was signed by none other than Adolf Eichmann. I can't think of another man who would have been less inclined to go along with this.'

'As I said Mary, there was a different code then. And his family, and my family had secrets.'

'I take it that he wasn't entirely happy about it then?'

'It would have cost my father a great deal, including their friendship. And it would have also put him in debt to Eichmann.'

'And that's why he helped him to escape.'

'He had no choice. And when others would have heard of it; they too wished to be helped by him.'

'So.... do you know how he felt about it?'

'I had always thought that my father's grief for all of those years was because he mourned her death; as did I.'

'Are you telling me that you didn't know?'

'Not until last year.'

'What happened last year.'

'I met David Hunter.'

'What! He told you this?'

'He showed me the photograph of his mother. I recognized her immediately. It was easy for me to get a copy; then I began my search for the truth. And for a way to keep the Von Treffen name, and her name, alive.'

Then a question forms in my mind that horrifies me; and I know that the answer could destroy everything I hold close. 'Does David know of this?'

'You are the only person I have told.' He begins to place the documents back into the leather folder.

My mind races as I work through the details. 'Meeting Katherine was never a coincidence, was it?'

'Only meeting David was what you call a coincidence. That was something so profound that if I believed in a higher being, then I would say that I was destined to meet him. But it is my belief that it was pure chance that led to our paths crossing.'

'But, since then....' The thoughts that come to me make me feel sick. 'Since then the whole thing has been contrived. You arranged for David to meet the Rossi's, and then to bring us to Italy. And you arranged to meet Katherine, knowing that she would....' I shivered at the thought. 'And you probably arranged for me to come here today.'

Von Treffen laughs. 'You credit me with powers that I do not possess. But I have arranged for as many things as I could to work in my interest. Others I have influenced to the best of my ability. That is the nature of my business; and it is also the nature of my family.'

'Please, tell me this.' I think about David leaving, and need Von Treffen to answer the second terrible question going through my head. 'Did my husband go along with your plans?'

He closes the leather folder and begins putting the files back into the safe. Then he turns to face me. 'Please forgive me for telling you this, but David....is weak. I control many people in my business, I make them succeed. But David will fail. He did fail.'

'Do you know why he left?' I ask.

'I believe that part of the reason is that he knows that he has failed; that he thinks what happened is his responsibility. I persuaded him to arrange for me to meet his sister; and I believe that he was overwhelmed with guilt.'

I try to keep calm at the thought of what Von Treffen had done to him, to the man I love. And I know then that he had destroyed our marriage. 'You said part of the reason?'

'He doesn't love you Mary. he cannot, for he is, as I said, weak.'

'Do you know where he is?'

'He is with his mother. where he feels safe.'

'Your stepmother.'

He smiles again. 'She died when I was seven.'

I stand silently as he closes the door of the safe and swings the painting back into place. My mind continues to race as I wonder how I might use any of this information against him. How I can stop him from taking Katherine's baby. Because now I hate him. I hate him more than I have ever hated anything. 'You do realise,' I say, 'that now you have told me all of this; you can no longer go through with your plans.' I try to sound more forceful than I feel. 'I won't hesitate to use it against you.'

'And I would expect nothing less.' He looks deep into me. 'I knew that you would not disappoint me Mary. You are indeed an interesting opponent, but I did not realise until now, just how worthy an opponent you would prove to be.' He reaches across and gently takes the photographs from me and holds out his hand toward the door. 'Shall we?'

We leave the small room and Von Treffen pushes the bookcase back into place, and I hear a soft click. I turn to face him and take a step closer. Standing less than a foot away from him, I can feel my heart beating against my chest, and I think of my bees, and I imagine the hum; the rhythm of the hive, and it calms me, and I can sense my heart falling into the same rhythm. I stare into his eyes, looking for something; anything that I can use; and he doesn't blink. An eternity seems to pass before I speak without looking away. 'David is your brother.' It takes what seems another lifetime before I can bring myself to say. 'Katherine is your sister.'

He doesn't move. He just stares back into me; showing no emotion. Then he speaks. 'The same blood does not flow through our veins.'

'But you want her child.'

'I want the child that has the strength of his grandmother.'

I think about David's mother, the woman I had met. Does she possess that kind of strength? Is she capable of that kind of love? She had doted on David, and at the same time had neglected, even rejected, Katherine. Is that because David reminds her of Alexander? But David is nothing like him. I hate to admit it, but David is weak and indecisive. He must have disappointed her. And then I see it. Alexander had admired her and even loved her, not for the love she had given him, but for the strength she had taught him. We all look for different things from the same person. It was possible that she had tried to do the same with David, but he had not possessed the same qualities as either her or Alexander. They had been kindred spirits. Katherine, on the other hand, did possess those qualities. But she was a female; and Elizabeth Hunter hadn't seen what alexander had seen. I step back from him, breaking the spell, and walk around to the other side of the table.

'Does she know that you are alive?'

'I am quite sure that she does.'

'So why....?'

'There is nothing to be gained for either of us. Only loss.'

I taste his sadness. 'What is there to gain from me?' I ask.

'I am glad that you have finally asked that question Mary. It tells me that you begin to understand.'

'I understand that you will take my friend's baby. That is enough for me.'

'Then do you understand that now I have been able to see what strength you have; and that you have the opportunity to change the outcome.' He walks around the table to stand in front of me, and as he passes it he picks up The Wind in the Willows book. 'Before you leave us, I have an offer for you. One that will allow Katherine to know that her child is safe and is loved. And one that will show you that I only do this to protect my child and my family.'

'Please continue,' I say.

He places the book back down again, next to me. 'You have given birth to two girls, to twins.'

'Yes.'

'And you very much appreciate the value of a new life that is part of you.'

Surely, he couldn't want one of my children? 'I love my girls.' I say forcefully.

He places his hands together. 'Mary, as I said, my sole intention has been to produce a worthy heir to the Von Treffen dynasty. One that is worthy of all that it represents.'

I pick up the book, and I remember my mother reading it to me as a little girl; and I think about the stories she would add that would always include the bees. The moral of the stories was always about love and loyalty to one's family, and what the bees were willing to sacrifice to protect their family; to the death if necessary. And I wonder if this moment now is what it was all for; if my being here today is my purpose, my opportunity, to show that kind of loyalty.

He continues. 'You will realise that I have no interest in the individual who provides that heir, other than they possess the ability to produce a child worthy of the Von Treffen name; and who better than the daughter of my stepmother. I had been willing to allow her to play a part in the life of the child, but she, and others, do not wish for that to be so. I believe she has the necessary strength and character to help raise the child.'

Katherine would not want any part of that. He has misjudged her.

He places his hand on my hand holding the book. 'but you Mary, you possess that rare strength which I not only admire, but wish to possess, to own. I want you to be the mother of our child; one that we will make together; and I want you to be my wife.' I step back and release my hand from his touch, as if it possesses a burning heat; and the book falls to the floor for the second time.

'I could not possibly....'

'I ask that you do not answer now. Think over my proposal; and think about Katherine. She will have her child, and she will be forever safe. There is still time for you to make the right choice.'

I have so underestimated him; and I feel helpless. He doesn't have the ability to understand the true nature of a mother's love. And he is certainly unable to comprehend a woman's love. Is there nothing I can use against him? Again, I race through my thoughts, looking for something, anything. And then I find it; just one small idea. 'I will tell her; your stepmother. I'll tell her all about your plans. I'll tell her what you intend to do.'

He stares into me once again. 'So, Mary, you still wish to play. Well here is my hand....and it is one that only you will hear, at this moment; and never again will I say it.' He bends down and picks up the book; and opens it to the front cover. 'I must read this again someday.' He looks at the page for several seconds, and then closes it. 'Perhaps not,' he says, and he looks up at me.

'I will take the child. That is inevitable; as I will use every resource I have, to make that happen. You may tell your story to whom you wish. But I would ask that each time you do so, you think on their lives. For once given it cannot be taken away. The offer will be open to you....' he smiles. '.... until I take my child.' He looks down at the cover of the book and runs his fingers over the title. He then opens it to the back page, where he does the same to the personal message written by the author. Keeping his hand on the page, he looks into me, and squeezes the page together, tearing it from the book. He then screws it into a ball and throws it to the ground. 'There is just one more thing before you leave Miss Swan.' He holds out the book to me. 'Please take this with my compliments. It is no longer of any value to me.'

As I drive over the bridge and away from the house, I begin to shake; and I find it hard to control the car; and as I round the lake a feeling of panic rises in me. I pull over to the side just before it joins the single road that leads me to the exit. I quickly open the car door and jump out and lean over and empty the contents of my lunch onto the grass verge. When I'm finished, I stand carefully, and shaking, I hold onto the car to steady myself. After waiting for several minutes for the feeling to pass and the fog that is filling my head to clear, I look at my watch. Did that all just happen? I have to make sense of it all. I get back into the car and search for the bottle of water I had brought with me for the journey, and after taking several mouthfuls of water, I look at the time again. It's just after 2pm. I still have time to get to the hospital and hopefully not be missed. I press the clutch, select first and slowly lift my foot. The car begins to glide forward, and a few seconds later I push the stick into second; and every few feet I begin to feel calmer. As I drive through the poplar trees, the sun flickers across the car with a steady rhythm. The gates loom up in front of me, and I wonder if they will open, and consent to give me the freedom I desire more than anything else.

They remain closed, and I begin to slow the car. The gates seem so much bigger than when I arrived, and they stand like tall soldiers. I have almost stopped the car, and one gate lurches and begins to slide open, and as before, the other follows suit shortly after. I anticipate my freedom by placing my foot over the accelerator, ready to press it with some determination. What I see the other side causes me to move my foot to the brake, and as I pass through the gates I slow to a stop.

In front of me are several cars, and as I look along the road I can see six or seven more. I sit motionless, my hands holding tight onto the steering wheel. As I stare through the windscreen the door of the lead car opens. I expect to see several of Von Treffen's men get out, only to tell me that I can't leave after all. Instead, I watch as Anatra steps out, followed by Edoardo and then Vittoria from the back of the car. I wish that the ground will open and swallow me. Anatra begins to walk toward me, and I can see from his face that he's not happy. I pull on the handbrake, check that the car is out of gear, and turn the engine off. There is silence. I know it won't last.

I wind the window down so that it's completely open. Anatra walks to the side of the car and stops at the window. His dark steel rimmed sunglasses reflect the sharpness of the blue sky. As he slides them off I expect him to ask for my driving licence and insurance. He stands for several seconds without speaking, and I continue to hold on to the steering wheel and look straight ahead. 'I'm sorry.' I hear myself say. Still he says nothing. 'I didn't mean to cause you any worry.' I add.

Nothing. 'Please say something Anatra. I can't bear this.'

He waves to the others, and they begin to climb back into their cars. 'I think it is best if I drive you back,' he says.

'Back where?' I ask.

'To the villa.'

'But I have to go....'

'Gaia has already gone. There is no need to worry.'

I can't believe how guilty I feel; and now I know that Gaia has gone to the hospital, I can bear it no longer. 'Oh my God, what have I done?' I let go of the steering wheel and bury my face in my hands. The strain of the past few hours finally releases into sobs; and as I close my eyes I see David, and Katherine, and then my mother. I feel a hand on my shoulder, and I know it is Anatra. There are no words, just the comfort of his soft touch.

'Please,' he says softly. 'We should go.'

I briefly look up at him and then slide across the bench seat over to the right and onto the passenger side. He opens the door, climbs into the car and immediately starts the engine. In one swift movement, he selects first gear, lifts the clutch and drives off in the direction of the other cars. I am not looking forward to the journey back.

∞ ∞ ∞

The kitchen at the villa Rossi is warm and welcoming; but I still hold on tightly to my mug of hot coffee as it brings a similar welcome warmth to my hands. Sitting with me are Anatra and Edoardo. 'What were you thinking Mary?' Anatra asks. 'Do you know how much trouble you caused?' I don't speak. I know that no matter what I say, I won't be able to make them understand, but I will have to say something; I'm just not sure what. 'I cannot believe that you of all people would be willing to put your life, and the lives of those around you, in such danger. And to also involve my niece.' He begins to raise his voice, and Edoardo places his hand on his brother's arm.

'Maria.' Edoardo says; and he smiles softly. I am sure that you thought you were doing the right thing. Am I right?'

'I was trying to help,' I reply.

Anatra goes to speak, but Edoardo squeezes his arm. 'That is understandable. We all wish to find a way to stop this. But did you really think that he would listen to you?'

'But he did listen.' I say, and immediately regret it. I had decided on the journey home not to tell anyone the details. And I remember what Von Treffen had said. *'Once given, it cannot be taken away.'*

'What did he say?' Anatra asks.

'That he would not change his mind,' I reply, and hope that will be enough.

'Did you expect anything else?' Anatra continues.

'I had to know.'

'Know what?'

'That I had done everything I could.' I lean forward to speak, and the coffee spills onto the table. 'I'm not just some helpless....' This time Edoardo places his hand on my arm.

'Maria. What you have done was very foolish. But it was also a very brave thing to do. I understand that....'

'Edoardo....' Anatra interrupts, but his brother holds up his hand.

'We all, through our lives, will do both foolish and brave things. Just as when we rescued Katherine. I am grateful that today we did not have to be foolish and brave again,' Edoardo says.

I smile at him. 'Thank you Edoardo.'

'As for my brother. He is angry because he cares very much for you.'

'Edoardo,' Anatra says as he scowls at his brother.

'More than he should perhaps.' Edoardo continues, ignoring his brother. 'Now, is there anything that this man said that may be of help to us?'

I look straight at Edoardo, and then Anatra. The details of the morning flash through my mind, and I know that I must tell them nothing. 'I wish I could say yes,' I lie, and the knot in my stomach returns.

I watch as the brothers look at each other, and Anatra says softly, his gaze lowered, 'Well if there is anything that you remember, please be sure to let us know. We cannot help you otherwise.'

'Yes, I understand.' I pick up my cup, and can feel my hand shaking, so I hold it with both hands, take a mouthful, then place it back down. 'I am sorry,' I say; and feel the tears stinging my eyes.

'There is one other thing Maria,' Anatra says. 'You will need to speak with Katerina. She does not know that you went to see Von Treffen.

I nod. 'You think I should tell her?'

'she will know soon enough; it would be better if it came from you,' he replies.

'I'll go and see her shortly.' The brothers stand, and I look at each of them in turn, and I can see their mother in both of them. Anatra makes an effort to smile, and they walk quietly out of the kitchen. I look at the wall clock and know that in less than an hour the kitchen will become a hub of activity, so I finish my coffee quickly and make my way up to Katherine's room. As I climb the stairs I realise that I have left the book that Von Treffen had given me on the kitchen table. I begin walking down the stairs to retrieve it, and stop at the bottom step, recalling the time I had seen David with the then unknown woman, talking secretly together. I realise now that it's possible that as well as them discussing the details of my dress, Vittoria could have been passing a message to David from von Treffen.

I continue into the kitchen and stop when I find Vittoria standing at the end of the table looking through the pages of the book.

'Wind in the Willows,' I say, and Vittoria looks up.

'Where did you get this?' she ask.

'I think you know,' I reply.

Vittoria opens the book to the back, and her eyes widen as she sees that the page has been ripped out. 'I am sorry I told them Maria.' I look at Vittoria. 'I told Anatra where you had gone.'

'Why?' I ask.

'They were worried, and I became scared.' She holds the book out to me. 'He told me that he could never love another woman as he loved her; his mother.'

I walk around the table, open the book and look at the torn-out page. 'What else did he tell you?

'Just that Maria.'

'He is not a good man Vittoria.'

'Si, I now understand that,' She replies. 'But I think he has found that love. He has found the woman to replace her.'

'Katherine, you mean?'

'No Maria, I think he has found you.'

I put my hands on Vittoria's shoulders and look into her eyes. 'I want you to promise me something.'

'Si Maria.'

'You must promise to keep what I tell you a secret.'

'Si.'

'He wants to have me as his wife.'

'Oh Maria, what will you do? You cannot marry him.'

'If I don't do as he wishes, he intends to take Katherine's baby. And there is nothing we can do to stop him.'

'You would do this for your friend?'

'My mother told me a story when I was a young child. It was about the bumble bee; and how he had been good friends with the rest of the bees. During the busy times, when the bees were collecting nectar to make it into honey, the bumble bee used to help them out before going off to collect her own nectar. But one day bumble bee was nowhere to be found. All the bees had come back to the hive feeling pretty tired. As they made their way into the hive they could hear laughing, and they wondered what it could possibly be. They went down into the hive and were horrified to find that bumblebee had eaten all their honey, and she had also killed all their babies. So, they took bumblebee to their queen and asked her to work her bee magic, and she changed the nature of the bumblebee and told her that she would be forever different from the other bumblebees, and just like the cuckoo, she would never have a friend again, and she would never have a home of her own.'

Mummy told me about the cuckoo bumblebee; and how it would invade a nest of bumblebees and kill their queen and destroy their eggs. Then it would lay its own eggs in the bumblebee hive and force the other bumblebees to look after her eggs. But when she had finished, she would fly off, sad and alone, with not a friend in the world.

'Von Treffen is just like that. But now he wishes to have a queen all to himself. He will take Katherine's baby; and if I don't do something, there will be no one there to protect it. She is my sister and my friend. But listen Vittoria. I am telling you this because I may need to speak with him again. I may need your help again; but I need to know that I can trust you.'

Vittoria thinks for a while. '*Si*,' she says, nodding her head vigorously. '*Si*, I will do whatever you ask of me. and this time it will be our secret.'

I turn to leave, and she holds my arm gently. 'Maria; you are the bravest person I know. Apart from *mio padre* of course.'

'Of course,' I reply, and we both laugh.

∞ ∞ ∞

I tap on the door to Katherine's room. 'Come in,' she replies, and I open the door and step into the room.

'Hello sis,' I say, smiling. 'How are you doing?'

She smiles back. 'Hi. I was thinking about going for a walk around the gardens. Beginning to feel a bit restless to be honest.'

'I remember that feeling,' I reply, and walk into the centre of the room. My eyes widen as I look around. 'Some things don't change,' Every surface is covered in clothes.

'If I had known you were coming up I would have made an effort.'

'Would you like me to....?'

'No, no thanks. It's.... comfortable.'

'I could walk with you if you like?' I say.

'I'd like that.' She pulls out a cardigan from a pile of clothes on the chair. 'Perhaps you could show me around Cesare's beehives. You've told me enough about them.'

'I don't know if that's such a good idea,' I reply.

'Oh, so they're just for you then Philippa Mary,' she says as she walks past me toward the door and rubs the side of my face. The times Mummy had done that, and I had hated it. but right now I want nothing more than to feel the familiar touch of her fingers running down my cheek.

'It's not that, and you know it,' I reply, following Katherine out of the door. 'It's more that you're pregnant, and they can be unpredictable when they don't recognise your smell.'

'Wait, you're telling me now that they can smell?'

'Of course they can,' I say as I close the door to the bedroom. We walk slowly along the corridor. 'Their antennae can smell, taste and feel.'

'So why wouldn't they like my baby?' she asks.

'They might love it; I don't know. But you're not used to....'

'Used to what?'

'Katie; you've never liked the bees.'

'And they'll know that?'

'Well.... yes.'

'Okay. Let's just walk in the gardens then.'

'Katie,' I say as we step off the veranda. 'Have you heard anything from Von Treffen?'

'How could I have done?' she replies. 'I have a thousand bodyguards making sure that he doesn't get anywhere near me.'

'So, do you feel safe?'

'Safe?' She asks as she slides her shoes off and rubs her feet into the cool grass. 'Not really. Do you?'

'I'm worried for my babies,' I reply. 'Things have changed.'

'Having twins does that you know. How were they today?'

'Okay, I think.'

'Okay you think?' What did they say; at the hospital?'

'I don't know.'

'What do you mean? They must have said something.'

'I didn't go.'

'Yes, you did. I saw you drive off this morning.'

'I didn't go to the hospital.' I turn to faced her. 'I went to see Alexander.'

'What did you say?'

'I went to....'

'I heard you the first time. And since when did you start calling him Alexander?'

'Can we go into the gardens?' I reply and walk out into the garden. 'I don't want anyone in the house to hear.'

Katherine slides her shoes back on and follows me. 'Why not? What do you need to say that they can't hear?'

I struggle to find the words. 'Katie, I want you to know that I love you and would never do anything to hurt you.'

'Now you're scaring me. please just tell me.... whatever it is you're going to tell me.'

I hesitate before I answer. 'He has asked me to marry him.'

'What? Are you mad? You can't be serious. Why?'

'You need to calm down Katie.' I walk toward her, and she raises her hands to me.

'And you need to tell me what's going on. How many times have you been to see him?'

'This was the first time Katie, I swear. The only other time I've met him was at the wedding.'

'Then why; why?'

'I will explain, if you let me.' I point to a bench in the far corner of the gardens. 'Can we go and sit over there?'

We sit at the bench and I tell her everything. I also explain how he had used David to lure us to Italy; and why he had used her; and I give her details of what his intentions were.

She is silent for several minutes, and I feel like I can't breathe.

'I've been so stupid,' she says eventually, and I let out a breath. 'I never realised that such people existed. When we used to talk about the books we were reading, and the characters; well, they all seemed so exciting; even the villains. But this isn't exciting; it's horrible; it's evil; he's evil'

I pull her to me and hug her. 'It will be okay Katie. I promise.'

'How can you promise that Mary? You don't know what's going to happen.'

'No, I don't. but what I do know is that he's alone, and we have each other, and we have the Rossi family and, for all I know, several thousand bodyguards.'

'Yes, but for how long can we rely on that?' she asks.

'We have one other thing Katie. If you look over there.' I point to the long hedge at the far side of the garden. 'We have something that has helped me survive some of the worse times of my life.'

Katherine peers at the hedge and then looks at me 'You can't mean....'

'The bees have always looked after me Katie. Think about it. they even saved my mother's life.'

She stands abruptly and begins to pace up and down. 'Then maybe I should go back home; to England; to Meadowsweet.'

'You can't. The legal papers he sent here banned you from leaving until after you've had the baby and the court has decided custody.'

'Well the bees can't do much about that can they,' she replies. 'Maybe I could sneak out.'

'Do you want to take that chance?' I ask. 'If they were to catch you; who knows what they would do?' I know that as well intentioned as the Rossi family are, they can't protect us forever. 'What if....'

Katherine stops pacing. 'What if what?'

'What if I did as he asked?'

'Now who's being stupid?' She sits down on the bench beside me. 'He's just playing you Mary, as he has all of us, until he gets what he wants.'

'I'm not so sure.'

'Okay. What if he really does... want to marry you, that is? Where does it end? And what about the twins? I bet he didn't mention them. And I don't want to lose you Mary. You're all I've got.' She stands again. 'And there's just the tiny detail of my mother.'

'You can't tell her about this Katie. You know what he said.'

'Just one other thing he wants to control. Is he trying to take over the world or something?'

I'm beginning to ache from not having fed Constance. I had enough milk for two, and I can only feed one, and I can't even do that right now. Have I done the right thing? This should be the most magical time of my life. I know that. But it is how it is. That's what Mummy used to say. Best get on with it.

'Katherine; I asked you once, when I first came to you house, about your father. You didn't want to talk about it then. It might be important.'

'I can only tell you what she told me. that he left not long after I was born. I'm beginning to wonder if she didn't kick him out, once he had served his purpose.'

'I've just realised something.' I reply.

'What's that?'

'She kept her name, her new name, that is. She kept the name Hunter, and she even had you and David registered under that name. she never took on your father's name.'

'Maybe she never married him.'

Or maybe it was her way of controlling things; as she taught Alexander to do.' I look down at the ground. 'David has gone home, you know.'

'What, to her?'

'So Alexander said.'

'And he would know.' Katherine points her finger at me. 'That's why she hooked up with my father; she just wanted an Alexander of her own. Let's face it; David is no Alexander. And I must have been her second attempt. Except for one small detail of me being a girl, she nearly cracked it.'

'And that must be why she kicked him out. She couldn't bear to go through that again.'

'You could be right.' She placed her hands on her mouth. 'Oh my God.'

'What is it?' I ask.

'She took my father away from me, and now her stepson; her protégé, wants to take my child. What is it with the Von Treffen's?'

'We won't let it happen Katie. We will find a way; I promise.' I catch a glimpse of Cesare appearing out of the hedge at the far side of the garden. 'Katie, I need to talk to Cesare. Are you okay for a while?'

'What is it?'

'Just something you said then.' I begin to walk across the garden. 'I'll tell you later; after I've spoken to him.' I go as quickly as I can, and as I approach Cesare I call out to him.

He turns at the sound of my voice, and I see that he's carrying an empty basket. *'Ah bella.'* He waits for me. *'Come sta?'*

'I am well Cesare.'

'Bien, bien.'

'But I am troubled.'

'I am sorry to hear that Maria. Is there some way I can help?'

'I'm hoping that you can.' I reply. 'I need to ask you about the Von Treffen family.'

His smile faded. 'We do not talk of them.' He replies, his voice sounding gravelly. 'Unless there is a need.' He turns away and continues his journey into the garden.

I follow, and I have to walk behind him as he moves along a narrow path with rose bushes either side. 'I think Cesare, there is a need.' He stops, keeping his back to me as he cuts several buds that have not bloomed, and he places them gently into the basket. 'Please Cesare; I need your help.' He continues his journey and I keep pace behind him.

'I cannot help you Maria. Not with this.' I'm startled by the anger in his voice. Could I be right? If I am, then it all makes sense. He stops again, cuts more buds from a deep purple rose, and continues along the path.

'If not for me, then for Annalise,' I say, and I stop, wondering if I have gone too far. He stops again, but this time he doesn't take any buds. I watch him as his shoulders lower. 'You said we were famiglia,' I continue. 'Isn't this what families do? Help each other?' He turns slowly to face me. 'She would want this Cesare. She would want to stop them this time.'

'You ask much Maria.'

'Yes, too much; I know.' I reply, as I hear the pain in his voice. 'It couldn't have been Alexander von Treffen's father. He would have been too young; and he only died twelve years ago.'

I wait for him to speak. 'Dieter Von Treffen,' he says.

'The.... Grandfather?'

'Si. He was....my friend.'

'Your friend? His reply surprises me. I didn't see that. 'You and the Von Treffen's; you knew each other well?'

'Many, many years past, *si*. My father brought this land from them. They would come back here in the winter months, and Dieter and I would play on the land; among the newly planted vines. They would stay here many times over the years.' He shuffles uneasily, and I feel claustrophobic amongst the roses. 'Then I met Annalise.'

'And that.... changed things.'

'We both fell in love with her.' He turns to the side to cut another bud, holds it close and turns it in his fingers, examining the petals. He softly kisses the petals, lost in a private thought. 'I loved her, and she chose me.' He smiles. 'And we married, and we had a son.

'Edoardo.'

'Si; my only son.' He places the bud into the basket. 'Dieter married also, and he had a son. But he still wanted her, and so he took her. And that was that.'

'And so you killed him.'

'*Si*. I killed him.'

'And for that you spent ten years of your life in prison.'

'For her.'

'But Annalise; she had another son.'

'*Si*.'

I watch as his eyes look into the past. 'But you named him....'

'She gave him the name.'

'Why?'

'Because she wanted him to be mine, my son.'

It starts to all make sense. Alexander would have known all of this. His sense of revenge went so much deeper than I could have ever imagined. 'Is Cesare your son? Now?'

'He is my son. Because of her, he is my son.'

I smile. 'Then she beat them; she never let them win.' I step forward and place my hand on his. 'How can I beat them Cesare? How?'

'The answer is not always there when you want it. But it will come. It will come if you are prepared to wait. Annalise waited, and she taught me to wait; many years. Can you wait *Bella*? Can you watch?'

'Yes.'

'Then that is what you must do. But you must trust your instincts. This much I have learned.'

'*Grazie* Cesare. Thank you.' I put my arms around him and kiss him on the cheek, and he laughs; his deep gravelly laugh. And it sounds musical. I turn and walk back down the path between the rose bushes. Then I stop and turned back toward Cesare. 'There is just one more thing.' I wait, knowing that I will cause him more pain. 'How did you know? How did you find out? What he had done. Did she tell you?'

'The bees told me.'

'The bees?'

'She would keep her diary in the blue hive; and I found it. She had told the bees, and they told me.'

I catch my breath. 'Thank you again Cesare. Thank you. When I return home, I shall tell my bees.'

Chapter 74

*And so the paint is on the canvas. There is no turning back. I have seen inside
your heart; what colours you have used. We dream of what we can become,
but can never truly know until the last stroke of the brush.*

Had she ever told the bees? Had Mummy done that? Did they know all about this? I
had woken her as early as I could. We had read the diary, but she had tired quickly.
Jemima called Doctor Sidle, as we felt we needed to know where things were going.
He was busy examining her, so Jemima and I waited anxiously in the kitchen.

'I never thought that we would get to this point,' she said.

'What point is that?' I asked.

'Where she would....'

'We don't know that yet, do we. Perhaps we should wait for the Doctor to tell us
what he thinks.'

'But it's going to come sometime, isn't it?' she replied.

I knew she was right, but I didn't want to think about it. 'I know, but I also know
that we will be alright.'

'You keep saying that, but you can't know that.'

I remembered what Cesare had said to Mummy. *The answer is not always there
when you want it. But it will come; it will come if you are prepared to wait.* And he had
asked her if she could wait. Could I wait? I knew the answer was there, and I thought
I knew where I had to go to find it.

There was a soft tap on the door. 'Hello; oh hello Miss Constance,' Doctor Sidle
said when he saw me, and he smiled. 'Miss Jemima didn't say you were still here.
And how are you.'

'I'm as well as can be expected Doctor. More importantly, how is Mummy.'

His countenance dropped slightly. 'Mummy, I mean Mary, is not doing so well.
Her heart is weakening. I think we need to admit her for further tests.' He sighed.
'She didn't recognize me this time. I think the dementia is progressing more quickly.
More than I would have expected. Are you able to take Mary to the hospital?

Jemima and I looked at each other. 'I think we can manage,' I said. 'How soon is this happening?'

'I have arranged for a bed at the end of the week. Is that okay?'

'That quickly,' I replied, then feeling guilty. 'Would you like some tea?' I asked, in an attempt to change the subject.

'That is most kind, but I am afraid I have a busy day ahead of me. I'm already late for my next appointment.'

'Oh, I am sorry Doctor,' I replied. 'How thoughtless of me.'

'Oh, not at all Miss Constance, you know that Mary is a very special lady; it's the least I can do.'

I waved goodbye and close the door. Back in the kitchen Jemima had started preparing some lunch. 'I need to go back to Italy,' I said.

She stopped what she was doing and looked up at me. 'But I thought you said you were staying.'

'It's only for a couple of days. I just need to sort a few things out, so that I can stay.'

'But why now? Mummy is going into hospital and she will need us both Connie,' She lowered her head. 'I need you.'

I walked over to her and placed my hands on her shoulders. 'Just a couple of days Jem. If all goes well, I'll be back before she goes in.'

'Okay,' she replied. 'I guess I'm just being selfish.'

'I just want to ask one thing,' I said.

'What's that?'

'Don't do anything before I get back.'

'You mean Jake.'

'I mean Jake, yes. Do you think you can do that?'

'Yes okay; but please come back.'

'I promise I'll do my best to get back as quickly as possible.'

I packed one bag and left it in my room, then I went into Mummy's room. She was still in bed. She had a book in her hands, but her eyes were closed. I sat next to her and waited, and after a few minutes she opened her eyes.

'Katherine, is that you?' she asked.

'It's Constance Mummy.'

'Yes, it is; how silly of me. Connie.' She smiled. 'I was dreaming.'

'What were you dreaming about?'

'Oh, Italy. Can we go and see her?'

'I'm going back there, Mummy.'

'To see Katherine?'

'To see the Rossi's. I leave in a couple of hours.'

She looked at me intently. 'What are you looking for Constance?'

'The same thing as you Mummy.'

'Then we need to finish the diary,' she said firmly. 'But take me out into the gardens; I need to feel the warmth of the sun.

Chapter 75

Diary; November 2nd 1970

As I watch Katherine sleeping peacefully in the hospital bed I think of Mummy. Several hours earlier; 3am to be precise; Katherine had given birth to a baby girl. My own delicate Jemima is still in the baby care unit. She isn't improving, and although I had been distracted whilst caring for Constance, I think of little else. I sip the tea I have made in the ward kitchen. I have to be content with a spoonful of sugar, as there is no honey. Von Treffen's legal team will be banging on the door of the hospital to take Katherine's baby at the earliest opportunity. Cesare had told me to wait, to watch for the moment; but I haven't seen it yet. I have asked Anatra if, when the time comes, he will help me; no matter the cost. He has said yes.

But the answer has not come. And it's beginning to feel as if it is too late. Cesare had also told me to trust my instincts; and I trust him. But I've seen nothing; not one thing that I can use against Von Treffen. Should I marry him? The thought feels me with horror. Perhaps once I've done that, and Katherine is safely away in England I can leave him. But I know in reality, that he will have thought of all the possibilities. If that's what I'm supposed to do, then I will have to face it head on.

Katherine stirs briefly, and I'm distracted from my daydreaming. Things will change when morning comes. The court has awarded custody to Von Treffen. We can appeal, but that won't change the fact that Katherine will have to let her baby go. And I had promised her that I wouldn't let her down; that I would find a way. I have this resolve in my heart that if he turns up at the hospital I will agree to marry him, but can I go through with it?

Chapter 76

The answer is not always there when you want it. But it will come. It will
come if you are prepared to wait. And we had waited.

I turned the page of the diary, only to find that it was blank, and I looked at my Mother. 'The diary ends there. Is that it? Is there another diary?' I asked her.

'There are no more diaries,' she said calmly.

'You didn't find a way to beat him. He took the baby?' I took a deep breath and stood up from the garden table. The sun was quite hot out of the shade of the umbrella. I thought of Italy. My Italy. I was beginning to feel exhausted from the journey through the diaries. The journey through my mother's past. I needed to know. I needed it to end. 'Can you remember what happened?' I asked her.

'I remember it dear. I remember it now.'

'The diaries, they brought it back?'

'Yes, yes they did.'

'You must have had a reason for not writing what happened. For not putting it in the diaries.'

She took the last diary from me and, closing it, she put it on the table. Then she placed her hand on the top of the diary. 'Do you remember what happened when Cesare read Annalise's diary?' she asked.

'He killed a man. He killed Dieter von Treffen.'

'Yes. And it was for that reason that I knew I couldn't risk the wrong person reading the diaries to find out the truth. So, I stopped writing. And when I came home, I put them in the hive; with the bees.'

'So.... will you tell me?'

'I have to Constance.'

'You have to?'

'Yes. You see.... I haven't told the bees; at least, I haven't told them what happened when I stopped writing.'

'And you really need to tell them? I mean, really tell them?' I said. Through the years I had seen many things that had led me to believe that the bees were very special to my mother. and since I had been home, and especially since I had read the diaries, I had become convinced by their magic.

'Yes Constance; my sweet Constance. I always knew that you would be the one who would become the Lady of the Meadow. And when I tell you, and the bees, the final part of the story; then you will understand. You see, the bees turn our telling's into sweet honey, collecting our memories like pollen. They are the keepers of our story.'

'Do you really believe that?' I asked.

'Yes, I do. As did your Grandmother, and her mother before her. They told the bees everything that had happened in their lives. But there was a time when your Great Grandmother nearly lost them. All of them.'

'What happened?

'Well, my mother told me the story of when my Grandfather died. He was a handsome man, bless him. She was angry; very angry. You see, she felt that he had died before his time. And she blamed it on the bees.'

'How so?'

'Well, she felt that they had lured her into thinking about them, thinking too much about their feelings. And she called them selfish; which is about the worse insult you can give to a bee.' I laughed lightly, and she continued. 'She thought that after all of the love and attention, and telling, that she had given them, the least they could have done was to tell her.... before. So that she might have at least been able to try and do something.'

'What happened?' I asked.

She refused to tell them about his passing. And so they began to leave; queens as well. And those that didn't leave.... they began to die; in their thousands. We got down to one hive before she broke.'

'What do you mean by broke?'

'She told them.'

'Told them?'

'She got up one morning; picked up her bucket, and went out to the hive. She placed her hands on the top of the hive, and she told them. She told them about the passing of the love of her life.'

'So, she saved the bees, and the hive?'

'Oh, much more than that. All the bees came back. All of them. At least the ones that hadn't died.'

'How did she know that they were her bees? The ones that came back.'

'Because the queens were all marked to identify them; and when they came back, the others followed.'

We sat quietly, as I thought about all that she had told me. 'I know what you want me to do; when the time comes,' I said.

'And I know that you will tell them.' She smiled softly at me; and I was glad that we had had this time. And I knew that I would tell them; I would tell the bees. And I remembered the last time I had been in the meadow with Mummy. I had been a little girl, and I had just returned from the hospital. I had known then of the magic of the bees, but I had not understood it. 'This is hard for me Connie.'

'Are you sure that you want to do this?'

'Yes, I'm sure. But may we walk to the meadow? I think I can only tell this the once; and they need to hear this too.'

We left the garden and walked across to the meadow gate. I placed my hand on the bar to open it, but Mummy put her hand on mine to stop me.

'May I? Just this once more?' she asked.

I stood back and smiled. She put her hand on the bar and tried to slide it open, but it didn't move. I thought her strength would fail, and I began to move forward, but she placed both hands on the bar and put all her frail weight behind it, and slowly it edged across and jumped several times before it was clear of its hold. She stood upright; a look of triumph on her face, and then she bent her body into the gate, and slowly it swung open. She walked unsteadily into the meadow, and I followed her through. As we walked closer to the hives we heard the familiar sound of the bees' welcome.

Now we were here together, she put her hands on the hive and closed her eyes. I stood the other side of the hive and placed my hands on hers. Together we could feel the life, the heartbeat of the hive. I waited for her to speak.

'Hello my babies,' She said softly. 'And how are you today?'

Mary's Story

I sit in the hospital chair for what seems an eternity, and when I see the first glimmer of sun touch the far side of the wall, I stand; my body stiff from being still for so long. I walk to the window and raise the blind, but Katherine doesn't stir. Looking out of the window at the surrounding buildings, I watch as their outlines become more defined as the sun rises, and it is like watching the invisible hand of an artist spreading colour and shape and shadow onto his canvas. My life has been such a canvas; except that the colours and shades have been added and painted over by those around me.

For just the briefest of moments, the room darkens again as a passing truck moves across the window. And I know; in that moment; I know, that my baby has left me. And I know that the waiting and watching is done, and I can see what I need to do. Cesare had been right; my instincts had been right, and as I turn to the soft sound of Anatra entering the room, and as I see his tears, I know. But I did not realise that I could be so sad and so happy all at once.

Anatra tells me that her poor heart just could not keep beating. She had been sleeping quietly when it came, and for that I am grateful. He takes me to her, and he sits with me, and we both cry until we can cry no more. Then I tell him what we must do. And he says no, and he argues, and he shouts, and we cry tears that we don't think we have. And then he says yes. And then I hold my baby.

∞ ∞ ∞

I sit with Katherine and watch as she quietly finishes eating; and I try to imagine life without my baby; and her life without her baby. I know that what I will tell her to do is the right thing; that she will have to say yes.

I am the strong one; I know that now. She would not have the strength to do this. I will tell her that there is no time. And when I tell her; the pain in her eyes nearly breaks me, but I stay strong; for both of us. I even think about how her pain will fool von Treffen. Fool him into believing that Katherine's baby is my baby. Fool him into thinking that her baby has died, and that Jemima is still living.

I tell her that it will have to be forever. And that is where the plan nearly fails. For just then, she hates me more than she hates him.

And he comes to the hospital; with his people. And I stand and watch as Anatra tells him that his child has died. And I know that I have done the right thing when all I see is anger. And I know that I have lost so much, but I have won. We have beaten him.

I say a silent prayer of thanks to Cesare. My Cesare. I love him so much. And later I thank Anatra. He explains how he had switched the details on the babies. He also tells me that if it is ever discovered, they will put him in prison and throw away the key. But he will never be found out. Because I love; I have loved, both of my babies for a lifetime. And I love Anatra.

Although my dear darling Katherine is no longer here, she also loved both of my girls as if they were her own; which was half true. I always knew that her poor broken heart would not last. When she died a short while after the girls twelfth birthday, she left a letter saying how happy she was to have had such a beautiful friendship. She also left me many pieces that she had crafted in the workshops of Meadowsweet. I still have the bowls she designed edged with bees. The ones she made to match my Grandmother's plates. And she said that although she never understood them, she always knew that the bees had given me the strength I needed, and she asked me to thank them for giving her the time that she had had with her secret daughter.

And so, my babies, I would like to thank you. And when the time comes, I know that my Constance will tell you the end of my story. Goodbye my babies.

Epilogue

I glance to my right to check on Jemima. She is sitting quietly, her head slightly bowed, and her eyes closed. I'm unable to tell if she is listening to the eulogy; and then I see her smile at the words that Edoardo Rossi is reading. He still stands tall; in spite of his advancing years. Gaia, his beautiful grey-haired wife, looks on with pride.

Of course, things will be different now, but I hope that it means they will be better. It doesn't matter to me that Jemima isn't my sister, and I hope that it won't matter to her; if she were to find out.

Looking over to my mother's coffin, I know that she has had her wish in the end. The slightly longer coffin sitting to the side of her is testimony to that.

Anatra had died the day after the love of his life. Yes, he had his wish too. Of course he did. Had he died of a broken heart? I'm not sure; but I am certain of the fact that Mummy had died knowing that she had been the love of his life. Even though dementia had robbed her of most of her memories. For some magical reason the bees had done that for her. It was their parting gift, you might say.

I had read in the diaries that David had said that he could never love someone forever. Maybe he had been right; but even though Anatra could not be with her, he had loved her for a lifetime, and that had been enough. He told me he had cared for Cesare's bees when he had passed away some years eight years ago, and when I had told him what his father had said to my mother, *'Should you ever need my help, the blue hive will give you the sweetness to satisfy you,'* he had taken me to the blue hive to find what his father had left there. We found a small package; a letter and a promissory note; the legacy of which would mean that Meadowsweet would never have to be sold or divided, and would ensure that we could stay there for a very long time. It had been a bittersweet experience; and when we had opened the hive, my mind had travelled back to when I had first retrieved the diaries; the beginning of my journey, and I had thought that it was a fitting end to magical journey. Or was I being too poetic?

Anatra and I had spoken for many hours, and he was able to tell me many things that were not in the diaries, and he had come back with me to Meadowsweet; to find his lost love. They had married six weeks before she died. And she was happy. Where was David, my father? No one knows. Amongst Mummy's papers I had discovered divorce papers that had been sent from some mysterious location many years before, which were the only sign of his existence. I hoped he was happy.

I feel my hand being squeezed, and I know that the man sitting next to me will experience all the love I can show. More than he can ever earn, or maybe even deserves. Perhaps that's unfair of me; for he has earned my love; and he is more than I deserve. That is my choice; my decision; my life; my dance. I look to my left and squeeze Gabriel's hand. Whatever we are to face, we will do it together. And that will be our dance.

My mind goes back to the moment this all started; when I received the message from Jemima in the small church in Milan. And I look up into the roof of this small church, searching for its soul; but the soft gloom shares no meaning, and leaves no impression; not one that would inspire an artist of some repute anyway. Then I see the bee, and I wonder if it is one of mine.

Mine. Yes; I am now the Lady of the Meadow; and we are less than a mile from Meadowsweet. I watch it as it flies in a broken circle and slowly makes its way down toward the coffins, and I draw in my breath as it lands on Mummy's coffin. I look across at Jemima, but she hasn't seen it. The bee wanders around the coffin for some time before leaving and heading straight for the open window. And then she is gone. I imagine her flying up into the air and looking down on the small church. I watch as she continues her journey across the rooftops and tree lined lanes of Wraysbury; dropping low and then lifting toward the sun as she checks her bearing. Then she moves ahead with some intent as she sees the familiar landmarks of Meadowsweet. As she flies between the tall chimneys of the house she drops low again, and picks up speed across the garden, where she slows to work her way into the meadow and bristle the tops of the tall grass. She chooses her hive carefully, knowing that her queen, and no other, will welcome her. She has news to tell. The sign of the black cloth draped across the hive needs to be explained; and she knows the answer.

Soon they will expect a new Lady of the Meadow who will tell them her story.

The End

Acknowledgements

I would like to thank my editor Bethany Brengan for her generosity and insight, and for doing what you do so well.

I am indebted to my friend Melsina Makaza *BA (hons) in Mental Health Care,* for being such a reliable resource of information, for her wealth of knowledge on Person Centred Dementia Care, and for her undying enthusiasm for this project.

My thanks go to Claire Preston for allowing me to share a quote from your amazing book about bees. Your thoughts on the philophy of bees were truly inspiring.

I am eternally grateful for the wealth of information to be found on the Internet, and for the nameless individuals who unselfishly share their love for bees and for the beauty of Italy.

Author's Note

The idea for this novel came from a conversation I overheard whilst in a university canteen. I happened to be on a writing course at the time, so I guess I was 'listening' more than usual. Two young ladies were discussing their hobbies, and one of girls went on to talk about her love of keeping bees. She spoke so passionately, and in depth about the bond that she had with them, and how much they influenced her life.

That brief conversation set me on a course of research, which consisted of my own conversations with friends who were beekeepers, numerous trips to the public library, the purchasing of several books, and many hours spent on internet sites discussing bees. It was also mesmerizing watching the many videos placed on Youtube detailing every aspect of beekeeping, which confirmed my belief that to those who are involved in this most fascinating of enterprises, it is more than just a hobby; it is a way of life. The passion I have seen displayed by all of those involved with bees leaves me in no doubt about the special relationship we have with this captivating insect.

In fact, as we have learned more about bees, we have come to realise that our very survival depends upon this selfless and hardworking family. Whether our view is one of fear or admiration for what is after all a miracle of life, we cannot deny its place in our lives. The fabrication of the bee's main product, honey, would in itself be sufficient to justify its existence, but when placed against the fact that every food we eat works its way back to the labours of the bee, it is truly staggering. My story cannot hope to change the tide of man's journey of destruction. It is just a small attempt to show the link between our own humanity and that of the bee.

I feel privileged to have been inspired to write a story based on this political, aesthetic, playful, bee. This retired bee. Why retired? Countless characters in history, both fictional and real, have spent their twilight days in contemplative solitude with the Honey Bee. Sherlock Holmes no doubt found them 'elementary' as he lived out his final days watching them in his Sussex Downs retreat. In between climbing Mount Everest and exploring, Sir Edmund Hilary kept bees with his brother, and would end his days beekeeping in new Zealand. Inspired by Sherlock Holmes, the novelist and travel writer, Paul Theroux, retired to the Hawaiian island of Oahu to take up beekeeping.

So, for me, this journey has been more than the completion of my first novel. It has also taken me into a world that has so many layers, it would take a lifetime to explore them all. My wife tells me I wil never retire. The prospect of keeping bees for those latter years leaves me sorely tempted. Will I write another story involving the bees of Meadowsweet? I will contemplate that as I put another teaspoon of honey in my   tea.

Kevin Carey